Praise for The Godmother . . .

"EVERY VICIOUS ABSURDITY on which she sets her sights does have a real-world counterpart somewhere; for appropriate testimony, read your daily paper . . . Scarborough makes her characters so real and their plights so poignant that we are with her all the way."   —*Analog*

"INTELLIGENT . . . witty takes on *Cinderella, Snow White, Puss in Boots,* and . . . other classic fairy tales."   —*Booklist*

"SCARBOROUGH'S EYES ARE WIDE OPEN, whether evaluating the society in an imagined spiral of decline, or reading Grimm's old fairy tales with an unblinking stare."
—*Port Townsend Leader*

"LOTS OF FUN . . . she securely grounds her tale by setting it in and around a believable social-services agency in Seattle and by making her protagonist sympathetic and realistic."
—*Publishers Weekly*

"ENTERTAINING AND EDUCATIONAL. A weird mix of Scarborough's two modes: fairy-tale humor and serious social commentary . . . a very dark look at some contemporary social problems."   —*Locus*

"A STUNNINGLY GOOD STORY, neither too heavy nor too light, with a careful balance between the harsh realities of modern city life and the romantic idealism of magical wishes."   —*Bakka Books*

"DELIGHTFUL."   —*The Olympian*

THE GODMOTHER

ELIZABETH ANN SCARBOROUGH

For Marilyn, Best wishes (3)

Elizabeth Ann Scarborough

ACE BOOKS, NEW YORK

This Ace Book contains the complete text of the original hardcover edition. It has been completely reset in a typeface designed for easy reading, and was printed from new film.

THE GODMOTHER

An Ace Book / published by arrangement with the author

PRINTING HISTORY
Ace hardcover edition / September 1994
Ace mass-market edition / December 1995

All rights reserved.
Copyright © 1994 by Elizabeth Ann Scarborough.
Cover art by Tara McGovern.
This book may not be reproduced in whole or in part, by mimeograph or any other means, without permission. For information address: The Berkley Publishing Group, a member of Penguin Putnam Inc., 375 Hudson Street, New York, New York 10014.

The Penguin Putnam Inc. World Wide Web site address is http://www.penguinputnam.com

ISBN: 0-441-00269-2

ACE®
Ace Books are published by The Berkley Publishing Group, a member of Penguin Putnam Inc., 375 Hudson Street, New York, NY 10014. ACE and the "A" design are trademarks belonging to Charter Communications, Inc.

PRINTED IN THE UNITED STATES OF AMERICA

10 9 8 7 6 5 4

This is dedicated with admiration, gratitude
and affection to Anne McCaffrey, who manages
very nicely without the benefit of a wand

DISCLAIMER *and*
ACKNOWLEDGMENTS

FIRST OF ALL, although Seattle is real, and the King County Police and other law-enforcement agencies are real, and Washington State does indeed have a social-services department, the police and social services represented in this book are definitely *not* real and in no way are meant to be taken as representations of the present agencies.

The background of this book is an alternate near-future projection of the sort of things that *could* go wrong in human-services organizations given an uncaring government, lack of funding and unqualified leadership taken to an extreme that has *not* occurred in Washington or, to the extreme mentioned in the book, anywhere else.

Some states and cities may have one or more of the types of administrative problems Rose Samson faces in her job, but the department represented is a fictitious composite. The Department of Family Services does not exist in Seattle.

I've also taken liberties with the administration of the King County Police, which has separate jobs for patrolmen and detectives. Thanks to the department for allowing me to tour, and to Hank Cramer for alternative police styles assistance. Also thanks to Whatcom County Search and Rescue, especially Neil Clement, Acting Director of the Department of Emergency Management; Sergeant Ron Peterson of the Whatcom County Sheriff's Department; Jerry Darkis, Search and Rescue 4X4 coordinator and man-tracker (who helped me find just the right camp for the seven vets); and Sherill Brown of the Sheriff's Posse.

Mostly, thanks to Becky Hoff, Sandy Charon, Linden Staciokas, Sally Brown, Marilyn Berry and John Swan. Their enthusiasm for helping others was what primarily inspired this book.

One

ONCE UPON A time in a beautiful city by the edge of the sea there toiled a young woman who did not believe in fairy tales. Fairy tales, she said, had no relevance to her life and none to the lives of the children she knew. She and the children she knew inhabited another realm altogether. "More like a soap opera," she explained. "You know, boy meets girl, boy and girl have children, girl quits job to raise children, boy loses job, boy loses girl, girl meets second boy, second boy abuses girl's children by previous marriage, children abuse themselves and their children unhappily ever after."

"You don't believe in happy endings, then?" a friend asked.

"No, I believe in happy moments," she replied, for she was even wiser than she was beautiful. Much wiser, as a matter of fact. "Which is why I love to come in here." Her gesture took in the interior of the shop, a place filled with rhinestone tiaras, Himalayan silver rings and silk kimonos, Indian saris sewn with golden thread and brilliantly colored gauzy Arabian thwabs. Not to mention the Victorian and Edwardian antique paisley shawls and velvet smoking jackets, the bustled skirts and flounced nightdresses that were the import stock making Fortunate Finery the most intriguing shop in Pike Place Market and by far the best

1

vintage clothing shop in all of Seattle. "That white ruffled skirt is absolutely gorgeous. I don't suppose it's a fourteen, is it?"

"I thought you didn't believe in fantasy," chided her friend, who was the proprietress of the fabulous establishment where the young woman liked to spend her lunch hours and much of what she laughingly described as her disposable income. "It's a three."

The young woman sighed and turned her attention to an ebony Chinese shawl embroidered with peacocks in emerald, cerulean, aquamarine and gilt threads. She draped it across her upper body and admired her reflection in the mirror. The greens in the shawl made her eyes look emerald instead of merely hazel, and the black brought out the reddish glints in her curly dark brown hair. By no stretch of the imagination did she look like a Chinese empress, but with her dimples and clean-scrubbed, open, heart-shaped face, she could have passed for a character in a Victorian novel. Not the tragic governess. The goodhearted cook maybe, or the nice, but slightly boring, welloff school chum of the heroine. "Oh, no, I never said that," she replied, reluctantly replacing the shawl around the shoulders of the mannequin. "Fantasies are essential. Escape is essential, or life would be unbearable. It's when you start believing in your fantasies that you run into trouble."

"Did you learn that in school?" her friend asked.

"No. In school they taught us that we would be able to make a difference. They tried to inspire us with the notion that by helping a single junkie, prostitute or wino we would make Seattle a better city and the world a better place to live in. To the best of my knowledge, that's a fairy tale."

"Had a hard day, have we, Rosie?" the friend asked.

"I've had a hard day ever since the new governor took office, cleaned house in the administration and implemented her idiotic idea of a budget. So has everybody else working in the social sector. Our staff has been cut by half, our budget is down to zero and our new supervisor is a complete idiot. Of course, we're not suffering half as badly as the clients except that they're quite used to suffering and if we don't watch out, we're going to be competing with them for street turf and cardboard condos."

"Oh, my, you *are* down. Here, have a chocolate. They're Dilettante." She referred to Seattle's premier gourmet chocolatier. She always kept a dish handy for her customers and her other guests, among them the panhandlers who brought her their pets to board when they had to go to hospitals or treatment programs—or got itchy feet. The city of Seattle would allow stray people to wander the streets, but animals found doing the same would be taken to the pound where they, unlike the people, would be fed and housed for a few days before being euthanized, if not claimed. Rosalie Samson had first met Linden Hoff because of the street pet shelter, back when Fortunate Finery was between Pioneer Square and the International District. Linden treated customers, street people and pets pretty much the same, and everybody was welcome to a bit of chocolate.

"I know, Linden," Rosie said, taking a bite from a truffle. "They always are." She sighed, half with resignation, half with bliss, as the truffle touched her tongue. "I *should* be jogging or walking or weight training on my lunch hour," she added after demolishing the morsel. "It would be much healthier, *and* less expensive."

Linden Hoff, who had heard it all many times before, clucked at her and opened the door to the ugly-brown clad UPS lady, who hauled a dolly full of boxes into the tiny portion of the shop that wasn't covered in racks of frilly, colorful, exotic, or merely amusing vintage clothes. "From England, Linden," the UPS lady said. "Don't sell everything before I get back, will you? Sign right here."

"I'll save you something special to make up for having to wear that godawful uniform, Lenore," Rosie's friend promised. As soon as Lenore and the dolly left, Linden pulled a box cutter from her pocket and went to work.

Rose watched with bated breath. The things from England were what set Linden's shop a cut above the others.

"Surely," Linden said while slicing open a box that with very little encouragement frothed frills and spilled fringes from the cut. "Surely life doesn't always go as you say. Boy isn't always an abuser."

"No," Rose sighed. "Equality is actually gaining ground. We are seeing more mothers doing the abusing these days."

"Well, there then, you see. That proves my point. Things haven't changed so much. It used to be wicked stepmothers and witches all the time."

"You've cheered me immensely. Oh, *this* is lovely!" she said, holding up a delicate chain with a small crystal globe hanging from it. She peered closely at the globe. Within it was a single golden seed. "What is it?"

"Mustard seed," Linden said, shaking out a sixties-style white Nehru coat with gold braid and ribbon trim. "You know, from the Bible verse about there being hope for whoever has as much faith as can be contained in a mustard seed . . ."

"Nope, don't know that one."

"Me neither, not exactly. Maybe it's not the Bible after all. Could be from *The Prophet*. Something spiritual. But anyway, back in the fifties and sixties, they were a very popular gift, and you were supposed to be able to make wishes on them."

"Hmph," Rose said, trying it on in front of the mirror. It accented the gold in her eyes. Funny, because it was small and delicate and rolled across her ample bust like a wagon across the foothills. Still, it showed up very nicely though it was unpretentious enough not to clash with the teal and purple flowered knit top and purple knit pants and jacket outfit she was wearing that day. In the winter doldrums after Christmas when the weather was usually gray and the mountains hidden by clouds and rain, the flowers and the bright colors helped cheer her. "How much?" she asked, fingering the little globe.

"I dunno. Don't tell me you might like it to make a wish on?"

"I can use all the help I can get at this point."

"What would you wish for?"

Rose thought about the clients she had to turn away because they weren't battered *enough*, that is, not in immediate danger of being murdered for a couple of days, of the budget cuts which allowed families to be put out onto the street and the disabled to have their benefits withdrawn. She thought of the stupid policy the new governor had pushed through the legislature that from now on the goal of family services was to protect the integrity of the family—that is, whoever was the strongest and in some cases had the biggest fist was to be protected and served by the agency. She thought of her caseload and that of her coworkers—all three of them, what remained out of an office of fifteen. "Reinforcements," she said. "I'd wish for reinforcements."

"Ah, then you're wishing for a fairy godmother, is that it?" Linden asked with a fond smile at her favorite customer.

"For the whole damned city of Seattle? Sure, why not?" Rose asked, fiddling with the little ball holding the mustard seed. "Anybody, as long as she's more competent than *Mrs.* Melvin Hager. We need all the help we can get."

"In the face of such a selfless wish, I can hardly *sell* that to you. Go ahead, take it. It's on the house. Come back tomorrow and I'll have all this unpacked."

"That's well worth a ferry ride on my day off. Right now I'd better get back to work. See you later."

In another part of that same city a fabulously wealthy young man had married a beautiful model and moved her into his palatial mansion overlooking Elliott Bay. This man had a daughter who was herself beautiful enough to be a model. In fact, the moment her stepmother's agent laid eyes on her, he begged to be allowed to sign her up.

The stepmother, whose career was waning, whose husband was younger than she and possessed of a reputation for playing around, feared for her identity if the girl remained in her house a moment longer. She sent to her Uncle Svenny for a hit man. Uncle Svenny had made his fortune in the most vicious end of the clandestine pharmaceuticals industry and had at his disposal many consultants in various related services. The hit man arrived promptly and she bade him take the girl out into the forest and dispatch her.

Snohomish Quantrill was the daughter's name. She had been named for the town that had given her father his acting debut on nationwide television. Her father had legally assumed the name Raydir Quantrill to fit his rebellious onstage image, but he was only rebellious for show. His real name was Raymond Kinsale and offstage he was fairly conventional, for a rock star/actor. Too much sex, drugs and rock and roll and not enough time for his kid.

Sno felt sharply again just how little time he did have for her when a complete stranger picked her up from school that day. Of course, even if he'd been her dad himself, she probably wouldn't have recognized him, all decked out in full biker leathers, a helmet and goggles. But he had the authorization letter the school required of any staff member her dad sent to pick her up, so she figured it was safe to go with him, even if he did look a lot like Darth Vader. He was probably a new guy or someone who'd been off on the road taking care of stuff for her dad. She hadn't been living with Raydir all that long this time, and his staff tended to have a pretty big turnover.

This was the first time anyone had ever picked her up on a Harley-Davidson, though! Usually Raydir just sent the limo. She got on behind the guy and jammed her head into the helmet he tossed at her. Hitching her school skirt up to her crotch, she hung on for dear life as he roared out of the parking lot. But she was not amused. This was not her idea of a great way to ride home. For one thing, it was December and she had only the unlined red wool parka her private school allowed as an overcoat with the uniform—anything to squash her individuality. Little did they know about the love beads lurking beneath her prissy white blouse. But the uniform, blouse, skirt, sweater and parka, was not made for riding bikes in midwinter.

Not only was it cold, but she quailed at having to cuddle up to a strange guy even for the time it took to ride the few blocks to the mansion. She was thirteen now, and looked older, even in the stupid school uniform, not that it mattered how old she was to some of the pervs Raydir hung out with. Even when she was a little kid, back when she and Mom used to live with Raydir on the road, she'd learned to be quick and smart about who she was alone with in a hotel room or on the bus. Her mom had warned her against certain guys, even back when she was four or five, but she was too little to be able to always duck them and her mom

couldn't always be there. That's why she and Suzanne—
Mom—had left Raydir the first time.

That and the bimbos. For the last three years they'd lived
with Grandma Hilda in Missouri. It wasn't exactly *The
Cosby Show*, just the three of them and Mom's boyfriends
and Grandma's art students hanging around after the beauty
parlor closed for the day. And Grandma Hilda had a great
vinyl LP collection of sixties oldies, which was how Sno
had come to know and love her favorite music, music that
had stories and melodies and rhythms that had nothing to
do with Raydir's kind of music.

She had her eyes closed and her cheek pressed against
the impersonal leather back of the driver. The wind bit
through her tights and ran right up her skirt, and shivers
raced across her shoulders despite the red parka. The wind
was too strong for her to be able to keep the hood around
her face.

Surely they ought to be home by now. But suddenly,
even through the Harley's roar, the traffic noise changed
and she saw that they were headed onto the on-ramp to I-5
headed north.

She tugged the dude's jacket. "Hey," she hollered. "We're
going the wrong way."

"Party," he screamed back at her.

Oh, yeah, that was right. Raydir had said something
about a party. She had just assumed she wouldn't be going.
Well, damn, if she'd known, she'd have brought something
to change into. Raydir didn't think of little details like that
and it was just like Gerardine, her stepmother, to be sure
that Sno arrived in her dorky red school uniform for the
party. Not that she cared about most of Raydir's parties,
or about fitting into the self-consciously hip crowd that
attended them. They weren't all that much fun, in her
opinion.

Raydir and all his friends thought they were so cool, so with it, but Sno was unimpressed. She was heavily into retro. While Mom was out on dates, Sno and Grandma used to make brownies and listen to the music, and Grandma would look deeply into the bowl of brownie batter and sigh, and after a while get out her protest buttons and tell Sno about the marches she had been on. So Sno loved more than the music; she was into the whole thing, the activism, the clothes, the marches, the—whatchamacallit—ambi-ahnce. She couldn't wait for bell-bottoms to come back. Fortunately for her, her hair was long, naturally straight and black, like Joan Baez's on her old album covers, so she had always kind of had a sixties look too. Raydir had sneered at such an unhip kid. Back before they left him for good, Mom had tried to please him by cutting Sno's hair a couple of times into a Mohawk and putting pink and purple stripes in it. Thank God that look was totally out now.

But Sno would have put up with it all over again if it meant having Mom back. The wind stung her face and whipped away the tears that otherwise would have trickled onto the leather jacket. Shit shit shit shit shit.

She was half afraid, riding in the open on the Harley, and halfway she just wished they'd hit something and she'd go flying until she crashed hard enough to stop the pain for good.

At least the wind and cold were numbing her now, and they had just exited toward Mount Baker. The mountains looked great today, clear and crisp with their new coat of snow, like humongous scoops of vanilla ice cream with chocolate sprinkles where the snow hadn't stuck yet.

And they were getting close. Closer all the time. This party was really off in the boonies. True, a lot of the rich people lived out toward the mountains, but mostly they didn't expect people to come to their parties after it started snowing and the roads got icy. Nevertheless, the bike roared farther and farther from the interstate, and, as the road sloped upward toward the mountains, and the sky grew darker, it grew colder and colder. Sno clung even tighter to the driver, small against his broad black leather back.

Even as she cowered against the wind, the nervous feeling that had been pawing at her gut sharpened into panic. None of this made any sense. Maybe the guy had been sent to get her. Maybe there was a party. But now that she thought about it, hadn't Raydir mentioned something about Kirkland? And Kirkland was just a little north of Seattle, not all the way up here.

Who *was* this guy? How had he gotten the authorization letter? Oh, crap.

Up a disused road, he ran the bike onto a trail in the woods. A trail. Not a driveway. And the woods didn't hide any big elegant houses with BMWs out front. He had to slow a little, and she thought maybe she could jump off and run away, but if she fell and hurt herself she'd have no defense against him at all.

Finally, he stopped and dismounted, kicking her shin as he scooted off the bike without paying any attention to her, seated behind him. Then, before she could hop off and run, he grabbed her wrist in one hand and jerked her off the bike. With the other hand, he reached into his leathers and pulled out a knife, which he flicked to reveal a long, glittering blade.

Two

IN AN EARLIER time in another part of the state in a village sandwiched between the sea and the forest there once lived a poor woodsman and his wife with their two children. Since the goddamned ecologists and their goddamned spotted owls had closed the forests, the woodsman no longer had any wood to cut to earn his living and his company had laid him off. For a time, he and his family subsisted on unemployment compensation, but as the program had been axed by the state during budget cuts, soon that means of providing food for the table also ran out.

"Let's go to the city where I can find work in my former employment as a topless dancer," the wife urged, but the woodsman would not hear of it. He had married his wife to take her away from all that, and besides, he didn't like the city. But all the jobs in their hometown were taken by other people who were out of work and their families, and soon it seemed that following his wife's plan was the only thing the woodsman could do.

At first the woodsman's children were not unhappy at the thought of moving. "Oh boy! Sevenplex movie theaters!" little Hank cried with glee.

"Chucky Cheeses, Chucky Cheeses," said his sister Gigi, who was only four but remembered birthday treats at the children's restaurant with all of the big mechanical animals and peanut butter and jelly sandwiches right there on the menu.

"Not unless your old man finds another job, kids," their father told them. "It'll be slim pickin's otherwise."

But their mother, who had to listen to them cry when they left behind most of their toys at the yard sale the family had before moving in with their mother's sister in Seattle, was more encouraging. "Yeah, sure, it'll be great. We'll go to the zoo and the aquarium and the children's theater at Seattle Center. Okay, Gigi, Chucky Cheeses too. But you kids gotta be real good. Don't give your Aunt Bambi any grief. She works nights and sleeps during the day and prob'ly Mommy will too so you got to be real quiet and real good while we're there, okay?"

The children promised that they would. Hank, who was seven, was aware that his parents were troubled and his daddy particularly was very sad. His daddy loved the woods, even though he chopped them down for a living.

"Maybe I can get out on a fishing boat," Daddy had said. "Let me give it a shot, honey. I don't want you back in one of them places."

His mother had smiled and stood real close to his daddy, like she was going to kiss him. "Those places aren't all that bad now, baby. That's where we met, 'member?"

And so the family moved to the city, where they all slept in the living room in Aunt Bambi's apartment.

It was summer when they moved there, and Hank hoped that his father would soon get a job fishing. Maybe then he would take Hank with him. Hank had always enjoyed fishing with his father when they lived in the village. And indeed, every day while Aunt Bambi and Mama slept and Gigi played quietly alone, Father took the #17 bus from downtown Seattle to the Ballard Locks to look for work, and every night he came home as Aunt Bambi went to work and Mama went to seek work.

When he had been a woodsman, Father's homecoming was always a happy time of day, but when he came home from the Locks he was always sad and angry—and he smelled like beer. At first he was just mad at the ecologists and the owls and the company that laid him off and the goddamn politicians. Then he started getting mad at Mama.

"Hank needs lunch money for school," Mama told him.

"Where do you think I'd get lunch money?" Father asked. "You were the one who was going to get a job. Nobody in port is taking on unskilled hands right now."

"I'm *trying*, honey, but I've gotten a little old, you know, and—"

"Put on a little weight, haven't you? Too porky for the clubs anymore?"

"I haven't gained that much!"

"Don't worry about it, baby, 'cause if one of us doesn't get a job pretty soon we're gonna be starving and you'll get skinny enough then."

"What do you mean, gonna?" Mama demanded. Hank didn't want to hear them yell at each other, and Gigi just stared at them with her eyes great big, looking like she was going to bawl. Hank shook his head at her not to. "There's no 'gonna' to it, Matt. While you drink up what little bit we've got left, Gigi and me are eating one meal a day and that's pancakes! God, I'm sick of pancakes. Hank gets his meal at school, but if you don't give him the money, he doesn't eat."

"What happened to free school lunches?"

"They went out when the administration changed, you know that. Your buddy, the governor who was going to make the woods safe for industry again, decided that there shouldn't be any free lunches for the kids of people who were too lazy to work. Like us."

"Don't you get snotty with me!" he yelled and looked like he was going to hit her.

Aunt Bambi slumped out of her bedroom then, wearing just a T-shirt with a pair of titties on the front of it. "Hey, you two. Knock it off or find someplace else to crash. I need my rest, y'know?"

The next night Father didn't come home.

"Hank, I want you to look after your little sister while Aunt Bambi and I are gone," Mama said. "Just go to bed and don't open the door for anyone."

"Not even Daddy?" Gigi asked. "Where's Daddy?"

"You heard me," Mama said. "He can sleep it off in the gutter if he wants to. Tonight's amateur night at the club, and I think the boss has his eye on me. If·I do good, things'll be better around here for a while."

"Where's *Daddy*?" Gigi demanded.

Mama let out a deep sigh and set down her purse to pick up Gigi. "Daddy's gone right now, sweetie. Maybe he found a boat to work on, eh? But I'll tell you what. If the nice man at Aunt Bambi's friend's work likes Mama's dancing, there'll be money again. We could go to Chucky Cheeses maybe to celebrate. Would you like that?"

Gigi nodded gravely, but after Mama left, she cried again for Daddy.

Daddy didn't find a boat after all, and two nights later he came home. His beard was grown out and scratchy and his breath smelled bad. Hank had to let him in, because Mama and Aunt Bambi were gone then.

"Hi, kids. Hiya, Gigi," he said in a slurry voice. "How's my little princess?"

Gigi started to cry.

"Aw, shut that shit up, baby," he groaned, and when she just cried louder he screamed at her and for a minute Hank thought he was going to hit her. Hank ran over to her and put his hand over her mouth.

"She'll be okay, Daddy. She's just kind of hungry. Mama didn't have time to make her pancakes and I don't know how. Maybe you could show me?"

"What the hell do I know about that? Cooking's your mama's job, not whorin' around all night."

"She's got a job—I think," Hank said. "She said she would bring home money."

"Well, that's something," Daddy said.

And for a few days there was money, but there never was enough to go to Chucky Cheeses, and Daddy always needed some to go to the Locks. Then one night Mama came home in the middle of the night, crying.

A few minutes later, Aunt Bambi came in too, and she was mad. "What the hell are you making such a fuss for? You know if you break the rules you get fined. You don't touch the customers. It's the law, Candy."

"That was a hundred-dollar bill, sis. A hundred dollars. Do you know what we could do with a hundred dollars?"

"Yeah, sure. Your old man could drink it all up in two days instead of one. Look, you're my sister and I love you, but I can't support all of us. The boss wants you to do that little favor for him. If you do it, he'll forget the fine."

"I don't traffic in drugs," Mom said coldly. "It's the law, sis. I'd get busted and I'd lose my kids."

"Fine. Great. We're going nowhere here. You'd be better off without these kids and they'd be better off without you the way you're going. And the sooner you lose that husband of yours, the better off you'll all be."

Mama cried and hugged them and said she loved her family, but things got worse after that. Daddy said he was taking a boat to Alaska and wouldn't tell Mama where he was going or when he was coming home. Mama cried all the time and went out every night and left them alone.

Then for a little while there was money, and Mama laughed more and bought some clothes and makeup and stuff and once took them out to Chucky Cheeses again. But then one morning a man brought her home and she was laughing like crazy and smelled funny.

The man didn't like Hank and Gigi, they could tell. And he came home with Mama a lot. Mama was almost never home then, and Aunt Bambi yelled at the children whenever she was awake. Mama had no appetite when she was home and no longer cooked for Hank and Gigi. When Hank tried to make pancakes, he made such a mess that Aunt Bambi hit him, and when Mama came home she hit him too.

After that, she cried and said she was sorry and soon they would have their own place and everything would be better. But Gigi started crying for Daddy, and Mama got mad again.

The man brought her home the next morning, and this time she looked half mad, half sad, the way Daddy used to. Or that was what Hank thought, anyway. Then all of a sudden she got happy and said, "Instead of sleeping today, I'm going to take you to the mall. How would that be?"

They were very excited about going to the mall. They left Aunt Bambi's apartment, in a development where all of the apartments looked alike, and took a bus—not the #17, but another bus. They changed buses many times so that it took a long time to reach the mall, and Hank tried to memorize all the bus numbers, but it was too confusing. Finally, they arrived at the mall. They had only been to one mall before, but this one was bigger, with lots and lots of stores.

There were benches where you could sit too, and although Gigi and Hank wanted so much to find out where the tantalizing aroma of chocolate chip cookies was coming from, Mama wanted to try on underwear at an underwear store. "You kids sit out here and wait for me," she said. "I'll just be a minute."

But lots of minutes passed and Mama didn't come back. Hank told Gigi to sit very still and be very good while he went in to find Mama. He thought maybe she'd yell at him, but he figured at least she'd be there. She wasn't. The lady at the store said she'd gone to try something on and hadn't come back. There was nobody in the dressing rooms either. The lady looked. She said there was an employees' exit in the back of the store and maybe Mama had gone to check the car. But there was no car.

Hank ran out to find Gigi, but she was gone too. He searched and searched, frantic to find either his mama or his sister, and then he saw the top of his sister's little blonde head and the flash of her Ninja Turtles sweatshirt. She was running like crazy right toward him, her fists full of something.

"Gigi, where've you been? Whatcha got?"

"Cookies, Hank. Have one!" she said, and gave him crumbled bits of cookie.

"How'd you get 'em?" Hank asked her, for neither of them had any money.

"They were just *sitting* on a counter," Gigi said. "And I was hungry, so I took one."

"Gigi, you can't just rip off cookies," Hank said. "You've gotta pay for them."

"That's right, little boy," a menacing voice said from behind him. "You have to pay."

Three

ROSE ALWAYS FOUND it remarkable that considering there were only about half a million people in the commercial city limits and twice that in all of King County, it seemed like there were, to paraphrase an old TV show, eight million hard-luck stories in the Emerald City. More per capita, anyway, than seemed possible from the population. Naturally, she knew that there were plenty of comparatively sane, conscientious and caring people in the city. There was always some group from Seattle going to build Peace Parks or help with relief to some embattled third-world country. Seattleites marched the streets in force against war and injustice, and a few of the wealthy descendants of pioneers actually put their money where their mouths were to improve the city both environmentally and culturally. The few shelters and soup kitchens remaining could not have stayed open except for the volunteers, caring people all.

Unfortunately, with her increased caseload and the longer hours she was working these days, Rose was usually too tired by the time she got off work to see any of her "civilian" friends, except for Linden.

Every morning she got up by six-thirty to dress, drive to the ferry terminal and make the hour-long ferry commute cross-Sound from Bremerton to Seattle. Then she usually worked a ten- to twelve-hour day before making the same trip in reverse. Day in and day out she listened to tales of murder, drug traffic, child molesting, battery and rape, not to mention the simple economic tragedies that cast people onto the streets.

Most of the time all she could do was listen and fill out endless reams of paperwork, or coach the clients to fill out endless reams of paperwork. Usually both. She used to be able to help people make the system work for them, but these days the system was getting its revenge, drowning everyone in fruitless paperwork.

Dialogues at work were sounding more and more like scripts from a black comedy.

"A foster home is not an appropriate placement at this time, Rose," Mrs. Hager said, handing back the stack of paperwork Rose had spent hours filling out. "Not when the child's father has become available to care for her."

"But the father's only available because he's out on parole for child abuse and molesting her older sister!" Rose protested.

"And you must remember that he *is* on parole," the supervisor told her. "Society considers that he is no longer a risk."

"You mean the sister moved to another state with no forwarding address so she can't protest the parole," Rose said, firmly damping down the desire to scream at the woman.

"Now, Rose, you don't know that," Hager said.

Rose wanted to shout, well, you would, you stupid cow, if you knew beans about your job, but she knew it would cost her her own job. Mrs. Melvin Hager was not one to tolerate even gentle criticism of her actions and zealously guarded her prerogatives at all times. Rose and her colleagues were not sure where Mrs. Hager had gotten her degree in psychiatric social work; the most popular supposition was that she had mail-ordered it from the Sears catalog back in the days when there still *was* a Sears catalog, but Rose was inclined to side with those who held that someone who dressed like Hager wouldn't have been caught dead shopping at Sears, even by mail, and the degree had to have come from Bloomingdale's at least.

Rose would have risked her job, if she thought it would do any good, but if she did, then Hager and the newly appointed division chief would just hire someone as wildly unqualified as Hager to take over. Then where would clients like little Polly Reynaud be? In the same place, actually, but without anybody watching over the situation who gave a damn or who would believe Polly when she tried to tell them about the games Daddy liked to play.

"How about if Polly stays with these people until the father is established in a counseling program here?" Rose asked. "Polly's been with these people for three years now, and she thinks of them as her parents. It would be traumatic to . . ."

"Just my point, Rose," Mrs. Hager said. "The child has begun to bond with others than her own family. All the more reason why she should be reunited with her father as soon as possible. Remember what the governor promised the people. This is a state agency which provides family services. We are responsible to and for the family and should at all times give the sanctity and sovereignty of the family unit the highest priority."

"Even when the family is a piranha like Reynaud?" Rose asked.

Mrs. Hager smiled a tight little smile. "It will all work itself out, Rose. Polly is herself a Reynaud, after all."

Rose didn't even ask what that was supposed to mean, but she was pretty sure it meant that if Reynaud was a daddy piranha, then Polly was a baby piranha and would learn to take care of herself. That was the way La Hager's mind worked. Rose picked up her report and left Hager's office, managing to close the door quietly instead of running screaming, tearing her hair and rending her clothing and engaging in other such elaborately inappropriate behavior, which might convey the wrong impression. Or not.

By then it was time for the department to close, though Rose still had a long night ahead of her, on call. Since she lived 'cross Sound in Bremerton, she had to stay the night on a cot set up in one of the interview rooms so she'd be available.

Her desk was covered with little yellow Post-its of calls received needing to be answered. She glanced through them, thinking that returning a few quick phone calls would make the time pass more quickly.

Of the business calls, none could be dealt with until Monday, but there was one personal message, and Rose picked up the slip with pleasure. "Call Lucinda Ellis," it said. "Lucky Shoe Stables, 547-8456." She dialed the phone quickly, before it could ring bringing another problem. It rang several times before a somewhat breathless voice on the other end said, "Lucky Shoe Stables, Lucinda here."

"Cindy? It's Rose."

"Oh, Rose! Good to hear from you. How's it going?"

"Busy but okay. How about with you? Are you enjoying the new job?"

"I'd enjoy anything that got me away from the bosoms of my loving family," Cindy said. "I'm house-sitting for a woman the owner of the stable knows, watching her cat and dog, and I'm teaching classes as well as exercising the horses. It doesn't pay much, but it keeps me alive since Paola threw me out of the house while she was contesting Dad's will. She keeps calling up, talking to the owner and trying to get me fired. Fortunately, the owner has a lot of horse sense, which is more than you can say for Paola."

"I thought surely she'd leave you alone once she took possession of the house your father left her."

"In my dreams. No, even though her lawyers got her and Pam and Perdita all of Dad's estate except the trust fund he set up for me, she's out to get that too and has it frozen while she's fighting it and meanwhile is making all the trouble for me she can."

"Oh, Cindy! That miserable bitch!"

"That's not the half of it. Wait till you hear the grounds she's using to contest the will . . ." They talked for several more minutes and finally Cindy ended with, "So what I wanted really, Rose, was to invite you up for a ride while I've still got the job."

"I'm not a very good rider."

"It's okay. We board some lovely thoroughbreds, and I'm teaching their owners to jump, but a lot of our business is just saddling up quarter horses with western tack for people who want to mosey around the park. Please say you'll come. I want to do something for you to thank you for all your help in getting away from Paola and company."

"Cindy, that is so sweet. And I'd love to come. I haven't been riding in a long time. Give me directions again."

The mall security guard had been really mad at Gigi for stealing the cookies, though when Hank tried to return the handful of cookie crumbs, slightly moist from being clutched in Gigi's hand, the man didn't seem to want them. He just wanted to yell.

"Is he going to put us in jail?" Gigi asked Hank in a whisper, not scared, just morbidly interested.

The man had taken them, Hank by his right hand, Gigi by her left, and hauled them back into the secret offices in the mall, where there was nothing pretty to look at and only metal furniture, and sat them down in chairs.

"Now then, what are your names?" he asked Hank, and Hank told him, even though he was afraid.

"You, young man, you're old enough to have memorized your address and phone number."

But Hank just shook his head. Aunt Bambi wouldn't let anyone use her phone but her, and no one had ever told Hank what the number was.

He told the man they lived in an apartment with his mother and his aunt and that Mama had left them at the mall.

"Well, then," the man said, and made a phone call. Some time later a policeman arrived. He wore a brown uniform and a windbreaker and had a clipboard and something stuffed under his arm.

"Now you're in for it," Hank hissed to his sister. "That cop's going to get us 'cause you stole the cookie."

"These're the culprits," the security guard said. "Cookie thieves."

"*Cookie* thieves?" the cop asked. Then, hunkering down in front of Hank and Gigi, he asked in a whisper, "How *are* the cookies here? Any good?"

Gigi stuck her thumb in her mouth, the way she did more and more often anymore, but Hank shrugged and said, "They're okay."

"Did you get enough? You still hungry?"

Hank nodded.

"Boy, me too. I missed my dinner. You kids want to come have a Big Mac and fries with me? My treat."

But when he stood up and reached for their hands, Gigi began to scream. Hank realized she knew that the cop was just saying he was going to take them for a Big Mac to get them to come to jail without a fight. He crossed his arms and glared at the cop to let him know he wasn't going to be fooled that easily.

The cop hunkered down again with an exasperated sigh and rolled his eyes at the security man. Then, from under his arm, he drew out something furry and looked at it as if it had come there all by itself. It was a teddy bear dressed in a policeman's uniform. Talking to the bear just like Hank used to talk to GI Joe and Gigi talked to her own stuffed kitty, left behind in Forks, the cop said, "Officer Bear, I think you'd better take over this investigation. See, the thing is, these kids have lost their mama and they're tired and hungry but they're kinda scared of me. Do you think you could tell them I'm okay?"

He waggled the bear up and down and turned it to face them. "Hiya, kids. I'm Officer Bear but you can call me Fuzz."

Gigi scooted forward a little bit, the tears stopping, though the thumb didn't come out of her mouth.

Hank looked at the cop. "I know it's really you talking," he said.

The cop winked at him but Officer Bear wagged into his face. "What's your name?"

"Hank. This is my sister Gigi. She's four."

"What grade're you in, Hank?"

"First."

"Do you like it?"

Hank nodded. "Most of the time."

"Me too. Most of the time school's cool. I had to go to police academy before I joined the force, of course, and that was lots of fun but what I really want is a real boy or girl of my own to go to preschool and kindygarden with, to color and count and learn the ABCs."

With this the cop turned Fuzz to Gigi and pushed the bear up against her arm. At first she drew back, but when the bear snuggled her arm, the thumb popped out of her mouth and she grabbed the bear with both arms.

The cop winked at Hank again. "I lose more good partners that way."

"Will you really take us for a hamburger and not put us in jail?" Hank asked.

"I'm just going to try to help you, son. Cops do lots more than put people in jail, you know. Ever see *Rescue 911?*"

Hank shook his head and the cop muttered, "Well, that blows that approach," under his breath.

"You got a gun?" Hank asked.

"Yeah, and handcuffs too. Wanna see them?"

"Can I?" Hank asked, and the cop—his name was Officer Fred—showed him the cuffs and even let him carry them when he and Gigi and the bear went to McDonald's. They had Big Deal Meals that came with free dinosaurs, and meanwhile they talked with Officer Fred about the mall. He had a little nephew, he said, and he wondered if this was a good mall to come to to buy him a present. He wondered if their folks brought them here real often and if it was near their house.

Hank told him that it wasn't, that their real home was by the ocean but they couldn't live there anymore because Daddy'd lost his job.

"Gee, that's tough," Officer Fred said. "What job did he have?"

Then he wanted to know about Mama and finally asked which store Mama had gone into when she disappeared. Hank showed him and Officer Fred spoke to the saleslady for a minute, then asked Gigi and Hank if they wanted to ride in the squad car and help him make a call on his police radio phone.

As they drove farther along on the freeway, there was a traffic jam and as it ended, Officer Fred showed them how the lights worked. Then he used the phone again and at last turned in to a parking space in front of a building with a green awning over the front and a sign that read AURORA CENTER. Two windows on the second floor were lit.

"Department of Family Services, Rose Samson speaking." Rose answered the phone with mingled dread and relief. Dread because you never knew what catastrophe might be on the other end, and relief because almost anything would be better than the boredom of staying in the office all night waiting for something to happen.

"Rosie! Hi. It's Fred Moran, remember me?"

Rose grinned into the phone, she was so pleased to hear hear the familiar name. "Fred! How've you been? Haven't seen you in a long time." Fred Moran had been the security officer at the department during the six years he was studying criminology, justice, psychology, sociology and urban anthropology at the university so he could be the best-prepared cop on the force. He came from a long line of Irish police, including his mother, but as a security guard at least, he had had nothing of the cynical macho bully often associated with a badge. Even with privately hired guards, some clinics were stuck with the stereotypical "cop" behavior around damaged, sometimes rebellious, sometimes hostile clients who had been or felt they had been shafted by the system. The guard Aurora had had before was one of that kind, and had to quit when one of the clients put him in the hospital with a broken neck.

Rose had been doing interviews with new clients when Benny Jackson, who had a drinking problem and an attitude, came in. Before he had been there a minute, he started swearing that he wasn't about to wait in line again.

One of the other counselors—there had been an office full back then—shrugged and grimaced in response to Benny's griping. And Rose had braced herself inwardly for an explosion when she saw the new guard approach Benny.

But instead of challenging the man, Fred had asked in an amiable way, "You running into some kinda problem here?"

And Benny had growled something and Fred said, "Well, let me see if I can give you a hand. Computers have been acting up today and things have been going sort of slow but . . ." And he continued to sort out Benny's problem in a way that was not just polite, but seemed as if he gave a damn.

He was like that with all the clients. "I really hate it that our security guard isn't on the state payroll," her boss back then said. "That guy goes above and beyond the call of duty all the time—he does case management and he gets paid minimum wage with no paid vacation or sick leave."

Friendly and personable as he was, Fred had listened more than he talked, and Rose hadn't realized he was leaving them until he'd showed up one day in his Sheriff's Department uniform and announced he had graduated from school and was ready for the streets.

This call was the first she'd heard from him since.

"Oh, you know how it is with us King County cops. We migrate all over the place for a while, learning the territory. I've been working the north end lately so I haven't been down your way much, but I'll be working out of the courthouse starting this weekend so I'll probably get to drop by once in a while."

"We'd love to see you," she said.

"Great. You'll have to show me all the good new places to have lunch downtown and fill me in on what's happening."

"Any time," she said, smiling into the receiver. She regretted that they hadn't become better friends while he was there. It would be terrific if that was still possible. For one thing, he was a pretty cute guy, although she seemed to remember he had been living with someone or something at one time.

He was continuing. "Listen, I've got a couple of youngsters with me I think need to meet you. Seems their mother took them to the mall and then got lost for the rest of the night. The place is closed now and still no sign of mother. The family moved recently too, and the kids can't remember the address."

Rose said nothing. What was there to say? If the children's own home could be found, they'd have to go back there as soon as possible even though an investigation should be launched, by all rights. Under the new system, children were always returned to their families first. "The family unit is *also* innocent until proved guilty," Hager was fond of saying. Nevertheless, Rose called around and looked into emergency foster placements and was pleased to learn that the Ogdens, a couple who had four kids of their own and a constant stream of foster children, were ready to shuffle their house around to make room for the children that night.

She heard the opening front door of the otherwise silent building and footsteps on the stairs—an adult's quick, deliberate steps accompanied by what sounded like a herd of children, and there they were.

"Hi, Rose, this is Hank and Gigi," Fred said. God, the new uniform was ever so much more becoming than the old one! But otherwise he looked much the same, his face neither handsome nor homely, his dark hair already streaked with gray, his hazel eyes intelligent and understanding. And his smile was the same old brilliant smile, broadening when he saw her. She was glad to see that the streets hadn't taken that out of him yet. Although, actually, if working here hadn't done it, nothing was likely to.

The kids were a small boy who might have been any-where from five to eight years old and a little girl three or four. The boy's hair was sandy blond and his face rather thin and nervous, his blue eyes darting everywhere, taking in the office, and back up to Fred's face for reassurance. The girl's white-blonde hair curled in little wisps at her shoulders and in bangs she kept brushing from her eyes with one hand, while in the other she clutched a teddy bear dressed as a policeman.

Rose hunkered down until she was eye level with the kids. "Hi, who's your friend?" she asked the little girl.

"Fuzz," she said loudly, then, as if startled by her own voice, stuck the thumb of her free hand in her mouth.

"He's a great bear. Where'd you get him?"

She looked up at Fred with big blue eyes. Rose's own eyes followed hers, and she smiled up at Fred too. She knelt beside Gigi and fingered one of the bear's paws. Fred's hands were long and well shaped, she noticed, the fingers slightly broader at the nails. "Officer Bear here is assisting us with our enquiries, isn't he, kids?"

Thumb still in her mouth, Gigi nodded gravely. Hank asked suddenly, "Will you call our dad in Alaska?"

"Oh?" Rose asked. "Is your dad in Alaska? What's his name?"

"Harry Bjornsen," the boy said promptly. "I'm Harry Bjornsen, Jr., really, but Dad doesn't like junior so I'm Hank."

Fred was nodding in a pleased way. "I'd rather be called Hank than Junior myself. Do you know which boat your dad's on?"

"Naw, he didn't tell us," Hank said. "Aunt Bambi says he isn't coming back."

"Who's Aunt Bambi?" Rose asked.

"We live with her," Hank said.

"What's her last name?"

Hank shrugged. "Just Bambi, I guess."

While she was questioning them, Fred said, "I'm going to go see what I can find. See you, Rosie."

"Okay," she said, and waved good-bye, as did the children, as he headed for the stairs.

She picked up her beeper then and drove Hank and Gigi to the Ogden house, where they were bedded down for the night while Fred initiated the search for their mother. Unfortunately for the kids, he was a very good detective.

Hank and Gigi went with Rose to Mr. and Mrs. Ogden's house where Mrs. Ogden gave them their own brand-new toothbrushes and pajamas and had her kids, two boys, move in together so Hank and Gigi could have one of their rooms. The kids didn't even seem to mind. They were already in bed by the time Hank and Gigi got there and seemed too sleepy to object.

And the next morning, there was Officer Fred at the lady's door. "Ready to go home?" he asked them, and took them straight back to Aunt Bambi's.

Mama looked really glad to see them and hugged and kissed them and admired Officer Fuzz and tried to thank Officer Fred but when he looked at her, he looked just the way Hank had been afraid policemen would look.

Aunt Bambi woke up after Officer Fred left, padded out into the kitchenette for a beer, took one look at them and said to Mama, "Shit. You're going to have to do better next time."

Four

THE FERRY GLIDED across Puget Sound trapped between two slices of brilliant blue, the sky and the water, with the snowy peaks of the Olympic Mountains behind, the Cascades ahead, the sharp white peak of Mount Baker up north beyond the San Juan Islands, the perfect cone of Mount Rainier to the south. It was one of those days that appeared on postcards that lured more and more tourists and transplants to Seattle. But, as was often true of such eye-appealing days, it was bitter cold, so Rose enjoyed the scenery from inside the ferry, warming her hands and her throat with a cup of cappuccino from the ferry's espresso bar while she listened to two musicians, Tania and Mark, play Irish tunes on a variety of instruments.

Rose didn't often get to hear the ferryboat musicians, since they only played the Bainbridge Island–Seattle route, and she normally rode the Bremerton ferry. But this morning, as sometimes happened, one of the Bremerton ferries had mechanical problems and wasn't running. It had taken her three hours to get home instead of just one. On the way over, she'd had no choice, since her car was still parked at the ferry terminal in Bremerton, but she chose to take the more reliable Bainbridge ferry on the way back. It took twenty minutes longer to drive to it from her house, but the trip across was only a half-hour instead of an hour.

Besides, this way she could see the musicians.

Had she known the trip home would be such an ordeal, she'd have arranged to have her cats fed and just stayed in Seattle to go to Linden's and then riding with Cindy. But she hadn't arranged for the cats and hadn't brought riding clothes, and Linden didn't open till eleven and Rose's shift was over at seven, so there should have been lots of time.

After dropping Hank and Gigi at the Ogdens', she had been able to sleep through the rest of the night in the clinic, then called in and reported off to Hager, who was taking call the rest of the weekend. Since Hager lived in Seattle, she needed only to carry a beeper. Normally, Rose would have had scads of time to get home, feed the cats, shower, change, and catch up on mail and phone calls, but because of the delay in the ferries she had had to rush. So now she enjoyed kicking back and letting the music refresh her.

Although soliciting on the ferries was strictly against the rules, only one or two of the more hidebound captains, afraid that the boats would become an extension of the panhandling street life in the city, prevented the musicians from playing. The passengers enjoyed the diversion. The music was usually instrumental—a harpist, a couple who played mainly Scandinavian music on accordion and mandolin, and Tania and Mark, who played fiddle, guitar, harp and hammered dulcimer, and sometimes other exotic instruments.

"Now docking Seattle," a voice on the intercom announced about ten minutes from the dock. On the left was the cityscape, the Space Needle, the Smith Tower which had once been the tallest building in the country, the modern skyscrapers mingling with the art deco remnants of another, kinder, gentler generation, the big E of the Edgewater Inn and the sign for Pike Place Public Market. Stretching along the waterfront to the right were the old wharfs now gentrified into gift shops full of jewelry, T-shirts, shell lamps, fudge, Mount St. Helens glassware, gourmet chocolates, Indian crafts and exotic imports, all of which could be reached by a walkway studded with seafood restaurants, and hung with brightly colored banners. Horse-drawn carriages lined the water side of the Alaska Way, waiting forlornly for the tourists who were not out on such a cold day. The trolley tracks sat empty under the Highway 99 viaduct, and beyond them cars prowled in the shade of the viaduct, searching for parking places. Rose was glad her office was right downtown and she seldom had to drive in Seattle. The traffic getting off the ferry was particularly bad, being routed far to the south, toward the Kingdome.

Along the waterfront, a shoal of giant orange cranes loaded and unloaded barges like so many spindly spiders storing food for the winter.

The ferry docked. Rose dropped a dollar in Tania's guitar case and followed the teal-and-purple parka ahead of her down the causeway and out onto the sidewalk outside the ferry terminal, across the tunnel walkway that ran under the viaduct and over Alaska Way, spilling ferry passengers out onto First and Marion.

One youngish boy Rose didn't know sat listlessly against the side of the tunnel, while on the other side a bearded, red-faced man in his forties or fifties greeted each passerby with a pleasant remark followed, if they waited long enough, with a request for change. The guy was a vet, and she wasn't sure what his trip was, but at least it didn't seem to be hostile.

She caught a bus up First to Third and Pine and walked over to Nordstrom's to buy a new pair of walking shoes before heading to the Market, past the Bon and the deserted Frederick's and Nelson building, and by the scrumptious

shops of Westlake Plaza. The usual steel drum band entertained people lunching at the patio tables set on the orna-
mental brick-and-concrete work that blocked off the street
as a strictly pedestrian area. A street preacher was exhorting
shoppers about the love of God. She happened to know
this particular proselytizer, from her former position as
a counselor at the Seattle women's shelter. She felt like
getting up and doing a little preaching herself about people
who claimed to be religious and did to their wives what this
guy had done in the name of morality. She kept walking.

The Pet Man, one of Patrick's clients, sat on the next
corner, his two lovable mutts and the gray striped cat sitting
beside him, his battered hat with a few coins and a dollar
or two next to him. A young woman in a skirt printed like
an Indian bedspread dropped a bag of dry cat food into
the hat and passed on. The Pet Man said nothing to her,
but one of the dogs sniffed the bag. Rose didn't think the
dog could be too interested. She knew how well fed these
animals were.

The Pet Man's menagerie was among the animals Linden
cared for from time to time. She licensed all of the pets
she cared for. Once the Pet Man had disappeared for six
months, and the Humane Society in Spokane had called
Linden because her name was on a dog's tag. Linden had
the dog flown back to her, but when the Pet Man returned,
he had avoided her for months, not wanting to tell her he'd
lost the dog.

As she neared the market, Rose heard the competing
musics of the street musicians who worked every available corner, doorway and level of the area. The clapping
gospel music of Gasworks Gus, an older black man, and
three young recently acquired protégés, the new washboard
band with the blonde woman and her guitar-playing partner,
all aggressively competed against by one of the crewcut,

orange-overalled Accordions From Hell group who seemed bound and determined to drown out other street music. She glanced in the window of the ice cream store, where Linden's songwriter friend Merle usually spent all day with his dog Pal at his feet, a guitar on his lap, a notepad, pencil, and a cup of coffee with endless refills on the table while he wrote songs. He wasn't there today.

She looked across the street, under the canopy of the market proper, where vendors sold fish and honey, flowers and tie-dyed T-shirts, rubber stamps and handmade silver jewelry. She would cross at First and Pike, she thought.

"Rose," someone said at her elbow. "Rose, it's me. Rose, please, have you got a couple of dollars? I'm really hungry."

The voice was male and young and did not yet have a good street whine to it. It sounded scared. And the face was familiar.

"Dico?" she asked, looking under the grime to the chocolate-brown skin beneath.

"Yeah."

"What did you do? Run out on the foster home?"

"What foster home? I've been on the streets since I turned eighteen."

"But I found you a placement . . ."

"Yeah, well, not fast enough. And I'd look for a job, honest, Rose, only I got no place to clean up, you know? I sure don't want to use the shower at the shelter. How about it? Couple of bucks for a snack?"

She took a five from her purse. Dico Miller wasn't a bad kid, wasn't on drugs or anything else that she knew of, and he did look thin. His parents had both been killed in an accident and hadn't left enough to bury them, much less pay their debts, and left their teenage son alone. No other surviving family members, no house, school over, no job, no prospects. She stuffed the five back and fished out a ten. "Get something to eat and try to clean up a little. I'll talk to a friend and see if I can get you a job, okay? Will you be here tomorrow?"

"Naw, I got an important appointment. Shit yes, I'll be here. What d'ya think?"

She ignored the attitude and crossed into the market, more preoccupied with wondering whom she could hit up to hire a former client than with the goodies at Fortunate Finery.

Then the crowd in the market jostled and assaulted her with noise, color and sensation from all directions so that she had to pay attention to keep from getting trampled or carried past the exit that led underground, into the belly of the market, where Fortunate Finery rubbed elbows with rock shops and comic shops, antique stores and Afghanistani imports, among others.

The fellows at the fish market were tossing humongous salmon back and forth while entertaining the customers with their patter. She stopped in at Tenzing Momo for some Tibetan incense, bought crocheted catnip balls for her cats, and then ducked around the corner to the ramp leading down to the next level.

The sandwich board was not out front; she noticed that right away. The door was closed, and the shop was dark even though it was already noon. She peered inside but could see no sign of Linden.

"Ahem," someone said behind her. A refined, ladylike, alto someone. "Excuse me," said the woman, stepping forward. She was as silvery and sparkly as a coho salmon leaping out of the bay into the sunlight. Her hair was every hue and tint of silver from gunmetal through pewter through dove gray to white and curled to well below her shoulders, held back from her face by a silver rose. Silver-gray eyes full of intelligence and cool humor regarded Rose politely before turning their attention to the door lock. She wore white tights and gray Doc Martens under a long, heathery wool skirt with a silver-embroidered lace petticoat hanging out from under it and a long, loopy sweater spun with silvery threads and topped with a drift of a sequined and rhinestone-studded silvery scarf.

"Is Linden sick today?" Rose asked.

"No, she's been called away," the woman said, over her shoulder. "I'm assuming management at present." She had a low, throaty voice, a torch singer's voice, Rose thought, like Eartha Kitt or Candice Bergen.

Merle ambled up, his dog, Pal, trotting along beside him. He stopped and stood with one long jeans-clad leg bent at the knee, and leaned against the door frame with his forearm. He was a tall man with thinning brown hair and bad teeth, but his quick brown eyes and soft musical voice betrayed him as more than an ordinary street person, however much he liked to play the role. He came from a good family and could have been anything, but he'd been an angry young man and kept being angry well into middle age. Now he was mostly angry at himself for letting all of his chances go by. The songs he wrote were good and true and best of all, Rose thought, not self-centered. Musicians all over Seattle performed and recorded them with Merle's blessing, but Merle, no matter what other gigs he tried, always ended up back at the market. Pal looked up at the silver woman and whined, a happy whine.

"Linden's not around?" Merle asked the woman.

The silvery lady turned and gave him the somewhat appraising smile he took so much for granted that he didn't react to it one way or the other. "No, but I am. You must be Merle and *this*," she said, patting the dog's head, "is

Pal. I've heard so much about you."

"You *have*?"

"Certainly."

"Excuse me," Rose said a bit more sharply than she intended. "Who are *you*?"

"I'm Felicity Fortune. I'm part owner of the shop, actually," she said with a faint trace of a British Isles accent—Rose wasn't sure of the exact origin. To Merle she said, "I'm glad you've come. This letter came to the shop for you."

He accepted the letter and ran his fingers over it for a moment without even looking at the address. "I came to ask if Linden could look after Pal. I decided to ship out on a tanker for a while, pick up a little money. I want to make a new tape but I want it to be a really *good* one this time."

Merle was always talking about that. Except for one, the tapes remained unrecorded, and the one he *had* made had been so overproduced you could hardly hear the songs. Another of Merle's fatal flaws, she supposed—he was a good musician but a lousy producer.

Felicity opened the door and said, "Sorry to keep you standing in the hall while I prattle on. Do come in." Her smile was warm and genuinely kind, quite out of keeping with the rest of her silvery persona. She was not, Rose saw, even particularly pretty. More what you would call striking. Her features were strong and determined—a patrician nose and a square jaw—and something about the set of them reminded Rose of Linden.

"Linden never mentioned anyone else owning the store," Rose said, feeling anxious about her friend's absence. "Is she okay?"

"Oh, yes, dear. Just had a bit of an emergency. Thought it best if I filled in for the time being. Let me guess. You must be Rose."

"How did you know?"

"The mustard seed," she said, pointing to the pendant that Rose had decided to wear that morning on a whim, just to keep her spirits up.

Merle remained outside the door after Rose and Felicity entered the shop. When Rose looked back at him, she saw that he was reading his letter. His lower jaw dropped and his eyes boggled, his head nodding rapidly as he reread it several times.

"Not bad news for you too?" Rose asked, experiencing her usual feeling that the whole world was falling apart at the seams.

"Oh, no. Rosie, you aren't going to believe this, but somebody sent Ace Jackson my tape. He wants to record two of my songs. He wants me to come to Nashville and talk to him about it."

"Merle, that's great!" she said, thinking how lucky it was that he had come to the shop before shipping out. "You really deserve it."

"Thanks," he said, his eyes still on the letter as he tugged at the dog's lead. "Come on, Pal. We got to think about this."

"Well, it's good to see somebody get a break," Rose said to Felicity. "I just hope he uses it to good advantage."

"Oh, I think he will," Felicity said, smiling that same assessing smile through the window at the retreating figures of the man and his dog.

"I wonder how he'll get the money to go to Nashville," Rose said, watching after them too. "Do you suppose Ace Jackson will send it to him?"

"Oh no," Felicity said with a rather surprising air of authority. "I *imagine* he'll find an unclaimed scratch tab which will suffice. He's ready for luck now, you see. He's outlived a lot of the influences opposing him. And he's

worked for it. That sort of people are still the easiest kind
to make lucky."

"Excuse me. I don't want to be rude or anything, but how
would you know?" Rose asked, her initial sense of irritation
with the stranger returning. There was something so theatrical about Felicity Fortune—so deliberately mysterious—
that Rose could not help but wonder if she was just *being*
weird or if she really *was* weird.

"I know quite a bit, actually," Felicity said, flopping
down in an overstuffed chair and making no effort to count
out the till, turn on the lights, or open the door for other
customers.

"Where exactly is Linden, then?" Rose asked in a tone
that brooked no evasion.

"If you must know, she wasn't quite up to the job here,"
Felicity said, playing idly with a peacock feather fan.

"You said you were part owner. You didn't *fire* her?"

"Oh, no. She's gone on for further training. She suggested you as a possible candidate too, and as a senior
member, I was sent to sort things out."

"A senior member of what?"

"A sort of sorority Linden and I belong to, one that helps
people."

"Uh-huh. Linden never mentioned any sorority, and we've
known each other a long time."

"Oh, she wouldn't mention this one," Felicity said, rum-
maging in the ridiculously small beaded evening purse she
carried at her side slung from a belt that seemed to be made
of fine-link chain mail. "She's just been a pledge until now.
Wait a bit. I have a card in here someplace."

She produced one that read, in calligraphy-style script,
"Dame Felicity Fortune, Godmothers (Anonymous), Fair
Fates Facilitated, Questers Accommodated, and Virtue Vin-
dicated. True Love and Serendipity Our Specialty."

Rose read it and chuckled with relief. "I might have known. That Linden. I never really figured her for a practical joker, but this is a good one. We were kidding around about this yesterday. Where is she really? Who are you? And please don't tell me you're the fairy godmother."

"Oh, no. I wouldn't put you on like that. I'm only *one* of the Godmothers and we're not exactly all fairies, not anymore. At one time, of course, that was true, but the fey actually found that human agents, properly seasoned, work out better. More identity with the subject. Just as many of you in your profession were yourselves the products of troubled childhoods so you now identify with your clients."

No wonder she was so theatrical! She was an actress. For some reason, maybe to give Merle his bit of good news, Linden had hired an actress to come in and play an elaborate joke on them all. Well, nobody could say Rose lacked a sense of humor. She played along, grinning to show that she knew what was happening, "Gee, that's very democratic of the fey. So okay, if you're who you say you are, how about my wish?"

Felicity nodded graciously. She was some actress, all right.

"Well," Rose said. "First of all, the division's budget could use one of those bottomless purses that were always turning up in the fairy tales. I don't suppose you've got one just lying around anywhere, do you?"

To her surprise, Felicity didn't do any fakey bibbity-bobbity-booing but snapped the peacock feathers of her fan together in a disgusted way. "That's it, throw money at it! Honestly, you Americans! And I thought you took your work more seriously than that."

"Money *is* serious," Rose insisted, drawn into earnest discussion in spite of herself. "Senate appropriations cut our budget by half this year."

"I'll look into it, though mind you, we don't do bottomless purses anymore. Too crude and very bad for the economy in general. Inflation and all that." She turned a shrewd gaze on Rose and for the first time, Rose saw that her eyes were very strange indeed—did they make holographic contact lenses these days? Felicity's eyes had that same crystalline look about them, and Rose thought for a moment that she could see rainbows in the irises.

"Also," Felicity continued shrewdly, and dead seriously, "a bottomless purse for your division would be of very little use to the persons it's meant to help if the money is spent under the direction of someone unsuitable."

Before Rose could protest that Linden surely must have briefed her about Rose's work situation, Felicity added, "I notice that you didn't ask anything for yourself, however. Your wish, in fact, was for reinforcements, a fairy godmother for the city of Seattle. Now that seems a little odd, Rose Samson. True, you don't believe I am who I am as yet, though you will, but have you no wish for yourself? I'd hate to think you were someone with a bit of that Messiah complex the pop psychologists are always on about."

Rose shrugged. "Maybe so, but I already have quite a bit compared to most of the people I work with. I've got a job, a home, food, and money enough to buy clothes from your shop if I want."

"Don't you wish for anything else? True love, maybe?"

Fred's face popped into her mind, but Rose said sensibly, "Felicity, no offense, but that's not something you get just by wishing." After all, she didn't even know if he was involved or not, or anything else about his personal life. She might not even like him if she knew him well and besides, real true love happened between the two people involved, not because some dingbat in motley silver waved a magic wand. Besides, there were lots of things more important than her own love life—or lack of it.

"I see," Felicity said.

"Look," Rose said kindly but firmly, "it's nice of you to encourage me, but lots of people don't even have the basics, much less two lovely cats and a vintage clothing collection. Sure my dad left us when I was a kid, but he continued to support us, and my mother was an alcoholic, but she sobered up before she died and we were able to deal with a lot of our issues together. Meanwhile, I've managed to make a very nice life for myself and I'm trying to help other people do the same."

"Survivor guilt, eh?"

"Will you cut that out? I'm just counting my blessings," she said. Before she could say any more Felicity, who reminded her a bit of a forties movie star with her dramatic gestures and grand, perhaps a bit matronizing tone, waved her own assessment of her motivations aside.

"Well, dear, there's nothing wrong with that, and mercy knows *I* would be the last to suggest there was anything wrong with you for wishing to bring blessings to others. It is, in fact, my raison d'être as well. However, if you could bring yourself to be a teensy bit more selfish and wish for something the wee-est bit more personal, it would be easier to prove my usefulness to you."

"I beg your pardon?"

"You *will* be wanting to put me to the test, *n'est-ce pas?*"

"*Mais non,*" said Rose, who could joke around as well as anyone. She was used to dealing with somewhat deranged people, and this woman seemed at least to be well intentioned. However, a reality check was in order. "Ms. Fortune, I'm sorry if you are under the misapprehension that, in passing time with my friend Linden, I somehow gave the impression that I wanted your help or advice. The truth is, as a social services professional employed by the City of Seattle and the State of Washington, I have rules to uphold, and one of those rules is that I don't tell you nothin' about nobody nohow no time, period. No matter what you show me, promise me, or give me. So please, let me disabuse you of any notions you may have that I will at any time break client confidentiality so you can prove—whatever it is you're trying to prove. Whatever you imagine you can do, the clients I have now, and my list by no means covers all of the people in the city who need help, have devastatingly real problems. Many of them face tragic, frightening, frustrating, humiliating, dangerous, even life-threatening situations every day. I—we—are trying to help them survive a little longer, in hopes that somehow they can last until improvement can be made."

Felicity Fortune was not the least put out, but dropped most of the melodrama, except for an eloquently raised eyebrow. "Well put, Rose Samson, and very loyal, I'm sure. But you'd be surprised what I can imagine, and what I've coped with. I notice you only say that you hope to help your clients to survive until improvements can be made—not until you can make them. Or they can make them."

"I'm being realistic," Rose said. "I can only do so much, the division can only do so much. Many of the clients could do more for themselves than we can possibly do for them if only they had the will or—"

"Or the luck?" Felicity Fortune asked, then waved the fan dismissively. "Oh, I know. I know. Luck is extremely unscientific, but like many unscientific things, it's also extremely useful. It also happens to be my business."

"Oh, cute! I get it! Your name is Felicity Fortune, as in good luck, and you make—ta da—good luck!"

Five

ROSE EXPECTED A disclaimer but Felicity Fortune simply tried to look modest. "Let's just say I—that is, we of the Godmothers—have made a study of its creation and have become somewhat—scientific—in reproducing it where and when it is needed."

"Oh, well, that's different," Rose said, settling down crosslegged on the floor and cupping her chin in her hands while nodding to Felicity Fortune to continue. Rose was a good listener. These days, other than filling out forms, listening was about all she *could* do. At least Felicity Fortune had a fairly original delusion. "Okay, so tell me. You're the fairy godmother, right? And you've come to make me and the city of Seattle live happily ever after?"

"I shall certainly try, with your assistance, of course. But first I think it is my turn to clear up any misapprehensions *you* may have about fairy godmothers and their historical role." Felicity Fortune now sounded less like an actress than a college professor. "The tales most people are familiar with tend to be highly revisionist. That is, the viewpoint taken is that of the person or people who triumphed in the situation in question, and any subtler details, random injustices or atrocities are swept under the rug."

"According to Bruno Bettelheim and some of the other authorities on the subject, the tales are metaphors for psychological processes," Rose said. "I have a lot of trouble with them even in that context. Are you trying to tell me that they are literally true stories?"

"Parts of true stories, yes. True as far as they go, yes. But highly adulterated, even by those Grimm boys, who like all boys were unduly fascinated by the gory bits. Actually, the real fault lies not in how they told the tales but the tales they left out. You see, the fairy stories mostly only tell about the cases in which we triumphed in our quest to bring truth, justice, happiness and a higher moral order to the universe."

"That *is* a tall order," Rose said. "I can see how if you've been doing this for a long time, parts were bound to have been left out."

"Yes, and those parts are what make us so unbelievable to a smart young woman such as yourself. Like you, we aren't always successful, and also like you, and I'm sure you'll take no offense that I say so, we do make mistakes. In a few of those instances, the tales have been altered to make us look good. For instance, there was the time Dame Agatha met a young woman and started to ask her for a piece of bread. Dame Agatha is actually notoriously bad at disguises and forgot to remove her jewels when she put on her rags. Besides which, she's a bit on the plump side. So when she asked the girl for bread, the girl, who it later turned out was having a bad episode of PMS so that the very *thought* of food made her nauseous, told Agatha she ought to be bloody ashamed of herself posing as a beggar when there were so many people in dire straits. It shows more intelligence than hard-heartedness, seen in that light, but before she could finish her sentence she had toads coming out of her mouth.

"Then along comes her flighty sister, sees Agatha's jewels, puts two and two together and decides Agatha's some dotty socialite with a bob or two to give away. She was dieting anyway, that one, so she gave Agatha a whole cake and as soon as she said, 'You're welcome,' right off her mouth starts dripping diamonds and pearls."

"The moral being that good manners pay?" Rose ventured.

"The moral being that manners are superficial and if you're going to impersonate a beggar you should bloody well take off your tiara first. The sister who dripped toads was ordinarily a bright and conscientious individual who read six books a week, carried medicines and food to plague victims, and privately donated to distressed families. Poor thing merely had a gruff way of expressing herself at certain times of the month, but there you were, the damage was done and she was spitting toads for the rest of her life. Being a resourceful sort, she wrote some of the earliest known papers on amphibian biology. Meanwhile, her flighty sister, who was a chatterbox, spouted diamonds and pearls until they became quite valueless and thereby bankrupted the royal treasury and the country as a whole. You never hear about that though, I daresay."

"True," Rose admitted.

"So you see what I mean. Of course, that particular example is neither life-threatening nor especially horrible, unless you have an aversion to toads, but we've dealt with many situations which were. Back in the days when these earliest case histories were compiled, there were, as there are now, plenty of wicked stepparents, starving and homeless people, abandoned and abused children and physically and mentally wounded war veterans. Besides which, there was quite a rigid class system. The unfortunates had no one to aid them save kindly individuals, who were very scarce.

"That is why the Queen of Fairy recruited us."

"The Godmothers?"

"Right."

"I don't quite understand. The little I've heard about fairies these days says that they were alien, spooky creatures who hated humankind."

"I don't know about alien and spooky, Rose dear, but humankind was even harder to love back then than it is now. Her Majesty, a *truly* great lady, though much misunderstood, decided that if it was ever to improve, someone must see to it that at least a few of the worthier specimens among the mortals were preserved against the depredations of the world. That is how our sorority was born. We are her agents, you see, and have continued to do her work throughout the centuries."

"That's very sweet," Rose said, gently. "But I'm afraid the Queen of Fairy couldn't even dream of some of the problems we have today—"

"On the contrary. People are not much different than they have always been, although they are, as you may have gathered, slightly better because of our efforts."

"There's never been a drug problem like there is now! It's epidemic! And there's AIDS and all sorts of other—"

"Ever heard of the Black Plague? I'm not denigrating the problems you face today, Rose, certainly not, or I wouldn't be here, but in my day a greater percentage of people died just from giving birth, malnutrition or working themselves to death than die of all of your diseases put together."

"Sure," Rose said, grinning. "And in those days you had to walk ten miles to school barefoot in the snow uphill both ways in the dark. I know."

"I beg your pardon?"

"It's something parents always say. You know. Life in the old days was harder than it was now. I don't see how it's gotten much better; maybe it did for a while, but these days everything, health care, law enforcement, ecology, the economy—just everything—is deteriorating very fast. I know, I know, it's not the Black Plague, but back in your day at least the environment was still healthy and, according to you, you had enough magic to make pearls and diamonds come out of people's mouths."

"Yes, the planet was healthy, but people weren't, and while we did have somewhat more access to magic, we did *not* have whole organizations full of young people like you to do all of the boring bits. Nor could we always help, even with magic. Sometimes we intervened too late, sometimes the forces we could arrange on the good side were too weak for really determined wickedness, and sometimes the whole world was simply aligned against those we would aid. But we always did try. As you are trying. And we do have methods and resources not presently at your disposal."

As Felicity spoke, Rose smiled at the surreality of debating the comparative damage of the Black Plague and AIDS and the comparative merits of social work vs. magic with someone who claimed to have personal experience of all of the topics. Oh well, at least Felicity Fortune wasn't claiming to be Madonna. Rose had processed six clients like that last week—an odd split between those who thought they were the rock star and those who believed they were the mother of Christ, with one breaking the tie who thought she was the rock star *and* the mother of Christ.

"Sounds great," Rose told Felicity. "If only it were true!"

"It is, believe me. You do have to believe, Rose. That's always been part of the equation, and as I told you, I'm perfectly willing to give you a demonstration. Ah-ah-ah! I didn't say I wanted you to violate any secrets. Perish the thought. But surely there's someone you'd like to help who doesn't need to be kept quite so hush-hush. Someone, perhaps, not covered in your line of work. An animal, perhaps? Even animals can use good fortune and true love."

"We-ell," she said, thinking of poor Cindy Ellis in danger of losing her job at the stable to her greedy bitch of a stepmother. "You don't happen to know any honest lawyers who take cases out of the good of their hearts or are willing to barter riding lessons for services, do you?"

"Not offhand, but give me a little time, Rose. Haven't been here long. Must do some networking. That sort of situation can be solved in a variety of ways—the best of which involve making certain contacts. In the old days, we always had to involve commoners, widows and orphans, that sort of thing, with the royal family. If you could get a prince or princess interested, well, there you were. The whole thing was easy to solve. Much more difficult in a democratic country."

"Well, but then there's always your magic wand, right?"

"At one time, certainly. But these days magic, like all natural resources, must be used sparingly. *Very* sparingly. Dame Prudence of the Accounting Committee monitors the expenditure of magical energy even more strictly than Puget Power monitors electricity. There is a great deal of need in the world and far less magic, so we attempt to conserve that resource whenever possible and use only as much as is necessary to get the ball rolling, you might say. Most of what we do these days consists of putting the right people and the right circumstances together, very much as I suppose you do in your job with trying to find the proper organization to deal with your clients' problems. But as you know, sometimes that will not suffice, and then we resort to magic."

"So you couldn't give me a bottomless purse if you wanted to?"

"I fear not. The mere mention of that device is enough to give poor Dame Prudence apoplexy. It is definitely *not* within my allotment. Even if it were, I wouldn't be so reckless. The larger magical withdrawals, like the overuse of any resource, involve costs which may easily outweigh the original benefit and result in highly unpleasant repercussions."

"I see."

"And that's only one of the problems. Magic also must be used only in aid of the worthy. There's simply not enough of it to punish wrongdoers these days."

"That figures. There aren't enough jails or counselors or any other means of dealing with them either," Rose said.

"Exactly. About all we can do in that line is to protect ourselves and those we are trying to help from them as much as possible, but mostly, the magic is only expended in aid of the worthy."

"So how *do* you choose who's worthy?" Rose thought every congressman who had ever tried to regulate the welfare system would love to have the answer to *that* particular question.

"Very carefully. If you're to use magic to bestow good fortune on an individual who might not have acquired it by other means, that good fortune must be balanced in their lives by their degree of need to begin with, or the amount of good they have done themselves or have the capacity for doing, to earn it, you see? That's one reason we so often help children and young people. With their lives ahead of them, they have the greatest potential for good and the most time to realize it."

"If you're all that magical, why let people get hurt at all? Or is it a question of not enough to go around again?"

"Partially that, I suppose, for there's certainly evil we all wish we could prevent. But often a spot of bad fortune can change someone very much for the better, developing empathy and compassion. If you can help someone out of one of those spots, then all that remains is to put opportunities to succeed at goodness in their way. Several of our more effective agents have been recruited during those periods in their lives."

"What if they never have the bad fortune? Is that good?"

"You're toying with me now, Rose. Of course, whether it's good or bad is entirely subjective. The real point is that if their fortune isn't bad, then they don't present a problem we have to deal with, and may be able to provide practical assistance to others."

"Sounds like you have a use for everybody."

"Not quite everybody. There are always a few who succumb to despair from the cradle on and will not recognize the possibility of good fortune when they see it."

"You can't help them?"

Felicity shrugged. "We're not what they need. At least, they usually aren't like the ones who actively enjoy the pain of others."

"The ones you can't fight?"

"I didn't say we can't fight them, just that we can't punish them."

"You could, you know, rehabilitate them. That's what we do these days."

"Do you really?" Felicity asked, cocking her brow again.

"Not always—well, very rarely, actually, but at least we're not trying to make two wrongs equal a right."

"Commendable, I'm sure, but I do wonder, dear, if you've considered that there are those who are not merely unfortunate or deranged but actually evil."

"Maybe. But there are so many people causing damage for other reasons that it's a little hard to tell who's who, don't you think?"

"You do have a point," Felicity conceded. "At any rate,

as I said before, punishment of wrongdoers is not our purpose. If we see to it that good is distributed to the deserving and the prepared, then we may assume that evil will be discouraged at the very least."

"Discourager of Evil," Rose said. "Doesn't have much ring to it."

"That's reality for you," Felicity said. "It lacks style."

"So, back to rewarding the really deserving, if we can be judgmental in the other direction for a moment. Were you the one who turned Ace Jackson on to Merle's songs? Did you use magic to do that?"

"Oh, no, dear. That was a friend of mine. Do you remember reading that Serena Starr, the country singer, had a dreadful childhood and would have been forced to stay with the stepfather who molested her after her mother's death except that she was discovered by Dallas Glover, the agent, and made a star? Serena was one of our girls. Clients, I mean. She was delighted with Merle's songs but felt they were more Ace's style than hers."

"Wow. But how did she find out about them? Oh. Linden, I guess."

Felicity Fortune nodded. "One of our most valuable trainees."

Rose took a deep breath. By this time, she was starting to take Felicity Fortune at her word. No doubt all this talk of wishes was the result of a wish-fulfillment dream, and Rose would awaken in her own bedroom in Bremerton. Meanwhile, why not see how far this crazy conversation would take her? "Felicity, I don't know whether to believe you or not, but you were asking about animals. Do you like horses?"

"My dear, I was a jockey as a young girl."

"Good. You and Cindy ought to get along fine. I was on my way to see a friend of mine today—she's just started working at a stable up near Gasworks Park. You want to come?"

"I certainly do," Felicity said, rubbing her hands together in the most theatrical gesture yet. "Lead on, Samson. The game's afoot."

"Where are you parked?" Felicity asked.

"I take the bus when I'm on this side," Rose said.

"Highly commendable. But perhaps this time you'll let me drive?"

"Okay by me," Rose said. The visit with Felicity had taken longer than the stop to say hello to Linden, and she wanted time for a trot with Cindy before dark. Maybe Felicity was a psycho, but she seemed harmless enough. Her delusion was apparently gentle in a codependent sort of way, and she must be a friend of Linden's, or she wouldn't have had the key to the shop. Besides, if by some wild chance she was one of the rare female serial killers specializing in the murders of women running vintage clothing shops, then Rose surely ought to keep her eye on her. And even if she wasn't exactly a fairy godmother, she had a fairly interesting view of nonsupernatural ways to network and help people. Any port in a storm, Rose thought.

Felicity locked up, and the two of them ascended the ramp into the market. The day was darkening already, and garlands of lightbulbs lit the vendors' booths. They threaded their way through the throng at the seafood vendor and out onto the street. A brisk breeze whipped pieces of paper and foam cups down First. Dico Miller still huddled on the street corner.

"I thought you'd have gone off to dinner by now," Rose said, then noticed Dico was cradling his hand. "What's the matter?"

"Hurt my hand."

"How?"

"Trying to hang onto the money you give me."

"Shit," Rose said. "Who took it?"

Dico shrugged. "I dunno. Didn't look too close. It ain't healthy."

"Felicity, I . . ." Rose started to introduce her to Dico and ask if she had a job for him around the store, but the silver-haired woman wasn't paying any attention. Instead, she was kneeling at the mouth of the alley and enticing a gray alley cat by rubbing her fingers together.

"Come here, you lazy puss. Yes, that's right. Come here."

The cat came purring, expecting a treat. Instead, Felicity scooped it up and began whispering to it.

"Felicity, this is Dico. Do you think you have a . . . ?"

"Most certainly. I have a very fine cat right here. Here you go, young man," she said, unloading the cat into the boy's arms, which made him swear when the cat, with unerring accuracy, landed on his sore hand. "Now you two take care of each other."

Rose rolled her eyes and nodded at Felicity, and Dico shook his head. Burdening the poor guy with a pet wasn't exactly her idea of helping him, especially with Linden unavailable to lend a hand if he was unable to feed the animal. But if Dico was dismayed, the cat took the situation in stride and had settled into the space created by the young man's crossed legs. It washed its white socks as serenely as if it was sitting on its own private windowsill.

"Here we are," Felicity said, stopping in front of a rounded boxy car, shaped rather like the old VW bugs but painted Porsche silver. It had a bumper sticker on the trunk lid that said, "Commit acts of random kindness and senseless beauty." The car bore no manufacturer's model name, nor did Rose recognize the make.

"Don't tell me. It flies," she guessed.

"No, but it *is* fueled by carbon monoxide from the exhaust of other vehicles, and emits oxygen fumes as its own exhaust."

"Wait a minute. That sounds suspiciously plantlike. This thing didn't start out in life as a pumpkin by any chance, did it?"

She was kidding Felicity in a way that would have been rather dangerous had the woman been seriously deranged. People got very upset if you made jokes about their delusional systems ordinarily, but Felicity just winked and said, "Really, Rose, you must allow me a *few* trade secrets."

"I like the bumper sticker."

"It's not original," Felicity told her. "But as Prince Charming used to say, if the shoe fits, wear it."

Six

SNO JUMPED BACK from the man and his knife. "Like, who *are* you?" she asked, panting. "What's your problem? Are you some kinda pervert or something?"

"Shut up," the man said, lunging for her. "Shut up and commere."

She could turn. She could run. But he was a tall man with long legs, and she was wearing a skirt. He could catch her in an even race.

"No," she said. "Uh-uh. I'm not making it easy for you. Look, mister, I don't know who you are or how you got the letter or why you picked on me, but you got a helmet on, I can't see your face. Just leave me alone and this never happened, okay?" He feinted at her and she jumped back, trembling. The fact that she was able to talk at all she attributed to feeling as if she was watching something on TV happen to somebody else.

"Give it up, little girl," the man said gruffly. "You got nowhere to run to, know what I mean? I can make it so you never feel a thing. I don't like hurting little girls, but you've seriously annoyed somebody with connections. That tends to be fatal, in my cultural milieu. So don't make me slash you to death, okay?"

He lunged again and Sno, who had not found his speech

57

at all reassuring, jumped behind the bike and shoved it
toward him.

He leaped back, then sprinted over the bike and caught
her wrist. Without thinking, she grabbed his wrist with her
other hand and threw him. Her judo lessons had finally
come in handy. He lay there on the ground, staring up at
her while she stared back at him, both of them unable to
believe that she had actually decked him. Then she took to
her heels and ran like hell.

Deep in the forest at that time there dwelled a group of
former soldiers, all grown much older than they had been
in the war, though no less troubled by all that they had seen
and heard and done. They had come to the forest to do a
sweat lodge and a lot of drumming, trying to bring peace to
their spirits, if not to the forest. There were seven of them,
these veterans, and they were called Doc, Doper, Chief,
Red-Eye, Dead-Eye, Drifty and Trip-Wire. Originally there
were eight but the eighth, the African-American sergeant
known for his stealth in ambush as Sneaky-Pete, had taken
a job as a personal security officer for an internationally
famous dance troupe of former inner-city children from
Detroit who were currently performing at a dance festival
in Port Townsend, Washington. So he couldn't make it.

Doc was out chopping wood that morning while Doper
and Chief were down at the river catching breakfast. They
had the cabin for two weeks and had only been here for a
couple of days. It was pretty well hidden. The cabin was
accessible by road most of the way, until the route to the
camp took off onto an overgrown side road that had been
washed out by a feeder stream, leaving a huge ravine that
had to be carefully negotiated, then the stream forded, in a
pack trip that took an hour or two. This time of year, with
the snowfall frequent and the roads plowed much less often,

the place was fairly remote. It wasn't so remote, however, that any of them felt foolish about not registering with the Park Service, especially since the register had disappeared, along with the Park Service building that used to be there just before you reached the Shuksan campground. Besides, they weren't doing anything dangerous or illegal, they had plenty of winter gear and lots of fuel and they all needed time away from civilization and together.

They hadn't known each other in-country. Hadn't even been in the same place at around the same time. Doc had served two tours early in the war as a medic, one tour largely in the Central Highlands with the Montagnard tribesmen, one taking classified hikes along the Ho Chi Minh Trail where it skirted Laos and Cambodia, with several also classified forays into those countries for a variety of classified reasons he still had trouble confronting. He'd spent a lot of the time since he'd been back getting drunk or high and getting over getting drunk or high, being in bad relationships, getting good jobs, jobs he loved, where people thought highly of him until he inevitably freaked out. Then he walked into his first vet center, talked to the counselor, participated in rap sessions and started working on his counseling degree while volunteering at the center himself. Now he was a full-fledged counselor, but this wasn't exactly a center-sponsored activity. This was something he was doing for himself, with friends.

Getting away. Clean air and water, beautiful scenery, snow, wood to chop, fires to build, singing and drumming, thinking, praying, talking to other guys, purifying himself in the sweat lodge. It had been great for the weekend. But something restless and dissatisfied inside himself, the cynical, asshole part that had controlled him totally when he drank, was sneering, "Okay. Been there. Done that. Now what?" Be still, he told himself, be still and experience this.

Then he heard the screams and tore off like a round from an AK-47.

Magic Flute

Taking money from street people like Dico Miller was only practice for bigger and better things, Nguyen Ding Hoa assured the Guerillas as the gang gathered on the fire escape of Ding's building and smoked the profits of their morning's labors.

The Guerillas blew smoke rings and nodded, cool. Like Ding, many of them wore their straight black or dark brown hair long, with a kerchief tied around their foreheads like an Indian headband. They were laughing and joking about the expressions on people's faces—the little black dude had about cried when they'd taken the money they'd just seen the woman give him. A ten! Most of those people didn't get that much all day.

Ding was doing a humorous impression of the poor geek when the window to his parents' apartment banged open and his mother's face appeared in the opening. "Ding," she said. "La dei."

"In a minute, Mom," he said.

"Now," his mother said firmly. She stood only four feet eight and weighed less than eighty pounds, but every ounce of her was made of steel springs.

"I'm with the gang, Mom," he said.

"You come," she said. He sometimes ignored her and his father. He would have liked to now, with his head light from the weed he'd been smoking and his friends giggling and looking on. But one glance at his mother's set face and he knew now was not going to be one of those times.

"Later, dudes," he said.

Le groaned. "Oh, man, you're not going to go . . ."

"Got to. Mom hasn't been feeling good. I better see if she needs me to get her something."

"Give her a hit of this, man," Huong suggested, holding out the joint.

"Hunh," Ding snorted in appreciation. He took the joint, then turned his back on the guys to climb in the window, blocking his mother's face from the gang and the gang from her.

"So, what's so important?" he asked her, when they were well away from the window.

"You!" she said, giving him a sharp one-handed shove that, although he towered over her, sent him reeling back into the living room, while all the time cursing him in Vietnamese. "You steal from beggars to buy drugs!"

"Mom, it wasn't like that, okay?" he replied in English, then switched to Vietnamese, "It's not like it's real drugs, just a little hash, like you had in Vietnam . . ."

His mother pushed him again and he sat down abruptly on the dilapidated foam futon that served as both a couch and his bed. She actually spat at him. "You who have had every chance are behaving like trash! Your father and I are both of good families. You think all he does is sweep out stores, but he was a doctor! Even when we were refugees, we did not steal. We worked. And we certainly didn't steal from beggars. You behave like a common shoeshine boy, roaming the streets and stealing! Is it for this we came to America, so our son could become a thief? Better we had all died under the communists. Better we had died in the refugee camps!"

"Mother, these street bums just have money given to them. They grew up here with everything. Most of them never had a war or the camps. They can share a little. We bust our asses in this country and get nowhere because the

Americans are so afraid of Asian kids being smarter and more ambitious than they are. You saw how it was with me. I couldn't get into the university."

"No, but you got into jail! We save you from prison in Vietnam, we bring you from the camps, and you go to jail here."

"Jail here is better than the camps, Mom. The people have so much and they won't share . . ."

"The UN doctor shared," his mother reminded him. "And the church group. And you used to share too, my son. You were a better person when you had nothing."

He closed his mouth and turned his face to the wall until she hurried off to her job. By that time it was raining harder than the usual Seattle drizzle and the gang had dispersed. He didn't feel like calling them back again.

He sat astride the duct-taped, patched vinyl seat of the rickety kitchen chair watching the rain run down the crack in the window and relit the joint. As he got quietly stoned, his mother's words and the disappointment and anger in her face stabbed through the smoke and through his own bitterness. Maybe he should have died in the camps, but somebody had promised him a chance.

It had been raining like this that day, another long dreary day in monsoon season, and he'd carried his rice bowl away from the quonset hut where his parents and the other adults squatted, eating their rice. The rain gushed through holes in the tin roof and beat so loudly that it sounded like a thousand drums.

Talking of their home, of the war, of family that was left behind and of what would become of the young people, talking of their bowels and their teeth and their skin diseases, the adults shouted in piercing voices between carefully savored nibbles of rice.

Ding could not bear it that day. The constant din of rain

made him feel as if he wanted to peel off his skin and run screaming through the barbed wire, but the cold and the dankness made his bones ache and his toes and hands and balls shrivel and shrink.

When he grew old here, what would he talk about? How it was during the early days in the camp?

He went to find his gang and eat with them. He had another gang in those days, his first gang, his friends, boys he had grown up with. Several of them had gone by then—Dao and Phuong had died earlier in the month from the fever that spread before the UN health officials came with their shots, several of the other guys were in the hospital, and Linh, the lucky devil, had been shipped out with his family to America. There had been talk that soon the Hong Kong government was going to return them all to Vietnam and turn them over to the communist government. It wouldn't be so hard on the ones who had no parents. The communists would train them to do something, take care of them, maybe give them jobs, but his parents would be punished, perhaps killed, if they had done even half what they claimed to help the Americans. Ding had not wanted to return to Vietnam. Not even if they made him president. He wanted to see America. He would make a good American, he would learn to drive a car and play a guitar and wear clothes same like the doctors from Seattle and Portland who had come with the UN. One of them sang a song all the time he was examining people and giving shots and Ding sang it to himself as he hunched over his rice, sheltering under the branches of a tree that overhung the barbed wire. He couldn't remember much of it, and began humming a Vietnamese song instead as he dipped into his rice bowl.

That was when he'd heard her.

"Please, son, share your meal with an old lady?" a tiny pathetic voice had whined near his elbow. He looked down and saw a wizened little woman with betel-blackened teeth staring up at him through cataract-clouded eyes.

"Where's your own rice bowl, Auntie?" he asked. His parents had taught him to treat every elderly person as if he or she were his own grandparent. His grandparents, of course, were lost long ago in Vietnam.

The old woman too had had her losses.

"My son died last week and gang toughs stole it from me with no strong son to protect me. Please. I'm very weak."

"Who stole it from you, Auntie?" he asked.

"Boys," she said. "Big strong boys like you, like my son. They've eaten it all. You can't get it back."

"No, but you will need your bowl. Here, you eat mine and I'll go settle with them." Part of him just wanted a fight.

She took his bowl and ate the rice hungrily, saying, "No. Don't go. It is enough that I eat now. You're a kind young man. And musical. Didn't I hear you singing?"

"Yes."

"What was that song?"

He told her the name of the Vietnamese song he had been singing, but she said, "No, the other one. Was that an American song?"

"Yes, Bac Si Baker from Seattle sang it always and I learned it from him."

"What is it? It is very strange."

Ding had known nothing then, nothing about music, nothing about America. He had told her, "It is the story of Lou-Le Lou-Ly but I cannot make out the words. When the Colonel remembers the work of my mother and sends for us to come to America, I will learn the meaning," he said, but he knew he was boasting. The Colonel didn't remember his mother. She had only been a secretary.

"Yes, that is so," the old woman said. "You sing well.

Do you play any instruments?"

Ding laughed a bitter laugh. "Where would I find an instrument here?"

"I have here a bamboo flute," the old woman said, withdrawing a slender pipe from her rags. "It is a worthless thing, except for the music it makes."

"How do you play it?"

"You blow softly—here—and finger the notes, like this," she said, and played back to him the Vietnamese tune he had been singing. "Would you like to try?"

"Yes," he said. And after only a couple of false tries, he played "Lou-Le Lou-Ly." When he finished playing the tune, he turned to the old auntie, grinning with happiness at his success.

Funny. What happened next he had never thought twice about until today, but simply accepted. He hadn't had anything to smoke then, he knew, but maybe he'd been delirious from hunger. He'd questioned things less back then, which was just as well.

For the old auntie had gone, and in her place was a beautiful lady, shining and smiling and he knew without asking that she was the goddess of mercy, Kwan Yin. He had heard his father describe her sometimes, and this was just how she should look. Lotus in one hand, jewel in another, flowing silken robes that did not dampen with the rain.

He wasn't sure if he was supposed to bow or grovel in the mud or what, but as he started to kneel she said, "No, no. The flute is a magic one. It is good for a wish. This wish I give to you because you kindly shared your rice with a hungry elder."

"I wish my family and I would go to America," he said.

"Tell the flute," she said.

He played his American song again, and when he looked

back, she was gone. He was not sure how else to wish to go to America, so that day he went around to all of the elders, asking them to tell him what they remembered of the Americans, especially if they remembered songs. Some remembered snatches, which he played on his flute. People were pleased to hear the music.

The next day, a letter from a Seattle church group came saying that the group was sponsoring Ding's family to move to Seattle.

Ding threw the remainder of the joint on the floor and crushed it with his toe, disgusted. Cheap shit. It was supposed to help you mellow out, forget, not remember.

Seven

DICO MILLER STARED after Rose and the silvery woman with amazement, then looked down into the whiskery face of the gray tabby cat in his lap. It seemed to be waiting for him to pet it, feed it, say something to it.

"What in the hell does that woman think I'm gonna do wit' you, pussycat?" he asked it.

The cat switched its tail a little and dug its claws into his bare knee where it peeked out of the fabric of his jeans, shredded by age rather than fashion.

"Ow! Shit, cat. I guess I could maybe sell you to Trinh Tran's Restaurant over there. You look like you been eatin' reg'lar, which is more than I can say for me."

The cat nudged his fingers with its head. It definitely wanted to be petted. Oh, well, its fur was warm. "Maybe I'll just sell 'em the inside of your fur and I'll keep it for mittens. Huh? You want to be mittens?"

"My fur is much warmer to you and me both with me inside it, genius," the cat said. "Besides, your hungry and cold days are coming to an end. You've got me now."

"And what might you be exactly, cat? Other than another mouth."

"Don't think of me as another mouth," the cat said, rubbing his hand some more. "Think of me as your mouthpiece. Stick with me, sonny, and I'll change your life."

67

About that time, it dawned on Dico that the cat was actually talking to him, or at least that he thought the cat was actually talking to him, which meant one of several things, all of them being that everything he'd gone through, the deaths of his parents, the loss of his home, being put on the street to be beaten by toughs, pressured to sell or use drugs, all of it had combined to drive him nuts. The cat just looked at him like, of course, you're nuts, sucker, whaddyathink? Who ever heard of a real talking cat?

He started to cry in earnest, right there on the street, his head down in his folded arms, which were hugging his knees. The cat jumped up on his shoulders, draped itself across his neck and purred in his ear.

"Come on," it said. "Pull yourself together. You got to find a grocer someplace and get us some chow and get me a flea comb and a proper collar."

"Kitty, you got any idea how much that stuff costs and how little I got?"

"And have *you* got any idea how much cats in cat-food commercials make for *faking* half of what I can do? Move your butt, mister."

When Felicity Fortune and Rose drove up to the stable, Cindy was totally surrounded by young girls who were looking on curiously while Cindy inspected the corn on a horse's foot and lectured her class on what might make a horse limp or walk badly and how proper shoeing could treat the problem. The stable was small, set in two tin-roofed buildings with a shed for hay, and Rose saw only four of the horses, but they looked quite well cared for. There was a sign above the barn door that read, "Lucky Shoe Stables, Horses Boarded and Rented by the Hour. Riding Classes, Beginners and Advanced. Inquire Within."

"So what will you do for Punkin's corn then, Cindy?" one of the girls wanted to know.

Cindy set down the horse's hoof and pushed back her wild mane of curly black hair with one wrist. Her hand had gotten rather mucky at some point. "As you can see, I've pulled off the shoe so it doesn't put pressure on the corn. The last farrier didn't see the problem developing and so gave her a standard shoe. Now we have to wait for a specialty farrier—one who not only recognizes foot problems but knows how to make the shoes to fit—to come and replace the shoe with one that will have a piece cut out where the corn is. Other kinds of shoes may include lifts on one side to compensate for turned-in feet, like orthopedic shoes. Relieving the pressure on Punkin's foot and not working her until she's properly reshod is about all we can do for now. Rose! You did come!" she cried, and waved across the heads of the girls. "Okay, gang. Class dismissed. See you Thursday."

She gave Rose a hug. Her arms were very strong, and her hands rather hard and callused. She shook Felicity's hand with a firm grip and shot Rose an inquiring glance while Felicity's own was inspecting the premises.

"What a lovely place!" Felicity said.

Cindy grinned. "Isn't it? The boss leases the bridle trails from the park but he has plans to buy real grounds for the trails some day. If I get my inheritance, I could buy in as a partner."

Felicity seemed to be having a conversation with the horse. "The horses are happy here. They are very well cared for."

"You bet they are," Cindy said, her voice full of pride, a tone Rose wouldn't have believed Cindy capable of when she first came to Family Services, half starved, dirty and neglected. She was still skinny, dusty, smudged with straw and horse sweat, but she had made a place for herself, however tenuous. "The first thing the kids learn is feeding, grooming and mucking out. Taking care of their tack, that sort of thing."

"Very sensible. Why expect the horse to do anything for you, after all, if you've done nothing for her, right, girl?" she asked, addressing the mare.

Just then another car drove up, a BMW with three giggling young women in it, clad in jodhpurs and hacking jackets.

"You there, girl," one of them shouted rudely. "Miss Carlson would like her horse saddled and bridled and two of your best mounts for ourselves. We will ride now."

"I don't believe this," Cindy said, staring at the girls pouring out of the car and sashaying toward the stable while making brittle little jokes among themselves. "It's Pam and Perdita."

"Your stepsisters?" Rose asked. "What are they doing here?"

"Trying to get me canned," Cindy said. "That's Kimmie Carlson, the parks commissioner's daughter, with them."

"Didn't you hear me, girl? I said to prepare our horses," the oldest girl, who had big, expensively coiffed but patently unnatural blonde hair, heavy lips and hard eyebrows snapped again, then said to the small, mousy teenager giggling nervously in the middle, "Really, she's just *standing* there. What a silly little bitch. I mean, I've heard of hiring the handicapped, but give me a break . . ."

"Hel*lo*, Perdita," Cindy said with fire in her eye. Rose saw her hand tremble against the neck of the horse she was stroking. "Hello, Pam. Kimmie, I had no idea you knew my stepsisters."

"*Such* familiarity from the hired help!" Perdita continued.

"Are you just going to stand there all day, or will you get our horses?"

"Otter is in his stall where he usually is and he'll be glad to see you, Kimmie, but no horse in my care gets subjected to these two."

"I *beg* your pardon, Queen of the Stalls, Miss Horse Manure 1996," Perdita said. "We have Mr. Carlson's express invitation to ride his horses and no stablegirl is going to stop us."

"That's right," the other blonde, who was mercifully quieter, agreed. "So get out of our way."

The Carlson girl, so often bullied herself, saw an opportunity to bully someone else. "Please do as you're told, Cindy. I'll saddle Otter, but Daddy said Perdita and Pam could ride Jelly and Salamander."

"Fine," Cindy said. "Then they can saddle them." She started to turn away, then headed for the stables. "No, I won't do that to Jelly and Salamander. Excuse me, Rose, Felicity."

Pam and Perdita followed her, making snide suggestions the whole way. After a bit Kimmie Carlson led a pretty chocolate-brown gelding out of the stable, and Cindy led a palomino and a pinto, saddled and bridled, behind her.

"Kneel down and help me mount," Perdita commanded.

Wordlessly, her lips tight, cheeks flaming, Cindy knelt and cupped her hands. Perdita kicked them out of the way and stood on first her thigh, then her head, kicking her in the eye on the way up, and the moment she was on the horse, kicked it too so that it ran away, almost trampling Cindy.

"Really, Cindy, what have you been teaching Jelly?" Kimmie Carlson asked.

Cindy was nursing her eye. When Pam started to open her mouth, Rose grabbed a short wooden footstool, plopped it down beside Salamander, and pointed at it. Pam mounted more carefully than her sister and trotted alongside Kimmie up the hill.

"That bitch. That effing bitch," Cindy moaned, holding her eye and trying to saddle an Appaloosa gelding at the same time.

"What are you doing?"

"I have to follow them. Those horses are my responsibility, even if Carlson is crazy enough to loan them to those barracudas."

"Here, dear, allow me," Felicity said, ably saddling and bridling the horse in, if not the twinkling of an eye, at least a good deal quicker than Cindy could have done it with one hand or Rose could have done it at all. "We may as well come with. Whom may we ride?"

"Floss and Andy, there," Cindy said, jerking her head toward two of the horses remaining. The only one not taken was the one with the malformed hoof. Felicity began saddling them, but before she could do so, Cindy was cantering up the trail, behind the other three riders.

Rose and Felicity were just mounting when Perdita, flopping all over the back of her horse, her feet out of the stirrups, hanging on for dear life, came galloping back to the stable, her sister and Kim right behind her and Cindy hot on their trail.

"Oh, help, stop, this beast has gone nuts!" Perdita bellowed. Jelly screeched to a halt when he saw the barn, reared once, and rid himself of his rider, who flopped ingloriously into a pile recently evacuated by either Floss or Andy, Rose wasn't sure which.

"Poor Dita!" Pam said, trying hard not to laugh as she pulled her sister out of the horseshit and wisely refrained from brushing her off.

"Kimmie, there was something wrong with that horse of

yours," Perdita said. "You don't know this—this stablegirl the way we do. Our mother put a roof over her head and fed and clothed her for years after her father died, and she has always been just as ungrateful, spiteful and malicious as she can be. Why, I'll bet she did something to the horse to make it throw me."

"I wouldn't do anything to one of the horses even if I thought he might kill you!" Cindy growled, jumping down and running to soothe Jelly, whose head Felicity now held. "Kimmie, I tried to tell you. My sisters not only don't know how to ride, they haven't the faintest idea how to treat animals properly. Poor Jelly, quiet now. Are you hurt? Perdita, you're lucky the park has so few trees. If I were Jelly, I'd have rubbed you off on one of the gasworks."

"Oh, you are *so* cruel," Pam said.

Jelly continued to fuss and Kimmie started to unsaddle him. "Why, look at this! There's a thorn under Jelly's saddle."

Perdita let out a squeal. "This is *it*, Cindy. I knew you were jealous of me, but I had no idea you'd stoop to hurting one of the horses to hurt me. Kimmie, you have to call your father right now and demand that this girl be fired, or the stable can no longer use the park. She is a menace and an attempted murderess and—and—should be reported to the Humane Society!"

"Oh, that's what you wanted all along, isn't it?" Cindy cried. "This was all just to get me fired. Kimmie, I'll bet you anything Perdita put the thorn under her own saddle just to have something to accuse me of."

"And be nearly killed for my trouble? As if!" Perdita countered.

Felicity clapped her hands three times. "Ladies. The horses are quite upset enough as it is without you screaming at each other. Kimberly Carlson, you and Cindy and I will return the horses to their stalls and groom them while you, miss," she said to Perdita, "and you," to Pam, "return to your auto and wait. Meanwhile, Rosalie will enjoy her ride as scheduled. Do I make myself clear?"

"Who the hell do you think you are, Mary Poppins?" Perdita snarled, but returned to the car.

"You can't go home again!" The hit man, who had read the phrase in a book somewhere and thought it fit the situation, yelled after Sno as she sprinted off into the woods. He tried to rise to chase her, but as the stunning effect of his fall wore off, he felt a sharp burning pain in his side and when he reached to touch it, his hand came away bloody. He had fallen on the damned blade himself. Who'd think the little bitch had it in her? He wound her red-and-black-checked muffler around his middle to stanch the blood, righted the bike and roared back out of the woods.

He barely managed to stay upright on the bike until he came to Bellingham, where he checked into a clinic, telling the receptionist that the wound was accidental. Even if she had called the cops, which she didn't, he still had the dagger, the wound was clearly self-inflicted, and nobody could nail him for that.

He'd lost a lot of blood but he wasn't about to risk a transfusion, so after they bandaged up the wound, he swung down from the examining table and stalked out again, snagging the blood-soaked black-and-red-checked scarf from the trash can on the way.

The next day he would mail the scarf, complete with dried blood, to Svenny's "niece," whose address was on the permissions letterhead he had shown the school. The scarf would reassure the "niece" that the kill had been made and get him paid. It would also establish evidence to connect to her in case she wanted to contradict him. Maybe she'd have second thoughts before hiring someone to kill her kids for her. Let her do it herself if she wanted the girl dead. She shouldn't have given the kid judo lessons.

Eight

The Big Bad

THE WOLF STALKED the underbrush, wary of larger predators while himself searching for prey. The scent of the forest was in his nostrils, snowy, clean, with a spicy-sweet fragrance of woodsmoke from a camp not as far from him as the people there might think.

. His body slunk through the branches without breaking them; his feet trod the ground without marking the fallen leaves that still lay bare under the trees and brush though snow lay farther from the trunks.

Farley Mowat would have loved this wolf. He was actually only looking for rabbits, squirrels, quail, even a deer if he could bring one down. He truly had no conscious designs on human beings—gone were the days when he killed them and took their ears and other parts for bounty.

But when he spotted the flash of red on the trail below and, slithering down to investigate, spied the little figure scrambling furtively up the trail with many glances behind her, old impulses he had hoped were dead rushed up in him. She was alone and stinking of fear, not of him, but of something else. Well, he thought as he grinned his lupine grin to himself, she'd change her mind about *that* pretty quick.

Without a sound he worked his way ahead of her, and

when she turned a bend in the path, he stepped out onto the trail in front of her.

"Hi, sweetheart, what brings you to this neck of the woods?" he asked, and closed in for the kill.

She didn't ask what he wanted or beg for mercy or plead innocence or go down on her knees or any of the things he expected. She sure could scream, though.

Sno snapped, screaming at the top of her lungs, picking up handfuls of snow and throwing them in the face of the shaggy-looking man advancing on her with his hands extended and a hideous grin. He had long hair and a long beard and his teeth were yellow, exuding smoker's breath. They looked sharp, and he looked hungry. Wild thoughts of werewolves skimmed the surface of her mind, careening like crazy colors as she screamed over and over again, as much in rage as in fear.

And then *he* lunged—God, she was really having a bad day—and as his hands closed over her throat, he was lifted off.

"Trip-Wire! Hey, Trip-Wire, buddy, come on away from that little girl. She ain't no gook!" another man said.

Sno wiggled out from under the man and stood back, both hands gripping snowballs so tightly the snow was melting. "What *is* it with you men today? Full moon? Huh? First that geek on the bike tries to stab me, and now—and now—"

And now rage overtook her and she began to shake and howl a little herself. The shaggy man looked shamefaced and buried his head in the shoulder of the man who had grabbed him, while five other men half-slid, half-ran down the hill behind them.

Thoughts of gang rape and torture murder danced in Sno's head.

"Who the hell *are* you?" everybody said in unison.

Later, back at the camp, wearing one of Doc's sweaters and a pair of jeans borrowed from Drifty, who was the smallest of the group, and wrapped in a camouflage quilt, Sno finished telling them how she came to be there. She felt better now. Nobody had tried anything funny. They'd fed her fresh fish and pots of coffee and shot warning looks at each other and protective ones toward her. Trip-Wire, the guy who'd scared her, had apparently had some kinda flashback and thought he was back in the Vietnam War and she was an enemy or something.

He was really sorry, she could tell. Especially when she told them that she had just escaped the weirdo on the bike with the knife.

"So, who was this guy who was trying to kill you?" the tall bearded one, Doc, asked. God, these guys were *old*. Older than Raydir, even.

"Never saw him before in my life," Sno told him. "And he was wearing a helmet, so I couldn't see his face. But something he said—"

"What?" Dead-Eye, the crewcut with the eyepatch, asked. "What did the bastard say to you, honey?"

"He—he said I shouldn't go home again. He said he didn't want to kill me, but somebody with connections wanted me dead."

"You think you know who it is?"

She nodded. "Gerardine. Raydir's wife. She hates me, and I never did anything to her, I swear."

"Gerardine?" asked Maurice, the black guy the others called "Doper," when they forgot that he preferred his given name. "The model? She's your stepmom?"

"Yeah."

"Well, darlin', it's perfectly obvious to *me* why the woman wouldn't be able to stand you," Maurice said. "You're competition, love. Absolutely *stunning*, and she is, frankly, getting *on* a bit. The woman must be thirty-five if she's a day."

"Forty-three," Sno said.

"No! You don't say!"

Sno nodded. "I mean, you can hardly tell, because she's always got on all the makeup and stuff. And I'm no competition—I don't want all those guys bothering me. I'm just thirteen, and I want to go to college. I like boys and all that, but only when they're really nice, and a lot of the ones at Raydir's house aren't. They just grab."

"Anybody bring the signal flares?" Doc asked. "We better call in the troopers."

"No!" Sno said. "They'll take me home."

"Not if you tell them what happened."

"They won't believe me," Sno told him.

"Because they'll think you're the spoiled rich kid of famous parents?"

"No, 'cause I got busted a while back for doing drugs and I'm on probation now. God, I wish I had a joint."

"Me too," the seven vets said in unison.

"But we're done with that stuff now," Doc said. "And you should be too. None of that crap's good for you, and we ought to know. Anyway, we have to call the troopers. You can't stay here."

"Why not?"

" 'Cause this is a men's retreat. We're living barracks style. There's no room for a girl."

"Huh!" she said. "One of those 'no girls allowed' clubs. That is so sexist and so *unfair*. Besides," she said, her voice dropping, "I've got noplace else to go. If you turn me over to the troopers, I'll be dead." Doc folded his arms and looked at the ground. The others avoided her eyes when she tried to plead with them. Her voice broke. "So, okay, what do I have to do to stay alive? Cook? Clean? Give you blow jobs? What?"

"Don't," said Doc, "tempt us. This is tough enough as it is."

"I can't go back there. I can't." The events of the day, the knife, the long bike ride, all closed in on her. "I thought I wanted to die when Mama was killed, but I don't. I don't. I don't."

Maurice stepped forward and enveloped her in a hug. "Oh, come on, fellows. I was getting tired of all of this singlemindedly hairy-chested stuff anyway. What's getting in touch with your warrior self good for if you can't protect a little girl in trouble? Can't she stay? She could sleep with me and, as you know, she'd be safe as with her own—well, safer than with her stepmom. She'd be the daughter, the little sister I never had."

"Oh, cut it out, Maurice, and let the kid go," Doc said. "We agreed that this was for us alone. We didn't even bring our own sons—we sure don't need a sweet young thing, even if she does have a mouth on her like a Marine. She'd get us all in deep shit."

"So what?" said Trip-Wire, who hadn't said a word since they returned to camp. "It's not like we ain't been there before."

"So?" Rose asked, when she and Felicity were back on 99 headed toward downtown Seattle. She had ridden away from the stable as Felicity suggested, because although she had qualms about leaving Cindy to the mercies of the stepsisters, the empty-headed Carlson girl, and the possibly psychotic Felicity, she had needed to clear her head. When she returned from her trot around the park, she saw that the BMW was gone, the horses were groomed, and Cindy and Felicity were chatting happily while oiling and polishing tack.

Cindy polished with a rather determinedly grim set to her mouth, a tension that was the aftermath of her encounter with Perdita and Pammie. Felicity proposed that they all go to dinner, and they repaired to Jake's Place where the food was so good it was almost magical, Rose had to admit. The meal lightened Cindy's mood a bit. Good meals were not something she took for granted.

After dinner, Rose was so sleepy from the exercise, fresh air and good food that she sat in happy, dazed silence, as Felicity and Cindy continued to talk horses until the restaurant closed, and they dropped Cindy off at the tiny basement apartment she was house-sitting on Burke Avenue North in Wallingford.

"So what?"

"So did you wave your wand, say any magic words, make sure things would all turn out right for Cindy?"

"No, but I promised to speak to her employer if those little tarts made trouble."

"That's *all*?" Rose surprised herself by blurting out. To her chagrin, she found she was actually disappointed. Felicity was such good company, and so practical and ordinary about horses and that sort of thing, that she had stopped thinking of her as a harmless nut and more as a charming eccentric. Well, she was British and apparently well off. Didn't that qualify her to be eccentric? But somewhere along the line, while talking to the woman, Rose had begun to accept all the stuff about magic the same way she would a friend talking about an interest in shell collecting or bungee jumping, which was certainly crazier than anything Felicity had brought up so far. And now she was unhappy because the woman had, naturally enough, not produced. So which of them had failed to keep both oars in the water, hmmm? Nevertheless . . .

"Yes, that, and I plan to bring her employer's establishment a great deal of business," Felicity continued in a quite sane way.

"I thought you were going to prove your magic powers to me," Rose challenged. Maybe it was wrong to try to get somebody to leap back into the chasm between them and reality again, but she was beginning to feel as if she had imagined their original conversation, and she wanted to keep all of this clear. Really, she ought to be glad Felicity hadn't driven her to a bluff somewhere and driven off, expecting the car to turn into a dragon or something.

"Just my powers. Remember, I told you that we only use the least possible magical force to do a job."

Rose just stopped herself from crying, "Aha!"

Felicity continued, "Your friend Cindy seems to me to be managing admirably on her own, despite the formidable opposition, and isn't that what you modern girls expect of yourselves?"

Rose felt defensive now on Cindy's behalf as well as her own. "You've got no idea of the hell she's been through, of what she's up against," she said.

"She told me. But she's persevering."

"Well, that's nice." Drop it, Rosie. Drop it, she told herself, but she found she had developed a morbid fascination with the subject, with confronting Felicity with the difference between what she believed she was and could do and what she was actually doing. "But weren't you going to prove to me that you were the fairy godmother by making everything like a fairy tale and providing happy endings?"

"I don't have to make everything like a fairy tale. It already is, if only you knew," Felicity said with a strange, grim set to her mouth. "As for my role, I'm here to help you and those who can benefit from my assistance. Even if I had unlimited powers, I couldn't do anything for some of your clients. Those who are more than a little mad, those who find their magic in chemicals of one sort or another, are not clear enough to receive or use the assistance I can offer. Neither can I undo the effects of AIDS or other terminal illnesses. I cannot replace limbs or restore life to the dead. But there are a great many good things remaining, including one thing that seems to be very much missing these days . . ."

"Yes?"

Felicity sighed and tossed her silvery hair, and took her eyes from the highway for a moment to fix them on Rose with a penetrating stare. "Romance."

"Romance? When what we need is soup kitchens and housing and medicine and treatment programs and shelters and education?"

Felicity shrugged. "I didn't say you don't need those things too, but nonetheless, just as much, romance."

That did it! Felicity was definitely out of touch with reality after all. In her most therapeutic voice, with a touch of the humor Felicity seemed well able to tolerate, Rose gently explained, "It *is* true, Felicity, that nowadays, in this country at least, we don't wait for princes to come to the rescue much anymore. They're in short supply these days, and it's a long wait and 'happily ever after,' frankly, is a literary device."

"How very sophisticated of you," Felicity said stiffly. "But honestly, Rose, what would you know about it?"

"Romance? I've had my . . ."

"No, the way relationships work in fairy tales. I suggest you do some research before you continue with the world-weary remarks as if you invented disappointment. It isn't becoming, it isn't therapeutic and it isn't useful."

"Well, excu-use me," Rose said, stung more than she would have imagined.

"Now, then, if you don't mind, I have quite a lot to do if I'm to be of help. Here's the ferry terminal. I think you'll find the 11:15 was late in docking and will be waiting for you if you hurry."

"Gee, promise me if we don't reach Bremerton by midnight you won't turn the ferry into a pumpkin. That's a long, cold swim."

"Very funny."

The wind was rising and the night sky spitting freezing rain by the time Rose drove up to her half-renovated house.

She'd stopped by the mailbox on the way, but there was nothing but a new Spiegel's sale catalog, three bills, and a postcard. There was, however, a plastic bag with the rectangular outline of a package poking its way through the bottom hanging from her doorknob. A furry face peered anxiously through the glass door and her senior cat, Oprah, a sleek brown Siamese mix, nearly tripped her as she stepped inside.

Dumping everything on the kitchen table, she scurried to turn up the furnace and use the bathroom, to which she was followed by Oprah and the other two cats, Sally Jessy and Phil, rubbing, purring, mewing at her not to forget her most important responsibilities. This in spite of the fact that they had dishes full of dry cat food and water at all times.

Since she didn't have to get up the next day and had slept in a bit that morning, she put the kettle on for diet hot chocolate and lit a fire in her fireplace. Her house had been a real find—a stone farmhouse, two stories, all wood interior with this terrific stone fireplace. She'd started a little remodeling with money she'd inherited when her mother died. Downstairs, the kitchen was roomy and convenient, the living room cozy with the fireplace as its centerpiece, a patio, a glassed-in porch, and a former bedroom she used as a library, plus a bathroom that was much more adequate since the remodeling. Upstairs were her room, a guest room, and an extra room in which she kept her vintage clothing and jewelry, plus a fourth former bedroom now made into a decadent master bath complete with double sinks, shower and Jacuzzi tub. She, of all people, did not need a *personal* fairy godmother, she thought with some satisfaction.

When the chocolate was made and the fire was laid, she turned her attention to the mail and to the parcel on the doorknob. Opening the plastic sack and peeking inside, she saw a package wrapped like a birthday present in shiny paper and iridescent ribbon. Opening it, she found a large secondhand volume of *Grimm's Fairy Tales*.

"Now how did she . . . ?" Rose muttered to herself as she flung the paper aside. There was no card and no inscription. Of course, the book could have come from Linden, with whom she'd had the first conversation about fairy godmothers, but Linden would have sent a card as well and sent it UPS. She always used UPS. But if it hadn't come from Linden, there could only be one other person, and that seemed close to impossible. She smiled. It was a nice book and a good joke anyway.

Settling down by the fire with cup in hand and cats fighting over her lap, she began to read.

Nine

SATURDAY NIGHT, DICO had to admit, was made warmer by the presence of the cat sleeping curled up against him, but in the morning, Rose's money was gone, the market was closed and he was as hungry as ever.

"Now what?" he asked.

"Watch," the cat told him. It flicked its tail while considering those strolling past the shops still open on the far side of First Street, past the bakery, the Middle Eastern Grocery and the various coffee bars.

Selecting its prey, it said, "Come along, stick close to me and don't be surprised at anything."

Then it scampered kittenishly up to a middle-aged lady with a good haircut and an expensive-looking jogging suit and stopped her by putting its paws on her knee and looking pleadingly up into her face.

"Oh, what a sweet kitty!" she said, stooping down to scratch its ears and whiskers. "You must belong to someone to be so friendly."

"Oh, yes, pretty lady, I do. My master is that clever young ventriloquist you see there. We had a nice house like you and lovely clothes and delicious food, but my master lost his highly paid computer job and now we depend on the kindness of strangers." The cat nudged the lady's hand and purred mightily while the woman curiously inspected Dico to see if he was moving his lips. "Oh, please, purrritty lady, if you could only spare a few dollars so my master could buy some toiletries and our bus fare to the laundromat so he could apply for jobs, we'd be ever so grateful."

The lady looked around but nobody else seemed to have heard the cat. She stared even more curiously at Dico, who gave her an embarrassed smile and shrugged, hoping she wouldn't call the cops.

"I don't know what your problem is, fellow, but this is a really clever cat and you're a marvelous ventriloquist. You two ought to be onstage instead of here in the streets."

"I keep telling my master this, pretty lady, but he's very shy because he is so poor," the cat told her. "Though proud."

"Look, there's an open mike tomorrow night at the University Pub. Why don't you and kitty come and sign up?" she said to him, opening her purse to extract a ten, which she placed in his hand. To the cat she said, "A clever boots like this sweet kitty will get you spotted, and someone might give you a job. Don't let him spend it on drugs or booze, will you, kitty?"

"Oh, *no*, pretty lady, I am my master's only vice. Isn't that so, master?"

"Uh, yeah. That's right. What the cat said," Dico agreed, nodding. The woman gave the cat a final scritch and stroke and, without another nod to Dico, was away down the sidewalk.

The hit man made it into Seattle Saturday evening, climbing painfully to his second-story condo on Queen Anne Hill to clean up and sleep. He awoke in desperate need of something to drink. He scarcely had been able to stay on the bike, the way his side hurt, and there was a liquor store just a couple of blocks away.

Now, the hit man was not himself an alcoholic, nor was he addicted to drugs. Those habits would have made him unreliable and therefore unworthy of his calling. No, he was simply someone who was good at something bad and didn't much mind the job in the ordinary run of things. There was something a bit missing in his makeup that made him look at other people's unwanted problems, be they relatives, former friends or business associates, as if they were motes in a video game and he was the eternal Pac-Man. He was not, as any psychologist would have insisted, purely evil, but neither was he very good. Mostly, he simply had the feeling that he was the only conscious person in the world and that all other people played out their lives unaware of him—unless he interrupted. So although he was very worldly and very wary, he was a little startled to be accosted on his quest to the liquor store by the bundle of rags huddled near a Dumpster.

"Spare a buck for a poor old woman, young man?" the bag lady asked.

Since he was in considerable pain, he was also not pleased to be accosted, nor was he feeling any more generous than usual, nor was he pleased to be intruded upon in his quest. "Fuck off," he growled under his breath and kept walking. But she was in front of him, groveling and whining. "Look, son, you look like you can spare it, and I haven't had a bite to eat in days . . ."

She was looking up into his face. He didn't like it when people did that. He dug in the pocket of his leather jacket, but instead of change, he brought out the blade. "Want to know how I got so rich, gramma?" he asked, and flicked it open.

She didn't even back off a pace. "Oh, Bobby," she said, sounding pleasantly surprised, as if she recognized him. She clucked her tongue at him as if he was writing dirty words on the blackboard instead of getting ready to cut her. "All these years, all these lives, and you've never learned, have you? Do you really still blame yourself for failing your queen so that she killed you in the prime of life? You were a very good huntsman and you did the right thing, you know."

"You're nuts," he said.

"Maybe," she said. "But you're a toad."

And he was. It was magic, it was something the wicked witch usually did instead of the fairy godmother, but it was within her power, and it was after all self-defense.

He didn't change in appearance. However, he dropped the knife and hopped in a startled way toward the Dumpster.

Felicity left him for a moment until she found, in a mud puddle toward the back of the building, a furious toad with an attitude that wouldn't quit. She pocketed the toad, fastening a Velcro strip over its warty head while it croaked indignantly, and led the crazy man to the emergency room entrance at Harborview. They had a psych ward. She hoped he had insurance.

Later, in another part of Seattle, she found another Dumpster, this one by a grocery store.

A harried-looking young woman in jeans and a T-shirt was just rushing out of the Safeway with a bag full of groceries. "Please, lady, spare an old woman a crust of bread," Felicity said.

The woman paused and dug in her sack. She looked a little scared of the bag lady but said civilly enough, "I don't have much in here but baby formula and Pampers, unless you'd like the pint of ice cream I bought for my kid?"

"Oh, I would love ice cream," the bag lady said. "It's been forever since I've had a taste."

"I could give you the money and you could go get something more nutritious," the mother offered.

"Oh, no, they won't let me in there. Say I scare off the customers. The ice cream will do fine. Though I hate to take it from a little child."

"That's okay. I'll go get him some more." She took it from the bag and handed it, gingerly, as if afraid the bag lady would draw a weapon or an accomplice would jump out and grab her. "To be honest, I probably wouldn't have stopped most days, but I got laid off this morning. I may need your advice on a good street corner for me and my kids pretty soon." Her voice sounded shaky and scared and her words just spilled out, nervously, as if she had to talk to someone.

"Oh, I heard about the layoffs. Just terrible, dear. Where did you work?"

"Boeing. On the assembly line. It was a good job, but it didn't pay me enough to save anything, not with two kids I'm raising alone, and now we won't even have medical insurance if one of them gets sick . . ."

"You poor thing. You're very generous to help me when you know you and your kids'll be in a bad way soon."

Her eyes were bright with tears now. She sniffed and said, "I guess we're all in it together, aren't we?"

"Yes, indeed we are. Oh, dear, I suppose I'll just have to let this melt and drink it. I have no spoon, you see."

"Just a minute," the woman said. "I have to go back in for more ice cream anyway. I'll get you a spoon."

The baby-sitter could wait another little while. There was still money to pay her and money for groceries. She thought of how she'd feel if she had to beg for somebody's ice cream. It wasn't like the old lady was asking for money to drink or something. She really was hungry. On impulse, the young mother whipped through the store and bought a bag of apples, a box of crackers, a pound of cheese and a sausage. All things that would keep for a while, that would feed the old lady for a few days. If she could digest such things. She almost forgot the box of plastic silverware and her own ice cream.

She took the things back out to the old lady, just removing the second pint of ice cream to put with her own sack. "There, that might see you through for a little while."

"Thanks," said the old woman, and grabbed the bag and turned around with it, as if she was so hungry she couldn't wait to chow down. The young woman shrugged and started for her car, but the bag lady hailed her again and said, "Wait, dear! You forgot this."

Now in a real hurry to get home to her children, the young mother turned around. She felt the bag lady press a piece of cardboard into her hand, along with who knew what germs, and then the younger woman popped into her car and headed for home.

It wasn't until later, when the baby was chewing on a brightly colored piece of something and she realized it must have been the cardboard the old woman handled, that she took it away from the protesting baby and saw that it was two Wheel of Fortune lottery cards. She scratched off the silvery coating and saw that each card was worth twenty thousand dollars.

Later, when she'd been able to redeem the cards, she returned to the Dumpster to find the old woman and give her some of the money, but she was not there, either that time or any other time the woman returned to the Safeway. But whenever she bought groceries afterwards, she bought a lottery ticket and though she never won so much again, she always won something, a dollar, two dollars, five, ten or fifty until she found another job. In the meantime, she helped her friends who had been laid off, and when they asked her how she was making do, she told them about the bag lady. But of course, it didn't work for everyone.

*   *   *

Later that night, toad in her pocket, Felicity returned
to her suite on the thirteenth floor of the Olympic Four
Seasons Hotel. The suite was a very posh suite, and very
cheap. There was no charge because the hotel, like most
hotels, never acknowledged that it *had* a thirteenth floor.
The only drawback was that Felicity had to walk up from
the twelfth floor and make her own door, but that was very
little trouble and required only a bit of healthful exercise
and quite minor magic.

Although she had a Chinese shawl from the shop draped
over the standard hotel table with her crystal set in the
middle, she still needed a few things to make her suite
feel like home. The phone, complete with two lines and
a message machine, and the television were adequate, and
her computer was set up for her to receive electronic mail
worldwide via GEnie and CompuServe, but she still needed
a police scanner and a fax machine. Right now her major
problem was setting up a terrarium for the toad. He could
stay in the bathroom for the night. She was put out with
him anyway. Some creatures never learned.

They barely got back from the mall when Mama wanted
to go again. "This time I don't want you kids calling the
police," Mama said. "It was so embarrassing that they'd
think I meant to leave you. I was just next door looking
at cards the whole time, and I got frantic when I couldn't
find you. Now this time, I'll take you in, and you *wait
for me*."

But Gigi cried constantly and Hank felt bad because he
couldn't quite believe Mama but he didn't want to think
she was fibbing either.

Just the same, as they rode the series of buses to get
to the mall, a ride which took them practically all day,

every time they left, Hank would lag behind and ask for
a transfer, which the driver gave him to shut the little kid
up and which he duly pocketed so they could find their
way home again when the security man asked and maybe
this time they wouldn't call the police and Mama wouldn't
be mad.

This mall was farther away than the other one and much,
much bigger. Hank carefully noted that the name of it was
a funny word that started with a *P* and then said "Center"
and that they went away from the water to get there and
toward Mount Rainier, which looked like the top of an ice
cream cone after you'd licked the ice cream all around.

He had paid attention to the questions the policemen
asked, and he also knew his house number and remembered
Mama's whole name and Daddy's.

Where was Daddy now? Hank missed him terribly. Everything had been all right when they lived in the country before
Daddy lost his job.

This time Mama took them straight to the McDonald's
inside the mall and set them up with hamburgers and fries
and shakes and told them not to move, she'd be back, and
not to come looking for her or talk to strangers, even those
in uniform.

Hank hoped she wasn't going to disappear again. He
watched her for a long time as she walked down the long,
broad corridor, then he saw a man step out of a store—
the same man who came home with her in the mornings
sometimes, and she walked off down the aisle with him,
his arm around her and his hand on her bottom.

"Come on," Hank said to Gigi. Gigi stared at him for a
moment and he said, "Come on or she'll get away again
and leave us."

That made his sister start to cry again but he took her by
the hand and dragged her down the mall, after Mama.

Ten

ON THE NIGHT the lucky (or unlucky, depending on your perspective) bag lady first appeared on the streets of Seattle, Rose Samson sat by her fire in Bremerton, reading the book that had (not quite) miraculously appeared on her doorknob.

Felicity was right. Rose certainly found these fairy tales believable—at least, all but the magic parts. Poverty, famine, wife battering, child abuse, cannibalism, incest (funny how it never mentioned in the Disney versions that the prototype of Cinderella ran away from her father to avoid becoming an incest victim, and in the original tale, Sleeping Beauty was raped by the king who found her, not merely kissed) and plague. What she found the most disturbing was the way the good guys and bad guys were so firmly separated, but then, children often looked at things that way, at least where it concerned the deeds of other people.

Not that these seemed to be for children at all. Had they been made into unedited films, many of the tales would have had to fight for a PG rating. Classic Oedipus and Electra complexes and sibling rivalry abounded. After the first twenty tales, Rose put the book down. It was too much like a busman's holiday, trying to read stuff that was so disturbingly familiar.

The girl in "The Handless Maiden." There'd been the

95

case of the twelve-year-old whose rapist had cut off her
hands to—what? To cut off her hands, Rose supposed.
Wantonly mutilating an already helpless victim. The girl
was fifteen now, and still in physical therapy provided by
the State, since the family had no money. In the Grimm
story, the handless maiden was the victim of incest. In real
life, in this case, the girl at least had the mercy of not
having had the rape and mutilation inflicted upon her by
her own family. Other kids, with other mutilations, weren't
so lucky. A hell of a lot of them didn't survive, the ones
who as babies had their heads bashed against walls, were
sat on stove burners or burned with cigarettes. Nope, there
was nothing old-fashioned about that story at all.

And Rapunzel. Two weeks ago there'd been the quiet
family who went away for a couple of weeks and forgot
and left a tap on. When a kindly neighbor noticed the water
running out the front door and called the utilities company
to shut it off, they discovered in an upstairs bedroom a
young girl left alone, filthy and neglected in a built-up
baby's playpen. Her hair was so long it might well have
never been cut and her nails were filthy and broken, her
skin lacerated. No loving rescuer for that child. If she was
sane a day in her life after that, she'd be damned lucky.

These were not airy-fairy stuff after all, but thinly dis-
guised, gossipy versions of news stories. Grimm always
painted the victims as good and kind and beautiful, of
course. The truth was that a child treated that way, one
who survived such treatment, had a much better chance of
growing up as twisted as the people who hurt it.

She realized uncomfortably that reading the stories was
giving her a little insight into other, more personal reasons
why she didn't like fairy tales, and she simply wasn't prepared to deal with it that night.

Instead, she put down the Grimms' tales and reached for

her secret vice, a romance novel, and read a few pages before she fell asleep. Felicity was right about that too. There wasn't nearly enough of this sort of thing in the real world. At least not for her. She knew some very sweet guys, but most of them were either involved or gay and the ones who weren't were friends. They confided their own romantic problems to her and she hated to wreck the friendships by trying to make more of it. Although—although there was at least one—Fred and the little girl's silly uniformed teddy bear popped into her head again. Was he maybe a little attracted to her? Was the suggestion to do lunch more than just a pleasantry? Of course, he was no doubt involved or even married or something, just her luck, or a total jerk. Maybe Felicity's craziness was rubbing off on her, but a little harmless fantasy never hurt anyone, and it was preferable to drop off to sleep remembering how glad he had seemed to see her again ("Hello, officer. Is that your nightstick or are you just glad to see me?" the old Mae West line intruded itself irreverently into her fantasy) than thinking about those god-awful fairy tales.

But if the fairy tales in Rose's book were Grimm, the Monday morning news was grimmer.

Thousands more people had been laid off and were lining up at the unemployment office. Gangs of Asian teens beat elderly people in the International District, as gangs of black teens and white teens and Hispanic teens vied for power, weapons and drugs, turning the streets into battle-grounds. Drive-by shootings on the freeway were making driving I-5 akin to playing Russian roulette. Police blotters were full of junkie mothers who sold their children to pederasts and child pornography buffs for a few dollars worth of crack. Hospitals were swamped with crack babies who couldn't track, couldn't respond, couldn't love, could do nothing but cry. And at work, Rose's desk was even more full of heartbreak than usual.

Polly Reynaud's father had been caught molesting the daughter of one of his beer-drinking buddies and was back in jail. Polly, instead of being returned to her former foster family, was with a new one that contained at least two older boys, both with records. Why in the hell hadn't Hager just *called* the former foster parents? They'd have taken Polly back at once. Then there was Yasmin Chu, who'd been in detox and trying to break away from her gang. Detox reported she had walked out in the company of six other girls. And poor Dico Miller, shivering on the streets, now had a cat to look after thanks to Felicity's marvelous magic. Boy, had she been a nut to fall for that. She was going to have words with Linden when she returned.

"Rose, pick up on line one," George hollered over the barrier between their desks.

"Department of Family Services, Ms. Samson speaking," she said.

"Hiya, Rose. Did you ever get any sleep the other night?"

"Fred!" Now, here was a bright spot in a bad morning. "It was great seeing you again. How ya doin'?"

"I'm fine, Rosie, but I'm pretty concerned about Hank and Gigi, the little kids I brought in to you the other night. They seem to be missing again—this time along with their mama."

"Oh, no!" she said. The picture of the little girl still clutching the uniformed bear was fresh in her mind. And quite aside from the realization that returning children to bad family situations caused harm to the children, it was also a pain in the ass to think you had a situation sorted out only to have to deal with it all over again a day or two later. "Damn. I was hoping to fit in a home visit this week to see what the situation is. Their mother seems to be a pretty absentminded shopper."

"Yeah, that was my impression too. And of course, they may all be out together having a good time somewhere, but the father returned from fishing in Alaska yesterday afternoon and when he got to the aunt's place, he found the kids and their mother gone. He says the mother's sister claims she's got no idea where the kids are, but when he pressed her she sneered at him, saying the mother ran off with a man she met at the topless club she works at."

"Did she know if the kids were still *with* the mother?" Rose asked. "Maybe she did get a new boyfriend, but she may very well have taken the children along. Perhaps she and the aunt had a falling out."

"You're being optimistic, Rosie. If that was so, why did she abandon them in the first place? My guess is that the boyfriend wanted her but not the kids and she dumped them and we brought them back just before she was ready to make her move, so she dumped them again."

Rose didn't ask what kind of a mother would do that. She had known scores of them. If only the new head of the department the governor had appointed had ever *worked* in any branch of social services at all, he would know how foolish it was to return hurt or neglected children to their families before investigating the situation. Unfortunately, the man's main qualification for his position was that he had contributed heavily to Governor Higgins's campaign. His background, she had heard, consisted of being extremely well connected politically with a group of highly conservative, fundamentalist religion–backed wealthy movers and shakers. She had heard he had no previous job experience that anyone knew of, but lived off a healthy trust fund from inherited stock in a chemical company of some sort. She had never met him, but he and his political cronies in the legislature and the state supreme court were responsible for the new rules that made the sovereignty of the family take precedence over the good of the children. And any man who thought Bitsy Hager would be a good supervisor was obviously uninterested in reality.

"I called on the aunt," Fred continued. "Even though I couldn't do anything about it all officially, she gave me the boyfriend's name. I have a feeling he may be mixed up in drugs because she was tanked and seemed afraid, initially, to tell me who he was, but she couldn't afford to be arrested for impeding the investigation either. One of the things that makes me most worried about the kids, in fact, is that the aunt, however much she denied knowing anything, did seem to take it for granted that something had happened to them, and that if she didn't cooperate she would be party to a crime. So she did disclose the boyfriend's name, but when I checked out the home and work numbers of the man, he wasn't at home and officially started vacation from work today. We're checking airlines and cruise ships, the Amtrak and bus tour companies as a matter of course, but haven't turned up anything yet. Meanwhile, since there's what you might call a pattern established, we're asking the assistance of the departments throughout King, Pierce, and Kitsap Counties in searching the malls, and just for good measure I've got a buddy in the department in Clallam County checking out the Bjornsens with former friends and neighbors in Forks."

"I'm so glad you called to tell me, Fred," she said. Most police officers wouldn't think of it. "If they come in for any reason, or if I hear anything, I'll call you at once."

"I'd appreciate that, Rose. I'd just let this go through channels but in the department's previous dealings with her, the new supervisor has been, shall we say, less than responsive to the needs of both the kids and the investigating officers."

"I understand perfectly. Was there anything else?"

"One more thing along the same line, as long as I've got you on the phone. Pete Hamish in vice tells me you were the assigned caseworker about two months ago when a thirteen-year-old girl named Snohomish Quantrill, the daughter of some rock star, was picked up for suspicion of soliciting and possession?"

"Oh, sure, I remember Sno okay. Not a bad kid really. Her mother died not too long ago, you know, and I think there's been a little tension between her and her father's new wife. The drug thing seemed to be still in the experimental stages, from what I could tell, and though your officer wasn't entirely convinced, I really think the soliciting charge was a misunderstanding. She said she was just hangin' on the streets to get out of the house."

"Well, she's out of it now. She's been missing since Friday afternoon."

"Missing? There was nothing about it on the news."

"Her father was just getting to bed during the morning news and, after a long hard weekend, finally noticed that the kid wasn't home, preparing for school. The stepmother has been at a fat farm since Friday morning, and apparently nobody else missed the girl either."

Rose groaned. "Oh, Jesus, I hope she's not on the streets again. She was pretty stoned when she was out there panhandling, and damned near got hysterical when the vice guy asked her if she was interested in doing what teenage girls on the street usually do for money. I'm not saying she's an innocent or anything—it'd be pretty hard to be, growing up in Raydir Quantrill's household—but she'd lived with her grandmother and her mother until her mother died recently and I think the drugs were sort of self-medication for her grief. If she did start hooking, I'd say it would be mostly to get the attention she doesn't get from her father. Not that she wants *that* kind of attention."

"Yeah, well, it may occur to her that going pro will get her the money for the self-medication and the attention, but her father slapped her in a private school and says she's been doing really well so far according to the school, but who knows? The stepmother's maid says the stepmom is a little more realistic about the kid and wouldn't put anything past her."

"Just what that kid needs. I got a little sidetracked talking about her, to tell you the truth. What I meant to ask you was if there was any chance she had been on the streets again. I hate to borrow trouble, but the first thing that I thought of was all those poor murdered hookers. A lot of those girls were underage."

It was Fred's turn to groan. "Yeah, that occurred to me too. But if she's been murdered, it seems to be unrelated, since the last anybody saw of her was when she was picked up from school by someone claiming to have come from her parents."

"It's Clarke Academy, if I remember correctly. Uniforms, security, very nice."

"Yeah. And *very* put out that the girl was apparently snatched with their full cooperation. The limo driver says he came to pick her up the same as usual, but she'd already ridden away with the guy on the Harley. The school claims he had a release letter identical to the one the limo driver shows every day."

"Maybe it was a boyfriend and they cooked it up between them," Rose said hopefully.

"Yeah, and maybe it was Evel Knievel come to take her to a rally. There's been no body found and no ransom note so far, so that's something. So let us know if you or anybody else over there hears anything about her or sees her, will you? Tell any of your clients who frequent the streets that the girl's father is offering a reward for information leading to her whereabouts."

"Be glad to," Rose said. "That's a good idea. It should turn up some leads."

"Too many, probably," he said ruefully. "Anyhow, call me if anything turns up, okay?"

"You bet," Rose said.

"Gotta go. Take care of yourself, Rosie."

"You too," she said, smiling. There was that warmth again, in his voice and in her own, that she hadn't remembered being there when he worked security. Joining the sheriff's department didn't seem to have changed him much. He was still interested in protecting and helping people, an attitude that often eroded in even the most conscientious officers once they burned out. She hoped that wouldn't happen to him.

She hung up and turned to face the client who had just come in. The client was a slightly heavyset black woman, her hair relaxed into careful waves. She wore a neat pair of slacks and a matching T-shirt under a waist-length purple jacket. On her feet were a pair of white nurse's oxfords. She set a sheaf of papers on Rose's desk.

"How can I help you?" Rose asked as pleasantly as possible. Nevertheless the woman, who had maintained a stoic and slightly angry expression until then, suddenly looked as if she was going to cry. Rose scooted the Kleenex box closer to her.

"I'm sorry to be here. Sorry to bother you. I never thought I'd have to come to someplace like this, but I need help for my kids. It's not for me. I held out as long as I can but, well, with the youngest being sick and me having to take off work to see to her, I—I . . ."

"Slow down," Rose said. "Tell me slowly now. You have a sick child?"

"Yes. Oh, she's better now but there's not enough food in the house to feed her and . . ."

"Easy. Okay, where do you work?"

"I *did* work at St. Barbara's Hospital, but I was fired last week. That's why I'm here. I haven't been able to go look for a job and I'm so afraid we'll—"

"Why did they fire you?" Rose asked.

"I've got the letter right here," the lady said.

"Wait, first things first. I'm Rose Samson and you are?"

"Paula Reece."

"Okay, Paula," she said and looked over the letter. "The hospital says they're firing you because your wages were garnisheed, is that right?"

"Yes, but—"

"Who garnisheed them?"

"The hospital did."

"No, I mean, who does the hospital have to give the money to?"

"To themselves. It's very complicated and really, really dumb." Paula Reece no longer seemed to want to cry. Instead, she was becoming indignant. "A month ago my youngest started running a fever and before I knew what was happening, fell into a coma. Well, I've worked at St. Barbara's for fifteen years, so of course I took 'Cilla, that's my youngest, Priscilla Anise. My other child is a boy, Malik. He's nine. Anyway, 'Cilla was diagnosed with bacterial meningitis. Ms. Samson, they had to fight for her life. She was on a respirator for a while and they had to do all kinds of tests and she was in the hospital three weeks. Thank God she even survived. And the doctors and the nurses, they were real good to her and looked after her real good. Supervisor said I should take however long I needed to be with her. But, well, then the bills came."

"And your insurance didn't cover it?"

Paula snorted. "Ms. Samson, I worked there fifteen years but I *got* no insurance. You know how much it would be for a woman and two little kids? More than I make a month."

"Don't you get hospitalization?"

"No, ma'am."

"I thought St. Barbara's provided it for their employees."

"Only for full-time. I'm a part-time employee."

"After fifteen years?"

"That's right, ma'am. I work thirty-nine hours a week, not counting overtime. Lots of us nursing assistants do and even some of the licensed practicals and RNs. I get no hospitalization, no vacation and I'm not supposed to get any sick time either, except the supervisor was so nice to me. But the business office made up for it. I went to see them about the bills and told them I couldn't pay. The woman I talked to just listened and nodded, but when I went back to work and went to pick up my first paycheck, and believe me, Ms. Samson, we *needed* that paycheck, I was told my wages had been garnisheed. Then today I get this in the mail, telling me I'm fired because the hospital thinks I'm a bad person for having my wages garnisheed and *they* were the ones who garnisheed them."

Rose read the documentation the woman had very wisely brought along to present her case. Doctors' reports on 'Cilla's illness, the bill, her work contract denying her hospitalization, the garnishment, and the letter of termination. Rose sighed, half in sympathy for Paula, half in disgust at her employers.

"Will food coupons help? I wish we could do more, but you see how it is." She indicated the office full of people.

"Anything you can do will help," Paula Reece said. "I am *not* a deadbeat, Ms. Samson, and I'm lookin' for a

job already. Every hospital in town is cryin' for help—
as long as it's only thirty-nine hours a week and you're
willing to work any shift. But yes, ma'am, food coupons
will definitely help in the meantime."

Eleven

PAULA REECE WATCHED the evening news with interest
born of relief and fresh hope. She had no sooner arrived
back home than she heard the phone ring. Harborview
needed her to start orientation immediately. She was to
work on the psych ward, something she'd never done
before, and because the work was specialized, she'd get
in-service training and be paid a little extra.

She had gone right over and started at once, just doing
little things. Little things were what most needed doing.
The patients weren't physically sick usually, and they had
a TV and stereo, craft classes, exercise machines, all kinds
of things to keep them busy besides actual therapy. But
they still needed vital signs sometimes, and the nurses and
therapists needed help putting the paperwork together.

The patients needed help organizing themselves too, filling their time with games or activities, and there were a lot
of special ways you could talk with them, not like a shrink,
just trying to help them know where they were and who
they were and maintain their dignity.

For some of them it wasn't easy. One of the new admis-
sions seemed to think he was a hoppy-toad and kept hopping and belching and trying to catch flies. Kinda like that
Renfield guy in the Dracula movie. Nice-looking man too.
Nice haircut, good clear skin, had come in wearing jeans

and a pricey-looking sweatshirt and a leather jacket that any boy on her block would die for. He had cut himself on a knife they'd taken away from him in emergency, though, and so his clothes were blood-soaked. They weren't damaged otherwise. It took Paula quite a while to persuade him to let her have the old clothes and get him new ones from the rummage closet.

The nice jacket had a big bloodstain, but she thought she could get it out, and he had blood under his nails, and while Paula was trying to clean the jacket, he soiled himself. Hoppy-toads didn't know much about toilet training, apparently. Even thirty-something hoppy-toads.

Finally she got him changed into old clothes that didn't fit too badly and would be easy to change and took his own down to the washer and dryer. They smelled awful, and not just because of the urine. Dried blood smelled nasty after it set.

She plopped the jeans and the sweatshirt and socks and his dirty undershorts into the machine with plenty of soap and bleach and started in on the jacket. The stain wasn't all that big and seemed centered around one pocket. There was a big lump in that pocket. She investigated. Something soft and something else, crinkly, like paper.

It was some kinda letter and a red-and-black-checked scarf, wool, thoroughly soaked with blood. Now that was funny, since the cut wasn't anywhere near his neck. Maybe he'd used it to stop his own bleeding, though she didn't think he'd have had the sense to. Still, apparently he'd got taken crazy real suddenly. That didn't seem right. Most people she knew who'd gone crazy had it come on for a long time, sometimes years, sometimes more, sometimes less. Strange. The letter was from some kind of record company and addressed to a school. She didn't read it. That was that poor man's business. Maybe she'd ask the nurse about it later. Maybe he was some kinda musician who burned himself out on drugs. That might explain how he got crazy so quickly. She already had the other clothes in the washer, and one of the patients was washing up dishes in the utility room and she didn't want to disturb him, so she stuck the scarf along with the piece of paper and the other things she took from the pockets into a brown paper bag and set them back in his closet.

It had only taken maybe half an hour altogether out of her day, but as she watched the news and the bulletin came on about Raydir Quantrill's missing daughter, last seen wearing a red school uniform, red parka, and black-and-red-checked scarf, it all clicked. There was a reward offered too, and she sure could use it.

But you were supposed to keep anything you found out about patients confidential, weren't you? She should report this to the hospital. On the other hand, what if whoever she reported it to took credit for her discovery and collected the reward? Then she'd never be able to pay her bills and clear her reputation. But on the *other* hand, if she violated the patient's rights by talking about him, the hospital might fire her and she'd have a much harder time finding another job.

She was caught between a rock and a hard place. She copied down the number on the TV, and, after debating long and hard about what to do, went to the phone.

Gigi had given the matter a great deal of thought and had decided she didn't like Mama anymore. Mama had made Daddy go away, and ever since she had been mad at Gigi and Hank. And Gigi did still like Hank, even if he was kinda bossy just because he was a boy and older.

She had heard him say she should stay there while he went chasing after Mama again when Mama plainly didn't love them anymore. But she thought that they might as well find the policeman who would give them another bear and buy them cookies and take them home right away instead of waiting around like they had before.

So she was looking around for him—not moving, mind you, just looking around—when she saw the wonderful house. It was behind a velvet rope in the middle of the aisle a little way up from where she stood. It looked like a Christmas house. Christmas hadn't come for them this year yet, to Gigi's mind, though everyone else had already celebrated it almost a month before.

Gigi had seen little houses like it before, made out of candy and cookies, but nobody had ever let her eat a piece of one. This one had candy canes and Oreos and gingerbread people and candy kisses and licorice sticks all over it. There was a sign by it, but Gigi couldn't read. She ducked under the rope and walked up the peanut brittle path for a closer look. She wasn't exactly hungry after the Big Mac, but a cookie would sure taste good. They had only had cookies when Mama left them in the mall before and Gigi took some and then the policemen bought some for them for dessert after McDonald's. Probably if a policeman came, he'd let her have part of this house. Probably. What good was it to make a house out of cookies if you didn't let little kids eat some?

She looked around. The mall still had lots of people, but nobody was paying any attention to the little house. She prodded an Oreo out of its frosting mortar and ate it.

Just then Hank came running up, panting and crying. "She did it again, Gi. She left us. She ran off with that man."

"Umm-hmm," Gigi said, and reached for a chocolate kiss.

"Stop that. You can't just take that. It's for display."

"No it's not," she said with a mouth full of chocolate. "It's for eating. It's good too."

Just then a head peeked out of the doorway and a man said, "Well, well, it wasn't a mouse at the door at all. It's a couple of cookie monsters nibbling my house."

"I'm not Cookie Monster," Gigi said. "He's on Sesame Street."

"She's sorry, mister," Hank said, pulling at her hand. "She's too little to understand. Our mama just ran off and left us. Can you go get the policeman to take us home?"

"Oh, sure, I can do that," the man said, coming out of the house. "But there's no hurry, is there? You say your mama just left you?"

"Yes, she left us in the mall again while she ran away with a man."

"Did she now?" he sounded very interested. "Well, gee, why did she do that?"

"She doesn't like us anymore," Gigi said through another mouthful of cookie.

"Now, honey, I'm sure that's not true," the man said. "Why, anybody would love a pretty little girl like you and a cool dude like your brother."

"Naw," Hank said. "Gigi's right. Mama doesn't really want us anymore—at least not till Daddy comes home from Alaska. I guess she'll like us again when he comes home."

"Oh. Well, then, I don't see that there's any hurry finding the policeman, do you? Truth is, kids, I put this house together to display here for Christmas and I was going to take it down tonight. I was feeling sad that not one kid had had a bite of any of this candy yet."

Gigi wiped the chocolate from her mouth—to her nose and both eyes and down along her chin. "We'll help you, mister."

He looked like a nice man. He was old like Daddy with mostly white hair and a little white beard and blue eyes— like a skinny Santa Claus.

"Is Christmas over, then?" Hank asked. "We went on vacation for it from school but we never did a tree or presents this year."

The man put his arm around Hank's shoulders. "You poor little kids. Yes, it was over three and a half weeks ago. Here, try a piece of window. It's sugar candy. I made all of this myself. I'm sorry if it's stale. I almost sprayed it with varnish to make it last and now I'm so glad that I didn't."

"Are you Santa Claus?" Gigi asked the question that had been second on her mind only to the chocolate ever since she saw him. "You got hair like him and a beard like him, but you dress like a regular person."

"No, honey, I'm not the real Santa, but I'll be yours if you want me to be. You see, I made this house to do something for boys and girls because I love to bake and I haven't got any children of my own."

"Cool," Hank said. "Can you help us find the guard to call the policeman to take us home?"

"What guard?"

"You know, the security man. He comes and takes you to an office and pretty soon a cop comes and gives us cookies and toys and takes us home."

"I've got a better idea," the man said. "I've got cookies and toys too. Why not just leave the cop out of it and I'll take you home?"

"No, that's okay," Hank said. "It's kind of complicated. I mean, I couldn't give you directions." He did, however, now know Aunt Bambi's address.

"Oh, I've lived in these parts a long time. I probably won't need directions if you can just tell me an address. Now then, why don't you kids help me break this down?

Eat as much as you want. I'm going to start making the dough for a new one for next Christmas as soon as I get home."

"You're going to bake cookies?" Gigi asked. It had been so long since Mama had baked cookies or anything else.

"Oh, yeah," he said. "I bake every day. In fact, I'll tell you what. Why don't you break off a piece of something here to see you through and we can stop off at my place and I'll put some chocolate chip cookies in the oven. It'll only take a few minutes and then you'll have some to take home."

He seemed like a nice man. As country children, Hank and Gigi had never been cautioned about strangers all that much. And nobody else seemed to want them. Maybe he would take them in and Mama wouldn't know where to find them and be real sorry. Then when they were ready to go home, they'd take her cookies and she'd cry and Daddy would come back and they'd move back into their own house and everything would be good again. The nice man could come and visit. And bring cookies.

Carrying handfuls of stale Oreos, they climbed into his car and he drove in toward the city, then turned into a place with a lot of houses that all looked alike. His still had Christmas decorations up. Reindeer on the lawn, lights glittering in the windows, a Santa waving from the front, candy-cane fenceposts with big red bows around them lining the walk to the front door and another gingerbread house, smaller than the one in the mall, on his lawn.

"I made the reindeer and the Santa and all the decorations myself in my shop," he told them as they got out of the car. He let them into the house ahead of him and locked the door behind him. "Come into the kitchen while I preheat the oven and get the first batch of dough out of the fridge, then I'll take you out to the shop to play with my toys until the cookies are done."

The inside of the house was funny and not nearly as pretty or inviting as the outside. See-through plastic covered the couch and chairs and even the lampshades.

It didn't smell as good as Gigi thought it would, either. She thought it would smell like cookies. Instead it smelled kind of—nasty.

Hank said, "Maybe we should just try to call the cops to let them know where we are so they can tell Mom we're on our way."

The man gave him a short, sharp, hard look, but then smiled and said, "Oh, I don't think the police will want to be annoyed by calls from a couple of kids. They're awfully busy. Besides, you might get your mother in trouble and they'd put her in jail and you in juvenile detention. You wouldn't like that, would you?"

"They wouldn't do that," Hank said. "They were nice."

"Fred let Hank play with his handcuffs," Gigi volunteered. "But I'd rather have cookies." She had been looking around for something and noticed all at once what was missing, what with the lights and the candy canes and reindeer and all. "Where's your Christmas tree?" she asked.

The man turned on his oven and took a bowlful of dough out of the refrigerator. He looked surprised at the question and Hank said hurriedly, "Shut up, Gigi. She doesn't mean to be nosy, mister. We didn't have Christmas this year at home, though."

"That's right, you said you didn't. How sad. Christmas is for children. Children *deserve* Christmas." He opened the door to what ought to be the garage and ushered them in, without turning the light on. "Well, don't worry, kids. I like to see to it that children get what they deserve." He chuckled, giving Hank a little shove. "I'll even let you play with my handcuffs."

Twelve

DING WOKE WITH a stiff neck. The rain had stopped. He opened the window. The fire escape was slick and cold, but the house oppressed him. And his dreams had been full of music. Returning to the living room, he opened the small wicker chest that served as a coffee table and also held his clothing and the few other belongings he had. He pawed through these until he reached the bottom, and pulled out the bamboo flute. He hadn't been able to use it in this country, of course. School bands wanted you to have real instruments, and his parents had scraped together enough to rent a metal and plastic flute for him.

He hadn't been allowed to play "Louie Louie" for one of his performance pieces either, though his recital of the song had amused his teachers.

Back then, he thought America was wonderful. The church group that had brought his family here helped them find a home among other Vietnamese. Later, the neighborhood expanded to include Laotians and Cambodians. The apartment was simple by American standards, but a palace compared to the camp.

And though Ding was happily enrolled in school, his father could not get a license to practice medicine in America, as he had hoped, and his English was not good enough for him to attend American medical schools or pass the required tests. He had to take odd jobs sweeping out shops, and later, when he had learned a bit more English, driving a taxi. Mother, whose English was better, did not work due to weakness from hunger and babies she had borne and lost while they were in the camps. For a couple of years after they first came to Seattle, however, she would wander around the house saying, "How I wish I had the beaded curtain that we used to have in the house in Da Nang," or "How I wish I still had the chest that my grandmother gave me. It would look well against that wall."

Ding used to think when he got here that when he became a famous musician he'd buy his mother replacements for the treasures she had lost . . . all but the little brothers and sisters who never made it to America.

Now she was plenty strong enough to go to work again and cleaned houses for American women.

He tried the bamboo flute, blowing the first few notes of a Vietnamese song. Back when he still played the flute often, his father always asked for Vietnamese songs.

He heard a knock on the kitchen window and saw Le's face and hands framed in the pane.

"Hey, man, everything okay?"

Ding remembered in time that his mother was supposed to be sick instead of bitching him out, and he said, "Yeah, she's just been kind of low. I think she's doing her missing Vietnam thing."

Le snorted. "That's nuts! It's a third-world country, man. My folks are like that too. Back in the camps they practiced English and here I can hardly get them to talk anything but Vietnamese. They think spending money on clothes is wasteful, and I'd dress out of the Goodwill bin all the time if it was up to them."

"Like the shoes, man," Ding said, nodding down at his friend's green velvet Doc Martens, now soaked and splattered with mud.

"I got those from my take of the car stereo money," he said, preening.

Ding thought the plain black DMs would have stood his buddy in better stead, but he said nothing. Being able to dress right was important—they'd all found that out in high school when they'd still accepted their parents' ideas about how they ought to dress. The hell of it was, up until then Ding had always loved school. He was quick and had a good memory and a talent for figuring things out. But the high school was a big one, mixed Asian, black, and white. And though he did well in class and earned praise from his teachers, the other kids, especially the non-Asian kids, made fun of him for being a show-off and a grind and dressing funny.

"Y'know," he told Le, "I feel like jumpin' somebody."

"Yeah," Le said. "Some Guerilla fighting! We ought to do it. Man, I'll never forget the first time I saw you lick that gang from school. There they are like with knives and knucks and all of 'em bigger than you. They thought they were going to whip your butt, man, till they found out the hard way you make Bruce Lee look like a sissy!"

"No sweat," he said. "It was just the stuff we all learned in the camps."

Two more of the guys climbed up the fire-escape stairs and sat on the landing by Le. By now Ding was leaning out the window, twiddling the flute in his fingers as he and Le talked.

"I remember that too, man!" Minh said. Like Ding, he wore his hair Apache style, with a kerchief headband. "Man, you were blood from one end to the other! What did your folks say?"

"Oh, that!" Ding laughed. "I never told you guys all of that story, did I? Well, the folks were about how you'd expect. Dad demanded to know what had happened, as if *he'd* ever be able to *bic* it, and Mom hissed at me and started attacking me with a washcloth and Bactine. So they go, 'What happened?' and I go, 'Some kids jumped me,' and I shrug, y'know? Well, once they figured out I wasn't gonna die or anything, they left me alone. It's not like they never saw me get beat up before, but back in the camps, that was okay. Things like that aren't s'posed to happen in America. But then, *later*, did I tell you what happened?"

He was sure he had, a dozen times at least, but they all acted as if he never had. He was a pretty good storyteller and mimic, and usually could crack them up.

"Well, later somebody called the house and I answered, because, you know, the folks were at work . . ."

The others nodded.

"So I go, 'Hi,' and this bitchy voice at the other end goes, without even finding out if it's the right number, 'Listen you, this is Mrs. Gloria fucking Maken and your savage son put my darling Teddy in the hospital with a broken nose, a broken jaw, a broken arm and a ruptured spleen. He's in intensive care right now and I intend to sue you for everything you have.'

"So I go, pretending to be Dad, y'know, 'Wow, I knew our boy did good but I didn't know he did that good! And you can sue all you like, lady. We don't have anything you'd want! So fuck you!' And I hang up."

"Yeah, go on, tell the rest," urged Hai, who was called Hal outside the gang. He had just climbed up the 'scape with three of the other guys.

"Okay, so later on, here I am doing my homework like a good little kid and there's this banging on the door. Well, my mom's home by then but she sees the uniforms outside the window and makes a beeline for the kitchen."

"My folks are the same way," Le agreed. "Since they were in that reeducation camp in Ho Chi Minh City, they don't want no part of uniforms."

"So like, I say, 'I'm not scared,' and I go to the door.

" 'You Nu-jin Ding Ho Ha?' one of the cops goes.

"So I go, 'Not me, man. Nguyen Ding Hoa lives in the next building.' "

"That's when they put you in the cage, right, Ding? Figured you was one dangeroso dude."

Ding grinned and nodded, but didn't say anything. What had actually happened was that the cops had then forced their way in, saying, "Not according to the school address, kid. You better come with us. You're being charged with assault with intent to kill. Your folks home?"

Ding was scared shitless but he shook his head and didn't tell them about his mother hiding in the kitchen. When they put the cuffs on him, though, she came running out, pounding on them and crying.

Later the church group intervened for him, sent a social worker to explain to the courts about the refugee camp and how his parents, who had come from Hanoi to the south to be free from communism, had fought and almost died after the fall of Saigon, escaped by boat to Hong Kong, and now came to the States to be shamed by their oldest surviving son. The court was lenient. He was put on probation and sent back to school, where he earned good grades once more until he half-killed another classmate in another brawl. *That* time he went to jail.

"Ding didn't care about that!" Le said. "The joint was nothing compared to the camps, was it, Ding?"

That was partially true. It was a lot like school and a lot like the camps. There wasn't anything there he hadn't been through before.

"I tell you, man, the joint was great compared to this dump." He jerked his thumb at the window to his parents' apartment. The "joint" wasn't an adult prison, but juvenile detention, and he was sixteen years old when he got out. He had completed his high school equivalency by then. His parents brought him the bamboo flute and sent him letters every day. He was sure they burned incense on his behalf.

They should have saved it for when he got out.

"I learned all kinds of good shit, man," he said, grinning.

"Yeah, we know," Hai said. "Like lock picking, hot wiring, how to take out car stereos, pocket picking . . ."

"My older brother knew all of that in Vietnam!" Le said proudly.

Ding was still grinning at his gang but inside he simmered with anger that the illegal things he had learned were all that was to be of practical use to him. When he got out, he sent applications for college. His grades were great, as usual, but he got three replies from the schools he applied to, and all of those were negative.

"What do they mean, they're full?" he asked his probation officer. "They take people all the time."

"They mean they're full of Asians, probably," said the officer, who was a sharp but weary-looking Laotian woman. She had told him about the informal quotas they had on Asian students then, and how afraid a lot of so-called smart Americans were that Asian kids would raise the grade curve "unfairly" or take all the positions in the best colleges. "Of course, you're trying out-of-state schools so far. You can probably get into Evergreen or even UW," she suggested. "They're more liberal."

So, sixteen years old with no place to go, too young to get hired for jobs, high school finished, too Asian and too bad for most colleges, he sat out on this fire escape and played the bamboo flute. And the gang, most of whom he'd known from a distance throughout school, began to gather around him.

Like him, they had no jobs; like him, they were outsiders everywhere, no matter how much they wanted to fit in or how hard they tried. And like him, they had grown up with their parents' wartime tales of bravery and treachery that they were not a part of. None of their folks thought their kids could have hacked it in the wars, none of them thought the kids could have been as brave or as strong as *they* had been. Ding and the gang were too Asian for the Americans and too American for their own folks. You couldn't win.

But he didn't need any of those other people now. He had the gang. They thought he was cool and tough, even tougher than they, and he knew that even the girls in the neighborhood were starting to notice him. Partly it was the idea that a guy who could kick ass so hard was also smart, could play music, sing and tell stories in a funny way. But mostly it was because, even if he didn't know what he was doing or where he was going any more than they did, he knew that he was damn sure going to do *something* and go *some*where and make somebody—preferably the whole effing city—pay for getting in his way. He and the gang would make sure of that.

"Come on," he told them, climbing out to join them. "Let's jump somebody."

"So, you guys were all in Vietnam together?" Sno asked, as she, Doc and Trip-Wire sat on a tarp spread over the snow and fished in the rushing icy river.

"Yeah. We weren't in the same outfit, though."

"I wondered. You all seem to know each other pretty well," she ventured. "Like you've been through a lot together."

Doc gave her a long look through glasses half frosted over. His beard and mustache had little icicles in them where his breath moistened the hair. "We have. But not in Nam. We've been in therapy groups together in one combination or the other for years. Or, I guess you could say, we're the ones who survived them."

"Yeah? Forgive me, but that sounds a little, you know, wimpy."

"Not when you consider that twice as many Nam vets have killed themselves since the war as died in battle," Doc said. "Including other members of groups we've been in."

"Sometimes," Trip-Wire said. "Sometimes having an enemy outside yourself is the easy part. It's all the enemies you've got crawling around inside that will do you . . ."

Trip-Wire wasn't scary at all now. He looked sort of like an aging biker with his long graying black hair and beard.

"You only say that because all of your outside enemies are gone now," Sno told him. "*And* you're an adult."

"Gee, thanks," Trip-Wire said.

"No, I mean, you can do what you want to. You guys don't know what it's like living with somebody who hates you no matter what you do to please her."

"Wanta bet?" Doc asked.

"Yeah, let me tell you about my ex-wife," Trip-Wire said.

"No, I mean really."

"Believe it or not, Sno, we were kids once too," Doc said. "My old man drank like a fish and, besides that, had religion. When he drank, his sense of direction was screwed up. He knew somebody'd been sinnin' because he felt so damn bad but he couldn't tell who it was so he beat the hell out of me on general principle."

"Makes me glad I didn't have an old man," Trip-Wire said. "My mother was nothing to write home about either."

Sno thought that over for a minute. For some reason, it never seemed like older people actually had *parents* even though she knew Grandma Hilda was her mother's mom.

"So you guys never really had families and you're kind of like family to each other, is that it?" she asked.

"Yeah, right. We're family. Maurice is the mommy."

"You," Doc said to Sno, ignoring Trip-Wire, "have been watching too many mini-series."

"Maybe," she said. "But they have to get their material from someplace, don't they? I thought all you macho types were supposed to hate gays." She herself, of course, growing up in the entertainment industry, had a much more cosmopolitan view of such things. But these guys were living in their military past, for pity's sake.

"Aw, don't believe that limp-wrist act Doper puts on," Trip-Wire said. "He ain't like that really. He's a good man. Ex-tunnel rat, so his nerves are real bad, but he helped save the hospital at Cu Chi. Silver Star, Purple Heart and the frag scars to show it. He's just like any of us except he's got a bitch of an ex-boyfriend instead of a bitch of an ex-wife. He's lucky he didn't marry the guy."

"Wow," Sno said. After a moment she asked, "Did it bother you guys, that they used to call you baby-killers?"

"Yeah," Doc said. "But you know what, it used to bother me when I was a kid that the others called me blanket-ass and stripe too, because I was a half-breed. You never really get over it, but you get used to it, and you grow beyond it. Why do they call you Sno? You look half Indian yourself."

"Not half. About a sixteenth, I guess. But I'm black Irish on my mom's side, except that Grandma Hilda was half German."

"And the Sno?"

"Oh, that was Dad's idea. He wanted me to have a celebrity kid name. He got his big chance on *Borderlands*."

"Yeah, I love that show," Trip-Wire said. "Especially the lady Mountie. Va va voom. She can come and get this man anytime."

"You're a fuckin' chauvinist pig, T.W., you know that?" Doc said, a little embarrassed in front of Sno, she thought.

"Huh? Whaddid I say?"

"Never mind," Sno said. "I'm used to it. Anyway, they make *Borderlands* over in Snohomish, so Raydir named me after the town."

Doc grunted.

"Actually, my stepmother is the only one who really bothers me now. She's all sweetness and light whenever anyone is around, but she hates me. I used to try to get her to tell me things about dressing and makeup because she's so beautiful and everything. I mean, when Dad first married her, after Mom was killed and I moved back in with him, I thought she was great. I wanted to be just like her. But the harder I tried, the more she hated me."

"Jealous," Doc said.

"Of me? I'm just a kid."

"So was Brooke Shields."

"Who?"

"Sorry. I'm showing my age again."

"She really got pissed off when her agent tried to get me to do some promo shots."

"She been working much lately?"

"I wish she was," Sno said. "I think it's the bimbos."

"What?"

"The babes chasing Raydir. They're getting to her. They got to Mom too, but we just left. Gerardine takes it out on me. Especially since I got busted. She acts like she's being so motherly but really she's glad. She calls me slut and junkie and stuff and honest, since I got busted and went to rehab, I haven't touched the stuff. Grandma Hilda would just die if she knew I'd been on drugs after all she and Mom did to try to protect me from it. I know that now. But I was so *bummed* after Mama died and one of Gerardine's ex-boyfriends—yeah, she's got *her* bimbos too, but those don't count, I guess—he got me to try a little. Said it would mellow me out. And I was *not* trying to turn tricks when I was down in the market. I just wanted to get some money for another line or two to tide me over. My allowance was gone and Gerardine wouldn't give me any more. The staff is all new since I was here before, so there was nobody I could hit up. I was just asking for change and that cop . . ."

Doc shot her a wise sideways look. "You didn't offer him a blow job too? Where'd you pick that up?"

Sno blushed. "No. I only said that so you'd know I was really desperate. People just say stuff like that back at Raydir's place. I don't even have a boyfriend."

"Keep talkin' like that and you will real quick, babe," T.W. advised.

"Look," Doc said. "It sounds to me like you got a lot to work through. We're doing a sweat tomorrow and it's guys only, but you could go in alone before or after if you want to. I'd recommend before. It may be a little smelly afterwards."

"Gee, thanks," she said dubiously.

"No problem. In the morning before, we'll be off in the woods, doing a rap session and that needs to be private too, and afterwards, we'll be here at the river, washing off, then separate vision quests and meditations."

"You'll be busy then," she said.

"Yeah, but afterwards we'll build a campfire in the snow and we can all come and talk about anything the day

Thirteen

THE ANSWERING SERVICE called Rose to tell her about Paula Reece's message and Rose called the woman back. "Paula, hi. Rosalie Samson. What's up?"

"I need your advice, Miss Samson—"

"Just Rose is fine," Rose said. She didn't much like formality. The creepy clients didn't have enough manners or respect to use it anyway, and those were the ones she wanted to distance, so she felt like she may as well use her first name with everybody. Besides, she found it easier to establish rapport with clients if she could use *their* first names and it was demeaning to them for her to do it if they couldn't.

"I just watched the six o'clock news and they showed a picture of that little girl who's missing, the singer's girl?"

"Snohomish Quantrill?" Rose asked. She'd been watching the news too.

"Yes, ma'am. Anyhow, the picture of that school uniform of hers?"

"Uh-huh. The red outfit with the black-and-red muffler."

"Yeah. Well, I seen a muffler like that."

"When?"

"Today, at my new job. Now, Rose, I know there's a lot of mufflers look like that but this one was black and red

127

too, just like that one, but what makes me worry that it might be related is, this scarf was all covered with blood. And I don't know, would I be violatin' that man's privacy to report it or not?"

"Oh, I don't think so," Rose said. "Haven't they told you yet that the confidentiality thing doesn't apply where you have good reason to suspect that the patient is a danger to himself or others or to property?"

"No, they didn't. I just started working there today and I guess they were kinda busy."

"Well, that's the rule. It's not just a hospital rule, it's law. So it's really your obligation to report it. Nobody could fault you for it."

"To the police?"

"Well, yes. I'd say without much delay. If the scarf is Sno's and the man either did something to her or knows where she is, she might still be alive. There's not a moment to lose, in that case."

"I guess not. But I sure don't want to call any police."

"You wouldn't be doing anything wrong, Paula, and you might be helping save a young girl's life."

"I know, Rose, but you don't understand how it is for people like me—they're apt to accuse me of planting it, anything. They shot my sister's boy just because he was the same age and color as a boy they were chasing. That child had never done anything wrong."

"Well, then, what shall we do?"

"Could you maybe call them?"

"I guess I could, but you'd have to talk to them just the same. I couldn't hide your identity, Paula. It's a kidnapping and murder investigation and that would be withholding evidence. Besides, there's a reward offered and *if* you're right and your information led to finding Sno . . ."

"Well . . ." Paula hesitated.

"Look, just before I talked to you the other day I had a call from an officer I know. He's a good guy and fair and he's involved in the case. I could see if he'd come and take your statement personally."

"That'd be good," Paula said. "But, do you think maybe that you could come with him? And maybe I wouldn't have to go back to work with him to find the scarf and that way they wouldn't think I was a troublemaker if it turned out to be nothing."

"I know how worried you are about losing this job, and from what happened to you before, we both have seen how unreasonable hospital administrations can be," Rose said in a careful, professional manner while she was thinking over whether or not she could go, ought to go. She and Paula had established pretty good rapport during their brief contact. Paula was exactly the sort of person Felicity talked about who could be helped—she had asked for food to keep her children alive and hadn't expected anybody to support her, but had gone right out, on her own, and found a job. Now she was understandably worried about losing it. And while Rose knew Fred Moran would cooperate with her as far as he could, the police had pretty formidable administrative snarls too. Paula's fears weren't unreasonable.

Rose was very tired. She had seen something like eighty clients that day, many of whom she couldn't help. She had only been home an hour or two. But there was a seven-thirty ferry she could catch if she hustled. "I'll tell you what. I live cross-Sound so it'll take me about an hour and a half to get back to the city. Give me your address and if I can't come with the police, I'll catch a cab to your place. Okay?"

"I'll be watching for you," Paula said and gave her the address.

She called the sheriff's office before she left and asked to speak to Fred. She expected a long hassle, that they would have to page him and give him another number to call her back, but he was still at the office and answered at once.

When she finished telling him about the conversation she said, "So, what do you think?"

"I think it's fairly slim but if you think it could be significant, well . . ."

"I promised Paula that you'd come personally and that if I couldn't come with you, I'd take a cab over to her place . . ."

"It would be great if you could come along and put Paula at ease. I'd really appreciate it. I'll pick you up at the ferry terminal at 9:10."

"Right." She refilled the dry cat food and cats' water to the brim and petted everyone, then threw a sleep-T, her toothbrush and some vitamins in her purse in case she missed the last ferry and had to stay over in Seattle with Patrick and his wife Gail. Pulling her last clean pair of jeans out of her closet, she tugged them on along with a man's dark green T-shirt, which she tucked in. She drew a vintage souvenir Indian-beaded belt through the loops of her jeans and threw on an oversized men's Norfolk jacket, just to look professional. A pair of beaded earrings from the market and her mustard seed, socks and running shoes, and she'd be ready for work tomorrow in case she didn't get to come home.

After grabbing her recycled kilim duffel purse, she set the security alarm on the house, ran for the car, drove to the terminal, parked, put money in the slot and ran aboard the ferry just as they were about to draw up the ramp.

She caught her breath and her dinner aboard the ferry, in the coffee shop. A foil-wrapper burger, a cup of espresso and a rather limp-looking salad should see her through the evening.

The moon tonight was a thumbnail paring, leaves of dark cloud obscuring the stars so that the water danced only with artificial light. The ferry glided through the water like some half-drowned ghost hotel, people moving eerily through its brightly lit rooms as it slid over the water.

Rose sipped her espresso and thought not so much of Paula as of Felicity. Of course, she had proved absolutely nothing and everything she said sounded crazy, but Rose could have sworn Felicity herself was neither crazy nor a pathological liar. She didn't sound like a deluded New Age guru either. And what if—what if what she claimed was real *was* real . . . wouldn't that be something? Then things could change. Inevitability wouldn't be quite so inevitable. That would be . . . refreshing, to say the least.

She didn't notice Fred at first because she was expecting to see him in a uniform and a patrol car, but as she turned the corner coming down the steps from the ferry terminal, a blue Ford Escort two-door on the far side of the street, beneath the overpass, honked, and the driver leaned out the window and waved.

Fred Moran smiled a slightly cockeyed smile as she slid in beside him. He was wearing civvies, slacks, a dress shirt and tie, looking very corporate except that in place of a sports jacket he had substituted a windbreaker with the KCP for King County Police on it. On the seat beside him sat a teddy bear in uniform.

"This looks like the bear Gigi had," Rose said, picking up the stuffie and straightening his badge.

"Nah, that's his brother, my *new* partner. I go through those guys really fast. Different service groups buy the bears and dress them for us to help smooth relations with children we encounter in the line of duty. In cases of domestic disturbance or child abuse, the bear gives the little guys something to hang on to."

"That's great," Rose said. "I could use one of those myself from time to time."

"Yeah, me too," Fred said, patting the bear's head and her hand at the same time. "That's why I always have a backup bear. I'll let you borrow him sometime if you ask nice." The flirtatiousness in the comment hung uncertainly in the air between them for a moment as he negotiated the turn out from under the viaduct and into city traffic. After a while, he said, "You look nice. I like the jacket, only somehow it makes me wonder where's the deerstalker cap and the pipe. It *is* the same kind Sherlock Holmes wears, isn't it?"

"Excellent, my dear Watson," she said. "Your powers of observation are finely honed. Speaking of sartorial splendor, you were wearing a uniform before. In fact, I think this is the first time I've seen you in mufti. Have you been promoted?"

"Sort of. It's your new progressive policing, ma'am. Since, as every patrolman knows, it's really the cop on the street who is the most important member of *your* police force at work, the administration in its wisdom has adopted a policy that's been in use in smaller areas for some time. Patrolmen learn detective skills and become crime scene investigators. You are lookin' at one of the same. That was why I called you the other day. I was investigating the crimes or potential crimes in our community, and their scenes, and everyone I knew associated with them. And I want you to know that we do appreciate your help with our enquiries, ma'am," he said. "Now then, tell me again about your friend and what she saw."

When they reached Paula's apartment, Paula was pacing the floor with anxiety. Rose had expected her to be shy and reserved around Fred but instead Paula practically dragged them inside, holding on to Rose's hand with both of her own and squeezing it urgently.

"I just remembered something real important," she said. "There was a letter in the pocket too. It was all crumpled up and bloody but I'm sure the name was some music company and it was to a school."

Fred asked, "What's the name of this patient again, and what are his ward and unit numbers?"

Fourteen

Hopping Mad

ROSE RODE WITH Fred to the hospital, but since he was on police business, she didn't go in at first. He called for backup and was met by uniformed officers. He was back sooner than she expected, shaking his head as he climbed in the car and slammed the door shut behind him. "Damn. I was afraid of that. The nurse doesn't want her patients disturbed by police and insists on a court order."

"No, that's not right," Rose said, opening her door. What she had told Paula was correct. The hospital had an obligation to cooperate if the patient was dangerous. She ought to know. She had worked at Harborview as the in-house social worker before going to work for the state. At the time, the state job was better. If the nurse was being difficult and making the police go through all the formalities before they could talk to the patient, then not only was Sno being put at risk, but more than likely Paula would be called on the carpet later.

"Where are you going?" Fred asked.

"If you don't mind, I'd like to talk to the nurse on duty."

"Well, be my guest if you think it'd do any good. I'll tag along and note your technique," he added, the tension in his voice giving way to a more lighthearted tone.

He allowed her to lead the way back up to the psych unit. She recognized the nurse from her days at Harborview and had had dealings with her a couple of times since, when she'd admitted clients and visited them later. Nadia Briggs was a fortyish, post-hippie veteran of the sixties peace and civil rights movements and was currently an activist for most other liberal causes including everything from environmental consciousness to women's rights, gay rights, animal rights and the right to die. Only her very determined jawline hinted at the steel that underlay the deceptively gentle flower-child manner. An air of professional competence was the only badge of office she wore besides a name tag. Her long light brown hair was loosely gathered at the nape of her neck and, like all of the psych staff, she wore plain clothes. Tonight it was jeans and a well-used sweater overlaid with a tapestry vest.

"Rose?" she asked, with a suspicious look at Fred and the uniformed cops standing behind her.

"Hi, Nadia," Rose said.

"Rose, I already told these officers that they'll need a court order to interrogate my John Doe. They can come back in the morning to talk to him. He's extremely disturbed and we've just got him quieted down."

"I appreciate that, Nadia, but I just thought you ought to know—well, did you watch the news this evening?"

"I caught part of it while I was getting meds out."

"There's a young girl missing—she was taken from her school on Friday afternoon after the kidnapper presented a letter from her father to the school. She was wearing a school uniform, including a red-and-black-checked scarf. One of the psych staff, another friend of mine, remembers seeing the letter and the scarf on your patient."

"That's breach of confidentiality!" Nadia said.

"The staff member was very concerned about that, which is why she asked me what she ought to do. I reminded her about what the code says about exceptions being made if the patient is a danger to others, and urged her to let me call Officer Moran, who's handled other clients of mine in a very sensitive and caring manner. It's winter out there, Nadia. My friend said the scarf the man had, the red-and-black one, was caked with blood. The girl may be badly hurt, alone, freezing. Your patient may have had nothing to do with it, but it sounds like he's at least met the guy who did. Please, the time it takes to get a court order may cost Sno her life."

Nadia cast a look of dislike back at Fred and the other policemen but led Rose and the others back into the ward. Fred shot Rose a surreptitious thumbs-up sign while Nadia strode ahead. "Not that you're going to get anything out of him by talking to him," she said. "He's very disturbed."

"I'd like to have a look at his effects first," Fred told her. "The scarf and the letter particularly, but also anything that might identify him."

Nadia shook her head. "It was kind of strange, really. He was apparently pretty well dressed and well groomed when he first came in, except for a recent flesh wound. But there was no identification on him, and God only knows how he came to *be* so well cared for. His psychotic break must have been extremely sudden, and that's a little unusual."

She unlocked a bin outside the room and extracted a plastic bag containing folded clothing and a wrinkled paper sack. Fred pulled on a plastic glove and shook out the paper sack, drawing forth a scarf crusted with blood and stinking.

"Great. It hasn't been washed," Fred said, though Nadia looked a little disapproving. He next extracted a folded and crinkled piece of paper, handling it with gloves, as if it were a priceless antique scroll. "This is it, okay," he said, grim satisfaction in his tone. He replaced the letter in the bag and handed everything to one of the uniformed officers. "I'll give you a receipt for those things," he told Nadia, which seemed to surprise her. "And I do need to talk to your patient, urgently, please. Now."

The patient was in a locked isolation room and as Nadia unlocked the door, Rose could see a form inside the room, squatting against one of the walls.

Before Fred was quite in the room or Nadia had closed the door behind her, the patient emitted a noise that sounded like a monstrous belch and leaped up and halfway across the room. The uniformed officers grabbed for their guns but Rose blocked their way to the door and meanwhile the patient leaped back, just as far, just as fast. The police kept their hands near their weapons but relaxed a little, and pushed their way past Rose. Fred waved them back again.

"It's okay," Nadia told the patient in a calm, everyday voice. "We're just here to see if you're okay. This man wants to talk to you. I'm sorry if we startled you."

"Reedeep?" the patient asked in a puzzled, slightly querulous tone, and began randomly hopping around the room, croaking.

Nadia had been correct about one thing. Questioning the patient was useless. But Fred didn't seem too disappointed as, a short time later, they left the hospital, the bag of clothing carried by one of the uniformed officers, while Fred tenderly carried the brown paper sack in his gloved hand.

"Thanks for the assist, Rosie. You were great," he said, sounding as happy as if he had a new toy.

"What did you think about the patient?" she asked, her question concealing the pleasurable glow his praise gave her. She *had* been pretty great, hadn't she? Of course, it was really just that she knew Nadia, who didn't much like cops anyway, but was not a fool or deliberately obstructive, merely conscientious. Her relationship with the nurse and the unit had always been collaborative, whereas Nadia still saw the cops as adversaries.

"It'll take some checking, but he's our boy," Fred said.

"You're sure?"

"The letter cinches it. Unless, by some weird chance, he just happened on it, he's the perp."

"But he seems too crazy to have planned something like that," Rose said. "Unless he's pretending and somehow, I don't think so."

"I hate to say it, but neither do I. But the only other alternative is that somehow or other he met the guy who did do it, who planted the stuff on him. That seems about as unlikely. Why not just get rid of it? No, I think he's our guy, he did the deed and then went gaga. There's the knife wound, for one thing. According to your girlfriend, it was already treated before he was admitted. Too bad the knife wasn't still on him. But if the wound had already been treated, maybe he got cut when he snatched the girl, which means he might have had himself treated closer to where he left her, so we can check that with area hospitals. That's about as close as we're gonna get to learning useful information from him for now."

"He *didn't* seem to respond well to your third-degree back there," Rose admitted.

Fred shook his head, wonderingly. "I don't know how anybody that nuts convinced the school to let him take the girl or the girl to go with him or how he even got himself checked into the hospital. Unless he's giving an Oscar-caliber performance, the guy's as seriously psycho as anybody I've ever seen. Is there some kind of technical name for it?"

"What?"

"You know, a guy thinking he's a toad?"

"A— You didn't happen to notice if there were any skin changes or anything, did you?"

"You kidding? That sucker could give you mega-warts if you got too close."

She smacked at him playfully. "You'd better can that kind of unprofessional stuff, officer, or I'll sic Nadia on you."

"Well, he was one froggy dude, you've got to admit."

"Yeah," she said. "Hmm," she added, a nasty suspicion rising in her mind when she remembered certain frogs from the fairy tales. Banishing the unwelcome thought that made her wonder if she was as crazy as Nadia's patient, she returned her focus to her most immediate interest in the case and said, "Well, at least since it *is* evidence, Paula won't get in trouble for breaking confidentiality, and finding the letter will certainly contribute information to finding Sno, won't it? And there's a reward."

"What? You get a kickback?"

"Of course not. But Paula really needs it."

"Yeah," he said. "She looked like she could use a break."

"Seriously, Fred, could you let me know what you find out? Because of Sno *and* Paula."

"I'll let you know what I can," he said. "Listen, do you have to go right back home?"

She checked her watch. "The last ferry's history by now. I'll call Patrick and Gail and see if I can stay with them tonight. That's what I usually do if I need to stay over when I'm not on call."

"Well, look, as soon as I turn in this report, I'll be off too. How about a cup of coffee—I mean, in addition to all the other cups of coffee I will of course offer you at the office if you'll hang on while I finish up."

"Okay, as long as I can hold the bear."

"You got a deal."

They passed by the desk right inside the courthouse door into a long corridor. Rose had been here a time or two before, once on a tour given to DFS employees. It was a large office complex composed of three big partitioned rooms, one devoted to crimes specifically relating to child molestation and abuse and rape cases. Adjoining that room on the left was another of the "detective's bullpens" containing perhaps fifty stations, this room devoted to other kinds of crime. In addition, on the far side of the first room there was a softly lit, hushed area that resembled the bridge of the starship *Enterprise* with blinking computer screens set in a circle around a room padded with carpet on the desks and the backstops. This was the communications center. Across the hall from these areas were the fingerprint labs and other evidence-processing facilities, including an awesome file room with six entire walls of black-bound, two-inch-thick folders full of evidence pertaining to the Green River killer, a case continuing to baffle all of the area's law enforcement agencies.

She drank her first promised cup of coffee in the break room while Fred filled out paperwork and sent the bag to the lab, and began scanning mug shots in the computer.

While he was doing that, she called Patrick's house to beg the guest room but no one answered.

Although the child protection and rape area was no doubt often very busy late at night, tonight there were only a few diehard detectives at their desks and no one waiting to be interviewed in the outer room. The fluorescents looked more garish than fluorescents usually looked, and their buzz was louder and more annoying. The loudest sound in the room, however, was the clicking of computer keys and the low murmur of voices on the telephones.

After a while, Rose wandered back to Fred's desk. He stared intently at the screen as it showed him first one face, then another. There was the click of his fingers on the key, then a pause. Click. Pause. Click. Pause. And another face would materialize, turning to show all angles in computer simulation from the original photograph.

"I thought you'd see several pictures at a time," Rose said. "Like pages in a photo album."

"That's right, it normally does, but I've already scanned in the photograph of the suspect we took tonight," he said. "The computer's only calling up possible matches. Wait. Look. That's him. Got him."

"Yeah, it sort of looks like him, but . . ." The face on the screen was sane, or at least if not, had a calculating, paranoid, different sort of insanity than the hopping, croaking psychotic she had just seen. The mug shot was of a man who resembled the pony-tailed, foot-fighting hero of a series of violent martial arts movies.

"That's him, okay. Robert C. Hunter, age thirty-eight, lists an L.A. address here. Let's read his biography. Not very long in terms of record. Brought up for drug dealing a couple of times, and released, one arrest for assault, but released, arrested for suspected murder, but released."

About that time, a detective from the next room passed by on the way to communications and glanced curiously at the screen. "Whatcha got goin' with Hunter, Moran? Don't tell me the sonofabitch is going after kids now?"

"You know this guy? I met him tonight, trying to eat flies on the psych unit at Harborview. Seems to think he's a toad."

"No kidding?"

"None whatsoever."

"Mercy me. How the mighty are fallen," the detective said with a low whistle, staring more intently at the screen.

"What?" Fred asked.

"Well, Hunter may be a loony now, but he is no ordinary loony, believe me."

"No?"

"He's an executioner. Six states have been trying to pin something on him for a long time."

"Nurses' aide found what looks like the Quantrill girl's scarf and the letter he used to snatch her still in his possession when he was admitted to the psych unit. He had a knife wound on the left lower abdomen that had already been treated when he was admitted to Harborview. If we distribute this picture to area hospitals, maybe we'll find out where he was when he got the wound."

"You sure he's crazy on the level? You can't sweat it out of him?"

"Nah, you can't do it to this guy," Fred said with a wink to Rose. "He'd croak."

"Maybe he's got a frog in his throat," the other detective said with a chuckle. "Otherwise, what you're saying is toadally out of character. Of course, I guess you could say he's been a toady for organized crime for some time."

"Stop! I surrender. Enough already. Can you give me what you got on this guy for tomorrow? I need to give Rose a lift—oh, Milt Bowersox, this is Rose Samson. Rose works at Family Services."

Milt nodded hello, but he was already on his way again to the communications room.

Fifteen

"WHERE SHOULD WE go?" Fred asked. "It's been a while since I've been foraging for food at this hour."

"All the Dumpsters usually *are* spoken for by this hour," Rose said. "But the Trattoria Mitchelli is open late and it's fairly quiet. Also, the garlic bread sticks are good if you're peckish."

"Peckish? Like an ostrich. Wanna split a pizza?"

"Now that you mention it, Paula did call before I could pop my Lean Cuisine dinner in the microwave. If you spend more hours on your feet, that means you've burned more calories and can pig out, right?"

"Hey, lady, watch it with that pig stuff," he said.

They exited the building together, out into a soft, chill drizzle that smelled of salt and was not unpleasantly cold. Overhead gulls wheeled and cried, and amid the occasional rush of tires on wet pavement, Rose heard the ferry whistle's deep tone far out on the Sound. Soft fog blanketed the Sound and muffled the mountains, swallowing the very tops of the tallest buildings.

The courthouse was only a short distance from Pioneer Square and as they walked past the brick pedestrian courtyards of the square, they saw benches filled with sleeping bodies, an occasional insomniac pigeon foraging on the ground beneath the trees. The round balls of the streetlights reflected back from the slick streets and sidewalks in long white streaks of light.

The totem pole in the little triangular park at the entrance to the square stood watch on a long line of benches, each with its sleepers, some with nothing but what they wore, some guarding hoards of trashy treasures in bags and shopping carts.

They walked in comfortable silence, hushed not so much from lack of anything to say as from the feeling that they were invading a vast, open-air bedroom. Once inside the darkened restaurant where soft lighting and the clink of glasses were enough to put Rose to sleep, conversation came more naturally.

Fred guided her to her seat with his hand light against the small of her back, a gesture she found more sexy than sexist. Before she had time to wonder about it and how nervous she ought to be after not having had a date in a long time, he said, "Funny, I think this is the first time I've been out for coffee socially since Heather and I broke up."

"George and Patrick and I brought Judy here for her termination party," Rose told him.

"Judy's gone?"

"Yeah, there's just the three of us and Bitsy Hager. You've already had the pleasure, I take it, from what you said over the phone."

"Well, indirectly. Catch me up, will you?"

She did, telling him about all the changes at the clinic since he'd left.

He gave a soft whistle. "Sounds pretty awful."

"It is. It's hard for us and it's brutal for the clients. We could sure use someone like you now."

"You could?"

"Of course we could. You were great with the clients, a great help to all of us."

His mouth quirked in a wry expression and his fingers played with the globe of the candle on their table. "Thanks. I was pretty clueless when I started."

"Nobody would ever have known from the way you acted."

He looked up from the candle, into her eyes. "I just watched what you did and followed suit." He shrugged.

"That's very flattering but it's also bull," she said. "I watched you before you even met me."

"Oh, you did, did you?"

"Yes, I did, and you were damned good. You always acted like you really gave a damn."

"I do," he said, still giving her the same kind of long, intent, listening look a counselor might give a client he was trying to understand. "So, you told me what the clinic's been up to, Rosie. How about you? What've you been doing?"

"Whoo boy, let's save that, shall we?" she said, thinking of the weirdness of the last couple of days. "I've mostly just worked, gone home, swamped out the house, petted the cats, and come back to work. You?"

"Got my master's in criminal justice and socioanthropology, quit my job with you guys to join the force just about the time Heather dumped me for an investment banker. I've been learning the ropes and earning my spurs, if you'll pardon the cowboy metaphors, ever since."

She gave him her own version of the patient, listening stare. He cooperatively allowed himself to be drawn out. He told her about his childhood, living in the bush in Alaska with a high school teacher father and a mother who had her doctorate in philosophy. "They never exactly treated me as if I was a child, more like I was their trapping partner or something. I got more discipline from our lead dog than I did from my mom. But it was a great way to grow up. When I was ten years old, they were killed in a bush plane accident on a trip to Fairbanks. I would have been with them but I had a bad earache and so I'd stayed with some Native friends."

Rose leaned forward and covered his hand with hers. "Jesus, Fred, what a terrible thing to happen."

"It just about killed me," he said, his eyes darting quickly to hers, then away, and his voice dropping. "I couldn't believe they were dead. I kept thinking they'd come back, and I wasn't about to let anybody make me leave. I had been driving dogs for a couple of years then by myself. Mom had started me with them from the time I was five. I'd known most of them since they were puppies and I was a baby. I hitched them up and we went looking for my parents. I loaded extra dog food, but it wasn't enough. Once we got started I couldn't seem to stop and I drove them on and on, down the frozen river, thinking that any time we'd see the plane, or see my folks snowshoeing over the next ridge, maybe hurt, but not dead, not both of them."

He shrugged and tried to smile to diminish the intensity of the memory, but the twist of his mouth and the raising of his brows didn't lighten his expression in the least.

"Lucky for me I had dogs instead of a snow machine. Dogs have more sense. The first time there wasn't food enough to go around they whined and howled that eerie yip-howl that malemutes have instead of a bark and went on strike. That brought me to my senses a little.

"I was maybe, I don't know, three days away from our cabin, and there was nobody else around. I had my Dad's rifle with me—Mom didn't like guns, in fact, she was a vegetarian most of the time, although she couldn't afford to be if Dad had killed a moose and the canned and frozen goods were running low at the village store between drops. She had a little garden and canned some in the summer, but the growing season is very short. Dad got her to carry a rifle on the sled, though, in case a moose or bear attacked the team. She'd shoot in defense of the dogs—or me—if not herself. So anyhow, I started hunting for food for the dogs, who were, of course, scaring away game for miles around with their howling.

"They weren't like the dogs in Jack London stories. These guys were spoiled pets, against the advice of all of our Native friends, and they were no more used to missing meals than I was. But like I said their howling scared the game, and the river was frozen too thick for me to be able to saw through the ice. I started snowshoeing away from them, out of range of their howls, so maybe I could find us a moose or a caribou. It was dumb, I know.

"I should have turned them. They'd have gone back, and it wasn't too hard to stay on course when you're running the sled on the river, like I was. Also, if I'd just stayed there, it was likely that somebody else with dogs or a snow machine or even a bush plane would have spotted me sooner or later. But I couldn't stay there.

"Before I had been sure I'd see my parents, and that kept me going. Now I was determined to get a meal for those dogs, so Mom wouldn't come back and think I'd been mistreating them. It had been pretty cold when I started. I hadn't minded too much because I was dressed plenty warm. But the weather suddenly began warming up and I got too hot and started peeling layers. I knew better, but I was in a funny state of mind then, kind of numb anyway.

"I didn't mean to discard my hat and mittens, but when they dropped out of my pocket I didn't pick them up. I peeled out of my snowsuit too, and I didn't want it to slow me down, so I hung it on a tree branch and just went on wearing jeans, long johns, two sweaters and my parka and mukluks. Then, of course, it started to snow. Heavy."

Rose said nothing, waiting for him to continue.

He held up his hands. The tips of the fingers were, she saw now, slightly discolored, whitish. "I was wandering around in circles, my hands stuck in my pockets, snow freezing to my face and hair as it came down. It sounds funny to say it, but I didn't mind. The ice on the outside matched the ice I felt inside, empty, hollow, abandoned and lonely as I'd never been in all the times I'd spent alone in our cabin while my folks went about their business back then. I stopped walking, forgot about the dogs, forgot about frostbite, didn't care anymore about my survival training. I wished to die or to see my parents, I didn't care which, but the way I felt then was just unbearable."

Rose swallowed hard and squeezed his hand.

"I would have died if it hadn't been for a woman who was passing by just then. At first I thought I *had* died and she was an angel, because her hair was white and iced up and flew like frozen ribbons around the edges of her parka's ruff, which was made from silver fox. She drove a team of malemutes and a sled piled with furs, and she tucked me into it. I felt even more strongly then that she was some kind of supernatural being, because I was so cold I couldn't even feel her touch.

"I wasn't so out of it, however, that I'd forgotten about the dogs. If this was heavenly rescue, then I didn't think a decent angel would let poor faithful dogs suffer for my neglect, and if it was human rescue, by a dog driver herself, she'd understand. I made her understand, through gestures and muffled shouts, that the team was down on the river. She nodded and drove in the direction I thought I had come from. My snowsuit marked the way and a short time later, her dogs began howling, catching the scent on the wind, and then my dogs began howling in response.

"The dogs jumped and made their 'woowoo' sound and licked at me as if I'd been gone weeks rather than hours, but I didn't have much energy for them. Then the woman did something I've never seen anyone do before. She righted my sled, knelt down and spoke to my leader, and then drove me on her own sled while my dogs calmly trotted along beside or behind her. She didn't take me back to the village. She took me to a cabin I never even knew was there. She didn't try to talk to me, or comfort me, but let me sit there in her cabin, and just watched to make sure that I never left except to feed my dogs. Sometimes we'd play games together, cards or dominos, but silently. I was in no mood for talking and I guess she knew it. I didn't want a stranger. I wanted my own folks. I guess she sensed that and just didn't force herself on me.

"Then one day there was a knock at the door and there stood my uncle Fred, the one I was named for, on snowshoes, in a State Trooper's parka, but looking so much like my father that I was hugging him before I realized it wasn't him. It was okay, though. He held me and talked to me in a voice very much like my father's and I started crying, outside the cabin, crying so hard the tears and snot turned to ice on my face and my eyes stuck together. Then my insides began to hurt, burning . . . it's hard to describe except to say that it was a lot like the way my hands had hurt as they began thawing. We went inside and my uncle stayed the night there, but the woman was gone when we went into the cabin, and when I looked outdoors again, her team was gone too."

He let out a long sigh. "To make a very long story slightly shorter, we took the team back into the village and called for a bush plane. It picked us up and took us back to my uncle's and I lived with him and Aunt Karen, who was a social worker, like you, until I decided to come outside and go to school. By that time it was okay to be away from my own. And hell, Uncle Fred and Aunt Karen had a slew of foster kids. Uncle Fred always told me he didn't know what they'd do without me because I'd been brought up to be pretty self-sufficient. I could drive the team, make a fire, hunt game and fish, when I was in my right mind at least, and had even helped build additions on the cabin. They always made me feel like they were the lucky ones to get me, and I played big brother to all the other foster kids. Rosie, my uncle and aunt couldn't have and never tried to replace my parents, but I really grew to love them, and I wanted to be as much like them as I could. So that kind of explains my interest in both police and social work, I guess."

"Fred . . ."

"Yes?"

"You never found out who the woman was, did you?"

He shrugged. "Maybe I was right the first time. Maybe she was my guardian angel."

"Or your fairy godmother?"

He grinned. "Could be."

"You know, I have a friend you really should meet."

"I'd like to meet a lot of your friends, Rosie," he said, reversing their hands so that he was squeezing hers.

But when she opened her mouth to tell him about Felicity, his beeper went off. "Damn. Gotta call in. Excuse me a minute."

She sighed and leaned back in the chair. The emotions his story, his eyes on hers, his touch, had sent tumbling through her were so turbulent she felt lightheaded. On the one hand, she didn't know whether she wanted to soul-kiss him or run from him, and on the other hand, she felt like she'd known him all her life and she had never been so comfortable having a personal conversation with a straight, unmarried, uninvolved male who actually seemed—no, was—interested in her. Maybe he'd tell her pretty soon he was HIV positive or only liked to do it with dogs or had actually become a Catholic monk; maybe she'd find out he told the same story to every woman he met (though he didn't have the demeanor of a womanizer from her experience, and she had had an unfortunate amount of experience back in her late teens and early twenties). But— she kind of didn't think so. She was terrified and filled with wonder at the same time.

He came back a short time later. "I need to go back in. The secretary at Clarke Academy definitely identified the letter as the one she saw and is pretty sure it was Hunter behind the goggles. But Rose, I . . ." He reached out and cupped her cheek in one hand and she covered it with hers.

"Yeah, I know," she said. "Me too." They exchanged a long look, then put on their coats and went back out into the cool, soft drizzle.

"Can I drop you somewhere?"

"No, I'll come back up to the station with you. There's a call I want to make."

While he returned to his desk and phone, she put in a call to Patrick—still no answer, so she resigned herself to sleeping on the call cot at the department—then, on impulse, dialed Fortunate Finery's number. Linden had always had her calls at the shop forwarded to her house, lest she miss a sale, since customers had the unfortunate habit of turning up sometimes on slow days only *after* business hours were over, during lunch, or before the shop opened. As Rose hoped, Felicity had continued the practice.

"Felicity Fortune here," the throaty Brit-tinged voice said.

"Felicity, it's Rose. I'm calling from the King County Courthouse. Tonight a friend of mine and I attempted to

Sixteen

THE MALEVOLENT GLARE of the toad would have been enough to convince the most dedicated skeptic that other than an amphibian soul lived inside the green and warty skin. It was also extremely silent for a toad, and watchful, its bug eyes daring the foolhardy to make toad jokes.

Rose stared at the creature in Felicity's bathtub with fascination and repugnance, although she normally didn't mind toads, and actually enjoyed listening to them singing around the pools and puddles near her house.

"Don't be rude, Bobby," Felicity told the toad sternly. "And stop sulking. Had I transformed you into something worthy of your human nature, you'd be something much nastier and far lower on the food chain."

Felicity had cheerfully agreed to pick her up at the courthouse and bring her back to her own place. Rose was still reeling from walking through a wall onto a hotel floor that wasn't there and entering the suite Felicity occupied, which looked like all of the other hotel suites except for the high-tech equipment and the crystal ball and the fact that it, also, technically wasn't there. She had carefully ducked Felicity's probing questions about the "friend" from the Courthouse. She wasn't going to talk to anybody about Fred until she (a) was sure what was going on and (b) sorted out her feelings, fears, and expectations and (c) knew

153

him better, not necessarily in that order. In the meantime, he had a few kids to find and she needed some sleep. It didn't look like it would be forthcoming soon. Felicity had showed her around the suite, proudly pointing out some high-tech equipment Rose was surprised to see there.

"What's the computer for?" she had asked.

"That's our communications network and also the GDB, or Godmother Data Base. We've put our collective memory on hard disk including a list of good deeds done, to whom, when, and where et cetera et cetera et cetera. I've got a fax modem hooked up to it but I miss my fax machine. So much faster and handier for sending photographs and such."

After the grand tour, Felicity had deigned to answer Rose's inquiry and had taken her into the bathroom to introduce her to the toad. "The man in the mug shot was named Robert Hunter. Is that why you call this toad Bobby?"

"Of course," Felicity said. "That's his name. Robert, Robin, Bobby the Henchman he has been throughout time, and he's one of those stubborn souls who never *ever* learns from their experience and thus is destined to remain a malignant cardboard spear-carrying figure."

"Well," Rose said, sitting on the edge of the tub and scratching her head, attempting to stimulate her brain cells, which had already received so much stimulation tonight they were getting numb with overload. "There isn't much job security these days. At least he's been reliable."

"How amusing."

"Of course it's not," Rose admitted. "Especially not now that you've interfered. We have a man who thinks he's a toad at Harborview with evidence on him that could help us find Sno, if only he could talk to us, and we have a toad who thinks he's a thug and evidently wants nothing more than to give us both a fatal case of warts. Please, Felicity, tell me, what *is* wrong with this picture?"

"I assure you that *I* had no way of knowing he was currently a murder suspect, at least, that he was suspected of murdering anyone you know. You refused to tell me what was going on in the name of confidentiality. So I was simply following my age-old practices and trolling for good to reward when who should I encounter but Bobby here. Well, he may have changed his looks, his age, his race, from one lifetime to another but I can see right through him. He was going to stab me. Now, while it is true that I am far too busy and my magical allowance is far too meager to waste it on punishment when as we both know, positive reinforcement is so much more effective, I am allowed to defend myself and remove menaces from— er—menacing."

"So you turned him into a toad?"

"Oh, no, of course not. I'm thriftier than that. It takes a great deal of magical force to compress matter from a large size into a much smaller size. The transformee is apt to be severely damaged or else, once condensed, explode in an alarming and unpredictable manner. And I couldn't very well make Bobby into a toad as large as the man he was. He'd be like something in a made-for-video horror movie and probably leap people to death or some such, left to his own inclinations. Energy is rather easier to swap around. As I've mentioned, his consciousness has already inhabited people of various shapes, sizes and colors and that sort of thing condenses quite handily, within certain limits. So I simply switched the toad's for the man's. Brilliant, eh?"

"Sure. If you can get Bobby here to tell us what he did with Sno." *What am I saying?* Rose asked herself. *I'm trying to get this woman to have a toad help me find a missing client! Okay, I've gone and done it now. Either this is a nightmare, or it's real and she's nuts and it's catching or it's not a dream and it's real and—it's real?* The toad was real, that was true, and the patient had been real. And walking into a hotel suite that wasn't there was real too. Maybe she'd just better continue to suspend judgment until she saw something she'd have to be committed for if she admitted she saw it.

"Oh. Hmm. That's a bit difficult," Felicity said. "Normally I could just give it a voice or, more usefully, give you the gift of animal languages. But I *did* rather squander that particular gift already."

"So much for thriftiness."

"Well, you were being so stubborn. I did it to impress you, I'm afraid. I was trying to make you believe me in some short, easy way, as you wanted. That never does work in the long run, but it seemed worth a try, so I did it."

"What?"

"Activating Puss."

"Excuse me? Activating what?"

"Puss. The cat I assigned to your friend, the street urchin, what did you call him?"

"Dico. Dico Miller," Rose replied and then asked, "What about the cat? Oh, come on now. You aren't going to claim it was—naaah."

But Felicity was nodding. "Puss. Sort of. Not the same body as the original, of course, but cats are natural nomads, spiritually, what with nine lives to live. The essence of Puss—intelligent, resourceful and street-smart, not to mention multilingual, creature that she is—fits well into the lives and personalities of many existing felines. In that way, dear Puss has been granted far more incarnations than the standard nine by Our Founder."

"The Queen of Fairy? Right?" Rose asked sarcastically.

"Brilliant! You're catching on. So anyhow, now and then, if Puss is not previously incarnated, one of us will activate her to help out a particularly hapless case, since she's quite capable of taking care of herself and a new friend. The spell invoking her is a little limited, but . . ."

Rose opened her mouth to say how ridiculous it was, and then she looked back at the toad, and saw it sneering at her with an expression that was never intended for an amphibian face.

"I've been working harder than I thought," she said, feeling a little dizzy.

"Yes, you have. And you need to let me help."

"You've already helped enough, I think," Rose said. "What am I supposed to do with all this great inside information you've given me? Call Fred Moran and tell him to come over and bring his rubber hose—if he squirts the perpetrator with it, maybe Bobby the toad will be so pleased he'll croak his guts out? If you hadn't been so damned helpful, the cops could question Bobby now and find out what he'd done with Sno."

"Tsk tsk, dear, you really are tired. I thought you people were trained not to assign blame. You're talking nonsense. If it weren't for me, Bobby would be back in his own body and many miles away from here and you'd never know he was involved. He'd also be free to hurt other people. As it is, the only problem really is to get him to talk, and that will be easy enough once we find Dico and Puss."

"Then what?"

"We'll have Puss interrogate Bobby," Felicity said, grabbing the toad and tucking it back into one of the pockets in her layers of silver-gray clothing.

"Sure. Why didn't I think of that? You say she speaks to humans; why shouldn't she talk to frogs?"

"Toads, dear. He's a toad. We must allow him the little dignity remaining him. As to your question, it's a mental

thing, dear. If you use that kind of magic to open someone up to understanding one other species, they're more
receptive to others. I have no doubt that Puss will, if she
applies herself, be perfectly able to understand Bobby." She
glared meaningfully at the toad. "Nor do I have any doubt
whatsoever that she will be able to make Bobby understand
that he had bloody well better tell her what he knows."

"Wouldn't it be easier to just switch them back again?
You know, make froggy—'scuse me, toady—a normal toad
again and make Bobby a normal, human-speaking psycho
instead of a large economy-size Kermit?"

"I'm afraid it doesn't work that way. The spell, being a
spell, lasts seven years, or until Bobby himself finds the
antidote."

"Being kissed by a princess?"

"A little more complicated, but something like that."

"So now what?"

"Why, now we go find Dico and Puss. Come along,
on with your coat and off we go," Felicity prodded with
nannylike cheery briskness.

"You have any spells or potions for staying awake for
someone who's worked all day, has to stay up all night and
has to work tomorrow as well?" Rose asked. It wasn't even
that she was tired so much as just that the weirdness of the
situation was getting to her. The constant feeling that she
had to be dreaming made her feel sleepy.

"Certainly," Felicity said. "The espresso machine just
finished cycling. Help yourself."

Rose poured herself a cup of the strong, hot brew, took
two sips, set it down, pulled on her coat and wrapped
her hands around the mug. "Oh, I forgot to say thanks
for the book," she said to Felicity as they stepped outside the hotel, bracing themselves against the chill of the
night.

"I trust you found it instructive," Felicity said without missing a beat.

"I found it—disturbing," Rose answered truthfully.

"Aha!" Felicity said with a triumphant bark worthy of Holmes himself. "I thought as much."

They walked briskly to Felicity's silverish generic oxygen-emitting automobile and settled themselves inside.

"Where are we going?" Rose asked.

"To find Puss and Dico. I have reason to believe that they'll be in the University District tonight."

"What reason is that?"

"Oh, I did a little networking and had one of our trainees suggest it to Dico. It's a possible way to get him off the streets and into something he can enjoy and make a living doing. But we'll see about that in a bit. You were saying you found the tales in the Grimms' book disturbing. I'd be interested to know why that is. Do you find them too violent?"

"Not really. Kids love that stuff. I know six-year-olds who are crazy about Jason and Freddie Krueger in the slasher movies."

"Is it the sexual content, then? That's what always seems to bother the churchy people."

"No. Kids who haven't been exposed to a lot of the same thing on TV or, God forbid, at home, won't understand it. The kids who've been abused could be helped by finding fairy-tale characters with the same problems. No, actually, what bothers me is something else altogether. You may think I'm being petty."

"Try me."

"It's the absoluteness of everything and all of that judgmental generalization that puts me off. I mean, everybody is either good and beautiful and industrious or lazy and ugly and bad, and people aren't ever mixtures of qualities—good sometimes and not so good at others, lazy when they're doing jobs in which they have no interest, industrious when they're properly motivated and . . ."

"But you're reading them as an adult, with adult perceptions," Felicity pointed out.

"I hated them when I was a kid too! I was seven years old when I got my first book of fairy tales, and it ruined my life. It's taken me years and years to get over it and . . ."

"You don't sound to me as if you're over it yet," Felicity said. "What on earth can have happened to make you feel that way? Or were you just an extremely critical reader as a child?"

"No. My aunt Zelda gave me an illustrated fairy-tale book for my seventh birthday. I had just learned to read and wasn't a very fast reader, and Zelda was trying to encourage me. She never approved of the books written in simple language with big print and not much text that were supposed to start kids out. She was reading *The Count of Monte Cristo* when she was ten and she thought I should too. Aunt Zelda thought I was a genius. Actually, I wanted someone to read to me about the pictures in the book."

"Why didn't your aunt read with you herself?" Felicity asked.

"She lived in New York and we lived in Idaho," Rose said. "Not much help. I could have used her then. I could have used almost anybody. My folks were splitting up. Dad was still living at the house, but he and Mother weren't talking to each other unless they yelled or talked in those overcivilized brittle little voices that are so full of tension I wanted to throw up."

"It's hardly fair to blame fairy tales for your parents' domestic problems, Rose," Felicity said.

"Oh, I know that, and I guess a lot of my attitude toward them is from my dad. He was a psychologist too, except he was world-famous and highly paid and had umpty-ump degrees. He didn't know much about kids, though. Not that he wasn't correct about everything! He was careful to explain to me that their breakup wasn't my fault and I was not to blame myself. Of course, any time I wanted attention from him, you know how kids will do, breaking something just to get him to fix it, even trying to get him to admire the Valentine I'd made for him in school, he couldn't be bothered. He'd just look away from me like he couldn't stand the sight of me."

"I'm sure he was preoccupied, dear."

"Yeah, you bet he was. With Giselle, his gorgeous blonde secretary who *happened* to look like all the princesses in the fairy tales."

"Oh, I see. But *that's* not what they mean. She would have been more like a wicked stepmother, surely?"

Rose shrugged. She didn't know why she was telling all of this to this dingy lady, but Felicity wasn't a client and Rose didn't feel that she had any particular secrets about a situation that was all too common among children these days—it was just that in this instance, the child had been herself and the memories still hurt. But she did believe in being open and honest about her feelings and believed in putting opinions in the context of the experiences that had formed them. It was all very rational when you thought about it. Probably her depth of emotion on the subject of fairy tales was making this whole strange situation with Felicity and toads and talking cats and such more powerful than it really was.

"Anyway, it didn't matter what he said or did because, like kids always tend to do, I knew the divorce was my fault, and he was leaving Mom and me because of something I'd done to make him mad. Then of course, I decided that the birthday party he and Mother gave me was some big symbol that we were a quote unquote real family again. All was forgiven, won't you stay home, Bill Bailey, and like that.

"If *I* were running things, that's exactly what it would have meant," Felicity said with what amounted to a growl. "I hope it was at least a nice party."

"It was, really. There was a store-bought cake, but it did have my name on it. I got a doll, though not the one I'd asked for, and a lot of clothes from Nana and Papa Samson. It was great. My parents even tried to be nice to each other.

"My father actually held me up to blow out my candles and called me 'Princess' like he had when I was little . . ." Her voice broke, embarrassingly, and she was afraid she was going to start crying, so she babbled blindly on. "I know it sounds dumb, but it was like in one of those stories when where the people get turned to stone and all of a sudden a kiss or a magic word turns them back again. Just that little bit of relaxation on his part, and I felt like he loved me all over again and I thought that's what being a princess *was*, being special, having your birthday every day. But as soon as the candles were blown out, we ate the cake and ate the ice cream, Mom threw the wrappings from my presents in the trash, it was all over. I wanted it to go on all the rest of the day . . ."

"Well, of course you did! And it bloody well should have."

"But it was like all of a sudden nobody was there, and I went from being a princess back into being a rock again. Finally, I found Dad in his recliner and I tried to climb into his lap with Aunt Zelda's book."

She sat quietly in the dark for a moment, watching the street lamps approach as the car rolled down the highway, the lights of the Space Needle, then the lights of the houses silhouetting the boats and gleaming on the waters of Lake Union. She had all the intellectual explanations of the effects of divorce on kids, knew all the therapeutic answers, but to her embarrassment, talking about that time still hurt. It sounded so dumb when she thought of all the little girls— and boys—who would have been so relieved if only their fathers would leave them alone. She knew, *knew*, that her reaction was perfectly normal, that the whole Electra thing was a process of childhood, that the children who were abused were in dysfunctional situations, but still . . .

"He wouldn't read to you, I suppose?" Felicity prompted quietly, her low voice softened by the rumbling of the tires and the rush of other cars all around them on the shiny black freeway.

"No. I thought he would for a moment. He took the book out of my hands and looked at the title as if he'd never seen it before, although he'd agreed when I unwrapped it that it was a great gift, then he said in that very logical, detached way he had, 'Rosalie, you're seven years old today. Too old for this make-believe stuff.' And he went back to watching the news."

"Well, it's bloody little wonder he couldn't get along with your mother! I certainly wouldn't have put up with such coldness."

"Oh, but he hadn't always been so cold. There was a time when he loved us and showed it, must have been, or I wouldn't have noticed the difference so much. And Mom had her share of problems too . . . she was drinking by then.

"I remember taking the book in to her that night too, and she already reeked of booze—the smell came out of her skin. She had this sleazy blue bathrobe with molting chenille flowers tufted all over it and she had changed back into it after the party. I can't stand chenille to this day. Before my father left us, she used to be kind of pretty when she fixed up, but later it was like she turned into something out of an old Betty Crawford movie, not one of the early ones, the ones where she was *old*. She forgot to wash off her makeup and had eyeliner and lipstick smeared on her face and her hair looked dead. When I was little it was sort of red-brown and curly, like mine, but sometime before the divorce she had it bleached and it grew out two colors, both of them ugly.

"But that night, on my birthday, she had been sober all day and had only just started drinking when I went into her room with the book. Except for the robe, she still looked nice and she smelled only slightly of booze and that was mixed with Emeraude perfume, which always made me think of the candy we used to make because it smelled like vanilla.

"I don't think she'd have read to me either, except that I told her I'd asked Father and he wouldn't, and that made her eager to show him up as a better parent, I suppose. She still cared about that, and about me, then. She pulled me up beside her on the bed and opened the book. She read the first story, and that was Cinderella, if I remember right, followed by Rapunzel and the one about the toads and pearls. But when we got to the fourth story Mama threw the book across the room."

"Whatever for?"

Rose shrugged. "Well, think about it. In every single one of those stories, it's the blonde who not only has more fun but is also supposed to be morally superior and probably, these days, they'd say she had greater earning power and was better in bed as well. The mean, lazy, rude sister is dark and *therefore* ugly. My Dad was Jewish and my mother was half Italian. Neither my mother nor I fit the description of anyone who ever comes out on top in those stories, with the possible exception of the Disney version of 'Snow White,' which was not in my book. In fact, one story, 'The Jew in the Brambles,' is downright anti-Semitic and between that and all of those damned heroines, Hitler could have easily used that book as an argument for blond Aryan superiority."

"That's a very political argument for a seven-year-old girl," Felicity said.

"Oh, that just occurred to me the other night. What struck me at the time was that since neither Mother nor I was beautiful and blonde, we must not be good or hardworking or any of the other things heroines were supposed to be. Maybe that was why Daddy was leaving us for Giselle the Gorgeous. God, I used to hate her guts!"

"Was she very unkind to you, then?"

"Oh, no. She was a living doll. Nice, funny, smart, always trying to do things for me. *Much* kinder than my Mother, who called her 'that whore' till the day she died. I mean, Giselle was *so* nice, better to me than my own mother as time went on, and I still couldn't forgive her, still hated her, still imagined gruesome ways to kill her and liked to torment her just to make her life miserable because she couldn't please me. I was a truly rotten kid where she was concerned, just like the ugly stepsisters in the stories."

"You just forget that. The ugly stepsisters hated Cinderella for no reason at all and, to you at least, your stepmother had taken your father away from you. It's not the same thing at all. Don't you know by now that villainesses don't *have* fairy godmothers?"

"No, really. I was a major brat. I mean, if it hadn't been for Giselle, I'd have had nobody. Father was still cold to me and Mom—well, she was much worse. Classic alcoholic split personality, so unpredictable I could never tell if she was going to cry all over me or slap me. Later, I used to come in the house and stand at the door and wait, trying to sense what kind of mood she'd be in so I'd know how to act to stay out of her way. One day she hauled off and gave me a black eye, which was just the ammunition my father had been waiting for to get me away from her. Not that he wanted me. He just didn't want her to have me—typical there, too, I guess. Fortunately for him and Giselle, they didn't have to put up with me for long."

"Now, now . . ."

"No, really, I was horrible. That's one reason I was attracted to working with disturbed kids."

"You've turned out pretty well, it seems to me."

"Thanks. I don't deserve the credit for it, so much as the school father and Giselle put me in while he went lecturing around the world about his work on Freudian motivations in militaristic government systems. The school was terrific. The women who taught there were what you might call free thinkers, very creative and really committed to getting to know every girl and getting through to her. Knowing who my father was, they nudged me into psych and sociology classes, and I studied hard to see what made my father behave like such a jerk and so—here I am. Of course, I'm not famous or important like my father was and I haven't exactly changed the world, which he did, really, but . . ."

"I'm sure he's very proud of you."

Rose shrugged. "Maybe he would have been. Maybe not. He and Giselle were killed in a skiing accident in Switzerland just before I graduated. I just kept thinking, 'Well, he managed to avoid seeing me do this too.' "

"I rather doubt that was what was in his mind when he died, but I can see how you'd feel that way," Felicity said. Then, to Rose's relief, she turned the topic toward a less personal vein. "As for the stories in Grimm's, you must realize, my dear, that they and those by Hans Christian Andersen, who was a Dane, after all, *did* come from lands where blondness was the norm and the national stereotype. I'm sure if they'd been written by a Chinese or an American Indian, they would have been rather different. In fact, they are, if you look at similar folk tales in those cultures."

"Oh, I know that, but . . ."

"Also, they were rewritten and interpreted primarily by the sort of dreamers who imagine that all beauty is contained in facial structure and the lines of the body, vast amounts of evidence to the contrary. I'm sure if you think about it, you'll realize that all of the good and kind and hardworking women you know are not beautiful and all of the beauties are not especially good."

"Well, of course not. Though some of them are," she said, her therapist's objectivity coming back into play.

The car rolled past the University of Washington and turned the corner, and suddenly Rose spotted a familiar figure running down University Avenue and a striped cat with white socks running along beside him. Rose rolled down the window and hollered, "Dico, wait!" as Dico and Puss ducked behind a building and a spray of machine-gun fire spattered the side of the car.

Seventeen

DING'S DESIRE TO jump somebody backfired. The jumpers became the jumpees, and Ding and his homeboys got their asses kicked by the Pele Patrol, South Pacific gangbangers who were two-thirds as tough and twice as big as the Southeast Asian boys. Of course, if the whole gang had come, it would have been no contest, but the homeboys had decided to cruise with just the part of the gang that had been on Ding's fire escape that afternoon. Le's older brother and his friends hadn't come, or any of the newer recruits. These days, well, at least before word of this battle got out, everybody on the southwest side wanted to be a Guerilla. Even the assholes who called them the Monkeys either to dis them or because they didn't know enough about English to know that a Guerilla wasn't the same thing as a gorilla.

Anyhow, the Peles *had* made monkeys out of the Guerillas, and the homeboys from the International District were looking for a way to save face when they saw the dopey-looking dude talking to the cat.

"Hey man, there's the victory feast!" Le hollered.

"Gross," said Hai, who was born in the States.

"You too sensitive, Hai?" Minh teased him. "Come on, let's get that cat. I'll show you how we ate in the camps, brother. You want to be a Guerilla, you gotta eat like one."

"Hey, man, there's cats at home," Hai said.

"I like the looks of that one," Ding answered, just to show them who was the leader.

The cat did not like his looks, however, nor the looks of the fifteen other homeboys out to kill its ass and jump its scrawny little master. It laid its ears back, as cats do, fluffed its fur up, as cats do, hissed, as cats do, and then yelled, as no cat in Ding's experience ever had done, "This cat is running before she gets wokked!"

Not only a talking cat, but one who told bad jokes under fire. A valuable cat, then.

The cat bounded away, closely followed by the kid, whom Ding had begun to recognize as the one from whom the gang had taken money earlier in the day. Ding and the Guerillas pounded after them, leaping and hollering and waving their guns, knives and baseball bats.

Then all at once a car pulled up beside them. Linh opened fire, the idiot, thinking the car was full of Peles pressing their luck.

The car screeched to a halt as bullets smacked into it, and the tires sputtered and hissed themselves flat.

Over all the other noises, a woman shrieked and shrieked, and right then, Ding knew they were in for it. The Peles didn't come lookin' for action with women in the car. These were civilians.

He hollered to the gang to beat it out of there but before he could turn and run, the driver climbed out of the car. He had seen her before, though only once, the night before he and his family had received the news that they were to come to the United States.

Just for a moment he saw her as she had been then, kind and beautiful, merciful and good. "Kwan Yin," he said, making a little bow over his steepled hands, but then she seemed to grow and sprout arms and legs and the belt around her waist was made of skulls.

"Is this how you use your good fortune?" the goddess of mercy in her wrathful aspect demanded. "How you use your gifts? You, who could enlighten and enliven the whole world, you choose instead to gather around you only a few other stupid children and you all behave like savages, terrorizing innocent strangers and animals?"

"Kwan Yin, you don't understand," Ding said.

"I understand that I chose you and your family to escape from that hole for a reason, and it wasn't this. I'd also like to know what you intend to do about my auto."

"Does it have a stereo?" one of the boys asked opportunistically.

"Shut up," Ding commanded. "Kwan Yin, I tried to make good use of my gifts but nobody would let me. The Americans call us names and act as if we were all their enemies. They hate us if we do well and if we don't, they shame us. My parents work at menial jobs and are given no respect. No matter how I excel, I can do nothing with my talents. Better if you had left me there in the refugee camp. At least there we all understood each other."

"Don't tempt me," Kwan Yin said, but there were fewer skulls spouting blood dripping from her girdle now and her color was less wrathful purple and more of a frustrated pink. "I chose to help you and your family to come to this country not because of your musical talent, but because even in adversity, you retained your kindness and humanity. Now that you have more, you've forgotten those qualities. You have dishonored yourself and your parents." Her words sounded eerily like those his mother had spoken earlier in the day.

"A 'gook' has no honor except what he can beat out of others for himself," Ding argued bitterly.

"I'm sorry that you hold such an opinion. I granted the wish of a decent boy who risked his own safety to feed and protect an old woman from bullies. Here you are the bully, picking on a poor boy less fortunate than you, since he has no parents and no home, and threatening to kill his only friend, a harmless cat, when you already have so much to eat you must constantly run around like a fool to keep from getting fat. Now I think you would have mugged the old lady in the camp for her rags."

"Not so!" Ding said. "In the camps we were equal. Here people have everything and they hate you if you don't have the same things but won't let you get any for yourself . . ."

"Ah!" she said. "I had no idea people were so evil. I suppose the group that sponsored your family did not really share, though they paid for your passage and for your home and clothing until you could get started."

"Well, sure, but they only did it to feel superior . . ."

"You seem very sure of that. Was that *your* only motive for being helpful?"

He dropped his head and stared at the splashes of slushy rain as they fell on the sidewalk.

"Ding, in granting you the chance to come to America, which you wished with all your heart, I did not guarantee that the struggles you had in the camps would be your last on earth. Life *is* struggle, you know that. Just because you're no longer in a Buddhist country, but in a country with more material goods, that fact is not changed. People struggle here too, and the course you have embarked on makes that struggle harder, not just for them, but for you. It is definitely making it harder for your parents, who endured much so that you might grow up away from the war they knew."

Ding spat, "They love the war. It is all they talk about. I will never be as good as they because I did not grow up in the war."

"Do you think that they loved the war so much or did they love Vietnam? And perhaps it is all they talk about because it is all they knew. Perhaps you *will* never be as good as they are, but if so, it is because you bring war with you in your heart. You have in you many gifts— for music and for people, to influence them for good or ill. Go. Contemplate your path. It is said that the road to honor is a rough one, but believe me, son, the road you have chosen thus far is no bed of roses either. It's just easier because your anger whips you forward toward worse disaster than even you have experienced. The calamities that befell your parents before were collective ones that fell upon you through fate. The calamity you invoke now upon you and your parents and your friends here is entirely one of your own making. Make something else."

"How?" he asked defiantly, expecting that there could be no answer.

"Make reparations to those you have harmed, give honor where it is due, and do not be deterred when obstacles place themselves in your path. Wait, and seek to look through and around them. They are there for a reason and have something to teach you. You can start the reparations by finding a phone booth and calling me a tow truck."

> *There was a godmother from Eire*
> *With curly long silvery hair*
> *Her name was Felicity*
> *She caused serendipity*
> *Which you may have thought came from thin air*

"My God, Felicity, what did you say to him? Where did you get that outfit you were wearing out there? I thought you didn't do magic if you didn't have to!" Rose talked fast, the push of adrenaline powering her tongue even while she shook with the aftermath of shock.

"I simply gave him a good talking-to and sent him home with his friends to do something useful. Young scoundrels."

"But—but you changed into someone different."

"Not really. I simply assumed the guise of Kwan Yin, as I did when I visited the refugee camps. Fairy tales in other lands not only don't have blonde heroines, they don't have fairies either, nor godmothers, but they *do* have motherly goddesses, and it all adds up to the same thing."

"You mean you do this all over the *world*?"

"Of course. Badly off as Seattle may seem to you, there are other places where things are much worse. Still, misery is misery, starvation is starvation, and thwarted talent and unused gifts are always a terrible waste. And speaking of terrible wastes, when the tow truck comes, do you belong to an auto club?"

"Not any kind that services *this* sort of car," Rose said, climbing out, now that she was sure the bullets had stopped flying, and rounding the corner of the building to see to Dico.

He was lying in a ball on the ground. The cat, who naturally was now pretending nothing had happened worthy of her notice, took turns washing her own fur and Dico's hands, which were still covering his face.

As soon as Felicity followed Rose over to Dico and the cat, however, Puss trotted toward Felicity to yowl plaintively for handouts and attention.

"Dico, are you okay?"

"Have they gone away?" he asked every bit as plaintively as Puss.

"Yeah. My friend scared them off. You're not hit, are you?"

"No, but d-don't c-come too close, Rose. I—I wet my jeans."

"It's a good thing I didn't have another cup of coffee at Felicity's, or I would have too. It's perfectly excusable to wet your pants when somebody's shooting at you, Dico. We'll find another pair for you someplace."

"Oh, I got some in my locker up by the ferry terminal," he said. "Who were those guys, Rose? Did you scare them away?"

"Not me. Felicity did. She knew the leader from before, and I think he owed her a favor."

While that was sinking in, Felicity was having a major petting session with Puss. "You can have all the crab and lobster you want, prretty Puss, prrrecious Puss" (the rolling *R*'s were accompanied by long strokes from nose to tail of the cat's rather ruffled fur) "if you can make this toad tell us what he did with a certain young woman."

"Everybody knows what toads do with young women, Feliciteee," Puss said to Felicity. "They put the make on them. They're worse than tomcats, who at least pretty much stick to their own species."

"I'll be damned, it does talk!" Rose exclaimed, though she didn't see the cat's mouth move or hear a voice with her ears but rather, inside her head. Oh, well, so it didn't talk. It was only telepathic. That was different. She would have been more flabbergasted, she supposed, had she not seen Bobby the toad's glare or Felicity in her Kwan Yin getup. What was a little catty conversation among friends?

"Well, this toad is different," Felicity told the cat. She pulled Bobby the hit-amphibian out of her pocket after glancing up and down University Avenue to make sure neither the tow truck nor passing pedestrians would notice. Actually, she needn't have worried, Rose thought. People talking to themselves and other invisible beings was rather common on the streets of Seattle. Either these were people who ought to be under someone's care, or Seattle was unusually full of Shakespearean actors memorizing soliloquies. Anyhow, on the weirdness scale, talking to cats scarcely rated a mention.

Or so Rose was thinking until Felicity pulled the toad from her pocket and, waving it at the cat, said, "Bobby, this is Puss. She will be happy to translate any utterances you may care to make on the whereabouts of the Quantrill girl."

"Reedeep," Bobby said.

Felicity looked at Puss, who switched her tail in an irritated way and said, "Untranslatable. I understand frog legs are a delicacy, by the way, Feliciteeee. I bet toad legs are just as tasty. Have you ever had any?"

"Why, Puss, what a thought!"

Puss licked her chops. "Yeah, ain't it? How about it, bug-eyes, you gonna talk?"

The toad embarked on a series of croakings and peepings.

"Come on," Felicity prompted. "What does he say?"

Puss's tail lashed from side to side, and her ears lay flat as she faced the toad. "He's saying you wouldn't really let me eat him. He says that wouldn't be playing by the rules. He says I should stay in my own story and stick to my own scenario and not interfere in his. He says fairy godmothers shouldn't interfere in stories they're not part of."

"*Does* he?" Felicity asked, sounding amused.

"Oh, yesss," the cat hissed, hunkering down so that her chin was on her forepaws and her back end was raised and twitching, ready to spring. "He doesss."

Felicity transferred her grip then, until she was holding the toad only by the scruff of the neck, legs dangling above the cat's outstretched paws.

The toad began croaking furiously as the cat reached up a claw-filled paw.

"Wait, Puss. What's he saying?" Felicity asked, stopping the cat with her free hand.

"Nothing important. Let me at him."

"Behave yourself. What he has to say is important; I can tell from the way he's carrying on. A girl may be dead or dying because of *his* blood lust, so please try to control your own."

"Oh, don't be so dramatic. The girl's okay."

"She *is*?" Rose asked, feeling lightheaded with relief. "Where is she? How long has she been there? What did he do to her?"

"He didn't do anything. She decked him with a judo move and the knife went through him. She ran away from him up in the woods somewhere north, on the road to the sharp white mountain. The big one. There's no word for it in toad."

"Baker! She got away from him on the road to Mount Baker. Can he be more specific?"

Puss asked him with more lickings of her lips and whiskings of her tail, and he answered with a few feeble peeps.

"He says maybe if you took him to the spot, he could show you the general area."

The toad began croaking more enthusiastically. "He says how about a deal, Felicitee? Now that he's assured you that the girl is all right—wait—he says he even warned her—how about you give him back his body?"

"Tell him I can't do that," Felicity said. "However, I can keep him safe enough that he can last out the seven years—past his life expectancy in the wild, especially since he's so unaccustomed to his natural toad's instincts and defenses, which could be fatal. I can also promise him unparalleled opportunities to have the spell broken, in the usual contractual way if he cooperates fully."

"You want me to say *that* in *toad*?" the cat demanded.

"Please."

The cat uttered a short nasty hiss.

"What was that about?"

"I told him."

"And?"

"He'll cooperate," Puss said, her tail twitch slowing down to a lazy J motion. "Oh, yes, he will."

Dico had been watching all of this through wondering eyes. "What a night, huh?" he said to Rose while Felicity and the cat continued to terrorize the toad.

"It sure is," she agreed. "What have you been up to, other than hanging out with talking cats, getting shot at, and, well—this?"

"Oh, this lady we met down at the Market said Puss and me should go to the open mike at the University Pub and gave us some money, so we took the bus up here. Except there's no animals allowed and the Pub threw us out."

"That's too bad. I guess you couldn't smuggle the cat in."

"No, I tried, but she got away from me and jumped up on the bar and ordered a saucer of beer," he said. After a beat or two, while they watched the cat and the toad in further dialogue, he asked, "Rose?"

"Yes?"

"I've gone crazy, haven't I? I mean, I'm imagining all this?"

"If you are, so am I, Dico," Rose said.

"I mean, I know your friend Felicity is actually the fairy godmother from all those stories and Puss says she is kinda like the born-again, what's the word?"

"Reincarnation?"

"Yeah, that, of the cat from 'Puss in Boots,' and that's pretty easy to believe, but what I don't get is why we're in it?"

"How do you know all this, Dico? Did Puss tell you?"

"Some. But mostly I just figured it out. My mom was really big on reading me fairy tales. I sure miss her, Rose. My dad too. But it's good to have Puss. Puss is really smart, though sometimes she's not very nice. But it's not too good to be nice on the street, Rose."

"No, Dico, it's not," Rose agreed with a little sigh and a new appraisal of Dico's perceptiveness. Dico was not exactly retarded, but he was not very smart either. That's one reason she'd been worried about him being on the streets alone. He was not highly employable and he was gullible. Maybe his current life was curing that—which was too bad in a way, since gullibility passed for innocence anymore—or maybe it was associating with Puss that made him seem suddenly a little wiser.

"I'd sure miss Puss now, but if she can help Felicity— I mean, the godmother lady—find that missing girl, well then, I guess I just gotta do without her."

Such self-abasement called to Rose's training and naturally helpful nature as an occasion to reinforce the youth's self-esteem. "Oh, I think Felicity intends that you and Puss stay together for a while, Dico, so I think you need to help us look for Sno."

Dico's face broke into a smile. "I'd really like to help you, Rose, and help the fairy godmother too. Between me and Puss, we'll find her."

"We'd appreciate your help, Dico, but right now, I think maybe you should come back downtown with us and we'll try to get you into the shelter."

"Not me. No way. I'd rather stay on the streets."

"Why? I mean, I know it's not the Ritz, but—"

"I had my dose of gettin' mugged and chased for one day. There's gangs hang out around there just waitin' for somebody to hurt."

Felicity, Bobby safely tucked back in her pocket and Puss twining around her heels, chimed in, "That's a disgrace, Dico. Never you mind. Rose and I will come with you and sort it out. Not that you don't deserve a home of your own, but if you don't feel the shelter is a safe haven, neither will hundreds of other people who need it."

Rose rolled her eyes. When she had wished for a fairy godmother, she had no idea she'd get one who was on a new crusade every two and a half seconds. And she thought *she* was an idealist.

The three of them plus Puss piled back into Felicity's car and were towed to the garage, where the garage owner demanded one hundred fifty dollars cash because he wasn't registered with the auto club Rose belonged to, and also told them he was backed up and it would take a week to get to Felicity's car. "And that's just until he finds out what kind of car it is," Rose said. "I'd like to be here for that. Are you sure you don't have any mechanically inclined magic?"

"I told you, I don't like to waste my allotment on trifles. New tires and a bit of body work and it will be good as new. He needn't even find out that it is somewhat—avant-garde. Meanwhile, the night is cool, but relatively dry. A bus is appropriate transportation for us to accompany Dico to the shelter and determine what further problems need addressing."

"Okay, that's fair enough," Rose said, and they walked up the Ave, as University Avenue is known, to meet the next available bus. At the bus stop with them were a blind man with a cane, but no dog, fortunately, and a man in a wheelchair. Rose immediately felt guilty for griping about the inconvenience of doing without a car.

Dico hid Puss in the long overcoat he had acquired, and she complained until they were within earshot of the driver; then Felicity told her to hush and Puss uncharacteristically obeyed.

After they boarded, the bus driver lowered a platform and the man in the wheelchair navigated onto it, was raised to the bus's floor level, and drove back to one of the special areas where the driver locked the chair to one of the other bus seats.

"It's a good thing we're along," Felicity told Rose. "That man is on his way to the shelter too, and he was beaten and robbed there two weeks ago."

"Wow," Dico said. "How'd you know that?"

"Yes," Rose said. "How did you? I didn't see you pack your crystal ball."

"I hardly need a crystal ball for such an observation. If you must know, quite aside from my special godmother attributes, I'm psychic, okay? It isn't an absolute require-ment of the job, but those who have a bit of a tendency in that direction find it quite handy on the job, and all the practice we get in this line of work is inclined to amplify such abilities. It's not magic, though, and it isn't like hav-ing wings or that sort of thing. It's rather like having the proper sort of personality to be a good salesperson or the right temperament to be an artist. The only really special thing about fairy godmothers, the only what you would call supernatural thing, is that we're quite long-lived."

"Like *how* long-lived?" Rose asked. "You're going to tell me you were 'born a hundred thousand years ago and there ain't nothin' in the world that you don't know,' like the hundred-thousand-year-old hobo in the song or the wandering Jew, maybe?"

"Don't be ridiculous. Nothing like that."

"But how old?"

"Well, let me put it this way. A little boy who got caught in the children's crusades and wanted desperately to go home again was one of my first projects."

"That's a good story, but anyone could claim that," Rose said.

"Could anyone get a toad to confess to a cat and get the cat to speak the human tongue to translate?"

"You've got a point there," Rose admitted.

Dico looked from one of them to the other and back to Felicity. "So how old *are* you?" he asked.

"I was originally born in Limerick, Ireland, in the time of King John," she said, "which was approximately nine hundred years ago, give or take a couple of decades."

"Hmph," Rose said. "And I suppose you stopped counting after you got to twenty-nine."

Felicity raised an eyebrow and smiled. "Naturally. Nevertheless, I'm a sweet young thing as godmothers go."

"Felicity Fortune doesn't sound like an Irish name," Rose commented.

"It's not a *Limerick* name," Felicity said. "My widowed mother and my sister and I moved to Limerick from Wexford when my widowed mother met and married a merchant. My father was a seaman, and Mother always said he had Spanish blood in him. She said it was he who insisted on naming my sister Theresa, a saint's name after all and not so unusual, and me Felicity, a family name he said. Of course, I was also named Mary Bridget, but Felicity was what my mother and sister called me—though I don't suppose the daughter of my mother's new husband thought it appropriate."

Rose thought that over as the bus rolled down 99, along a trail of white lights on one side, a trail of red lights on the other. On the right side of the bus, city lights played against the water; on the left side, the Cascade Mountains were a darker blackness against the night, beyond the lights of Seattle, Bellevue, and Issaquah in the east.

The bus threaded its way down and through the bus tunnel and out again. Conversation hushed, and the bus grew quiet except for the rush of its tires on the pavement, Dico's intermittent snoring and Puss's purring from within his jacket.

Rose was only partially listening. "There," she said, as the bus rounded a corner near the courthouse. From the jail entrance emerged a beige-overcoated young man with lank blond hair and a two-day beard. He began pacing back and forth, carrying on an angry conversation with himself. Rose regretted her earlier frivolous thoughts about soliloquies. This was no actor. Despair and degradation radiated from this man like the smell of decay radiated from, well, a corpse left three days in the woods in the middle of summer, she supposed, but she had never seen one and, shuddering at the thought when she remembered Sno, never hoped to. Like the smell of decay emanating from the fruit freshener of her refrigerator most of the time, she decided instead.

Puss peeked out from Dico's coat, sniffing at the man who was walking beside the bus, just outside the window. "Oh, look, there's Ed again, Dico. I wonder who's in charge today, Eddy or John Lennon."

"Eddy, I'd say," Dico replied, watching the man. "Definitely Eddy. When he's Lennon he wears them little glasses and walks a lot cooler."

"You know him?" Felicity asked.

"Oh, yeah. I see him around. He's crazy. He used to be in the loony bin, but like they closed the place down. Lotsa folks like him out here because of that. They said institutions wasn't a good place for folks but hey, I'd act crazy if it'd get me a warm place to sleep and three squares a day. These folks too sick to even do something against the law so they can go to jail once in a while."

Rose added, "The city streets are full of these folks. People thought closing mental institutions would be a humane thing to do, but it was intended that the money instead go to more personal supervision in a societal context. Instead, the money got filtered into other areas of government and now there's no place for people like Dico's friend there. They wander around the streets too bewildered to seek what help is available. Is there anything you can do for them, for him?"

"Dico, Rose, Puss, my dear friends, I'm a fairy godmother, not God, the Goddess or a god. Not even Wonder Woman or Superman. Rose, I can do no more for people like that man than you are attempting to do already—try to help him stay safe, and warm and fed."

"You can't—make him sane, think of some wonderful job only he could do, something like that?"

Felicity shook her head. "No. I could buy him a hot dog, though, or give him a new pair of shoes, if you like."

"Hey, me too," Dico said. "I'd like a hot dog and new shoes. I spent all my bread on the cat here."

Puss hissed, "It wasn't enough."

Rose told Felicity, "I might be able to adopt Puss or help support Dico, but what about everybody else? My salary just wouldn't stretch that far."

Felicity was silent for a moment, then said, "Well, then, we'd better see what we can do about this shelter, shall we?"

The bus wheezed to a stop in two more blocks and they got off, followed by the man in the wheelchair.

"I have another question," Rose said, as they stepped into Pioneer Square.

"Yes?"

"Well, you *do* have a crystal ball?"

"I do."

"Then why don't you use it to find Sno? Or at least see if she's alive?"

Eighteen

IN ANOTHER PART of the city, Gerardine Quantrill was doing just that, although she wasn't doing anything so archaic as gazing into a crystal ball. She should have heard from the hit man by now. He was supposed to send her evidence of Sno's fatal accident. Nothing so messy as her heart, which could not, after all, be identified, at least not by Gerardine. Her head would be ideal, if only there was somewhere to keep it. That way they'd never find any dental records. But then, they knew she was missing, presumably kidnapped by a bad drug connection, which was true except that it was Gerardine's connection, not Sno's.

Gerardine had also had the bright idea of having him dismember the corpse, then mail her Sno's right hand, which had a little heart tattooed on the wrist. She'd suggested that to Svenny when she'd called to make the connection with the killer. She appreciated Svenny's expert opinion, but he had not been especially brilliant on this occasion.

"What ya want that for?" he asked.

"Identification," she said. "So I'll know he did it."

"You think he'd dare cheat me? *Me*?" Svenny had asked.

"He could mail it as if it were a demand for ransom," she said.

"Gerry, honey, you're too kinky for crime. You'd make a better psycho. You'll get your token but you leave that up to me, okay?"

But she hadn't got her token, and when she called Svenny had told her (a) he hadn't heard anything from the independent contractor he had referred to her to help with her little problem and (b) never to call him again. Not a good sign.

So she had to assume the hit had failed and the brat was alive. She should have known by now that if you want something done right, you have to do it yourself and you certainly didn't leave it up to a man. But it was easier to lie to Raydir about her concern for the dear girl if she hadn't actually seen her die. Ah, well, she'd always wanted to be an actress as well as a model. No time like the present. Now all she had to do was find the little twit.

She showered, stripped and entered the big meditation room she had designed on the top floor of Raydir's home, a room that overlooked the Sound and the mountains. Growing up a beauty in a series of foster homes had had its disadvantages, including male guardians and "brothers" who were all too interested when she was all too young. Some of them just used her, but many of them had hurt her, either accidentally in the process or deliberately and joyfully, something she had grown to appreciate in time. But at first, before she attained her sophistication and knowledge of how to use the foibles of those around her to her own benefit, she had learned to leave when one of them crawled on top of her. She could go still inside herself and travel wherever she wanted. See whomever she wanted.

But not all psychics are good psychics, and astral travel has been used by great sinners as well as great saints. Gerardine sought Sno like an eagle seeks a rabbit, from on high, with unerring instinct, and she found her, living in the woods with seven men, mere men, easy to manipulate and easy to blame.

"What makes you think I *haven't* found Sno in my crystal ball?" Felicity asked, facing Rose. Meanwhile, Puss jumped out of Dico's coat and began trotting down the street toward Crazy Eddy. Dico hurried after her, still well within sight, if not earshot, of Rose and Felicity, who had stopped to face each other.

"Well, if you had, why take so much interest in the investigation?"

"Just because I can find her doesn't mean I can help her alone. It is necessary for several reasons that the investigation take place."

"That's pretty enigmatic. Are you sure Sno is—okay?"

"For the time being, yes, I believe so. But she needs finding very soon."

"Well, where is she?"

"In the woods, probably not far from where this one"— she jiggled her pocket, and the toad croaked—"left her. I can't tell much except that she seems to be well. If she's following her archetype, she has protection and shelter."

"Excuse me? If she's following her archetype?"

"Yes, if her story continues to parallel the one of 'Snow White.' "

"Ex*cuse* me?" I should have expected it, Rose thought with a certain sense of fatalism. "Would you care to elaborate? Do you mean to tell me that Snohomish Quantrill, a budding delinquent and potential prostitute with a substance abuse problem, is Snow White, and is now safe in the woods with seven little men?"

"No, not really."

"That's good."

"But I wouldn't be at all surprised, although the men may not be exactly seven or all that little or, for that matter, may not be men. This is the age of equality, after all. And Sno Quantrill isn't Snow White, not in the way Bobby the hit man is Robert the huntsman. Bits and pieces change around depending on the time and the other people involved and *their* stories. If you read enough of the so-called folk and fairy tales, you'll see that it happened in them too—partially because the original reports of these events became confused with time and telling and possibly because similar things keep happening—differently, depending on circumstances. I think a lot of the trouble you may have recognizing the archetypes comes from having stories set down on paper, instead of being transmitted orally, as they were originally. When things are told from person to person they're much more fluid. Set down on paper, it appears that if one version is right, that no others can be. Life isn't like that."

"You're very Jungian, aren't you?" Rose said after a while. "Jungian analysis is all full of archetypes, and I know there've been some books written from a Jungian viewpoint about fairy tales."

"The tales," Felicity said, "were first. Jung didn't invent them—he simply made use of them. He didn't invent the archetypes; they've been there all along. Ask any observant person who has lived beyond eighty years without getting senile. They will tell you human beings tend to do certain types of things and act out certain events in certain ways over and over and over again. Take that old lady detective of Agatha Christie's for instance, Miss Marple."

"Oh, yes, I used to love that series on television and I read most of them when I was in my early teens," Rose said. "I had no idea you were interested in murder mysteries."

"One has to do something while waiting up for girls to return from dances and such."

"You know much more about modern things than, well, than I'd have thought, I mean, if I'd believed in you from the beginning."

"Dear, I haven't been dead or asleep all these years. I've been doing exactly what I'm doing here, wherever I seem to be needed. We have agents all over the world, of course. That's why that young man, Ding, knew me already, and I was able to get his attention."

"Yes, and I want to know more about that sometime, but you were saying about Miss Marple."

"Oh, well, obviously, just that she always solved her mysteries by remembering, no matter where she was or what sort of strange murder case she was involved in, something very similar that had happened to someone she remembered as being like someone else from her hometown of St. Mary Mead. Agatha Christie may have invented a wholly mythical London, but she knew a good deal about human nature."

"So, can you only help with people who are like Snow White or some other fairy-tale character?"

"Oh, no. But there are a lot of fairy tales and a lot of similarities, and the kinds of problems the characters in the fairy tales have are the kinds godmothers are best equipped to deal with, thwarted love, the warped parent-child relationships or sibling relationships that require dramatic intervention to salvage the lives and futures of important personalities who can someday exert positive influence on those around them."

"Sounds like what I do, though we're not usually quite so optimistic about the end result."

"Yes, dear, but you must deal with great masses of people while we—ahem—*usually* only try to assist one person at a time. You have little time for truly individual attention and quite limited means without access to some of the methods we may employ. You try to cope with problems even we cannot solve *with* the help of magic."

"Well, that's pretty depressing," Rose said.

"Being depressed about it is the last thing you should do," Felicity told her. "Hope, my dear, is an essential ingredient of wishes. Where all hope has vanished, there is no possibility of wishing. We, of course, represent the last frontier of hope. You're rather more accessible to most people, providing they can stand the red tape and the competition from those not truly in need."

Farther down on Yesler, Dico had stopped to talk to Eddy. At this time of night, the park benches and doorways of Pioneer Square contained sleeping bodies, young men, old men, one or two women, drunk and sober, sick and well, crazy and sane, black, Native American, and white, all huddled up, all homeless with their sleeping bags, coats, shopping bags and carts.

"What can you do for them?" Rose asked.

"What could I ever do for a mass of refugees? For the victims of the Black Plague?" Felicity said. "As a group, not a great deal except help develop leaders who will understand and assist with the problems in a human fashion. As individuals, sometimes a little, sometimes quite a lot, depending entirely on the person. Even the smallest thing can be enough to encourage someone who has decided to give up hope."

They were passing along the triangle with the totem pole in the center, opposite the underground tours, and passed a bench containing a lumpish-looking blonde woman with dirty hair and an old Indian man. Felicity reached into the depths of her layers, pulled out two little plastic sacks and set one beside the woman, one beside the man, then knelt

down and whispered something in the woman's ear. The
woman barely stirred.

Felicity then whispered something in the Indian man's
ear. He snorted and swatted, then chuckled.

"What?" Rose asked.

"I told her where to find an unlocked public restroom
where she could clean up in the morning with the things
I gave her. We'll unlock it before we return to my place."

"And the man?"

"Oh, I told him a joke."

"I'm not even going to try to figure that one out."

"Come back here tomorrow and you'll see," Felicity
said.

They started walking more quickly to catch up with
Dico, Puss and Eddy, who were about a block ahead of
them, approaching the shelter.

All of a sudden, a car full of people pulled up to the curb
next to Dico and Eddy and they all piled out, catcalling and
yelling names as they surrounded the two men.

Puss darted out from the flurry of feet yowling, "Oh, shit,
not again!"

Rose took off at a run toward the melee, Felicity behind
her yelling, "Rose, be careful! You're not Wonder Woman
either!"

But Rose wasn't paying any attention to anything, including her own safety. Maybe the fact that the young men
surrounding Dico and Eddy were white, well dressed and
clean-cut looking led her to think they'd listen to reason,
though she should have known better, but she started shouting, "You leave them alone!"

"Hey, man, *these* scum may not have any money but *she*
does," one said, and they began converging on her.

Felicity stopped just short of where Rose was being surrounded and concentrated very hard.

*   *   *

Ding hadn't thought about disgrace in a long time, but he thought about nothing else as he and the homeboys made their way back to the International District.

He wasn't disgraced in the eyes of the homeboys. They'd all seen Kwan Yin too, although the more ignorant and Western among them had to have her significance explained to them. They were all unusually quiet on the way home.

They drove in the old Ford station wagon of Le's elder brother and were almost to the exit when Ding felt a sharp, sudden impulse.

"Get off here," he told Le. "Now."

Felicity quickly ran through a list of magicks she still had left. She could turn the gang of whitebread ruffians into stone, but since the spell would last seven years, that was likely to attract undue attention and divert the imaginations of the medical community from the real problems that should claim their skill. Ditto if she put the lot of them to sleep. Her toad-changing magic, of course, was used up on Bobby. In the end it seemed best to cast a mental net and try to pull in all who could help or who owed her favors, meanwhile blowing loudly on the police whistle she always carried in her pocket and bracing herself to defend herself and her friends with all of the martial arts skills at Kwan Yin's disposal. Unfortunately, the persona lent itself more to the silken-robe-and-lotus sort of thing than to practical skills, so she attempted to look like David Carradine and hoped that would suffice until real help could come.

It was also problematical to blow on a police whistle while emitting fierce karate yells, but she did her best as she leapt into the fray—just in time to see a tire iron heading for her skull.

*   *   *

Le turned at Ding's insistence and when Ding saw the
gang of toughs surrounding something or more likely somebody, when he saw Kwan Yin and her handmaiden standing
by, when he saw the talking cat streak away from the men
loudly calling, "Help! Help! My master has been set upon
by ruffians!" when he saw the handmaiden swinging her
purse like an Argentinian gaucho's bola as she ran toward
the white gang, and when he saw Kwan Yin, with a mighty
leap worthy of a Ninja Turtle, enter the fray, he opened the
door of the speeding car, dove out, rolled, jumped to his
feet and passed the vehicle on his way to join in.

"After me, Guerillas! JUMP!" he yelled and Le's car
slammed into the other gang's car, as the driver bailed out
slightly before he remembered to put the brake on.

This required no great feat of leadership on Ding's part.
Seeing Kwan Yin had accomplished a couple of things for
the gang. First, it made them realize that their leader had
even better connections than they had imagined, and second
they realized that, all previous appearances to the contrary,
there was someone very powerful of their own culture on
their side as long as they watched their asses and cleaned
up their acts. It was Ding's role as leader to show them
how to go about this, and his instructions could not have
been more emphatic. Then there was always third, which
was that they just really *liked* jumping people.

Ding kicked aside three of the men and saw that the
others had cornered one cowering guy in a trenchcoat along
with the cat's master, the black guy, who was trying to
shield the handmaiden, who was bopping the hell out of
one of the white guys with her purse, while another guy
was about to clobber Kwan Yin with a tire iron. Before
Ding could intercept the iron, it turned back on the guy
wielding it and began to thump hell out of him.

He saw the black guy dive past him and the flash of a knife and saw the black guy pile on top of the guy who *had* the knife and that he, Ding, was the knife's intended target before the black guy intercepted the attack.

About that time the white guys decided this was no easy way to have fun and began hauling each other back into their car, the Guerillas still beating on them as they fled, using knives and bats. It was way too crowded to shoot any of the bastards without downing an ally with friendly fire, and the homeboys, a little more savvy than the military, realized this and used their firearms as clubs instead. Ding stepped on the wrist of the guy with the knife, causing him to drop the knife. Ding picked it up, then pulled the little black guy off. The white guy ran with his buddies back to the car, and the lot of them sped away, taking the front fender of Le's brother's car with them, rattling in their wake.

The black guy was shaking. Ding clapped him on the back. "Thanks, man. You saved my life. I'm glad we didn't kill you a while ago."

Dico stopped panting long enough to say, "Me too."

Ding saw Kwan Yin watching him as she helped Rose pick up the items that had been flung from her purse in the fury of her attack. "Look, I'm real sorry about jumping you, man, and scaring your cat," he told the kid. "Sometimes you just get pissed off at the world and take it out on the nearest person, you know?"

Dico nodded. Fifteen minutes ago he wouldn't have known but, now that it was over, he had to admit half-choking that guy had felt pretty good. "Yeah, I think so."

Kwan Yin continued to watch Ding, her head nodding very slowly in encouragement and conditional approval.

"My name is Nguyen Ding Hoa," Ding said, making a slight bow to Dico.

"Dico Miller," Dico replied.

"Dico, my folks work night shifts and I was going to fix them breakfast. Would you like to come home with me and meet them?"

"I'm kinda a mess right now to go meetin' people, besides, I offered to help . . ."

Dico looked back to Kwan Yin, but she was smiling and nodding.

"Well, okay, but I need to clean up and change and . . ."

"No sweat, man," Ding said, though he could smell the acrid scent of urine on Dico. It was nothing new to him. "We got plumbing, at least, and you and me are about the same size. Now, this is Le, Hai but you can call him Hal, Minh, Chi . . ."

"What about Puss?" Dico asked, suddenly remembering the cat and looking around for her. "Puss? Puss? Now, I know that damn cat didn't let nothin' happen to her. Come on, Puss, we got invited out to eat."

A small whiskered face peeked out of the alley. "Ssst. You go on by yourself, Dico. I got my own rats to kill. Your new buddy may be okay, but I remember his previously expressed dietary preferences, if you get my drift. Meet me here tomorrow."

Dico nodded and turned back to Ding. Ding started to look to Kwan Yin for approval, but by that time she and the handmaiden were no longer there.

Nineteen

WHILE DICO AND Ding were talking, Eddy was talking to himself in an extremely agitated fashion. He had risen to his feet and had started running toward the shelter entrance.

"I wonder what possessed him to come wandering down here at this hour if he's staying at the shelter," Felicity said.

"They probably just released him from jail," Rose said. "They tend to do a lot of the paperwork at night and as soon as it's finished, they release the prisoners—and people like him are left wandering at two and three o'clock in the morning. It's stupid, but it's the system."

"We'll see about that," Felicity said, as she and Rose left Dico to the attitudinally altered Ding and his friends and followed Eddy to the shelter's dark alleyway entrance. "Why is there no light at the doorway?" Felicity asked.

Rose shrugged, wondering if Felicity thought of herself as a building inspector as well as a fairy godmother.

The shelter was in a converted store. Its front door was for some crazy reason boarded up so that it could only be entered through the alley. Swaths of newsprint were taped to the picture-window front.

"We'll need a disguise at this point," Felicity said. "Your outfit'll do, given a bit of judicious fitting and smudging. Pull your shirt out and do something or other with that jacket. Tear it or something."

"No way," Rose said. "It cost me fifty bucks at your shop, and wasting a perfectly good coat is not my idea of a way to help the homeless." She pulled it off, turned it wrong side out with the lining rucked up in the back, and threw it over her shoulders. "Better?"

A yellow-toothed, straggly-haired bag lady stood before her dressed in a droopy collection of rags including what appeared to be the soiled trousers from a men's plaid polyester leisure suit, scuffed and torn saddle oxfords that had once been black and white, mismatched sox, a wrinkled and torn flannel shirt over a Huskies sweatshirt, topped by an army fatigue jacket and a daisy-covered vinyl rain cap from which greasy ropes of iron-gray hair drooped. She was carrying half a dozen plastic supermarket bags bulging with items Rose couldn't see.

"You're still too neat," this apparition told Rose. "Muss your hair."

Rose did so and they entered the shelter. It took a moment for Rose's eyes to adjust to the darkness. It was a good thing she didn't move before they did. Two or three years ago, shelters used to have proper beds for people to sleep in and bathrooms and cooking facilities. This one offered nothing but a place indoors to spread out and catch vermin and infections from the other denizens.

The sound of coughing, sneezing, sniffing and whimpering mingled with other voices, querulous, cranky and whiny, if not openly hostile. Several people were muttering and arguing with themselves like Crazy Eddy. The only warmth in the place was body heat, and the room smelled of backed-up plumbing, urine, farts, vomit and rancid body odor. No wonder so many preferred sleeping on the streets.

The place was an absolute breeding ground for disease, a sort of petri dish for people, with whole families piled together under one sleeping bag or on top of one bare mattress. The kids could be incubating tuberculosis, leprosy, plagues for all she knew. She wondered if the federal government's free vaccination programs had arrived in time to protect these kids before they were out on the streets, never mind their parents.

Rose felt a flush of shame that she had been unaware of these dismal conditions before. She had visited this place three or four years ago, shortly after she began her present job, and had somehow imagined, despite knowing about the budget cuts and diminished services, that the shelter had stayed the same. She blithely continued to send people here without ever returning to inspect it herself or volunteering to do anything for it. The fact was, by the time her day was ended and she rode back across the Sound, she was filled to the roots of her hair with misery and needed badly to escape it. No doubt everyone else who should have concerned themselves with the deterioration of such places had responded in the same way. With economic times so hard, many people were working extra hours and extra jobs just to try to keep going, and had less money and less time to help the less fortunate. There was still the fear that poverty and homelessness were contagious, and at times Rose wondered if the fear wasn't valid.

But this dump was no escape or haven for anyone.

There didn't seem to be any sort of coordinator or supervisor on the premises, which wasn't surprising, since no coordination or supervision of the facility seemed to have occurred for some time.

"I had no idea," Rose whispered, turning to Felicity, or at least to where Felicity had been standing. Then she realized the door behind her was ajar, and she stepped back into the street to see the bag lady/Felicity pull a cordless phone from one of her plastic bags and speak into it. A minute later, a city utilities truck arrived, and six workers climbed out, set up barriers and opened a manhole. Two of the workers, a man and a woman, flashlights in hand, entered the building, and through the open door Rose saw one of them picking his way back to the bathroom while the woman set to work on the antiquated steam heat registers on the side and rear walls of the building.

In a very short time the two utilities workers emerged and the woman said to Felicity, whom she apparently recognized regardless of the rags, "That's it, Godmother. Just a tad plugged. The bathroom's a mess, though."

"No problem," Felicity said.

"That was the easiest job I ever had fixing this sort of pipe, to tell you the truth," said the woman, who was probably in her late fifties and was dressed in a coverall with a nametag that said "Morales." "You didn't have anything to do with that, did you?"

"No, dear, you just have a magic touch. You'll make a fine commissioner next election."

"Gracias, Godmother."

"De nada, dear. You will remember to send an inspector around regularly now, won't you, and a repair crew if necessary?"

"I will attend to this personally, Godmother, to show my appreciation for what you have done for me and my family."

"That eases my mind considerably, Esmeralda. Please tell your workmen there will be a van arriving shortly with hot coffee and breakfast. Another alumnus is in the process of buying the restaurant next door to convert to a soup kitchen."

"That is very gracious, Godmother, but I think we are finished now."

"Then adiós, Esmeralda, and give my love to your children and grandchildren."

"Adiós, Godmother."

Rose watched all this open-mouthed. "Wow, that's what I call networking. You wouldn't want to run for mayor—no, governor, would you?"

"Certainly not. My sort are guerilla do-gooders, vigilante busybodies, an underground composed of like-minded associates, most of whom are alumni, beneficiaries from past forays. Our tactics would never withstand the scrutiny of the press, or the paper-pushers for that matter, and except for fixing the utilities, which came out of the city budget—the part reserved for the mayor's birthday party—the activities are privately funded. I'm afraid the mayor will be appalled to learn that she's serving an inferior vintage of champagne to the one she originally ordered, but we must all make little sacrifices. Speaking of which"—she withdrew from her plastic bag scrub brushes, face masks, rubber gloves, sponges, disinfectant and cleanser—"you and I will now go clean the loo."

Twenty

HANK THOUGHT THE woodshop was cool, with all the tools and paints tidily lined up and hung above a long, spotless wooden bench. Dad's tool shop had had sawdust all over everything. For a garage, this was pretty great. Hank wondered if the man had more tools down in the basement. Maybe the big fancy power tools. There was a key in the door lock. It made him really want to go look and see what was in there.

Gigi was more fascinated by the cutouts of gingerbread people, some of them bigger than she was. Single sides of these in various stages of being painted were stacked against the walls a couple of feet deep all over the garage. The completed ones had two sides—a back and a front, and in between the cutouts the man had made sides so that each gingerbread man stood on his own and formed kind of a box.

After she'd seen that, though, she was ready to go back inside. "Let's get him to call Mama now," she said to Hank.

But Hank was still eyeing the basement door, though he pretended not to be. Instead, he nodded at the tools. "I wonder if he'd teach me to use these things," he said. "Dad always said I was too little."

"When we were home, we *were* littler," Gigi said. She felt very old now. She walked back to the door and tried to open it but it wouldn't open. So she knocked. No answer. So she pounded.

All at once it opened wide and she fell into the kitchen, banging her knee on the doorsill.

Before she could think to cry the man said, not very nicely, "What's all the racket for?"

"I want to bake cookies now," Gigi said.

So they did, but the cookies were funny-tasting.

"Let's call Mom," Hank suggested later.

"It's too late," the man said. "Your mother will be in bed."

"No, she won't," Hank said. "She works at night."

"Then she'll be at work. Give me your number and I'll call from work tomorrow. You two can stay here while I'm gone. I've got a big TV and some toys and lots of stuff for you to play with, except you are not to go into the basement under any circumstances. Do I make myself clear?"

"Yes, sir."

"Good. Just make sure you mind me on that score and everything will be fine. Meanwhile, I'll put you two to bed upstairs. Here, have some warm milk with your cookies."

"I'd rather have cocoa," Gigi said.

The man nodded accommodatingly.

He even had a separate room for each of them, with big beds like Mom and Dad used to have.

"Tomorrow night, when I come home, I'll bring a Christmas tree and presents," he promised as he tucked Gigi in. She was suddenly very, very sleepy.

"I don't have a nightie," she said.

"You don't need one here," he said. "But take off your clothes so you don't get them dirty in your sleep."

And that night she had a very strange dream. She dreamed a teddy bear crawled into bed with her but it was very big and it kept trying to bear-hug her and ran its paws all over her and kept checking her bottom to see if she'd peed the bed—that's what it said it was doing. Except it didn't have paws, it had hands and sometimes it pinched. When she woke up, she was crying and her bottom hurt.

But downstairs in the big house, bacon was frying and Hank opened the door to her room and said, "Come on, lazybones, wake up. *He's* making us waffles in the shape of gingerbread men."

Gigi felt very sleepy as she pulled on her shirt and pants and followed her brother downstairs.

They ate bacon and the waffles shaped like gingerbread men with butter and lots of syrup and peanut butter because they wanted it and orange juice and hot chocolate. It was the biggest meal Gigi had had outside of a fast-food place since they'd left home—and that seemed like such a long time ago, back when she had been very little.

The man didn't say they had to brush their teeth or wash their faces or anything, but when Gigi had to go to the bathroom it hurt really bad and she came back crying about it, expecting sympathy. Instead, both the man and Hank told her not to be such a big baby.

The man was wearing a suit and tie that morning, and looked important.

"Now, until we can find your parents, you kids are welcome to stay here," he told them. "Tonight when I bring home the Christmas tree, we'll get out the ornaments and trim it. Tomorrow, I've arranged with Santa for a special surprise visit since you missed Christmas this year."

"And by then Mom will probably be here, huh?" Hank asked, sounding almost disappointed at the prospect.

"Sure," the man said, picking up his briefcase. "Now, remember what I told you yesterday. You can go anywhere in the house but the basement. It's dangerous down there, and I think I've given you enough to enjoy yourselves with that you can respect my wishes. The key is in the lock, and you could disobey me, of course, but if you are good children, you won't do that and you won't get hurt. I also don't want you messing with the phones because you might—accidentally, of course—call long distance and cost me lots of money. So I've put them all away in a safe place. Now I'm going to go and lock you in for safety's sake. I expect you, Hank, to take good care of Gigi and I want everything neat and tidy when I come home for our Christmas party. Understand?"

Hank nodded, but Gigi, who still hurt, just whimpered and sucked her thumb.

The last thing the man said when he left was, "Now you remember what I said about staying away from that basement."

Bluebeard

The man who looked like Santa Claus in a business suit locked the door from the outside so his precious merchandise couldn't get out. He walked through the Christmas decorations and out to his car, and headed for the freeway. He could hardly contain himself, he was so excited at this new find. Usually you had to travel to another country or to some unsavory ghetto, risking who knew what diseases to get what he had happened upon not quite by accident. A collector's dream.

Not that he hadn't done a certain amount of preparation. There was this house, of course, with all of its little secrets. Only his most avid fellow enthusiasts, ones on whom he had lots of insurance against being tattled on, knew about this place. Even his wife had never known about it.

He also had good bait. The gingerbread houses were not easy to make and assemble, and he could enjoy only the delicious pangs of frustration as the children came and went, attended by parents. There was pleasure of a sort in that, of course, but nothing like this.

It was risky, though. These were not some immigrant youngsters from South America or India sold by or stolen from their parents and smuggled in for the pleasure they could give the man and his friends. These children were local, lost, maybe being hunted for by the police. However, if he was generous with his luck, and shared them with his more influential friends, he would have allies who dared not betray him, no matter what disposal he had to make of the children eventually. He drove up I-5 to Seattle, where he was touring the downtown facility.

He was proud of his work, aware that he had helped the new administration turn this whole sorry liberal business around, using state money and facilities to return things to their proper status. Admittedly, the so-called caseworkers were rebellious at times, disliking the necessity of returning the family to its proper prominence, the father particularly to his rightful place as supreme head of the family. The man was a father himself, but the woman he had chosen to be his mate had gotten some strange ideas in her head during all of that women's liberation crap, and then had misconstrued what the children told her about his loving and mutually satisfying relations with them. She knew better than to try to take him on in court—not to mention that she knew he'd make her very, very sorry if he caught her—and had simply disappeared with his little ones. Since his appointment, he had been too busy changing the system to court anyone else. However, the very changes that had robbed him of his family, the changes that allowed women to leave their husbands and the courts to tell a man how to treat his family, would make it easy for him to find another nice situation when he was ready. Single mothers with many children were quite the norm now, and many of them would be glad enough for a roof over the family's head to refrain from having too many difficult opinions on what *he* should do.

He entered the downtown facility and was immediately fawned over by that silly woman he had personally appointed to be supervisor. She had become politically active in support of Mrs. Bob (Florence) Foster, the antifeminist, antiabortion, pro-family, pro-industry candidate for state legislature, and while campaigning for Mrs. Foster, had developed the hots for the current governor and campaigned for him as well.

The governor, who was not a particular man and who had very conventional tastes in sexual entertainment, had hinted strongly that the lady should be rewarded for services rendered by a job suited to her skills and background. She had a degree in psychology dating from 1959 from Spokane Evangelical Women's College, or SEW as it was known to alumni. She also was a minister in a mail-order church, which gave her the alternative credentials necessary. Quite a find, actually. She wasn't just another playmate of the governor's but was an effective agent for the sort of changes both the governor and he wished to make in the current system.

However, she fawned all over him and made eyes at him the whole time he was there, and he couldn't wait to get away. He did notice a young woman in gray half-nodding over her paperwork. He had a word with Bitsy Hager about her and learned that the girl was one Rosalie

Samson, a chronic troublemaker who resisted the new policies and tried to go behind her supervisor's back. Hmm. This was where it took a strong hand, a firm grip, to steer the department in the proper direction. He could replace her, at no cost to the state, with one of his volunteers from the Washington League of Religious Women. He made a note to that effect to leave in his evaluation for Mrs. Hager. In case she missed the point, in Hager's presence he stared at Samson's back for a significantly long moment with a kindly, concerned, but regretful air. Then he looked back at Hager with his best careworn expression of resignation.

Following the inspection, he found a pay phone and made a call to a colleague who also had an office downtown. He had had an extra bounce in his step with the anticipation of sharing his find with this like-minded enthusiast.

"I've found something extremely tasty," he told the colleague. "When can we meet to discuss it?"

The colleague was very eager, but heavily committed all day and all night. "I have a meeting with the Bainbridge Planning Commission this evening and need to take the six-thirty ferry right after my appointments today. If you'd care to ride over with me, I think we could be relatively anonymous."

"We could just stay in your car."

"Oh, no. Watching the children cavort on the ferry is one of the few joys of my day. It will be crowded and noisy, so if we're discreet there should be no difficulty."

The man who looked like Santa Claus was somewhat uneasy with this arrangement, but then, the risk of being found out, the sauce of danger, added to the pleasure of the sport, something he felt as keenly as did his colleague. It was amazing how unaware—how dead, really—other people could be as long as you conformed outwardly. "I'll meet you in the rear, then, of the six-thirty boat."

"I'll look forward to it."

Rose felt as if she had lived through a week by the time she dragged herself to work that morning. Cleaning the filthy bathroom at the shelter had given her time to come down from the adrenaline rush that had kept her going throughout the night. Her consolation was that between the excitement of the tenderness that had unexpectedly developed between her and Fred and being shot at by a gang who subsequently rescued her from being beaten by another, she probably wouldn't have been able to get to sleep anyway.

She didn't begrudge the work at the shelter, though. Felicity had scrubbed as hard as she had, and was the first to tackle the toilets, and Rose found herself attacking her share with more zeal than she'd ever devoted to her own bathroom. Maybe it was self-defense against the germs, which probably had microscopic muscles the size of Arnold Schwarzenegger's by now, judging from the dirt and the stench. By the time the place was clean and the erstwhile residents began filing in to prepare for another day on the streets, the place was clean, smelling of disinfectant and restocked with soap and toilet paper. Rose used some of each herself before she and Felicity left. At some time during the night, Felicity had taken from her pockets more packages of toiletries and laid a package beside each sleeping person. From outside, the world's two most seductive smells, coffee and bacon, invited the shelter's occupants to come out to the sidewalk for breakfast.

"This is really something, Felicity. Some of these folks will remember this for a long time," Rose said.

"Only those who are able to move along," Felicity said. "The others will come to take it for granted. The medical team will be in later to see to those who are too sick to leave."

Felicity made another call from her portable phone before they left, and in another few minutes moving vans began arriving with plastic-covered mattresses, bunk beds and bedding. A laundry and diaper service truck with Chinese lettering on the side followed close behind.

"Who's paying for this?" Rose asked.

"The people who run these businesses can afford it," Felicity said.

"You are the biggest blackmailer I've ever met," Rose said. "But it's great."

"Nonsense," she said. "If someone hadn't done something similar for the people helping out here, they might be in worse shape than those in the shelters. It's less like blackmail and more like tithing—except instead of going to some bloke who decides how to distribute their hard-earned cash for them, they come right in and intervene with their own goods and services to help people directly. I've also instructed my alumni to be on the lookout for those among the clientele there who are capable of serving the food and doing the cleaning and maintaining the facilities for the others, so they may be hired to do so."

"You're *sure* you won't reconsider running for governor?" Rose had asked at the time.

Felicity laughed too, looking at Rose's smelly, dirty outfit and dust-smeared face and hair. "If you can say that now, I'd have you for my campaign manager. I'm pleased that what we've done here tonight has helped, but it's only one night and one shelter and over the long run, there may be, will surely be, complications and shortcomings and abuses, just as there always are. A clean bathroom, a hot meal, a warm place to sleep and a bar of soap don't cure everything. Such things don't make reasonable people of the insane, find jobs for the unemployed, or cure drunkards and drug addicts of their addictions. Not even magic can do that, and what we've done here isn't magic. But it is a start."

"Unless I start cleaning up now and get to work looking more respectable than this, I'll be joining the ranks of the unemployed soon myself," Rose said ruefully.

As they headed back up the steep incline to Third Avenue to catch the bus, a young man in jeans and a sports jacket was stopped by the man from the park bench the night before. "Hey, buddy, don't walk so fast. I got a good joke to tell ya."

"Yeah? What?"

"Well, there was this old lady lived all alone with her ol' tomcat, see, and all of a sudden poof! here comes the fairy godmother and she said, 'Because you've been a nice ol' gal I can give you three wishes. Whaddaya want?' So first the old lady wants to be rich, then she wants to be a babe again, and hey, presto, she is. What do you think her third wish was?"

"I don't know. What was it?"

"If you got fifty cents I'll tell you. I'm not panhandling, mind you. I've gone into business as an im-prom-too standup comedian and thas my cover charge."

"Fifty cents, huh? Okay," the younger man said and dug into his pocket.

The bus came then and Rose didn't hear the punch line, because Felicity pulled her aboard among the throng of morning commuters on their way to work, all of whom made as much room for Rose, who did not smell like her namesake, as they possibly could. Felicity had reverted to her pristine silvery self, which hardly seemed fair.

A shower did Rose good, but her clothes were out of the question. Felicity loaned her a pantsuit of soft dove-gray lamb's wool and a plushy pewter turtleneck to wear under it, plus rhinestone and silver star-shaped earrings, which went fine with the mustard seed.

Before she let Rose escape to work, she insisted that she borrow her own makeup and her own "Magique" perfume, which Rose used very sparingly since she seldom wore perfume. Although it had smelled rather musky in the bottle, once it touched Rose's skin it immediately assumed the sweet vanilla-floral scent she preferred.

"Now then, with this," Felicity said, draping a silky white gauze scarf ornamented with sparkly crescent moons and stars sprinkled across it, "and this"—she added a gray tweed Irish walking hat with a dove's feather cockade— "you're set."

Rose pulled the mustard seed out of the neck of the turtleneck and returned the scarf and hat. "I'm a caseworker, not a starlet getting ready for a dance in the rain with Fred Astaire. Let's not overdo it, hmm?"

"Really, dear, I don't know how you're going to find romance if you don't try to look like a princess occasionally."

"Sorry, Felicity, but I'd think you of all people might understand why some of us have to be socialists at heart."

Bed of Straw

"I really hate to do this, Cindy," Pill Putnam, the owner of Lucky Shoe Stables, told Cindy Ellis. "You're the best hand I've ever had and if things were fair, I'd be offerin' to make you my partner, not firing you. But without the use of these trails, I got no business. You understand, don't you?"

"Sure, Pill," Cindy said, half angrily, half dejectedly, but trying not to blame her friend or make him feel any worse than he already did. "And now you understand what I've been up against with the three P's."

"The three P's?"

"My stepmother, Paola, and my stepsisters Pam and Perdita. They'll go to any lengths to make my life miserable."

"It was one of them give you that shiner, wasn't it?" Pill asked, pointing to the eye that Perdita had viciously kicked while Cindy was helping her mount.

"Yeah."

"You thought about getting a lawyer? That there's assault."

"Lawyers cost money, Pill."

Pill spat out a sunflower seed, which he gnawed on to give the impression of chewing tobacco. He talked like a Texan but was actually a former cowboy stuntman who had moved to Washington from Venice, California, to pursue his dream of running his own stable. He didn't even eat meat. And he took a lot of vitamins, which was what prompted his fellow film wranglers to hang him with the handle "Pill."

"Well," he said, and spat another seed. "Hell."

"Yeah," she agreed. "Hell. For sure."

"Look," he said. "I haven't got enough to pay you two weeks in advance, but I'll keep Punkin here until the farrier comes to do his shoe and you can find another place to keep him."

"Thanks. I wish you had a stall for me as well. My house-sitting gig ends tonight. Everything I own is in my pack."

"I can give you a few bucks for a locker, but I don't know what else to do. I'd take you in, but the wife is a little jealous of you, you know."

"Jealous of *me*?" Cindy asked. "Jealous of me? Why? I'm officially homeless, jobless, and if I could find someone who could afford to take proper care of Punkin, horseless."

"Let me check with the accountant and I'll see if I can buy him from you if you really want to sell," Pill said, ducking the more uncomfortable part of the conversation. "He'll be fine once the farrier gets that new shoe on him, though. Meanwhile, I'll tell you what. If you meant it, about the stall, you can bed down in the vacant one just for tonight. Meanwhile, I've got a few things to do. Why don't you lock up tonight?"

"Thanks, Pill."

"It's the least I can do." He shrugged. "I'm sorry."

Twenty-one

THE DEPARTMENT WAS so swamped with clients Rose began feeling like an assembly-line worker. Recent layoffs at Boeing and Microsoft, an outbreak of salmonella and spinal meningitis in the schools, and the usual abuse, both sexual and violent, kept Rose filling out forms and talking to a steady line of people. She was seriously drooping by the time she heard Hager in the open office behind her desk, saying, "Attention everybody! This is our division head, Mr. Hopkins, and he has come to watch us work today. I trust you will all be on your best behavior."

Rose didn't even look around. She was too busy trying not to throw up at Hager's kindergarten-schoolteacher manner and too sleepy to pretend to be alert for the benefit of the division head, who was one of the idiots responsible for the new "policies" that put children like Polly Reynaud and the Bjornsen kids in jeopardy. She did her job and ignored him, and barely noticed, later, the triumphant expression on Hager's perfectly powdered face.

Her thoughts were a jumbled kaleidoscope of images from the night—Fred stroking her cheek, the cat interrogating the toad, the gunshots, the cat's tail disappearing behind a building, the shelter, Fred at the computer, the frog-man in Harborview, well, toad-man actually. These impressions intruded on her consciousness so that she lost her ability to track her thoughts through the labyrinth of all the routine things she had to say and questions she had to ask, and she suspected she was making no sense. By the time she was finally able to break for lunch, she scarcely could pair a face with each form she had filled out that morning.

In the back of her mind, she had been wondering if and how she ought to explain to Fred that she knew where he should start looking for Sno. Somehow, she couldn't see even that unusually cooperative cop being really understanding when she told him her tip came from a toad. Maybe that was why she didn't give it the priority it deserved. But during her lunch break she called the King County Police and asked for him.

"Hi, Fred. It's Rose. Look, about Sno . . ."

"Rosie! Hi! You sound as tired as I am."

"I didn't get any sleep last night," she said.

"Me neither, and I've got a coffee buzz you wouldn't believe. It's been pretty crazy around here, but I was just about to call you with an update about Sno's case. We got a court order and sent someone over to photograph the man at Harborview early this morning and faxed it to area police. They took the photo and a description of the guy's wound around to hospitals and clinics up and down the corridor from the border to Portland. One of the emergency room nurses at a clinic in Bellingham gave us a positive ID on the photograph of our frog-man as being the same guy she treated the night Sno Quantrill disappeared."

Rose took a deep breath, then suggested, without explaining the source of her hunch, "Gee, it would have been real easy for him to take her into the woods then, up by the mountains, where nobody could see them."

"Could be. We find a lot of bodies in the woods. We're checking closer to the highways meanwhile, though."

"If it's in the woods, you'll organize a search party, won't you?"

"Not me, no. Though I'll probably be coordinating with whoever does organize the search. It won't be King County, though, if the perp was last seen in Bellingham. From the information we have now, we know he took her from her school at four P.M. to someplace in Whatcom County and turned up eight hours later at an emergency room, alone, with a knife wound in his side. The poor girl's probably bought it, but we've got to proceed as if we can save her."

"Maybe the fact that he's injured means she got away from him, Fred."

"Maybe. But if so, why hasn't she showed up?"

"I don't know, but maybe she got lost and is waiting for someone to come and find her. I've just got this feeling she's still alive, Fred."

"Funny you should say that, because, all evidence to the contrary, I've got the same feeling. If only we could narrow down the search area so we knew where to start."

Poisoning the Apple

Gerardine's own search had been satisfactory. She'd seen the little bitch, sitting on a riverbank looking like a girlish version of Huckleberry Finn instead of the conniving little whore she was, but Gerardine knew how to take care of her.

Really, she shouldn't have bothered with Svenny and his incompetent hired help to begin with. She was plenty smart enough to commit the perfect crime herself. Dusting dope with strychnine didn't exactly take a degree in chemistry, and Gerardine actually *had* had some chemistry classes—she took them in conjunction with her cosmetology courses. What with all her modeling, she was great at disguising her looks too. It was easy in this case, since she wanted to appear to be a back-country hippie hiker lost in the woods. She simply washed off the makeup no one, not even Raydir, ever saw her without. The change was incredible.

Her lips were a quarter of an inch thinner, she had no lashes or brows, and without her contouring brushes her face simply looked long and flat, the cheekbones not so pronounced or interesting. Dark circles stood out under her eyes and an unattractive mottling of reddish veins flecked her cheeks and nose.

She was seldom seen without one of her outlandish wigs, but chopping bangs in her own white-blonde hair and bundling the rest up in a bandanna covered by a stocking cap provided good cover. Then, with a turtleneck up under her chin and her lithe body wrapped in layers of patched down and flannel, she ducked out the back way. She had already ordered a trail bike to be readied for her use, and this she loaded in the back of Raydir's van. Thus equipped, she headed for the Mount Baker Highway.

Without any expenditure of magic at all, Felicity could smell other magicks, particularly what Dame Erzuli La-Chance, the Haitian godmother, referred to as "bad juju." Yes, it was about time for Sno's stepmother to make her second murder attempt, right on schedule. In this life, in this version of the story, the stepmother apparently once more had some sort of magical powers—from the strong but ill-defined scent of them, probably they currently took the form of an underdeveloped psychic ability, and that was what Felicity scented. More to the point, however, the stepmother undoubtedly had a working vehicle, which was more than Felicity could say. She could scalp that young scamp, Ding, she thought in a flash of unprofessional irritation.

Fortunately, her name wasn't Fortune for nothing. She had the best luck of any hitchhiker in the history of Puget Sound. When she caught the first whiff of Gerardine's powerful negative force, a smell which quickly faded to the north, she stuck Bobby in her pocket, walked down the stairs, and stepped out into the lobby and the entranceway in time to see a cavalcade of motorcycles pull up. After lengthy good-byes, most of them roared away, but one man with a gray-black bushy beard and long hair had paused a bit longer.

"Excuse me, but are you by any chance going north?" she asked. Then she looked again. She hadn't exactly cheated. She hadn't *meant* to magically call up another of her former charges. Not when the telephone was so cheap, especially local calls. But she saw past the beard now, looking into the man's eyes, and he gave a start of recognition as he saw her too.

"Godmother! Where you goin', babe? I'll take you anywhere."

"Hello, Haisley. I'm delighted to see you. North will do nicely for now. Toward Bellingham, I should think."

"I was just headed up there to pick up my rig and join the 4X4 search and rescue team. Got a kid missing in the forest, and it's going to take a *massive* search."

"You sound thrilled."

"I *love* doing this stuff. It's like maybe a way to pay you back for what you did for me when I was a kid. You don't look a day older, by the way."

"You are a very nice boy, Haisley. Have you got an extra helmet?"

*   *   *

Two Warnings

A telephone was ringing somewhere in the house. Hank knew they weren't supposed to answer it, but it kept ringing and ringing and ringing. Finally, he thought maybe the man wouldn't mind if he just went to find it and hung it up. That should be okay, as long as he didn't answer.

But then, maybe he should answer. Maybe it was the police, or even Mama.

Gigi was watching TV. The man had a big TV and lots of tapes, but right now she wasn't watching tapes. His VCR setup was a little complicated for her, though Hank thought that as soon as he dealt with the darn phone he'd be able to figure it out.

No, she was watching a talk program. The *Susan Buchanan Show*.

"Today Susan will be talking with the mothers and teachers of children who died from abuse inflicted by child molesters. In some cases the molester was a friend or relative. In that case, why didn't the parents, teachers, or neighbors see the warning signs? Speaking of which, just what *are* those warning signs? If the children were harmed by strangers, why weren't they taught to avoid dangerous situations? And, most importantly at this time, how can you and your children avoid becoming victims? We'll have questions from our studio audience who will share their opinions and experience with us. But first a word from our sponsor."

The words went right by Hank as boring adult stuff. "What are you watching *that* trash for?" he asked as he passed by the room. "Cartoons are on."

"Susan's dress is pretty," Gigi said. " 'S pink."

Girls!

The phone was silent for a time and then began ringing—

this time Hank could tell it wasn't just one phone but several. The sound seemed to be coming from underneath the floor.

Oh. Then the man had taken the phones to the basement, where he didn't want them to go. What could he *have* down there that was so dangerous if he didn't even lock the door? Was it really dangerous or was it some big surprise—maybe like Christmas presents?

Fred Moran was still wearing his detective hat, covering cases he had become involved with as a patrolman. He had been delighted when the department made the radical switch in operating procedure. A couple of years ago, the guy in the uniform had been the low man on the totem pole and it took years of street work to be "elevated" to detective. The detectives talked on the phones a lot and saw little of the street once they made the grade. The flaws of this system made up for the flaws of the previous system, in which a cop worked the same neighborhood from the time he was a patrolman on up the ladder, and maybe got to know everyone in the neighborhood, including the criminal element, a little too intimately.

If patrolmen never did any detective work in the neighborhoods they patrolled, obviously they could be more objective as detectives. Just as obviously, however, they lost track of who the people they were protecting were, how various segments of society and various subcultures and communities throughout their jurisdiction functioned. People felt better if they were dealing with someone they knew.

So the new theory held that the cop on the street was not just the foot soldier, but the primary link with the community, the one who knew the ropes. Initially, talented patrolmen trained in detective procedures as crime scene investigators, or CSIs, but as they gained knowledge and experience, the boundaries of that role expanded to include the sort of investigations Fred was conducting now.

"I'm sorry, Mr.—"

"Bjornsen. Harry Bjornsen. It's on those three hundred forms I've spent the whole goddamn week filling out. Now you tell me something. Where's my family? Can't a man go out to earn an honest living without coming home to find his family is lost and no so-called cop in the whole damn city can find them?"

"Mr. Bjornsen, we're doing our best. Your wife's sister says your wife left town. She doesn't know where, but she's assuming the children went with her."

"Christ!" Bjornsen said.

"Mr. Bjornsen, I hate to make this any harder on you, but how was your marriage going before you left for Alaska?"

"What the hell is that supposed to mean?"

"It means, sir, that it is not unheard of for a disgruntled spouse to snatch the children and take them to another state."

"You think that's what she's done?" he asked, dismayed. Then he dismissed the idea. "Nah, she wouldn't do that. We weren't getting along, but we were still trying to work it out when I left. She knew I was pissed but she also knew I left because I had work and would be bringing home a paycheck. We all needed this check." He waved the check in question in the air for emphasis. "That's what started the trouble in the first place. Everything was fine before I lost my job. Then we had to give up our house and come over here to live with her sister. Her sister ain't the best influence, if you want to know the truth. She works at a topless joint, and my wife used to too. She got it in her head that she had to go back to it."

"So the children might have been left unsupervised with

you away and both the mother and the aunt working, maybe?" the cop asked.

"Could be, I guess. Hank's only seven but he's a good boy, looks after his little sister. This has been pretty hard on them, I guess. We've all been on edge."

"Mr. Bjornsen, are you aware that your wife took your children to the University Mall and left them there?"

"She wouldn't do something like that!" he said.

"I'm sorry, but she did. I brought Hank and Gigi home myself when I was patrolling the University District. A mall security guard called me. DFS had a difficult time locating your wife, but she claimed the children had run away from her and she had no idea where they were."

"Why didn't you do something about it?"

"What would you suggest? DFS has been backed up trying to cover cases where the children are being physically and sexually abused to the point that their lives are threatened. Your children appeared to be healthy and reasonably well cared for. If we'd arrested their mother, then who would have cared for them? The aunt?"

Bjornsen snorted. "Not Bambi-baby. She let us know all the time what a drag it was to have us around, especially Hank and Gigi." He rubbed his eyes wearily and also, Fred suspected, to rid them of any subversive moisture that might be gathering to betray him.

"So where do you think your wife might have gone, Mr. Bjornsen?"

"Do you think I haven't called all those places?" he asked. "Bambi wouldn't tell me. If she'd gone to her folks, Bambi would have said so. She's taken off with some guy."

"Do you have a picture of her and the kids, Mr. Bjornsen?"

"Yeah, in my wallet," he said and pulled out a miniature

of a family portrait. "The kids look different now—hell, they probably look different than they did when I left, but my wife hasn't changed much—well, not at home. At work she wears a lot of makeup and fixes her hair up puffy, but that's her."

The woman in the picture looked pretty similar to the one who had answered the door the morning Fred had returned the children. "May we borrow this?"

"Sure."

"We'll take it around to the malls and see if anyone remembers seeing any of them during the weekend. If she dropped them at a mall once, she might have done it again. The people at one of the fast-food joints might remember seeing your kids. Hank and Gigi really love their Big Macs, don't they?"

"Oh, yeah. They both love McDonald's, and Gigi—my little girl—Gigi loves Chucky Chees—" His voice broke and he looked down for a moment, then back up again. Now he looked belligerent and angry, though not particularly at Fred. "You find them, Moran. You find my kids and get them back to me."

Candy Bjornsen had another nightmare. In it the phone rang constantly, even though she and Harry had taken the kids camping in the woods. She couldn't find the phone, but when she got up to go looking for it, she noticed the kids were gone. Then, over the shrilling of the phone, she heard Gigi crying and screaming and when she went looking for her, a tree fell on top of her. Pinned under the tree, she saw Gigi come running while a big bear who looked strangely familiar chased her. Hank ran behind the bear, trying to hit the bear with a stick. Harry was no place around.

Candy opened her eyes and she could still hear the bear

growling. The side of her face was sore and tender to the touch and one of her teeth felt sharp.

Something heavy was weighing her down.

Not a bear paw. She was in a bed, in a room with a carpet and walls. There was blood on the pillow, though, she saw that right away, and then she saw the arm across her middle. And then she remembered.

"Oh, shit," she moaned, and tried to slide out from under the arm without waking Shane, her new boyfriend, her supplier, the one who liked partying and didn't like kids. The one who had given her the pink ice tennis bracelet and the swollen jaw last night. She was still wearing the bracelet, but was otherwise nude. There were other tender places on her body.

The beating he'd given her was no more than she deserved, she knew that, but not for the reason he thought. He was pissed because when they'd made love after he gave her the bracelet, she accidentally called him Harry. What did he expect? She'd been married to the same man for ten years. It was a habit.

But she hadn't resisted or cried out when Shane walloped her, because she knew she'd earned every blow and then some. The drugs had run out for the time being, and she remembered leaving the kids—remembered the other times she had left the kids, and she wanted more than anything to be away from this man and back home, not at Bambi's, but in Forks, with the kids and Harry, the way it used to be.

She slid to the floor and froze until she heard Shane grunt softly in his sleep behind her. Then she pulled on his suit jacket—it was cold in the apartment—and padded out into the front room to use the phone. It rang and rang and rang but Bambi didn't answer. She must have turned it off, and even if the kids had made it home, they were forbidden to use the phone. There was one other option. She dialed 911.

Following the Trail

"Puyallup Center? That's Pierce County." Fred gave a low whistle. "Long way from downtown."

"That's what the lady said," the communications supervisor said. "Puyallup Center. She was wondering if two little kids who answered to the names of Hank and Gigi Bjornsen had been picked up from there and if so, had they gone home. Johansen went with Bowersox to question the merchants at the mall. Good thing we've started photographing kids when they're found wandering around like that. Saves time when they 'disappear' again, don't it?"

"That's a fact. Where was she calling from?"

The communications supervisor handed a card over to Moran. "Uh—yeah. Here's the number. It's registered to a Shane R. Triplehorn. Queen Anne Hill address."

"Did the caller identify herself?"

"Negative."

"Might be our runaway mama. I'd better take more backup on this one than a teddy bear."

"Hold on there, buddy. You may not remember, but there's quite a few of us in this room and gee, you got to share some of the crime with us or we're gonna feel left out. You got a previous engagement, remember? Smitty and I will go find mama. So you go liaise with SAR in Bellingham about the Quantrill girl. Poor guy. All that fresh air and stuff prob'ly going to rot your lungs."

"I'll try to be brave," Fred promised. "But, please, Chuck, if you find those kids, call up the SAR office, will you?"

"No problemo."

Twenty-two

SNO SAT ON the tarp along the bank of the river, listening to the water rush. There was a line in the water, but she wasn't eager for a fish to bite it. The guys were in their sweat lodge out in the woods, but she could hear the drums thumping across the clearing. They were comforting, like the bass vibrating from the rehearsal room at Raydir's, giving the house a heartbeat. This wasn't frenetic or fast, though, just a steady throb that was soothing, lulling her to sleep late at night. Well, that and something from Raydir's liquor cabinet.

She had been sitting there most of the day, watching the silver of the water's sparkle, listening to the ripple and the thump, smelling smoke rising from the sweat lodge, thinking about things.

"Hi there. Didn't know anybody else was out this far," a woman's voice said behind her.

She turned to see a washed-out-looking hippie woman with a backpack standing behind her, appearing like a ghost in the clearing where no one had been before.

"Sorry, didn't mean to startle you," the woman said. "My old man and me live up the river a ways. I'm just going to town to bring in supplies. Can I bring you anything?"

"Oh, no. No, thank you," Sno said.

"I didn't know anybody was staying around here now."

"We're only here for a while," Sno said. "Or rather, the guys are. I'm their guest."

"Oh, yeah?" the woman asked and raised an eyebrow.

"Nah, nothing like that. It's kind of a spiritual retreat for all of us."

"Cool. I don't suppose you'd need anything to help you stay, like, mellow?"

"Maybe," Sno said, with guilty pleasure. This would be a great time to get stoned. She didn't think the guys would get too bent out of shape if she did a little something, especially if she scored enough for all of them. "Whatcha got?"

"Whidbey Gold," the woman said, grinning. "Primo stuff. Grown by independent botanists under optimum conditions of light, soil and temperature. It's cheap too."

"Damn," Sno said. "I just forgot. I came from school and I don't have any money on me."

"How about your friends?"

"They're all occupied elsewhere."

"Bummer," the woman said. "But I'll tell you what, since we're neighbors and like that, I'll give you a sample joint, okay? When I come back, if you like it, maybe you can borrow some cash from one of your pals and I'll lay enough on you to keep you all in touch with the cosmos."

"That'd be really cool," Sno said, but she was starting to feel jumpy. There was something a little weirded-out about the woman, despite the fact that she seemed like a very cool and groovy person, as Grandma Hilda would have said. Something oddly familiar too. And distasteful. But hey, she was being nice. Free pot.

"Here you go. Don't bogart it. Save some for your buds, okay?"

"Sure," Sno said. "Thanks."

"No problem," the woman said.

"Have a good shopping trip," Sno said. "See you later."

She didn't see the woman's cruel smile as she turned away, or she would have recognized it.

A Plot Overheard

Exhausted from her long night and day, Rose left the office after work and walked down to the ferry terminal, paid her fare, glad to see a ferry in dock so she wouldn't have to wait, and followed the crowd of commuters aboard. She ached in every bone, her head felt filled with glue and feathers and light from sleeplessness, and she congratulated herself for finding a boat, even though something seemed vaguely strange about it. She was just thrilled to get out on the Sound, away from the city and, she hoped, far from the influence of fairy godmothers with designs on her time and energy.

As commuters often did, though usually later at night, she commandeered one of the long, padded benches for herself and stretched out on it with her coat under her head for a pillow.

She didn't notice who sat on the benches on either side of her, and the tops were too high to see over while she was lying down.

She drifted off quickly but she didn't sleep as soundly as she expected to. She kept seeing faces, Felicity's, Sno's, Fred's, Paula Reece's. She had, she knew, an overly developed sense of responsibility. Even Felicity accused her of that, though it didn't make the godmother any less willing to exploit it.

"So when can I see the pictures?" A man's voice carried to her ears, from the next bench.

"I haven't taken any yet but I'll get some tonight. You'll

like them, they're beautiful. And I was lucky to get a boy *and* a girl." There was a sort of drooling, lascivious tone to his voice that made Rose slide slowly up in her seat and listen a little more closely.

"There are possibilities there. How receptive do you think they'll be?"

"Oh, they'll be receptive," the other man said smoothly. "And they'll do what they're told."

Rose did not like this conversation. It was not so much what was said as the way it was said. Maybe it was just her profession that made her look at things this way, she told herself. Maybe she'd been seeing too many pederasts on a day-to-day basis. Probably this was just some father and a photographer getting ready to take the kids' pictures for the yearly Christmas card. But she didn't think so. And she wasn't sure what to do about it.

She listened a while longer but the conversation didn't get more or less incriminating. In fact, the men changed topics entirely to talk about politics—the school tax bill, from the sound of it. It was too dull. She tried to stay awake, but the night before had thoroughly done her in, and she drifted off again, only to be awakened by the announcement, "Now docking at Bainbridge Island. All drivers will please return to their cars now."

Bainbridge Island? Shit! Her car was in Bremerton. She had been so sleepy and confused she'd taken the wrong ferry. That was the thought that awakened her, but movement from the pederasts in the seat next door kept her alert. They must be getting off here. She peeked over the top of the seat to see the two men were leaving. Ducking back down for a moment so that they wouldn't spot her, she then rose and followed them to the stairs leading to the car deck. If she got their license numbers, the police could check them out, at least.

That was easier said than done, however, especially for someone in her blurry state of mind. The ferry was awash with commuters this time of the day, and she lost the two men in the crowd. She stepped aside and stood on the cement platform that separated the stairs from the main car deck and tried to look over the heads of the other passengers to spot her quarry. The two men looked much like the other business commuters—suits, haircuts, and she only saw their backs. One was white-haired and, she thought, bearded, medium size, relatively fit, the other brown-haired and of a similar size. Just when she thought it was hopeless, she saw the white-haired one climbing into a car, then spotted his companion in the driver's seat. Pushing her way through other commuters, she threaded through the other cars, now being started, to write down the license number. She had to fumble in her purse, standing in the river of thrumming cars, for a pen and something to write on and ended up scribbling the number on the flyleaf of her copy of Grimms'.

She finished getting it just as the first car began leaving. As she started scurrying out of the way of the cars, she glanced up to see the brown-haired man staring back at her in his rearview mirror.

She ducked back up the stairs and onto the ferry. What to do now? Her soul cried out for sleep, and there was often a commuter bus between Bainbridge and Bremerton. She debated for a moment and decided reluctantly against it. The bus would take her to Bremerton but not to either her house or her car, which was still at the ferry dock. No, the only thing left to do was to ride back to Seattle and get on the proper ferry the next time.

Who *were* those men? How urgent was this? Ought she to try to contact Fred's office from the boat? Well, no, because all she had really was a license number and a rather vague conversation, plus a feeling about the conversation that in her present state could just as easily be a delusion. Not that she thought it *was*. You just couldn't go to the police with your womanly intuition and some citizen's license number.

She supposed she'd been thinking too much lately of the missing kids—Sno and the Bjornsen children, Hank and Gigi. The man had said he was lucky to have a boy and a girl, and that fit the Bjornsens. So did jillions of other kids all over the country.

"She was taking down my number!" Throckmorton bellowed. "That stupid bitch was taking down *my* number." He watched the rearview mirror intently, but the girl had gone. He almost missed the crewman's signal to drive off the ferry and ashore.

"So what?" Hopkins said, as they drove up the hill to the parking light at the intersection for the former City of Winslow, now called Bainbridge, like the rest of the island. "She can't do anything with it."

"She heard us talking," Throckmorton said. "She must have been sitting near us . . ."

"Well, I did suggest we have our little talk in the car belowdecks," Hopkins told him. "But no, you had to have your—er—cupcakes and eat them too. Besides, unless she had a tape recorder with her, which I very much doubt, she has absolutely nothing on either of us."

"That's easy for you to say. You've got your own little secret hideaway. I'll be the one who's harassed. It's *my* license plate number she took. And I'm a prominent man, I have my career to think of." Panic rose in Throckmorton's voice.

Hopkins bitterly regretted at that moment having someone who knew his public life as well as Throckmorton did also privy to his secret. Always before, the graphic films he had of Throckmorton and various young subjects, as well as still photographs, had provided sufficient insurance of the man's silence about those of Hopkins's amusements he shared with fellow enthusiasts.

Of course, they knew nothing about the basement—the little game with the lock was suspended on those rare occasions when other adults were present. The door was only left unlocked as a variation of Russian roulette he liked to play with the children—naturally, he never risked it with the older, more sophisticated ones. Any of those who might be a threat went straight to the cage in the basement after they had been useful. But with the younger ones, it was interesting to see how long it would take them to disobey, how long their fear would keep them from trying to contact the authorities (he did have a special code on his phone required to get an outside line, just in case, but the children didn't know it), how frightened of him they would be when he came home. A little hide-and-seek added a certain fillip to the other activities.

This could be something rather more serious, however, and they would be involved together. Hopkins didn't much like that but since he had pleasanter pressing matters awaiting him in his very private residence, he decided to await further developments before making a decision on this situation.

"You think I'm not concerned about the implications for my own career?" Hopkins asked, but his mind was working much faster than his calm and soothing speech indicated. "Tell you what. Turn here."

"What? I thought you were coming back to my place to give me the particulars."

"I was, but since you're so concerned about this, I thought we should try to cruise the parking lot and look for the woman coming off the ferry. Obviously, she wasn't driving or she would have gone to her car instead of back upstairs."

"Makes sense." Throckmorton pulled back into the parking lot.

"What did she look like? I didn't see her."

"Curly brown hair and dressed in gray," Throckmorton answered. "That was all I could make out in the mirror."

The description reminded Hopkins of someone he had seen that day enough for him to be even more uneasy than he had been before. "She doesn't seem to be getting off."

"You don't think she's going to make a report in Seattle, do you?"

"Why would she do that? But I'll tell you what. You have a car phone, don't you?"

"Of course."

"I'll go back to Seattle and look for her on the ferry. If I see her, I'll find out where she lives, where she's going, and deal with it. If you see her, you take care of it here. Either way, I'll call your car phone in forty-five minutes and find out if you've learned anything or tell you what I've learned."

"Fine, but we'll have to be discreet. You know how easily monitored car phones are. As a matter of fact, it's better if you call me at home. My wife's on business in Portland."

"How clever of you to think about being overheard at this late hour," Hopkins said sarcastically, then added, "Try not to get too paranoid over this. It's probably nothing. Perhaps license plates are a hobby of hers."

"Norman?"

"Yes?" Hopkins asked.

"What did you mean when you said deal with it?"

Hopkins smiled politely, as if telling a clerical worker how to handle paperwork. "Use your own judgment."

*   *   *

On the trip back, Rose thought, she could at least get some rest. There were very few people on the return trip, and once more she stretched out on a black padded bench, this one with a table and a shoulder-high privacy wall between it and the bench on the opposite side.

She was too sleepy to pay proper attention to where her purse was, and too fast asleep to notice when it was moved, searched and replaced.

She did notice, however, when the ferry docked in Seattle, that one of the few other passengers on board looked very much like the elder of the two men she had followed to the car deck. Furthermore, she had the distinct impression that he was aware of her behind him, though she couldn't say why. And there was something familiar about the stiffness of his shoulders and the way he carried his head.

Never mind. She would call Fred, by which time she could get on the Bremerton ferry and go home.

However, the phone at the ferry terminal was out of order, so unless she wanted to use the ship-to-shore, she'd have to wait until she got home.

By that time the Bremerton passenger ferry was docking, and she boarded and slept sitting up, since the benches were all occupied.

Hopkins had found the girl easily enough—he hadn't even needed the description once he saw her sleeping at the table benches in the stern of the boat, but she fit it well enough. He had noticed earlier in the day that the gray pants suit looked far too expensive for someone on her salary. So, Ms.—Rose something—was going to cause him trouble personally as well as being a thorn in his side professionally. He had taken care of the professional end earlier that day, and he could take care of this as well, if need be. Better if he delegated that little task though.

Her purse was within reach. He rifled it as quickly as possible, but it was rather large, and made heavy by a book of fairy tales. He lifted this and it dropped open. The license number was written on the flyleaf. While pretending to read the book, he quietly tore out the page and slipped it in his pocket.

Searching her wallet was somewhat trickier, even though the stern was almost deserted. Just when he had found her driver's license and was getting ready to note the number and her address, a crewman came in with a vacuum cleaner and began vacuuming the floors a couple of yards away.

Hopkins pocketed the license along with the page of the book, and, making a face as if the noise was bothering him, moved to the bow of the boat and stayed in the crowded cafeteria until the ferry returned to its Seattle terminal berth and he saw the girl disembark with the meager straggle of other passengers.

Waiting to board were hordes of commuters returning to Bainbridge, but the girl marched past these. Hopkins expected her to go down the steps to the street level or cross the overpass tunnel to First and Marion, but she did neither. Instead, she reentered the terminal and promptly disappeared through the ticket gate to the Bremerton area. Why had she taken two boats? It must mean she'd deliberately been spying on them! He checked the driver's license in her pocket. At least there was a good reason for her to go to Bremerton. She lived there.

Not wanting her to spot him again, he left the terminal and walked over to the Federal Building at First and Marion to make his call from one of the phone booths. He got Throckmorton's answering machine, which fortunately had a very businesslike message instead of something cute and prolonged, with music.

"Hi there, yer honor," he said in a breezy, folksy voice not easily recognized as his own. "This is Samson's Nursery in Bremerton calling you about that rosebush you wanted. It's in but it's going to take a lot of pruning." He checked the address on the girl's license: 1249 Beach Drive. He couldn't give too many clues and he assumed she was listed in the book. "It'll be $12.49 with tax. Call me if you have any trouble finding us again. Just drive along the beach till you see our sign." As an afterthought he added the ubiquitous, "Have a nice day."

Hank poked into the upstairs rooms. Besides his bedroom and Gigi's, there was what looked like a nursery for little babies and a master bedroom with a mirror on the ceiling and bathrooms for every bedroom.

He had to go while he was in the master bedroom and just because it was close, he decided to use the john there. The door was tightly closed and there was a red light beside it. Was that how you knew if somebody was already in there? Hank wondered. Couldn't they just say so?

He cracked the door open. It wasn't shiny and tiled and mirrored as he expected, but black inside, dark, and it smelled funny, like chemicals, and had clotheslines strung with hanging things. There was the sound of dripping. His fingers automatically found a light switch in the usual place beside the door and he flipped it.

The flapping things were pictures! Oh, so that was it. The guy was a photographer and this was the darkroom. Oops. Maybe he shouldn't have turned on the light, Hank thought. He knew enough about darkrooms from TV that you weren't supposed to go in them because pictures were developed in there and the light could hurt them. He peered into the trays in the bathtub, but it didn't look to him like there was anything in there. How about the hanging ones, could they be hurt?

He stared up at the clotheslines over his head and tried to make out if the pictures were okay—they all looked like naked baby pictures at first, and then he saw that some of the naked kids weren't infants and then that there were men with the kids. Doing stuff. Weird stuff. Some of the kids in the pictures were crying and some were tied up.

He knew right then that he and Gigi had to get away, had to go find a cop even if they couldn't find Mom.

He tried to remember if they had driven past a mall or a shopping strip or a town of any kind on the way to the man's house. He thought there might be a 7-Eleven down the street.

"C'mon, Gigi, we gotta go," he said. And just then, they heard the car drive up.

"Why?" she asked. "I wanna make cookies."

"No, you don't," he said. "The man's a slime bag. He's going to do bad things to us."

"Is he a pedalist?" she asked, nodding at the television. "Susan Buchanan says pedalists do sexy things to kids. I guess like Mama does at the dance place except it's not just dancing. Pedalists hurt you and maybe even kill you. And, brother, you know last night when I hurt?"

"Tell me later, Gig. We gotta hurry now," Hank urged. He grabbed her hand and dragged her through the kitchen to the garage door as he heard the front door open, and pushed the garage door carefully behind them. They could hide behind the gingerbread cutouts, but he'd be sure to find them then, as soon as he turned on the lights.

There was the basement door, nothing between them and a place to hide except that little key in the lock. The one place the man had said not to go. Why not? Then he heard

the phone ringing and thought he knew. He didn't want
them to go down there and use the phone to call the police.
Let people know who they were. Hank thought Gigi was
right and the man who had seemed so nice *was* actually one
of those creepy pedalists. A dirty old man who did nasty
things to kids. He might already have gotten to Gigi.

Dragging his sister with him, Hank crossed to the basement door and turned the key in the lock. It opened easily.

He tugged Gigi after him with a "shhh" and closed the
door behind them quietly. He started to go back and take
the key, but he was afraid the man would see it missing
and know immediately where they were. He didn't feel any
lock hole on the inside of the door so he could lock them
in either, so the key wouldn't have helped. It was very dark
in there, and it smelled worse than the sewer, worse than a
dead rabbit lying on the road, worse than the beach at low
tide. The phone had stopped ringing.

"Peeyew," Gigi whispered but just then the man's voice
called out.

"Hank? Gigi? Where are you? I have a surprise for you.
Where are you? Taking naps, maybe?" The voice faded.

"Quick," Hank said. "He's going upstairs. Let's go
downstairs while he's going upstairs and he won't hear
us."

"It's *dark*," Gigi whimpered.

"The phone is down there," Hank said. He had to hand
it to his little sister. She shut up immediately.

But by the time they felt their way carefully to the bottom of the stairs, Hank heard the door from the kitchen to
the garage open.

"Hey, kids! I like hide-and-seek as much as anybody, but
I need you to come out now."

He was trying not to sound mad but Hank could tell that

he was. There was a shuffling of boards, crashes, curses and then silence.

Hank and Gigi scooted over behind the stairs. They could hear the hum of a freezer and felt its outlines and its coolness. They ducked behind it and hid, waiting, beneath the stairs. They could hardly breathe, it stank so bad down there.

The door opened.

"Oh, no," the man said. "Oh, no. I bet I know where you are. You've done it now. You went the one place I told you not to in my whole house. You rotten kids! I told you not to come down here. I told you that key was in the lock for a reason. I could have taken it out, but I *trusted* you and you let me down. I only wanted you to stay upstairs for your own good. There are things down here that could hurt you. But I'll tell you what, if you come on out now, come back up the stairs in the dark, all by yourselves, I'll forget all about this. We'll make cookies, we'll talk, maybe we'll even have a party. Wouldn't that be fun? But you've got to come out first."

Gigi shifted beside Hank, and he tried to put his hand over her mouth and instead hit her in the face.

"Ouch!" she said.

"Oh, kids. I've been working all day. I'm too tired to play hide-and-seek with you. Come on up the stairs now and be good. I hear you. I know you're down there. You disobeyed me. I told you this room was locked."

His foot fell on the first step. "Come on, now. Don't make me come down after you."

Hank thought fast. He was scared of the man, but coming down here had been a mistake. There was no door down here, and he couldn't find the phone in the dark. They'd have a better chance later. Down here nobody could even hear them if they screamed.

"We were playing," Hank called up. "We're sorry, mister, but we were playing hide-and-seek and my stupid little sister came down here to hide. I guess she sort of turned the key by accident and didn't know it was the door you said not to open. Turn on the light so we can come upstairs without hurting ourselves. We're real hungry."

"Me too," the man said. "But I'd rather not turn on the light. You got down there in the dark, didn't you?"

"Oh, no," Hank said. "We turned on the light, then turned it off again."

"Liar, liar, pants on fire," the man chanted. "You didn't turn on the light. Don't lie to me, Hank. I don't like little boys who lie."

Gigi began to whimper again, then to cry, then to howl. "Please, mister, turn on the light. My sister's really scared. We'll come up the stairs, but we can't see." Hank didn't want to face the man on the stairs in the dark. He stood up and told Gigi to shut up and pulled her around the corner of the freezer.

"Too bad. I told you and told you not to come down here."

"It was an accident. We're sorry. But the room wasn't locked. Really. Please, turn on the light."

"Have it your way," the man said. "We were going to play nice games that feel good, but the games are going to be rougher now because you disobeyed me. I just wanted to see if you were good children who deserved presents or more lying, sneaking little brats who need to be taught a lesson." The light flipped on, and as soon as their eyes adjusted to it, both kids began screaming. Above them, floating down over the terrible sights they saw all around them, like something out of a horror movie, the man's voice said calmly, "Meet my former pupils. They wouldn't stay out of the basement either."

Robbed

Rose dragged herself into her house, and was halfway to bed before she remembered that she needed to call Fred's office to give him the license number. She was actually relieved to be able to leave a message, since she didn't have to explain the whole thing that way. She could simply leave her name and number and tell him that she thought he should check out the number she had written down. But when she dipped into her purse for the Grimms' to leave the number, she found that the flyleaf had been torn out. She also noticed that all of her ID cards had been dumped out of her wallet and were scattered over the bottom of her somewhat oversize handbag.

She supposed in her present sleepy state she could have done that herself, but she had a large, chilly doubt about that. Instead of leaving the number she said, "I— Fred, this is Rose. I think I've been robbed. On the ferry. I had a license number I wanted you to check out, only it's missing now. I'll call you back later or you call me." She pawed through the cards and found all of her credit cards. No money was missing from her purse. Her driver's license was gone, though.

She had done all she could for the moment, and she was still too tired to be able to function. Wearily, she threw her purse on the floor and flopped onto the bed, where she was promptly pounced on by three very vocal and active cats. For once she ignored them.

Twenty-three

THE "BAD JUJU" scent faded until Felicity could no longer detect it as she and Haisley turned off the highway five miles north of Bellingham to the search-and-rescue office. One of the women in SARA—the Search and Rescue Auxiliary—had driven Haisley's 4X4 to the office so that he could join the group immediately.

Felicity asked Haisley if she could possibly borrow his bike to get around town.

"If it was anybody else . . ." Haisley began. "But, bein' as how it's you, take it. Just bring it back here when you're done or if you want to ride it back to Seattle, call me and I'll come and pick it up."

"You always were a sweet boy," she said, kissing his furred cheek. "And a brave one too. I do hope you find that girl."

"Me too, Godmother, me too," Haisley said, but he was already heading for the headquarters building to start loading supplies in his vehicle.

Felicity paused only long enough to smell the faint whiff of bad magic still drifting toward her from the east, then revved up the bike, patted the pocket with Bobby in it and took off for the forest.

Normally she would have left the search and so forth to the thaumaturgically challenged, as they were called these days rather than mere mortals or mundanes. However, this whole matter was far more complicated than she anticipated.

Although she was a far cry from the popular conception of a flying fairy godmother borne aloft by gauzy appendages sprouting from her shoulder blades, Felicity realized she was nonetheless winging it at this point. The problem was, the stories kept mutating. They were rather like viruses in that respect. She was beginning to feel less like everyone's surefire chance and last great hope and more like a shot in the dark, which might or might not accurately target the heart of a problem with some sort of assistance.

Whatever was she to do for Dico Miller? Puss didn't seem to have the magic she had had in the old days, before mass media, when people were far less used to talking animals and far more respectful. These days, people assumed the creature was some sort of technological trick, she supposed. Ding had not turned out well, either.

And then there was Cindy Ellis. What to do about her? No doubt the stepsisters would see to it that she lost her job. Cindy had come so far toward taking care of herself, getting a skill, finding love, even equine love and building her own self-esteem. It would be a shame to have all of that taken from her because an inept fairy godmother was busy doing the job brave people like Haisley and his search-and-rescue friends had trained for. But then, brave people didn't have toads with inside information, as she did.

She smiled, thinking of Haisley. A very nice man, in spite of the rather ferocious biker persona. At the last minute, he had insisted on playing the gallant and lending her his leather jacket as well, though she was perfectly capable of altering her attire—that bit of magic was one of the rather basic tools of godmotherdom, and gave her a distinct advantage over, say, Superman, who needed a phone booth. One had one's image to live up to, after all. But she accepted the jacket so as not to hurt Haisley's feelings. She had been rather surprised to see him as a biker, rather than a CEO or something, after all the attention she had given him during his childhood as an Army brat in Germany, where his father, a heavy drinker, began beating him. She saw something fine in him then, and she saw it now. Of course, it was perfectly feasible these days that he was both a biker *and* a CEO. They hadn't discussed his career.

That was one of the problems with these times, she decided. People changed roles, changed careers, changed families so many times, and there were such a *lot* of them, some good, some bad, most extremely mixed, that it was rather difficult at times to know with whom you were dealing.

In the old days, despite all the wars and plagues and such, life had a slower pace and things were a bit more boring on most days, so that the pivotal people and the pivotal incidents in their lives stood out from the crowd. You always knew who everybody was back then, and the mean-natured ones were not often salvageable and the better-natured ones were not subject to so many temptations to go bad.

Like Ding and his gang or, for that matter, Sno Quantrill, who should be as pure as the driven snow, but who in fact, according to the papers, had had a few problems with drugs. Ah, for the old days, when one could intervene and manage a crisis before the crises of several other stories intruded upon one when one had not finished with the first.

As she told Rose, the individual problems were no different than they'd ever been but because of the larger population, they got jumbled and doubled and tripled up until it was hard to tell whether you were supposed to change someone's dress and give them magic footwear, put them to sleep for a hundred years or turn them from a marionette into a real boy.

She drove past the malls lining the highway near Bellingham and followed the wide thread of highway until it narrowed, farther out into the country, paralleling the tumbling blue Nooksack River much of the way.

The foul scent of psychic power gone wrong became stronger and pulled her more surely the farther they went, past Maple Falls and into the Snoqualmie National Forest, on past the town of Glacier. As they zoomed through Glacier, however, the smell suddenly became overpowering as a van passed them in the westbound lane. Felicity sighed. So. The stepmother had come, had done the deed.

She followed the fading scent as far as the deserted state park facility and stopped.

Parking the bike, she extracted the toad from the pocket of her inner garment, and held him aloft to give him a good look around.

"Does this look familiar, Bobby?" she asked. "One reedeep if yes, two reedeeps if no."

Silence. Godmothers were fairly tireless, but she had had a particularly full night and no sleep since, followed by an exhilarating but fatiguingly lengthy motorcycle journey. She was in no mood to tolerate amphibian stubbornness. Sighing a deep, put-upon sigh, she resorted to tougher tactics.

"Bobby, it pains me to resort to this, but if you fail to cooperate, you will compound your foolishness in losing your form for seven years by forcing me to call upon Puss. Normally I hate to threaten people, but you must admit it's only just, since by your actions you've threatened the life of an innocent—very well, relatively innocent—girl. It would inconvenience me greatly to have to return to Seattle and call Puss before I can convince you to show me where you lost her. I am already most displeased with you since, as you know, you have been through this in many lives.

"Perhaps you don't realize all the implications of your actions. You see, most people learn from their past mistakes and in future lives go on to grow into better people. Others, who don't, become ogres. Puss, if you'll recall, has her ways of dealing with ogres. So what do you say?"

"Reedeep."

"Yes, I rather thought so. Reedeep, indeed. Now then, I'm going to let you go, and you're free to hop away and be a toad for the rest of your life if you like. But if you'd like any sort of advancement opportunities in your present position at all, I advise you to stay close to me and be of all possible assistance in locating this girl. Understood?"

"Reedeep."

"It's amazing how quickly one picks up languages in the company of a native speaker. I'm pleased you feel that way. Very well, you lead and I will walk behind you. We'd best leave Haisley's bike here lest I accidentally squash you."

The toad answered that by making a giant leap forward, leading her up the road. Felicity, pocketing Haisley's keys, trod carefully behind the amphibian.

The walk was long, and it was nearing evening now. The wind picked up and blew fresh snow around, covering the trail made by the tracks of the van that had passed them in Glacier. Felicity altered her footgear so that it had tall warm wrappings and extra socks and soles that gripped even on ice. She was very glad for Haisley's jacket, not because she couldn't come up with one of her own, but because a generous gift was always warming. She pulled white woolly mittens and a faux silver fox hat from her pockets, donned them and kept walking. The tire tracks stopped altogether then and Bobby hopped forward, onto a narrow trail, just wide enough for a motorcycle, leading into the forest. In the snow that had penetrated the needles of the trees to carpet the ground around them, Felicity saw the occasional track of a bike. The van had had one strapped to its back.

At a certain point on the trail, pretty much indistinguishable from any other point, Bobby stopped and reedeeped meaningfully. Here Felicity stopped as well, sniffing the miasma of Gerardine's negativity lingering like the stench of vomit in the snow-cleansed air.

"Is this where Sno escaped you?" she asked the toad, who reedeeped in the affirmative.

"And I don't suppose you have any idea where she might be now?"

The toad gave her two rather mournful reedeeps.

Felicity sat down on a fallen log and searched for an impression of the girl. She felt some powerful emanations coming from the southeast, but they were masculine. Underlying these was a persistent aching numbness masking other emotions; fear, anger, despair? Possibly the girl, but the overlay was too strong to tell. It wasn't far, though, and if the emotions did belong to the girl, at least she was alive. For now. If the woman in the van had made contact, the girl was in danger, but the men were close, they were protective. Felicity was not overly concerned. The wicked stepmother's tricks had been thwarted before, and they could be thwarted again. She stood up and dusted off her seat and stuck Bobby back in her pocket.

"Well, then. I suppose what I need now is a story other than the literal truth to tell the searchers and help point them in the right direction. And something rather obvious to mark this spot."

A little later, at a phone booth in Glacier, she placed a call to the Whatcom County Sheriff. Somewhat to her surprise, a voice said, "Sheriff's Department, Sergeant Moran speaking."

"Sergeant Fred Moran of the King County Police?" she asked before she thought about it. She had read Rose like a book, though of course she was polite enough to say nothing, and knew about Rose's feelings for Moran. Now, even on the phone lines, she read the same sort of feeling in his heart for Rose, and it made her proud.

Moran's had been a very dramatic case, and she enjoyed remembering herself in her role as a benevolent version of the Snow Queen, preserving the grief-stricken boy until the ice would melt from his heart so it could one day, now, hold love. Felicity sighed a deeply satisfied sigh. She was a sentimentalist, a romantic, loved cute animals and adored Disney's movies, if not the company's politics. So sue her. She was a fairy godmother, and it went with the territory. Somebody had to believe in something these days, and she believed in love.

"Yes, ma'am. What can I do for you?"

"Sergeant, I heard on television about your search and I just wanted you to know that—well, I'm an amateur astronomer, you see, and I was out with my telescope in a campground just past the town of Glacier, on the way toward Mount Baker, when I saw a motorcyclist pass by. There was a young girl wearing a red outfit and a helmet riding behind him. I thought this was a little strange, you know, because the poor girl didn't have on slacks, and I thought it was most inappropriate. As I was returning to the highway, about an hour later, a similar motorcycle passed me on the highway, but there was no girl. I also thought the rider looked rather distressed, and I wondered where the girl had gone. I suppose I should have called then, but one always thinks there's a rational explanation and, er"—this was the biggest lie in the whole call—"doesn't want to get involved. I hope that is of some help to you now."

"It is, ma'am, thank you. That should help a lot. Now, then, may I have your name, address and phone number?"

But Felicity had already hung up, a smile of satisfaction playing on her lips.

Anonymous or not, her information was acted upon promptly. As she roared through Maple Falls, she passed a small convoy of 4X4's heading toward Glacier and points beyond. She caught a brief impression of Haisley's mind, jazzed up, ready to spend the night in his car, searching by headlamp until it was time to curl up under a blanket in his front seat. He was not a CEO after all, but after a rough start he had turned into a very good and caring man. The touch with his mind made Felicity more cheerful than she had felt in some time, ready to take on the problems of the world single-handed if need be. Though with people like Rose and Haisley and Fred around, her battles would never be fought without comrades.

Gigi kept screaming and screaming and Hank wanted to throw up as the light flooded the basement room. It looked like something out of one of the horror movies Hank and Gigi's parents would have never let them watch, back in the days when they still cared.

The walls were ringed with shelves, upon which sat big gallon mayonnaise jars with distorted heads floating in them. The telephones were there, four of them, next to rows of teeth on a big, long, bloodstained table, along with neat piles of bloody clothing, sorted into shirts, pants and underclothes. In one corner of the room, a long, rectangular hole the size of a grave had been dug, and this was filled with white stuff from which the strong chemical smell came. And dark brown stains were splattered everywhere. *Blood* stains.

Now that they weren't running, they noticed other smells too—it reeked as if somebody had peed and shit their pants. Probably the people whose heads had been cut off.

"You see what happens to disobedient boys and girls who don't do what they're told after their friend has been so kind to them?" the man asked, coming down the stairs, slowly, one at a time. He crossed to the table containing all the teeth, calmly picked up a portable telephone and tucked it in his jacket pocket before turning to the cell with an evil grin.

They kept screaming and crying, Gigi's crying choking into short, gasping sobs as the man came down the last step and toward them.

"Well, well, how convenient," he said. That was when Hank noticed that their hiding place under the stairs behind the freezer was really a little room. There was a barred door standing ajar.

The man reached into his pocket. Hank thought he would pull out a gun, but instead he pulled out two pairs of handcuffs. "See, Hank? I told you I'd let you play with these. You can get very well acquainted with them."

Hank tried to duck and wiggle away but the man was fast and caught him. He was very strong for such an old guy. He cuffed one of Hank's hands to one of the bars, and the other hand to another. "If you're good, I'll give you something to eat and drink from time to time and let you keep your clothes on until I say otherwise. Meanwhile, I think you're a bad influence on your little sister here, so she and I are going upstairs. I have a few things to teach her."

"Nooo!" Gigi howled and hit at him but she was no match for the man. Hank tried to kick him but the man scooped Gigi up under one arm and carried her, squirming and screaming, back up the stairs.

Twenty-four

CINDY WAS JUST bedding down, spreading her sleeping bag in the stall next to Punkin's, when she heard the rumble of a motorcycle's engine outside the stable. She pulled her hacking jacket on over her T-shirt and jeans and slipped into her moccasins. Who could this be? Pam and Perdita come to play some nasty trick? A scout for a gang of drug-crazed bikers come to rape and murder her? It wasn't Pill, because he didn't own a motorcycle. Nobody else had a reason to be here late at night. She grabbed a pitchfork and held it at the ready as she peeked around the barn door, trying to see past the glare of the headlamp to make out the rider. The rider dismounted then and stood silhouetted by the light, legs akimbo, helmet under the arm, a scarf flying from the neckline of a leather jacket. Very Lindbergh.

"Cindy Ellis? I know you're in there." Ooops. Very Amelia Earhart.

"Who is it?" Cindy asked. A woman's voice, given Cindy's family situation, was not necessarily reassuring, and she couldn't tell to whom the voice belonged because of the noise of the engine, which the woman had neglected to shut off.

"It's Felicity Fortune, and there's not a moment to spare. I can't imagine why you're hanging around here when there's work to be done, lives to be saved."

"Lives?" Cindy stepped out into the light. "Can you shut that thing off?"

"I beg your pardon. I got caught up in the urgency of the moment. As I said, lives are at stake! There's a massive search going on, and Search and Rescue are badly understaffed. They desperately need volunteers, and your horsemanship skills would be of great use."

"Felicity, I appreciate your concern, but I don't even have access to a rideable horse. Punkin hasn't got a new shoe to fit his corn yet. Besides, I couldn't ride all the way up there. I'd need a horse trailer. I don't have any gear . . . shoot, I don't even have a home, thanks to the three P's."

"Details, details!" Felicity said with an airy wave of her hand. "In the wise words of one of my former godchildren, dear, 'Don't sweat the small stuff.' "

"But, Felicity . . ."

"I wouldn't dream of letting darling Punkin miss this opportunity to show his stuff. Bring him out here, please."

Puzzled, Cindy went to Punkin's stall, put a hackamore on him, and led him out of the stable.

"Now, then, which hoof is involved?"

"Left front," Cindy said.

"Very well." She looked pointedly at Punkin's feet for a moment, and the air between her face and Punkin seemed to shimmer and shift, as if alive with sound waves made visible. When Felicity looked back up, she said, "Now, then, that's a fine job of blacksmithing if I do say so myself. Get on his back and walk him around. We must make sure the strain of being improperly shod hasn't hurt him."

Cindy did as she was told, and found to her relief and pleasure that Punkin now was able to walk, even trot, without a limp or a trace of hesitation. Sliding off his back with a pleased grin, she said to Felicity, "Wow! How'd you do that?"

"We Godmothers are nothing if not versatile. It isn't iron, of course. Our founder has never quite reconciled herself to iron, but it's sturdy stuff and the spell should be good for at least twenty-four hours. Now, then, you must join the search party on the Mount Baker Highway with all possible dispatch. I noticed that they were inadequately equipped with horses and had very few volunteers despite the urgency of the search. More may be joining tomorrow, but by then it could be too late for poor Sno."

"But I can't ride Punkin all the way up there tonight!" Cindy said.

"Of course not. You must have a horse trailer." She looked around, her gaze finally reluctantly returning to Haisley's bike. "Well, there's nothing else to do, is there? This is going to take a great deal of transformation magic, hideously expensive, but what must be done must be done. The usual hour for the end of the spell is midnight, but since we're making a late start, it will have to be dawn in this case."

"I'm afraid I don't quite follow," Cindy said. Maybe Punkin's improvement was an illusion. Maybe this woman was out of her gourd. She seemed nice enough, but . . .

"Holy cow!" Cindy cried, as the motorcycle Felicity had ridden in on was suddenly transformed into a four-wheel-drive Toyota Land Cruiser with a state-of-the-art one-horse trailer already hitched to the back.

"You haven't time to change now, dear, but you'll find good hiking boots, a woollen cap and mittens, long underwear, and a down jacket—oh, and extra socks and some freeze-dried food and a flashlight, inside. I trust you can provide your own sleeping bag."

"Sure!"

"Find Haisley Henderson and tell him Felicity Fortune sent you. He'll see to it that you get on with the search team. Pay particular attention to the area in and around the Shuksan campground and picnic area, past the ruined State Registry Department and restrooms. If you are not assigned to that area, see to it that it is not overlooked and is inspected most thoroughly. I'm sure the searchers are very competent, but they have quite a large area to cover. If you are ignored, which I doubt given the caliber of people on the search, inform a Mr. Lightner, the tracker, that you were tipped off by the lady who sent in an anonymous report to Sergeant Moran. Tell them she was very shy, but anxious that all of her evidence be taken into consideration. Also, suggest that the girl may have found refuge with other persons camping in the area for a prolonged period. Now, then, off with you!"

"But, what about you? This is—was—your transportation."

"I borrowed it from Haisley. It will revert to its original form as his motorcycle at dawn. Meanwhile, I have a few other things to do, and I can bloody well take a cab. Oh, by the way, what is your stepmother's address?"

Sno decided to save the joint until she really needed it. She tucked it in the pocket of the flannel shirt she had borrowed from Maurice and continued watching the river, wondering what it would be like to live up here for good, far away from people or maybe with only one other person, and have to backpack your supplies back and forth from town. She wasn't sure she'd like it, but living along this river in the snow and the fir trees was sure more appealing than going back to Raydir's. Funny, that hippie woman was probably the same age, size and weight as Gerardine, but how different they were. Anyhow, they seemed that way. Maybe a few of the right drugs at the right time in her life would have done Gerardine some good.

Just then the line began to bob, and she grabbed the pole and started reeling in a fish. It was a very big fish and almost dragged her into the river, and without knowing it, she began squealing and yelping with excitement as she splashed in the icy water and back out into the snow, trying to land her catch.

Half-naked guys poured out of the woods and down to the bank to help her.

Dinner that night was fresh fish rolled in bran flake crumbs and seasoned according to a recipe Doc said he got from his grandpa.

Sno felt fine for a while, and then she was bummed at the thought of ever having to leave this place. The guys were doing some more after-dinner bonding around the fireplace, a process which seemed to involve talking about guns by model numbers and flamboyant names. These were really good guys, but she was personally on the other side of the gun issue. For that matter, she was against the war in Vietnam—retrospectively, that was. But she didn't want to hurt their feelings, so she slipped on Maurice's multicolor down jacket, stepped outside into the frosty, star-filled silence of the night, and strolled toward the river, fishing the joint out of her pocket as she went. Halfway there, she stopped to light up.

Invisible Writing

Rose awoke after deep and murky dreams to the sound of her own voice answering the telephone, which was what that ringing in her dreams had been. Glancing at her bedside clock, she saw that it was only about eight o'clock in the evening. She had come right home, fed the cats and fallen into bed.

She was still trying to wake up when her message finished. If it was an important message, she'd grab the bedside phone, but she wasn't about to wake up for just anybody.

However, to her annoyance, she couldn't make out whose voice was on the other line. It had a funny, muffled quality to it, and the words weren't very clear.

She groped for the phone, knocked it off, retrieved it and hung it up as the message ended. Wearily she dragged herself erect and padded down the stairs to the hall where she kept her machine. She punched the button, and the muffled voice began again.

"Spying on others isn't nice, Rose Samson. But if you spy on us, then we'll have to spy on you. We know where you live. We know where you work. And we know how to get ahold of you if we want to. Stay out of what doesn't concern you, or you'll be sorry."

Well, if that wasn't adding insult to injury! Rifle her purse, take away her puny little piece of evidence, and her driver's license too, dammit, which was no doubt how they traced her. They wouldn't get away with that.

So she was good and mad when the phone rang a second time. She picked it up and said "Yeah?" into it.

"Rosie? It's Fred. I'm up in Bellingham, at Search and Rescue headquarters. We finally got a couple of breaks just in the last few hours. First, we got a call in Seattle from a woman who said Gigi and Hank had been dropped off at Puyallup Center. A couple of officers are out on that now and also trying to pick up the caller. If it's the mother, we may be able to find the kids quicker. Then another woman called here just now and said she'd seen a motorcyclist and a girl in red out past Glacier. That narrows our search down to only a few thousand square miles."

"Oh. Good, that's real good news," she murmured automatically.

"You sound funny. Are you okay? What's this about you getting robbed?"

"Could be I have something on Hank and Gigi too, or it could be just a coincidence, but I had a threatening message left on my answering machine. It wasn't just a prank. I— well, I was so sleepy I got on the wrong ferry and went to Bainbridge before I remembered I left the car in Bremerton last night. While I was riding over, I overheard two guys talking on the ferry. Call it an occupational hazard, but it seemed to me they were discussing a pair of children, a boy and a girl, and just from the way they were talking, I couldn't help feeling these guys were pederasts."

"Whoa, and they think cops are suspicious."

"I know, I know. But with the Bjornsen kids missing again—well, anyhow, it was on my mind, and I was afraid if I didn't follow up I'd hate myself later so I followed them to their car."

"You *what*?"

"Calm down, I didn't ask for a ride or anything. I just copied down a license number. Only they saw me. And I think one of them followed me back to the ferry terminal, got on the Bremerton Ferry after me and took my driver's license out of my purse while I was sleeping. Anyway, it's gone. And there was this weird message on my phone machine."

"Oh, yeah? How weird?" he asked with a rather comical leer in his voice.

"Well, not that kinda weird. Not if it was the guys I heard on the ferry. I'm over the hill for that type." She recognized his levity as an attempt to relieve tension—a certain black sense of humor was common to both social services professionals and cops as well as nurses and, she supposed, soldiers and anyone else whose work fell into the "It's a dirty job but somebody's got to do it" category.

"What did these two guys look like?"

"They were, you know, suits. Businessmen, executives, yuppies. One was younger, middle-aged, the other was older, with white hair and I think a beard. I just got vague impressions, really. I was very sleepy and mostly I just saw the backs of their heads and heard their voices. I caught a glimpse of the face of one of them in the rearview mirror, but that was all. I was so out of it, in fact, that I probably would have forgotten the whole thing except for losing my license and the threatening call."

"Sounds like it's a good thing you didn't. Do you still have that license number?"

"No, that was the other thing. I wrote it down in a book, and they tore the page out. But wait a sec. I've got an idea." She rummaged in her purse again for the torn book, and carried the phone with her while she went into the room she used as a library. She was in search of one pencil with an unbroken lead, and at length she found one.

"You okay?" Fred asked.

"Yeah. Just a minute. I think I can have the number for you after all. Did you ever make rubbings of numbers and writing from impressions on the page in back of a torn-out page?"

"What do you mean, did I ever? That's part of Detecting One-oh-one."

"Oops. Sorry, I'm still half asleep. Forgot I was talking to a professional." She rubbed the side of the pencil lead lightly on the page that had been behind the torn one. The numbers emerged, white against the gray of the pencil lead, just above the words "Once upon a time."

"Here it is. JZZ 666."

He double-checked it with her and said, "Okay, I'm going to call back to the office and ask them to trace this. Meanwhile, you better report it to the local constabulary."

"I will. But *mañana*. Please. I'm a little weirded out, but that's not really why I called you. I thought it might be a lead—he *did* talk about 'finding' a boy and a girl. Could be our missing kids."

"And of course, it could also be wishful thinking."

"I've been having some unusual luck where wishful thinking is concerned these days," Rose told him.

"Really?" he asked in a suddenly softer voice. "I've been doing some myself, but I don't know how much luck I'm having." A beat of silence, then, more briskly, "Anyhow, I'll get that number traced, but you stay out of it from now on, okay? Tomorrow somebody can check up on it and see if this guy can help us with our enquiries, as they say, but meanwhile *you* keep your doors and windows locked tight. You hear? Leave the rough stuff to us."

"Yes, officer. But I think they're just trying to scare me. They'll know soon enough that all the evidence I've got has already been passed on, and there's no other reason for them to pursue me."

"Maybe not, but be careful anyway, Rosie. Do you own a weapon?"

"Not a gun, but I'll be sure to hide the kitchen knives so they can't be used against me. Will you call back and let me know who that license belongs to, at least?"

"I promise I'll call back, okay, but I think you'd better leave the police work to us. Although, if you're really crazy about it, you could come up here and help us search the woods for Sno Quantrill. The sheriff's posse, the Explorer

Scouts, and the majority of the back-country horsemen, the usual SAR recruits, have gone to be in the Cereal Bowl Parade at Disney World in Florida, and half the 4X4 club has gone to the bowl game. The military normally would help out, but they're on red alert already with this new trouble in Costa Rica."

"That shows how in touch I am with the world," she said. "I didn't know there *was* any trouble in Costa Rica. But I've got a lot of comp time coming. I'll check in tomorrow and try to get away."

"Great," he said. "So, maybe I'll see you?"

"Yeah," she said softly. "That'd be nice."

"Bye, then. Remember, lock up."

"Bye."

Rose hung up, then changed the message on her answering machine. "Hi, this is Rose at 555-2468. Just wanted to let anyone calling in know that I just spoke to the police and gave them the number of the license of two men on the ferryboat who first aroused then confirmed my suspicions that they were up to no good. The license number I gave the police is JZZ 666. Have a nice day."

If any of her friends called and got that message, they'd be no more puzzled and amused than usual, although they might vaguely feel they didn't get the joke.

Then she went into the kitchen and pulled out all the carving knives, all the steak knives, and on second thought, remembering some of the movies her teenage clients enjoyed when she was counseling at a youth shelter, grabbed the blender and the Veg-O-Matic as well and locked them in a closet. She'd have to take her chances her foe wasn't into microwave murder.

She went to the bathroom, had presence of mind enough this time to brush her teeth and wash her face, and returned to bed.

Wrath of Bluebeard

"Now, then, young lady, time for you to take a bath," the man told Gigi. She shook her head emphatically, her thumb firmly in her mouth.

The man had taken her up to the master bedroom, the one with the mirrors on the ceiling, and after locking the door finally turned her loose. She found a corner and hunkered down there, watching him.

"Are you worried about what happened to Hank?" he asked in his nice voice again. Now she knew it was false, that he was a bad man. But if she played like she didn't know, maybe he would be nice and maybe she could find a way to get away.

She nodded.

"Hank was naughty. He disobeyed. I told you kids and told you not to go down there. I knew you'd be upset by my basement."

"Are those dead kids?" She took her thumb out of her mouth long enough to ask.

He pretended to laugh. "Dead kids? Dead kids? I guess they do look real, don't they? Is that what scared you so much?"

He advanced on her, as if to hug her. Or squeeze her to death. She scooted back until she was half under the bed.

"Poor Gigi. I'm sorry you were scared. Do you really think I'd keep dead kids in my basement? Those aren't real kids, not really. All that stuff down there is just for effect, like in the movies. You really thought it was real, though, huh? I'm surprised at you, Gigi. How can you think I'd kill kids? I love kids. I love you. Now come here and give me a kiss and get ready for your bath like a good girl and we'll play a little game."

Gigi scooted backwards until her legs were under the bed. The smell of the man's aftershave didn't take away the bad smell from downstairs. He grabbed for her but she wiggled under the bed, which was high enough for her to crawl around under. She crawled to the middle, beyond his reach.

"Oh, little girl, you're asking for it now," the man said. "I guess you've got your own game going. Okay. I'll play yours and then you'll play mine." He laughed, as if he'd said something funny. She heard the bed wheeze above her and then, all of a sudden, he popped down to eye level below the bed, there was a blinding flash, and he had a fistful of her hair. It burned and hurt and little knives ran into her head. She screeched and screamed and yelled and turned over and held on with her hands and feet to the underside of the bed but he kept pulling.

Then suddenly an arm was around her neck, choking her while the hand continued pulling her hair. She coughed, gasped, and finally, blackness filled with little blue and red stars overcame her.

Right beside her ear, a telephone rang.

Twenty-five

RAYDIR QUANTRILL STRAPPED on his axe, tugged the phones up over his ears, and prepared to vent his frustration and sorrow in his art. The studio was darkened. He had set the controls himself in the sound booth before coming down here to play and to listen to his own echo until everything else in his life was no more than background static.

He knew he was a little stoned. He had to be. His kid was missing, and her mother, who was maybe the only woman he'd ever had who gave a shit about him, was dead. And Gerardine—well, if he stayed straight long enough, he would have to admit that behind that beautiful face and body there was one scary female. He'd fallen for her at first not only because she was gorgeous but because her ego was even bigger than his. Shouldn't be the problems with insecurity he'd had with Sno's mother.

He'd been fairly crazy about his gorgeous new wife to begin with, and after Sno's bust had even stopped getting zoned for a while. That's when he began to see that Gerry had this *thing*, this model thing, about her looks. And something uglier, something he did not even want to think about, that settled on Sno.

The kid was way fucked up. The only thing he could think of to do about it was the school. That had worked pretty good, kept her out of trouble while he was on the road, and better, kept her out of Gerry's way.

Yeah. The whole idea was fuckin' brilliant. That's why they were now looking for his kid—or, face it, his kid's body—up in the mountains someplace, where some psycho had done god-knows-what to her.

He'd never been able to protect her. He'd never had time to help her. The truth was, he was so busy, so wrapped up in his music, his love life, partying, that he never knew she needed help until it was all over.

"Nonsense," a voice in his earphones challenged. "You bloody well know now." He saw no one, though anybody could have snuck into the control booth.

He was too stoned to worry about it. He just took it for granted that if he heard a voice, somebody was there, somebody who thought he ought to have an answer. Somebody who was blaming him, holding him accountable.

"Oh, for pity's sake," the voice said, reading his mind again as if he had physically opened his mouth to broadcast through the mike. "Your only child has disappeared in the forest in the middle of winter and you're sitting here feeling sorry for yourself, thinking everything is about *you*. Pretty soon you'll have yourself convinced that she'd be better off dead because you're such a terrible father."

"What the hell am I supposed to do?" he half-demanded, half-cried, realizing as he spoke that underneath the druggy fog he was actually pretty upset about it. "I can't join the search. I can't confront the son of a bitch."

"Can't you?"

"No. I offered to equip a plane with infrared, rent a chopper, anything to help, and they told me, real nice and while acting like they wanted to ask for my autograph, mind you, but real clear, to butt out, stay home and wait to arrange for the funeral."

"And of course, you always do what you're told and obey all the rules, don't you?"

"Well, no, but it's my kid and . . ."

"Precisely. But don't you suppose that if you gave your real name instead of your stage name and dressed a bit more practically for the enterprise, those heading the search might fail to recognize you? And if you showed up driving the sort of 4X4 vehicle they find particularly useful and offered humbly to help the search in any way you could without interfering with anyone—and you must refrain from interfering with the searchers if they're to find your daughter and only do what they tell you will be helpful—don't you think that perhaps it would be a good thing to be there when and if they find her, in whatever condition?"

His head was suddenly clear. That was exactly what he wanted to do. He unstrapped the axe, pulled off the phones and sprinted up the stairs into the control booth, but it was as dark and empty as ever.

However, one of the playbacks suddenly switched on and a voice said, "One thing though, Raymond. You mustn't tell your wife."

Meanwhile, unnoticed by Quantrill or his mysterious caller, a toad was loose on the premises. Like many toads, it was about the size of a coffee mug, it was green and it was bumpy. But unlike most toads, it had a bad attitude and it was, at this point, hopping mad.

It also had the mind of a seasoned murderer and a karma to match, it wanted revenge, and it wanted to start buying its way back to humanity. And the toad knew just the bitch who ought to foot part of the bill.

The toad had never been in this particular mansion before, but it had seen the inside of its share of fancy places, and locating the bitch's bedroom was no problem. She was sleeping like a baby. The toad gave an extra mighty hop and leaped right into her face. She opened her eyes and they were looking, a bit crosswise, into the eyes of a killer with a grudge.

The doll was no dummy. She figured out immediately, in her witch-bitch way, that this was no ordinary amphibian she was dealing with.

"Who *are* you?" she asked.

Shit! He could almost wish that fuckin' cat was here to translate. How could he tell her he was the dude who took the fall for her when she tried to have her own kid killed?

Then she sat up, and he fell off her face. "Oh, no, it can't be . . ."

Well, if her conscience or whatever was bothering her, it ought to. "You got it, babe," he reedeeped at her. "Sorry I didn't send the scarf."

She didn't act shocked or panicked or any of the things you'd expect of most women. She simply eyed him like he was a lab specimen she was about to dissect—and he'd have to be careful about that—and said in a cool, sweet voice, "Now, I wonder how you got in that shape? I hope you're not here expecting me to catch flies for you or something as payment. You didn't follow my instructions, and by now the little twit's told people all about both of us. If I hadn't gone to a great deal of trouble to mix a little poison with her favorite smoke and expended a lot of mental and physical energy to find her and get her to take the bait, everything would have been ruined by your unprofessional behavior." She leaned over the side of the bed and picked up a high-heeled shoe, which she raised slowly over his head.

He hopped down off the bed, and she was out and after him. He could hop faster than her famous long legs could run, but she knew the house better. He made a terrible mistake, however, when he hopped through a door into a cool, watery, inviting place filled with plants.

He realized his mistake when he saw the toilet.

"Got you now," she said, as she flashed past the full-length mirror. He hopped into the tub as she stopped cold, gazing into the mirror.

He eyed her from the far side of the tub with increasing satisfaction. "That ain't all you got, doll," he told her.

Whether she heard him or whether she had caught a glimpse of herself in the mirror long enough for it to register before she stopped to stare, he didn't know and he didn't care, since she got the point. "Warts!" she cried, running frightened fingertips over the brown hairy spots starting to appear on her perfect nose, her perfect upper lip, and her perfect cheeks in sort of a frog's-butt-shaped pattern. She moaned and wept hysterically. It didn't take a genius to figure out she was not only no longer the fairest in the land, or even the house, but unless she found some magician with a miracle wart cure, her modeling days were over.

"Sayonara, sweetheart," he said as he leaped behind her and out the door while she pawed her blemishes.

He had thought to find Felicity but when he saw the 4X4 pulling out of the garage and Raydir himself behind the wheel, he had a better idea.

He hopped in.

"She did *what*?" the man yelled into the portable telephone. With the other hand, he held Gigi by the hair. The more she struggled, the worse it hurt, but she knew she had to get away from him, *had* to, that he wanted to do bad things to her, kill her, maybe *eat* her and Hank both, like the witch in the fairy tales. Susan Buchanan hadn't said exactly—well, Gigi hadn't exactly under*stood*—what it was people like this did to little kids, but she wanted no part of it.

"Okay, okay, calm down. Listen to me. I know this girl. She works at DFS—I recognized her. No, I don't know if she recognized me too, but it seems to me that if she did, she wouldn't have needed the license number. But listen, I spoke with her supervisor only yesterday about her for something altogether different and I planted a not unwelcome hint that she get canned. So if she did recognize me, and tries to implicate me in anything, it'll seem like sour grapes."

He didn't talk for a minute while he shifted Gigi against him, almost sticking his arm in her mouth. "Well, what *about* you? It stands to reason if she can't hurt me she can't hurt you either. All she has is a license number, even if she is broadcasting it on her answering machine and has given it to the police. Have they showed up yet? When and if they do, have your attorney slap a suit on the woman for harassment. No, well, I can see where you wouldn't want it investigated. That does present quite a problem for you. I think you'd better take care of it." Somebody squawked like Donald Duck on the other end of the phone. "No, there's no point in bringing her over here. I already told you, the place is occupied at the moment. No, blackmail photographs are *not* a good idea and certainly not *here*. Listen, leave it alone or shut her up, but the deal was, if she was over here, I'd take care of it, if she's over there, you do it. I don't care how you handle it, just leave me out of it!" The man was shouting by now. "No! No, don't bring her here. I'm telling you, nobody comes here unless *I* bring them. You're getting hysterical. Stop threatening . . . !"

He was holding Gigi too tight, his arm cutting off her breathing, so she bit it. He threw the phone in the air and let go of her hair to grab his arm. Then she ran through the bathroom and into another room and opened the door and was out the door and down the hall while the man yelled behind her.

Should she go back to the basement and get Hank? No, then the man would find her for sure.

Instead she ran only as far as the front door and tugged, but it wouldn't open.

Locked.

A window. A window. An open window?

No—it was too cold. No open window.

But she had to get away. Had to escape the man. Had to help Hank before the man killed him. She tried the door again and heard the man yelling into the phone, "Don't do anything! I'll call you back!"

Break the window? How? It was only glass. Breaking a window would be bad, but he was bad too and she hated him. The fireplace. That heavy thing Daddy and Mama used to use to poke the fire back in Forks. It would break the window, and she could pick it up by herself. She did and crawled with it up onto the sofa and swung with all her might at the window. It broke the glass and sailed through it, the window shattering and falling out in big pieces of glass. Gigi climbed out of the broken place in the pane, not quite avoiding all the broken glass, and ran as fast as she could down the sidewalk, between the rows of reindeer and the Santa whose smile looked mean to her now.

It was dark outside, with no streetlights, and in places the sidewalk wasn't finished. She ran down the street and ran and ran, hoping someone would see her, someone would take her to a policeman or home or anywhere else. Her ears whirred and her legs ached and she got a stitch in her side. She looked behind her and didn't see anything coming, so she ran up to a house and knocked on the door but nobody came. About that time, she saw a car coming and she thought it must be the man, so she stepped off behind a big patch of weeds and huddled there, and when it had gone, she started running again. She kept doing this and kept doing it, but nobody ever answered their door.

She had not started to read yet, and certainly couldn't read the "Development Under Construction" sign that had been there for years, ever since the developer had gone bankrupt and been unable to finish the project.

So she kept running, knocking and ducking out of sight when a car came by until she knew not how much later, long past dark, when she hid beside one of the houses and didn't immediately get up and run some more. Instead, she fell asleep and dreamed of running and being chased by monsters.

She had no idea how much later it was when she woke up, though it was still dark. She tried pounding on the door again, still with no luck. But she must be getting someplace soon. She'd come so far, it seemed to her. A few more steps, and she saw the lights on the highway ahead of her. She could no longer run, but she walked with dragging steps toward it. She didn't feel like she could go any farther. Why didn't anybody find her? Maybe the man had given up by now. The lines of houses ended, all of them darkened for as far back as she could see. She no longer saw the reindeer in the man's yard.

Near the highway, a river of car lights flowed past her. She had no idea how to get to them.

Suddenly, a car pulled up beside her. She turned, hoping for help, as the car stopped, but it was the man. This time she was too weary and sore to even try to outrun him.

Quietly, grimly, he slid out of his car and ran around it to scoop her up. Nobody else was near, nobody heard her crying. He held on to her as he gunned the car forward, onto the freeway.

"I don't want to hear a word out of you, little girl," he growled. Even though he talked quietly, he sounded madder than she'd ever heard anybody sound, even Daddy when he hit Mama. His eyes had gone funny now too, and his eyebrow kept jumping all by itself. "You've cost me hours and hours of valuable time and now you'd better be a real good girl and not draw attention to yourself. I didn't want to bring you with me but your little escapade has had me out looking for you most of the night and I don't have time to take you back now. We're going to take a little ferry ride, won't that be nice? We're going over to Bremerton and we're going to take care of a nosy young woman and make sure she doesn't make trouble for anyone and if someone else has beat us to her, and we find him there, we'll take care of him too. If not, we'll make a little tour of it, up to Bainbridge Island. He has a very nice home there. You'll like it. I'll let you play in the hot tub if you're good."

A sob escaped Gigi before she could stop it.

The man turned and glared at her. "And if you're not, both you and your brother will be very, very sorry."

Rose knew something was wrong by the way the cats were acting. They sat up, alert, tails lashing and ears and whiskers atwitch as they seemingly looked through the walls. She had just awakened as one of the animals walked across her face to go stand on the windowsill and look out into the side yard. Rose felt as if she was going to snap if she moved too quickly, every muscle aching and stiff and her head heavy with exhaustion as she turned toward the window and raised herself on her elbows. Dawn was breaking over the tops of her bare-branched apple trees. She rolled across her bed to get a closer look, but could see nothing but the yard, looking a little frosted around the edges, but otherwise much the same as usual.

Sometime during the night she had been vaguely aware of the phone ringing and her message machine going off, but she hadn't been able to wake up enough to answer had she wanted to. Nothing could have awakened her but furry feet with the threat of claws lurking in every tread padding across her nose and forehead.

Cats made great alarm clocks.

Normally she would have had to arise fifteen minutes from now to get up and go to work anyway or call in sick if she preferred. Actually, she felt sick. She knew that calling in would cost her not only in terms of pay, which the state no longer gave to employees who were sick but not hospitalized, and in the fact that once she returned to work there would be twice as much to plow through, and she would be placing an extra burden on Patrick and George. She had had a long weekend. And, oh yeah, she had comp time coming, since the state no longer paid overtime. Well, that solved that. She'd go in to work, coordinate with Fred and Felicity about when the search was to start, and work until time to begin.

She got up and padded to the bathroom, tripped and impeded at every step by darting velvety pillows hurtling themselves broadside at her bare legs and screeching at the tops of their lungs that they hadn't been fed in weeks.

She didn't have time to do more than brush her teeth, wash her face and take vitamins. To dress for work, she needed slacks and something businesslike. For a horseback search, jeans, a sweatshirt and a jacket. She pulled on the latter, plus a pair of cowboy boots and socks that would go okay at the office too, grabbed a blazer and slacks, and stuffed them and Felicity's clothes from yesterday into a sack.

She'd have to steer the car to the ferry on autopilot and get her coffee at the espresso bar on board the boat.

The car was parked in the circular drive that led through the apple trees, formerly an orchard that was now her front yard. She never locked it in her own yard, as she usually had several loads of stuff she shuttled back and forth between the house and the car and was always forgetting something, including her keys. She slid behind the wheel and closed the door, and was vaguely aware of something flashing in the rearview mirror just before the business end of a gun barrel was pressed against her right temple. "Don't you know driving without a license is against the law?" a voice asked.

Dico was in hog heaven. Ding and his friends took Dico back to their neighborhood, and they were completely different from how they'd been before. They acted now like Dico was one of them, well, almost, and they were real nice to him. They sat on the steps visiting for a while till Ding said he needed to go inside and make supper for his folks, who would be getting off their night shifts soon.

"You cook, man?" Dico asked.

"What about it? Where I'm from, we were lucky to have food . . ."

"I can relate to that okay. Naw, I'm not dissin' you, Ding. I'm impressed. Whaddaya cook?"

"Rice mostly. Here it's easy to get good shrimp or a little fish sometimes, but the folks don't like to eat too heavy before they go to bed. After so many years of eating light, too much disagrees with them."

"Where you folks come from?"

"I was born in a camp in Hong Kong after my folks got out of Vietnam."

"No shit! My daddy—my real daddy—got killed in Vietnam. My stepdaddy and my mama got killed a little while ago. But your folks got through it all okay. That's good."

"Yeah," Ding said, wrinkling his nose. "Look, you want to clean up? The bathroom's through that door, and I'll loan you some clothes."

"That," Dico said, "would be great."

While Dico was cleaning up, Ding was busy in the kitchen.

"Hey, man, that smells great," Dico told him. "Where'd you learn to cook?"

Ding shrugged. "Here. When I finally had enough food. Me, I like burgers and tacos and pizza, but the folks still want the same kinda stuff they had in the camp."

"You guys camp out?" Dico asked. "That where you know the cat lady from?"

Because he didn't seem to be prying, didn't seem to know, and maybe, having been on the streets himself for a while, could understand, Ding told him a little about the camp.

"Heavy," was all Dico said then. He wondered about it, though. His mama had told him once Daddy had confessed to her in a letter that he had a kid by a Vietnamese woman. That made Dico feel sorta related to Ding, in a funny kind of way.

Later, when Ding's mom and dad came home, they ate as Dico had not eaten for months. He polished off his fifth plate of rice, fish and vegetables and ate two more eggrolls while Ding's parents kept offering him more until he began worrying that he'd eaten them out of a week's worth of groceries.

"This sure is nice of you folks," Dico said. One reason he was eating so much was that he was hungry. The other was that he knew he had better save at least half the fish for Puss or he'd never hear the end of it.

Ding looked a little embarrassed, and somewhat pained, at the way Dico acted toward his parents. Dico explained about his—what would it be, cousin?—in Vietnam that he knew about but hadn't met.

Mrs. Nguyen shook her head sadly and looked at her husband. "My sister had such a child," Mrs. Nguyen explained. "But she and the child were both killed."

Dico asked how that had happened, and pretty soon they were telling him all about it, all about Vietnam in the old days before the war, and the war, and working for Americans while friends and family members worked for the Viet Cong. They talked and talked, well past the time when they should have been sleeping, getting ready for their night jobs.

Dico only noticed once that Ding looked bored and angry, but then, later in the day, as the parents continued to talk, he saw that Ding had taken out a tape recorder, no doubt hot, and was taping everything his parents said, while meanwhile making notes in a spiral notebook.

Twenty-six

CINDY ELLIS WAS happily received by Burt Stalling, the leader of the Back Country Trail Riders and coordinator of the sheriff's posse. It was nearly sunset by the time she reported, but the searchers would continue as long as possible, until darkness forced them to stop.

"We can use more hands," Burt told her. "Especially experienced trail riders. Only a few of the folks who were able to come from the Eagle Scouts and the local trail riders have been out with us before, so we'll have to do a little on-site training when they get here. We've got miles of highway to cover between Glacier and the ski lodge just to find the start of the trail. Now, normally I pair up two or more riders to take the trails, but since we're short and you have a vehicle, I think I'll send you out with one of the 4X4 teams. A rider can sometimes spot something from horseback a walker doesn't see."

Cindy, remembering Felicity Fortune's instructions, said, "Could you tell me who Haisley Henderson is, sir? My boss gave me something to return to him."

"Sure. In fact, I'll post you with Hay. Good man."

About that time, another 4X4 drove up and a tall, rangy man in his late forties got out. Cindy was immediately impressed by the REI couture he sported. She'd been mooning over the catalog, wishing for just such a jacket as he wore, but the cost was way more than she could see spending. Especially now, without a job.

Burt greeted the man.

"You Stalling?" the man asked.

"Naw," Burt said, with a wink to Cindy to show he'd pulled this particular joke many times before. "Just pausin' to assign this young lady to her post. Just kiddin', son. What can I do for you?"

"Name's Ray Kinsale. Neil back at SAR headquarters said you could use another 4X4 and told me to report to you for assignment."

"You've had CPR and first-aid training?"

The man nodded. There was something about him that seemed familiar to Cindy, but the man wasn't speaking or moving enough to give her any further clues as to where she might have seen him before.

"Okay, then. You might as well get trained by Hay Henderson too. I like having three on a team if possible. Missus H. was gonna have to go search too since we're so shorthanded, even though she's our top base-camp organizer. This way we can keep her at base with you two pups for Hay to train."

Cindy didn't mind being called a pup but the other newcomer looked surprised, even a little shocked, as if he never, ever considered himself in those terms. He smiled a tight, tense smile, just a little. Cindy thought if he ever relaxed he might be pretty nice-looking.

She and the newcomer convoyed out to the former site of the ranger station just west of Shuksan campground where Hay Henderson was beginning his leg of the search. How had Felicity *known* Hay Henderson and Shuksan would go together? That was the place Felicity had told her about. Shouldn't she have just told the SAR coordinator? Wouldn't that have done more good? Cindy shook her head wonderingly. Well, she hadn't, and any woman who could make a jeep and horse trailer out of a motorcycle could pretty well do as she liked.

Hay Henderson, a hairy biker-looking guy, turned out to be a good and patient teacher, assigning each of them to comb a yard at a time of the assigned area.

"We're looking for a sign, any evidence that the girl or the perp have been here," Hay told them.

"Red," Cindy muttered, remembering Felicity's words and scanning the trees and bushes, looking for a flash of that color.

"What?" Ray asked.

"She was wearing red, the TV said," Cindy repeated, guessing that the TV would have made routine mention of the girl's clothing. "I was just telling myself what to look for."

"A school uniform," Ray said. "Do we have to go so slow? I mean, anything could be happening to the poor kid. Can't we speed things up?"

Hay shook his head and said, "I know how you feel, buddy. But slow and steady is the best way. We got everybody on it we can, and we'll have more in the morning. Meanwhile, we don't want to stumble around and mess up a clue we miss because we're in a hurry. Comprende?"

Ray had exhausted his supply of words for the moment and nodded, close-mouthed. He looked truly miserable, though, and Cindy felt sorry for him.

"Okay, let's boogie," Hay said.

Cindy had Punkin saddled and ready by then and mounted up while Ray and Hay—sounded like a team of stand-up comedians—beat the bushes from as high as they could see down to the ground. They covered the Shuksan campground and the stretch of road between it as the light faded so much that Cindy suddenly realized she scarcely could see color.

They found red cigarette packages, used condoms, paper cups and McDonald's yellow-and-red cardboard boxes. They found several discarded articles of clothing including a herringbone patterned sock, a bra much bigger than any schoolgirl was likely to wear, and a black tractor cap with the legend "Over the Hill" on its crown. But no red cloth, none at all.

"Okay, gang," Hay said. "That's it. We'll hit the picnic grounds tomorrow at first light."

Sno tried to light the joint, but it was wet. All it would do was smolder. The rain drizzled lightly·down and didn't help matters at all. Here by the river, the feeder creek rushed over the rocks as loud as one of Raydir's concerts, and for a while she sat with her arms hugging her knees, the cold and damp seeping up from the ground, through her jeans and soaking her butt.

The fragrance of the woodsmoke drifted toward her from the cabin and she yearned toward it with part of her, while the other part wanted to be alone, away from all those guys who at least had each other and their memories of a war that was over way before she was born. They could say what they wanted to about it; at least something had happened then. At least their enemies were people from another country, not in their own families.

Well, that wasn't exactly right either. Doc's father had been an alcoholic, and Maurice's mom used drugs and tried to sell him to her boyfriends—even though he said he ran away, Sno wondered. Trip-Wire had the crap beaten out of him every day of his life before he joined the service and had taken the opportunity to beat the crap out of somebody else until the anger was all gone, leaving just that jumpy, scared feeling he projected when you talked to him. He tried to make out like he was so bad but really, he was so scared. She could dig it.

In the basement of the abandoned Whatcom County Courthouse, at the circular console in the middle of a room surrounded on all sides by glass offices, Fred Moran hung up the phone after trying one more time to get through to Rose. No answer except the mocking machine message she'd left for the men she'd met on the ferry.

Fred tapped a pencil on the desk, turned it around and tapped it again.

"Anything wrong?" asked the deep, radio-announcer voice of Neil, the coordinator.

Fred shook his head slowly, chewing the inside of his lower lip. "I'm not sure."

It had been a long night but Fred was used to working nights, preferred it in fact. More action and less bureaucracy to deal with, usually, although this night would have dragged interminably had it not been for swapping lies with Neil and talking to Rose, then to the Kitsap police about the license number she was now broadcasting on her answering machine. Johansen and Bowersox hadn't found the kids, or he'd have heard from them by now. Smitty and Chuck hadn't returned yet from going to check out the caller at the Triplehorn residence.

Normally, he would stick around and continue keeping an eye on the progress of this search while waiting by the phone for news of the Bjornsen case, but now he felt increasingly that he should have been more concerned when Rose told him about her encounter. The Search and Rescue folks wouldn't be able to discover anything until daybreak anyway, which was not for a few hours at this time in the winter.

He made a decision. He had already given all of the information King County had about the frog-man and the crime. Rose was not due at work for another hour and a half. She should still be home. He told Neil, "If something breaks, you can reach me by radio. Meanwhile, I need to go downtown, maybe over to Kitsap County to check something out."

Neil, who had a hand and an ear devoted to the telephone while the other hand traced a line on a map, nodded absently and waved the phone at him.

Fred drove south, getting caught in the heavy morning traffic outside the Boeing plant near Everett so that it was almost eight-thirty by the time he reached downtown.

He stopped in at headquarters to fill out more paperwork and pick up the ID on the license number Rose had requested. Winston Thorndyke Throckmorton. Wasn't there a *judge* by the name of W. T. Throckmorton? There had been some stink about him working in King County after he moved to Bainbridge Island, which was in Kitsap County. Fred remembered, because he had once been a witness in Throckmorton's court on a breaking-and-entering case. A couple of the detectives in the domestic abuse department had warned him against the judge, who they felt had a habit of dismissing cases of child molesting and domestic violence. They said he never seemed convinced by the evidence, even when it had been collected with the same care given to a drug bust. Child-molesting cases. He remembered what Marilyn Wallace, a detective sergeant, had said: "I don't think Throckmorton believes in child molesting—he acts like we're telling him dirty stories for the shock value every time we present evidence."

"Hmph," Leon Rodriguez, another detective with the same complaint, had replied. "Either he doesn't believe in it or he doesn't see anything wrong with it. His concern for the privacy of the accused seems to me like something personal."

Fred had listened to them, presented his evidence, which was taken, he thought, in an intelligent manner that led ultimately to a conviction, and forgotten about it. Now he felt as if someone had punched him in the solar plexus. *Did* the judge not actually believe people molested children, despite a steady parade of evidence to the contrary, or did he simply not believe it was a crime because it was, as Rose suspected, something he did himself? And if he was in heavy denial about one crime, how would he feel about committing another? Fred rang Rose's house again, with the same results as he'd been getting since he called her before.

By then it was eight-thirty. DFS opened for business at eight. She should be there by now.

He identified himself to the man who answered the phone, someone he didn't recognize, and asked to speak to Rose. The man put him on hold and in another moment a voice he recognized as that of *Mrs.* Hager, Rose's supervisor, answered. "Miss Samson is no longer with the department."

"Since when?" Fred asked.

"I'm not at liberty to discuss that."

"I spoke to her before she left for work this morning, and she didn't mention changing jobs," Fred said. "This concerns a police investigation, ma'am. Can you tell me where I might reach her?"

"I have no idea, nor could I divulge such confidential information over the telephone if I knew. If you'll excuse me, officer, we have our own highly important job to do."

And she hung up. It crossed his mind to make like the guy from *Lethal Weapon*, hop into a patrol car, storm into the place, cuff Hager and grill her "downtown," but that·

was movie and TV stuff, not real life, and besides, he didn't think she *did* know where to find Rose. But he was pretty sure Rose had had no idea she'd been canned when he last talked to her. If he didn't find Rose pretty quick, he'd do a little bit more digging into why Hager knew Rose was not coming to work before Rose did. Unless they'd had words on the phone within the last hour, at least. In which case, what would Rose do? Go out to breakfast? Unlikely.

He signed off duty, indicated that he'd be available on his car phone and could be reached in Kitsap County for the next few hours. By then he just had time to catch the 9:15 car ferry to Bremerton if he hustled.

Twenty-seven

THE GUN WAS no longer at her head when Rose drove the car onto the first available car ferry after a long delay. It was stuck in her side, so the ferry crewman loading the boat couldn't see it. The man with the gun had been in such a hurry to make the ferry that they were the first to board, despite the fact that this morning only one car ferry was making the commuter run and the 6:40 did not run that morning, while the 7:40 ran almost an hour late and didn't load until almost 8:26. She knew the time precisely. The gunman kept asking her for the time as he prodded her. Despite the winter wind outside the car, she was sweating so badly her hair was soaked. Normally inside the car she took her coat off on the way to work, but of course, the gunman wasn't particularly concerned about her comfort.

She tried, briefly, to establish some rapport, to do what the experts suggested and get him to think of her as a human being rather than as some *thing* which was in his way.

"I understand why you're doing this—that my phone message about your license number threatened you, but honestly, that's all it was, a threat. If you hadn't rifled my purse, the whole thing would never have escalated the way it did."

"*I* didn't take it," the gunman said. "*He* did. And I'm damned if I'm going to take responsibility for his stupidity. As for you, you should have minded your own business."

"I was," she said. "I'm a social worker. Really, I had absolutely nothing on anybody, except that the way your conversation was going made me think of a case I've been working on with a friend of mine who's a policeman. I'm sure you're a perfectly nice man who would never dream of harming a child . . ." Right. And *she* was Mother Teresa. He was such a nice man he had a gun in her ribs.

"That's right. I don't harm children, I *love* children, something you self-righteous busybodies never consider. Children like to be loved—who doesn't? They *crave* contact, ask for it, beg for it, only because you think it's wrong, because you're afraid of the competition from the smooth skin and the clear eyes and the soft hair . . . there's nothing wrong with loving children, no matter what laws you man-haters manage to have passed. After all, we feed and support them, clothe them, pay for their schooling; why shouldn't they love us? If you think I'm going to let you ruin my life because *you* feel threatened by my sexual preferences, you're quite mistaken. And if Hopkins thinks he will survive watching *my* ass get fried without getting burnt himself, he's mistaken as hell."

"I see."

"Do you? You gave the police my license number, but I know a thing or two about evidence, my dear, and if you aren't there to present it yourself, there's nothing but hearsay . . ."

"There's the tape on the answering machine of my police friend . . ."

"If he remembers to save it. And even then, what else is there? No, you will cost me my photograph collection, which I will have to destroy or hide, but I'll be all right.

Especially since I am going to see to it that Hopkins is forced to help me take care of you and will therefore be only too happy to assist in seeing that those who would persecute both of us are able to harm *neither* of us."

She didn't ask what he intended to do about her. She didn't want to know.

By the time the ferry came, it had been a very long two hours and her bladder was about to burst. Maybe she could get him to let her use the head below decks, if not on the passenger deck.

"No tricks," the gunman warned as she nosed the car forward, stopped where she was told, just behind the chain separating the car deck from the cold, olive-green waters of Puget Sound.

"No worries," she said.

"See that there aren't," he told her. "I can't kill you here, but one peep out of you and I lock you in the trunk."

She didn't see how he could really do that, but if he got lucky she supposed he could get away with it. The crew didn't frequent this end of the boat until the end of the run, when they tied up at the dock, and at this hour, passengers who weren't upstairs on the passenger deck were catching extra sleep in their cars or were deeply sunk into early-morning-commuter hypnosis and paid little attention to what was happening around them. She could scream, maybe. Somehow, with the gun trained on her at close range, that didn't seem an option.

Once they were parked, she said, "I have to pee. Bad."

"Hold it," he told her.

"I can't hold it anymore. It's going to be really messy and stinky in here pretty soon. If we're stopped, it'll be suspicious," she added.

"Don't be cute," he said. "If you think I'm letting you go up to the powder room to discuss our relationship with the other ladies, you must have formed a very low impression of my intelligence."

"No, but there's a head between the staircases. You can stand guard. Please. I really have to go."

She hadn't used this head very often. The interior was battleship-gray and the fixtures extremely utilitarian and rather grubby. It was just a long, narrow closet with the toilet at the back and a basin in the middle. Mops and pails were often stacked to one side.

He came in with her. "Okay," he said, facing her. "Go."

"I—can't," she said. "Not with you watching."

"Then do it in the trunk, I don't care," he said, opening the door and motioning her through it.

"No, really, I have to but I can't . . ."

"Out." He pointed the gun at her. This was the most extreme case of piss-or-get-off-the-pot she'd ever heard of, much less been in, she thought, but discomfort and desperation won out over fear.

"No. *You* get out. Shoot me in here or drag me out screaming, but you're going to make a lot of noise and draw a lot of attention to yourself. I don't know what you think you're accomplishing by all this, but I'll be damned if I'm going to die from a busted bladder or humiliation."

"I could just shoot you through the knee or the arm," he said, and she could see that her rebellion was going to cost her. As long as she seemed docile, he might relax around her. If she caused trouble . . .

"Or you could just go outside and let me do this in peace," she said, and it was no effort to allow a pleading note to enter her voice.

"I have bullets that will penetrate this door," he told her.

She just stared at him. He fumbled with the door and backed out, pocketing the gun.

Damn, too bad this was a ferryboat bathroom without a handy window to sneak out of. The first thing she did was to lean over and turn on the faucet, allowing the water to trickle; then she relieved herself, after which it was much easier to think of an escape plan.

She could just start screaming, but the bathroom was encased in the heavy steel of the interior hull, the ferry's engines were loud, everyone but the few crew members below decks was locked behind closed car doors and rolled-up windows. If she made a run for it, this nut might start shooting through cars to get her and hurt other people. If she led him upstairs, where there were more people, possibly she could get away, get help. Didn't any of the senior crew carry a weapon for security?

What she needed was, as they said in the movies, a distraction, but she didn't think throwing a rock to make noises elsewhere was going to do the trick this time. What she needed more was a SWAT team, but she would have settled for Felicity, who was AWOL just when she most needed a fairy—or even a ferry—godmother.

As soon as Felicity emerged from Raydir Quantrill's sound room, where she had used an ancient Tibetan technique similar to that used by Yoda in *Star Wars* to make the musician overlook her presence and heed only her words, she sensed Rose's distress. She also sensed Fred's, since at one time he had been as close to her as Rose was now. There was so much pain, so much suffering, so much despair and desperation in a city the size of Seattle, that even she could only differentiate between the general miasma of anxiety and anguish and the specific difficulties of her own associates. She stood in Quantrill's Japanese garden overlooking the Sound and listened with her heart and mind.

She heard Rose, quite clearly, across the water, and Fred somewhere near it. She had to get to them. Her car was still at the mechanic's. Perhaps she could use a bit of her magic to nudge things a little, maybe even have the mechanic deliver her completely repaired car to her here in the next minute . . .

"What do you think, Bobby?" she asked, patting her pocket, which, to her surprise, was empty. In her concentration on concealing her presence, she hadn't noticed the toad's defection.

From behind her, someone coughed politely.

Felicity turned and groaned when she saw who it was: a woman, like herself of indeterminate age, with carefully coiffed pale hair, wearing a gray-and-moss-colored Harris Tweed business suit with a Nottingham lace collar and cuffs peeking out of the jacket and a clean handkerchief of similar make in her breast pocket. Silvery half-glasses perched on her nose, though she certainly could have afforded contact lenses, and she carried a briefcase and wore dark tights and sensible walking shoes.

"Dame Prudence, how very nice to see you!" Felicity greeted the chairperson of the Godmothers' Accounting Committee with less than her usual sincerity.

Dame Prudence raised carefully penciled brows over eyes that were pencil-lead gray rather than Felicity's own opalescent silver. "I'm delighted that you think so, Flitters. I was afraid that after our last encounter, your enthusiasm for my appearing in the middle of your projects might have been somewhat diminished."

"Nonsense, Prudence; we all have our jobs to do, and your intervention taught me a valuable lesson."

"Then I'm a rather poor teacher," Prudence said acerbically.

"Wha— Oh, dear, you don't mean I've done it again?"

"Yes. You've reached your limit for this project."

"But I've been so careful!" Felicity wailed. "Really, I've been extremely strict. Really, *really* strict."

Prudence cast a cold, gray eye at the now-empty pocket. "Have you? Transformations rather than simple stasis spells to protect yourself?"

"It wasn't a real transformation, simply a little personality migration."

"Giving an alley cat the power of speech so it could indoctrinate a homeless and rather simple-minded young man into its amoral mode of behavior?"

"Puss is *not* that sort of a cat, Prudence. I know you dislike cats, but if you didn't always have your head in your ledger you'd know very well that I didn't create Puss. As for the amoral behavior, I wonder what Her Majesty would say if she heard you talking such perfect rot. You've been reading too many of Georgie MacDonald's bowdlerized versions of your own escapades."

"Getting huffy with me will avail you nothing, Flitters. You're cut off. Starting now."

"But the assignment isn't *over*, and I'm just receiving signals that my current goddaughter as well as a former godson with whom Rose has every chance of finding true love are in desperate trouble."

"You should have thought of that before you went about giving human speech to stray cats."

"But it isn't fair," Felicity protested. "Rose needs me . . ."

"She should have wished more wisely."

"More selfishly, you must mean. Because up until now she hasn't wished for anything for herself. She wanted me to help the people she serves in this city. She is a remarkable young woman . . ."

"What about the true love, your former godson?"

"That required no magic on my part whatsoever, not even an introduction. They did it all themselves. But now I'm afraid something terrible may be happening to Rose while you detain me with your spell-pinching pettifoggery."

"Felicity Fortune, that is unfair! I want to serve as much as your goddaughter, by using my own talent for stretching the remaining magic as far as possible so that more people can have a bit of luck now and then. I simply can't allow you to go squandering it to spoil one girl. I have a duty to the sorority to rein you in, and you've admitted yourself that you need checking."

"But it *isn't* just one girl. Don't you see? And she's certainly not spoiled. On the contrary, she's so unselfish it's nearly pathological. She hasn't wished for anything at all herself. Please, Prudence. My vehicle is being repaired . . ."

"By an ordinary mechanic? Flitters, how could you?"

"He won't notice, honestly. I, uh—"

"You used magic for that too? My point exactly! I can give you a lift to wherever your goddaughter is, but that's *all.*"

They rode in silence for some time, while Felicity picked up increasing signals of distress not only from Rose and Fred but a wildly frightened one from someone she didn't recognize—a child, though, she was sure it was a child. What could she do to help at a distance? Surely there was someone she could call on . . .

"Flitters!" Prudence drew her up sharply.

"You surely don't intend that I shouldn't make use of the magic I've already set in action, Prudence?" Felicity asked. "That would be wasteful."

"I suppose so."

So Felicity reached out with her mind until its waves were intercepted by the alert whiskers and questing curiosity of one of her established allies.

* * *

Puss was way ahead of Felicity. Figuring she'd been temporarily abandoned by her counselee, she was not about to starve. The territory around Pioneer Square was new to her, but she was enterprising. Unfortunately, she realized— a lacerated ear and a painfully torn claw later—that other cats were equally enterprising and *did* know the territory around every restaurant and any other establishment containing either food to steal or both food and people to bestow it.

She patrolled a bit farther afield—though not so far that she couldn't meet Dico again when he returned, as she hoped, with a share of the food from dinner with Ding.

Down at the foot of Jackson Street, where it met the Alaska Way under the viaduct, she saw a long line of cars stopped, waiting, all heading into one parking lot. There were people in each of the cars. Surely most of them liked cats and many had something to offer in the way of tribute.

She sprinted across the near lane and leaped onto the hood of a car and down, and she was across the road. She followed the cars as they surged into a parking lot bounded on the far side by the gray-green waters of the Sound, which smelled deliciously as always of salt and fish.

Hopping up onto the walkway near the terminal as the cars filed in and parked, she watched. One big white boat was already halfway out in the water, and the drivers and passengers of the cars were settling down as if they expected a wait. And to help them wait, right beside the terminal, was a fast-food restaurant, a place from which came the lovely aromas of frying meat and ice cream. Sure enough, the driver of the first car, a man by himself—not an awfully good risk, Puss thought—climbed out of his car and strode back toward the restaurant.

But there was a very tall fence, and he didn't come out again.

She decided after smelling the goodies in the restaurant for a few more minutes that perhaps more direct action was required. After all, people were impressed by a cat who could speak their language, and the godmother had never said that Puss could *only* use her skill to help Dico.

She certainly had observed enough human panhandlers to know the lines, which she would modify for her own purposes.

She saw a car with a man and a child in it. Now, this was a good setup. If she played hide-and-seek with the child, the child would cry when Puss seemed to have disappeared for good and the man would buy it ice cream. Then the child, overjoyed to see the kitty reappear, would share the ice cream. Some cats were afraid of children, because they ignorantly petted too hard or sometimes you found a bad one who would try to hurt you purposely. Also, they ran in packs. Puss figured being able to talk to them ought to shock them out of any ill intentions until she could get away. Besides, she was basically an optimistic creature and firmly believed there were lots of cat-loving witnesses who might come to her rescue and even offer her a home. Not that she needed or wanted one. She did all right on her own, and now she had Dico to look after. It was different back in the days when she was having kittens, before she'd had her hysterectomy. Kittens needed homes, a proper start in life. She had adopted cat-mad families then long enough to have them take responsibility for finding homes for her children.

The last one had taken her to the vet when her kids went for their checkups, and that was the end of her career as a mother. After that, there was no reason really to accept the restrictions humans imposed, even for expediency's sake.

She was a bit ambivalent about humans, actually. She loved eating regularly but hated the monotony of a cat-food diet, loved being petted, hated being restricted to one family who could come and go as they chose while making sure she didn't have the same options.

Really, the free life was better, and with Dico she had the best of both—plenty of pets, a new gift that ensured she could always get something to eat, and companionship. *He* might have a hard time finding warm places to sleep, but she never did, and with him as a security guard or at least a watchperson, she could now sleep in many spots that weren't safe for her before.

She approached the car with the child and the man, very cautiously going to the child's side. She rose on her hind feet and put her front paws on the windowsill, looking over the top with only her ears, eyes and nose showing. The child, who had been turned away, curled against the window and was, as Puss expected, both shocked and pleased to see her.

"Shhh," Puss told her, and the little girl—it was hard to tell sometimes, but Puss felt that this was a little girl— nodded very slowly, as if she too had a secret. She didn't seem a bit fazed to be addressed by a cat, but children were more practical about such things than adults, as Puss was well aware. Adults wasted a lot of time trying to figure out how and why a cat could be talking to them, whereas a child simply figured that if a cat was talking to them, then cats or at least some cats must be able to do so, and that was that.

Puss's plan was only spoiled because this child was already crying and the man wasn't doing anything. Probably the best thing to do would be to move on to the next car, but Puss had that quality that cat-haters failed to realize was a trait of her species—she was inherently sympathetic to human misery. Her instinct was to curl up beside this child and soothe her with purrs. This child was very upset, and Puss sensed that it was over nothing trivial.

"Why are you crying, child?" Puss asked through the glass. The little girl looked fearfully behind her.

"Ah, the man. Your father?"

The child shook her head.

"I don't suppose ice cream would help?" Puss asked.

The child shook her head again. She was very quiet, for a child. She must be quite frightened indeed.

"Help," the child said through the glass, so quietly that had Puss not just said the last word herself she'd not have recognized it.

The man beside the child roared then, and Puss reluctantly hopped down lest he see her. He did not seem like her kind of person. Poor child.

Oh, well. She saw misery every day. She had better luck two doors down at cadging a bit of a breakfast muffin with cheese, ham and egg enclosed. Two cars later she began to feel she had been unfair to single men, as one spotted her, opened his door, and quite voluntarily and without any prodding on her part, deposited a lovely dollop of ice cream on the pavement for her edification.

Naturally, she was not intending to speak to this person at this time, since it appeared to be unnecessary, but as she was licking her paws clean and contemplating rubbing against the trouser legs that hung out the door as the man watched her, she received a message.

"I beg your pardon?" she said aloud, without thinking about it, looking up from washing behind her ear as the summons entered her mind.

"Ah, Puss! I've found you. Now listen carefully. Rose is in trouble out on the water, and I don't know why. I need you and Dico to look for her and also—there's a child in trouble there somewhere. I—um—I'm going to be a while getting there but I'll be down soon, and I shall require assistance from you and Dico."

Puss, having had little chance to develop her psychic abilities beyond an uncanny knack for finding food and sunny spots, was confused about how to respond to the mental touch until it was gone. Fortunately, so was her ice cream. With a brisk whisk against the trouser legs, she bounded off in search of Dico.

She found him where he had left her. He looked a bit guilty and quite sleepy, but glad to see her.

"Hey, Puss. Look what I brought you."

Fish! And there was no time for it now.

Quickly, she apprised him of the situation and led him back to where she had received the mental summons. The cars were just beginning to drive onto the ferry as the two of them ran past the toll booths and into the parking lot.

Twenty-eight

SNO WAS ONCE more by the creek bank, once more alone, once more left out because she wasn't a guy, because she wasn't from Washington, because she'd never seen a war. Damn men. You couldn't talk to them. Oh, as long as you listened it was fine. But as soon as you tried to talk to them about something important to you, they turned off and acted bored.

All she'd done was ask who lived up the creek, and did they know her.

"Look," Trip-Wire said. "You're an okay kid, but no more women, all right?"

"I didn't invite her to come over and cook supper," Sno said. "I just talked to her. She said she lived up the creek. All I wondered was if you knew who she was."

"Sno baby, ain't *nobody* lives up the creek, with or without a paddle," Maurice told her, chortling to himself as if he was being really cute.

"She said different," Sno told him.

"Doc, you know what you said earlier about the 'Yards," Red-Eye interrupted, as if he hadn't realized anybody at all was talking. "I think if we'd had more of them . . ."

She tuned them out then, just like they'd tuned her out. The impulse she had to tell them about her joint and to offer to share completely vanished, and now here she was again, sitting on the creek bank while they were in their stupid sweat lodge playing their stupid drums and talking about a stupid war which happened way before she was born and which they were stupid to have gotten involved with.

After they'd gone this morning, she dislodged the joint from the place where she'd left it to dry next to the fireplace, and now it was ready for her to mellow out with. By herself. They could all get stuffed.

She lit the end and stuck the joint in her mouth and took a long, long drag.

It didn't smell quite right, but then, she wasn't all that experienced with it. She noticed that the end of the cigarette was yellowish. Maybe somebody had cut the weed with curry powder, by the look of it. Weird. She hoped it would still make her high.

With her next puff, she realized that this was very strong stuff. Her face felt like she was wearing one of those cleansing masks that dried on your skin to suck out the blackheads and pimples. Even her neck felt stiff.

She reached up to touch her face, and her arm jerked and cramped. So did the other one. She tried to get up, but her legs were cramping now too. She screamed, but her mouth wouldn't move far enough to let the sound out, so the scream stayed trapped inside her as her whole body jerked and shook in one long agonizing spasm.

Felicity heard the scream halfway down I-5.

"Oh, my word! It's Sno!" she cried.

"I beg your pardon?" Prudence said calmly.

"One of the girls I was trying to help. She's dying. Oh, please, Prudence, just a bit more magic. It's life and death . . ."

"Isn't it always?" Prudence asked in a battle-weary tone that any of Sno Quantrill's companions would have recognized. "We're on our way, and that's the best we can do, unless you'd like to stop and call 911?"

"Don't be ridiculous! Half of Whatcom County is already searching for her. She's been missing in the woods for days. And she's not the one we're headed toward."

"Do you want me to get off at the next exit?"

"No. No, Rose is in deadly danger too, and there's a child, and Puss and Dico won't be enough . . . all of that *and* Bobby's gone missing."

"What?"

"Bobby. The executioner. The hunter. The hit man. The little toad. I can't imagine what happened to him."

"Flitters, I think you need a vacation. A cheap one, mind you. Your mind is wandering. I thought you had two people in deadly danger, and you're worried about a *toad*?"

Felicity gave her a very cold look. "It's not as if he's a real toad, Prudence, even if there was anything wrong with that. He's an enchanted hit man, or at least contains the personality of one in the body of an innocent creature, and I'm responsible. Oh, dear, oh, dear."

"What do you want me to do, Flitters?" Prudence demanded.

"Loan me one of your own magicks," Felicity said immediately. Prudence sucked in her breath, shocked. "Just one," Felicity said. "I simply can't help everyone without a little magic."

"If I give you one of mine, how will you spend it?"

"That," Felicity said, "is an excellent question."

Having grown up around animals, Fred was amused by the antics of the enterprising alley cat going from car to car begging food. It surprised him a little, when, in the middle of eating ice cream, the cat suddenly looked up, made a couple of almost-human sounding utterances, and then ran away as if a pack of dogs was on its tail.

He shrugged. Cats were like that, operating on a logic all their own, but for an alley cat to leave food freely offered and safely guarded he suspected it took considerable provocation. The car ferry from Bremerton was late this morning, and even after it arrived, the cars did not immediately begin unloading.

Fred opened the car door again and stood watching, trying to see what happened. One of the loading crew from the parking lot passed by, and Fred asked, "What seems to be the problem?"

"Somebody didn't return to their car," the orange-vested woman said, shrugging. "Probably asleep on the passenger deck."

Rose had begun to wonder if the car deck bathroom had any kind of an independent air supply. It was cold in there, and stuffy. She wondered how she could make a weapon from the mop or a bulletproof vest, maybe, from the bucket half-blocking the way to the door.

Periodically the man with the gun would knock on the door, quietly, so as not to draw attention to himself. After a time she felt the ferry stop, though the engines continued to run, and over them she could hear faintly the static noise of an announcement being made on the intercom, once, twice, three times. The man kept knocking on the door until finally he got tired and stopped.

Could he have gone away? Was it a trick? She sat on the stool, completely dressed now, a while longer, gathering the courage to open the door and find out, while the deck shook beneath her. Surely that was the sound of cars unloading? She was parked at the front end of the ferry—they must have had everyone drive around her and then pushed her car off. Would the crew members have found her assailant and forced him to deal with the car? If so, he should be gone now.

She'd been cooped up so long it was hard to believe she was free, but she shot the bolt on the door and peeked around. For a fleeting moment she saw the back end of the last two cars, one of which was her own. Two crew members were arguing with her assailant, who was walking beside the car. Belatedly, Rose realized that the hard, pointy object digging a hole in her hip was the car keys.

She stepped out onto the deck and headed for the staircase when the orange-vested crew members on the bow waved the first two cars in the long, snaking lines aboard the ferry.

Just as she was about to slip past them, onto the ramp and to freedom, a tear-smeared little face steaming up a car window caught her eye. The blonde curls—little kids tended to look a lot alike at that age but—wasn't that Gigi Bjornsen?

Fred watched as the cars unloaded around the disabled vehicle, then saw the last car being pushed out, while two crewmen talked to a man who was presumably the driver. Poor bastard probably couldn't get it started, but why wasn't he in it?

Fred was curious both by nature and by training, and he was a great believer in synchronicity. He was looking for Rose, whose absence had not been explained, and before he'd even started searching, something else a little odd was happening. He knew they were going to start loading the cars pretty soon and he'd be in the way, but a cop had to do what a cop had to do, and *he* had to know who the guy was whose car had been pushed off the ferry and why he wasn't behind the wheel when it was pushed. The closer he got to the side parking lot where the car had been pushed and the crewmen were arguing with the man, the more familiar the man looked—and sounded.

"Why, hello, Your Honor," he said, greeting Judge Throckmorton. "Having a little car trouble?"

"Who the hell are you?" the judge demanded.

Fred pulled out his ID and badge, peering around the judge to the license plate of the car. "Fred Moran, KCPD, sir. Maybe I can be of assistance here."

"Yeah," said one of the crewmen, a burly, balding redhead who was clearly angry above and beyond the call of duty. "You can arrest his Honor here for obstructing traffic."

"If you want to prefer charges, sure, but the state generally doesn't push it in incidents like this."

"We had to drag him away from the door in front of car deck head and then he says he lost the keys overboard."

"Not enough coffee yet this morning, I'm afraid," the judge said, changing tactics and smiling ingratiatingly at Fred.

Fred was jotting down the license number already. "Yeah, me neither, sir. I understand. Mind telling me whose vehicle this is, sir?"

"Why it's my—" Fred thought he was going to say "mine" and stopped. That must mean he knew that the police would know his own license number. Which meant that he had called Rose's answering machine. ". . . a friend of mine's. Mine—" He paused, trying, Fred thought, to see if he could come up with a story that would stand up to investigation.

"You know how it is, sir. I'd like to call your friend and just make sure, especially with the registration locked inside and all. Come with me and we'll call you a locksmith."

"Officer, you know me, obviously, and therefore you

know where I can be found. I'm rather late for an appointment because of all this. Could you handle it, do you think, and come by later for me to deal with the details?"

"Sure, after we call your friend and get authorization for a locksmith. We're going right to the courthouse, and it will only take a couple more minutes of your time to deal with this. You can call your appointment from there."

The judge's shoulders seemed to slump a little, and he stuck his hands in the pockets of his green quilted down jacket. "Of all the idiotic . . ." the judge began, as the crew members returned to the ferry. The last of the cars waiting in the parking lot pulled around Fred's car, which was also obstructing traffic, and drove over the ramp into the maw of the boat.

Fred opened the car door and reached for the cellular phone, but as he took his eyes off the judge, the man suddenly began walking briskly away from the car.

"Judge Throckmorton!" Fred hollered.

"Do it without me," the man said, and quickened his pace. Fred jogged after him. He had found long ago while working at a convenience store, when people didn't want him to check their ID, that this kind of arrogant behavior often hid fear of being caught—in the case of the irate customers, for bad checks. In the case of the judge, he didn't know for sure, but he had a good idea it involved Rose.

He caught up with the judge and grabbed his elbow. "I'm sorry, sir, but I do have to detain . . ."

The judge turned on him with a snarl, his hand whipping out of his pocket, displaying the glint of metal. Fred couldn't reach his own piece in time to keep from being blown to kingdom come.

But about that time the cat he had seen before streaked between them and clawed its way up Fred's leg as a young black man ran headlong into the judge, knocking the gun from his hand.

The judge's gun dropped and spun on the pavement, and Fred, the cat still clinging to his leg, rolled and pounced on the weapon before rising to pounce on the judge and his assailant.

"That wasn't what I'd call a great career move, Your Honor," he said to Throckmorton. "Now, then, I'm charging you with assaulting an officer with a deadly weapon for beginners. Why do I have the feeling I'll want to add a thing or two after I've checked that license number? You have the right to remain silent . . ."

"Hey, cop," Dico said. "Can I get up?"

Fred, panting and a little scraped up, covering the judge with his own gun while pulling his off-duty revolver from its holster, said, "Yeah. Thanks."

"Go find another cop, Dico. This guy's too tied up to hear about the little girl and the distress signal Felicity's been getting from Rose," the cat said in perfectly clear, if somewhat nasal, English. "And look. The big white boat's way out in the water. Now we'll never catch them."

"Guide us," Doc said, eyes closed and every pore inhaling the heat and giving forth sweat, cleansing mind and body. "Heal us, Great Spirit."

Maurice was drumming slowly and steadily as a heartbeat.

"Send us a vision," Trip-Wire said suddenly. "Something to make the nightmares go away."

"A vision," Dead-Eye repeated, feeling a little silly but trying to get the hang of this new-age stuff.

"A vision of a totem animal," Doc said.

"RRReeedeep," came the noise from the tent flap and

with the next drum beat, a toad squatted among their sweating bodies.

"Rrreeeeedeep," the toad repeated, and hopped back beyond the tent flap.

"The sign has been given," Doc said.

"You kiddin', man? That was nothin' but a toad."

"Follow," Doc said.

They exited the tent and, to Maurice's surprise, the toad sat a little way away until he saw them, and saw that they saw him, and then hopped back toward the creek bank, periodically turning around to croak again, as if summoning them, hopping faster and faster into the clearing by the creek until Doc was the first to spot her.

"Jesus, it's Sno!" he told the others.

"What's wrong with her, man?"

"Convulsions or something," Dead-Eye, who was also a paramedic, said. "We gotta get her to a hospital."

Twenty-nine

CINDY FOUND RAY a bit of a trial.

"I just can't understand it," he was muttering.

"Excuse me?" she asked, continuing to search from horseback the area above the heads of Hay and Ray, who were both on foot.

"I mean, I know it happens all the time, but I still can't feature the kind of sleazeball who'd run off with a little kid . . ."

"You mean the missing girl?" Cindy asked, thinking of the picture. "She looked more like a teenager to me."

"Still, she's a kid."

"It's not like that's any protection," Cindy told him grimly. "If she's been killed by a stranger, that's at least better than having your own family try to do it."

Ray shook his head. "No way would that happen to that girl."

"Don't be so sure," Cindy said. "I mean, my stepmother and stepsisters never sexually molested me, but even before Dad died they did everything they could to make my life miserable—Pam and Perdita used to beat me, burn me, force me to do all the dirty work. Even tried to poison the pony my father gave me, but I found out in time. I was sixteen years old then. I left home—well, the house I grew up in, which my stepmom claims is hers. I've never

305

been back, but Pam and Perdita, those are my stepsisters, came over and hassled me in front of an important client till I lost my job."

"Bummer!" Ray said.

"No kidding. I used to wonder why they should hate me so much. If it hadn't been for Rosie, I don't know how I'd have gotten by. She found me a place to live where nobody hassled me and I could finish school and work in a stable to pay for riding lessons. She also told me that the steps hating me wasn't my fault or anything I did, that they were jealous and greedy and the surest way to let them win was to blame myself or buy into what they were trying to sell me about what a low-life scum I was. They wanted Daddy's money, and that was it. Well, I can do fine without it if I can just find a place to live and ride. Some kids aren't so lucky, though. This girl was kidnapped by someone who had authorization to pick her up from her parents, according to what the Seattle policeman said. She was a teen. Maybe she got away. A lot of times kids are little and it's their own blood parents who are molesting them, hurting them, maybe their dad's doing it and their mom's pretending nothing's happening."

"You sound like you've made quite a study of it," Ray said.

"Well, you tend to, when you've been through it yourself. Rosie says the more you face up to your past, the less likely you are to repeat the cycle of abuse."

"Not everybody does either thing," he said. "Take me. My old man was after me all the time—"

He sounded casual, but Cindy knew the feeling behind the admission was anything but. Maybe he could only tell her because she was a stranger sitting high up on a horse and he'd never see her again.

"But I don't try to screw my kid. Her mother would have said I screwed everything else instead. But not my kid. Not *my* kid. It's not right. She needs me to protect her. A couple of guys I know—well, sometimes my crowd is pretty, you know, out there—they got after my little girl and I lost 'em. History. But her mother took her away anyhow."

Cindy nodded slowly and kept riding, Punkin stepping forward one foot at a time. She was listening so hard she almost failed to catch the glimpse of red caught on a bush, a little tuft of wool.

They called Hay, who called in the tracker, and down the same narrow deer path, a few feet farther from the campground, they found a red thread.

It was all she and Hay could do to keep Ray from mauling the evidence. Hay gave him a serious talking-to while Cindy, riding parallel to the tracker along an old logging road, kept watch for further evidence that would help the tracker "cut sign," or establish how far the girl had gone since their initial clue. Being on horseback was limiting in one way. For Punkin's safety, Cindy could only ride in cleared areas and on established trails. But there was always the possibility that the girl or her assailant had found the better marked trail and diverged from the deer path to follow it.

It began snowing just as she reached the gully in the road caused by erosion from the feeder creek, which even now sent a ribbon of water along the bed of the washout. She was wondering if Punkin could safely jump the gully or go around it when she heard something, almost like a bird cry, but more guttural and with an anguished, frightened note to it.

Hard as she listened, she didn't hear it again, however, but she turned Punkin's head to return to Hay and report it, just in time to see not only Hay, but the tracker, Jim, and Ray trotting toward her.

"Good," Hay said when he saw her. "Didn't think it was you."

"You heard it too?"

Hay was beaming. "Yeah. And if it's our girl, she's still alive."

Ray wasn't listening. Before any of the others could act, he was sprinting around the washout and up the other side, running down the trail.

"Shit! Damn fool!" Hay said, the grin disappearing as he shouted. "Hey! Kinsale! You're going to mess up the trail and we'll never find her!"

But by that time Jim was way ahead of him, jogging after the overexcited searcher.

Hay got on his radio and called base camp, telling the coordinator what they'd found and heard and asking for a medical team to join them and an ambulance to be standing by out on the road.

"An ambulance?" Cindy asked gravely.

Hay shrugged. "No tellin' what we'll find. Wouldn't it be awful if the poor kid had survived all this time, and just when we're about to find her she's attacked by a bear?"

"Let me ride on ahead," Cindy said. "I can go faster than any of us, and I promise I'll keep to the middle of the trail and keep my eyes open for signs."

"Want to take a firearm with you in case there is a bear?"

"I never learned to shoot," she said, shaking her head. "I was too afraid I'd find an excuse to use it on certain people."

"Keep in hailing distance of Jimbo, then. He'll radio back your position and what the condition is. And watch out for bears and catamounts."

She patted Punkin's neck. "She's got radar for that kind of thing."

She led Punkin around the washout, both of them slipping in the mud on the way up. The snow fell in little distinct flakes on the mud of the trail, melting so slowly that she could see each crystalline pattern before it sank into the trail.

By the time she had remounted and caught up with Jim and Ray, Ray dragging behind Jim now even though Ray was trying to run and Jim was jogging at a steady measured pace, the snow was falling faster.

The trail was seriously overgrown, and she was about to turn back when she heard a rustling in the bushes ahead. At first she thought it was just a toad that came hopping out, heedless of the horse, but she soon realized that the disturbance was too loud and varied to be caused by a toad. It sounded like feet, branches cracking, voices and a sort of a gurgling snore. "Hello!" she called, dragging out the vowels. "Do you need help?"

A voice, not a girl's but a man's, called back, "Help!"

She rode forward as far as she could and saw the men, seven of them, carrying a litter as carefully as they could. On the litter was the agony-twisted body of a girl, covered with a poncho that kept sliding off.

Cindy felt a moment of panic. What had these guys been doing to the poor kid, and would they try to attack a woman on horseback? "What happened?" she asked.

"We don't know. She was like this when we found her."

Cindy rode back to find Jim, who radioed into base camp. Meanwhile, Ray rushed forward. "Sno!" he cried, and to the men, "What did you do to her?"

"Not a goddamn thing except try to save her life. Who the hell are you?" one of them demanded.

"Her father," he said.

As if the whole situation hadn't been confusing enough already! The men yelled at each other until Jim suggested in his quiet but deadly authoritative way that their primary objective should be continuing to transport the girl to medical assistance and finding out what was wrong with her before it killed her.

Once more the procession hoisted the litter made of a sleeping bag. Because of Sno's contorted position, they had to carry her on top of it.

They all trotted ahead, still arguing, which was something Cindy couldn't bear. She let them get out of earshot before she mounted Punkin, then noticed, after they walked a few steps, that the horse was limping badly.

So much for magic horseshoes! Punkin had lost her shoe someplace along the trail. Damn! It would be a long walk home, Cindy thought, releasing Punkin's hoof and remembering that her shiny new rig was going to turn back into Haisley Henderson's bike now that the search was over. She would do fine, but how about poor limping Punkin?

She was still kneeling beside her horse when a toad—surely not the same one—hopped back out of the bushes at the same place she had seen one before, and then seemingly deliberately squatted in front of her and dropped something. She picked it up. It looked like a marijuana joint. Evidence, maybe? Why did the toad have it? It couldn't have thought it was a fly, and toads did *not* build nests.

The toad looked at her expectantly, its buggy little eyes watchful.

"Wait a minute," she said to it. "Fairy godmother—magic shoe—you're in the wrong fairy tale, bud, and I am not *about* to kiss you."

The toad gave her what would have passed for a scornful look, had it had eyebrows, and hopped ahead on the trail. She followed, leading Punkin.

The ferry motored across the Sound, a steel band playing its entire repertoire on the bottom of the hull. Safely concealed by the other cars parked between her and the car in which she had seen the little girl, Rose watched. This time she was going to be smart and notify the authorities. The police could meet the boat in Winslow, and Rose would just have to risk being wrong. If the little girl was Gigi, the man would have a lot of explaining to do. If not, Rose would have a possible lawsuit on her hands.

But that was an improvement from her situation twenty minutes ago.

The car deck was only about a quarter full, with more room between the vehicles than usual. Almost all of the passengers had gone up to the deck above for coffee and papers. Though the flow of traffic from Bremerton to Seattle was enormous at this hour, the flow in the opposite direction was often sparse.

Despite her resolve to report the car rather than take further risks herself, she needed to make sure of the license number and the appearance of the driver first. She walked briskly forward, as if going to her own car, and stopped at the car closest to the driver's side of her target.

Bending down as if she were opening the door and preparing to enter the car, she turned to see the driver's face. Twice before she had seen him only in oblique views, several times she had seen grainy photos in the newspaper. But he had turned at the disturbance her presence made beside her car, and now she was looking him full in the face. This was the governor's good buddy, Norman Hopkins, the family man himself, head of the Washington

State Department of Family Services, her boss.

He did not look happy to see her.

She turned and glared at him as hard as he was glaring at her, then stared open-mouthed at the gall of the man. He held the little girl on his lap by her waist. She was clad only in cotton underpants now, and she was bleeding, blood smeared on her arms, legs, and face, her curly blonde hair matted and wild. Her little jeans and T-shirt lay crumpled on the passenger seat, and bruises like blue socks circled her ankles and wrists.

Thoughts of letting a third party handle this safely totally fled Rose's mind. "Open this up right now, you son of a bitch!" she screamed in a most unprofessional and nonempathetic manner.

The door shot open, slamming her back and pinning her against the adjoining car while Hopkins emerged. "Miss Samson, I have already demanded your removal from the system, and this sort of behavior shows me I was right."

"Wrong!" she hollered, not so much out of emotion now as to draw attention to them. "Your behavior with that child shows *me* that you're dead wrong."

"I am—removing that child from an unsuitable home where she sustained the injuries you see. I was simply examining her for further wounds."

"Right. And I'm the Playmate of the Month. For one thing, you wouldn't remove a child from an unsuitable home if you saw its parents dismembering it with a chain saw. For another thing . . ."

Before she could get to the other thing, she saw the little girl slide out behind Hopkins and scoot toward the front of the boat.

Hopkins saw her too and grabbed for her but Rose blocked him and they stumbled over each other trying to reach the child. Rose screamed and screamed but her voice was lost in the engines and the drumming on the bottom of the boat.

The little girl was screaming too, a high-pitched child's scream that pierced the noise better than Rose's did. Peripherally, Rose noticed crew members running down the stairs, but meanwhile Gigi's tiny, shivering body stood outlined against the gray-green waters chopping against the bow of the car deck.

Hopkins leaped forward to catch the child, and Rose tried to wiggle around the car door to summon the crew, but Hopkins suddenly grabbed her wrist and dragged her forward with him.

He ducked under the chain, towing her along, but she grabbed it and held on. In another moment, the crewman who was running toward them would be close enough to help.

He pulled with both arms, hard, tugging her so that her fingers started to slip. Her nails broke on the chain, tearing back to the quick, and she felt the skin burn off her hand as she tried to hold on, while he gripped her other arm and tried to walk himself forward along her.

Then suddenly a little body hurled itself between them, and he let go of Rose and tried to grab the child. Releasing his grip, he stumbled backwards, and Gigi, still trying to reach Rose, ran behind him. He fell backwards, over the lip of the boat and under it, hanging by his knees, dragging the child with him. Rose lunged forward and caught at Gigi's leg as Hopkins's scream was abruptly cut off, and the little girl bellowed as she followed him overboard.

Thirty

DAME PRUDENCE'S CAR roared past the tollgate at the ferry terminal, where she of course paused to deposit the ferry fare before roaring on into the parking lot.

One lone man stood by his car in the vast but otherwise empty lot, which led to a sheer drop into Puget Sound. The ferry had gone long ago. At the lot's exit, a police car with a prisoner in the back and a witness in the front rolled out of the lot and onto the street, its red light flashing. Atop the hood of the solitary car, a cat sat licking its paws.

"There, Flitters. You see?" Prudence demanded in her infuriating way. "Two of your emergencies have resolved themselves quite nicely without you making stones speak or the Space Needle fly or any of the other extra tricks you seem to think you require. The Quantrill girl is found . . ."

"And in critical condition and perhaps will not survive," Felicity retorted.

"That is up to her now," Prudence said more gently than Felicity actually noticed at the time. "The Ellis girl helped find her, thus enhancing her self-esteem . . ."

"And she will have plenty of healthful exercise as she has to walk her poor lame horse to a home she no longer has . . ."

"And your Officer Moran has just apprehended one of the principals in a child-molesting ring, a man who has

314

used his position to protect others from justice."

"And in the process, he's missed helping his true love, who . . . oh!" Felicity suddenly felt a burst of terror and saw through Rose's eyes as, far out in the Sound, she was dragged forward, after the little girl and the man who even now was being sucked under the ferry. The crew members still weren't close enough to save any of them.

Prudence asked, "Felicity, what is it?" as her colleague, who had gone deathly pale and stone-still for a moment, suddenly burst from the car and ran toward the water.

"Rose! The child!" Felicity cried. "Save them!"

Prudence gave a very slight disgusted shake of her head, then said, "Oh, very well, just this once." She waved her hand and repeated a passage from the navigational engineers' manual.

"What's going on here?" Fred Moran demanded as he strode up to them. "I heard you say something about saving Rose. What do you two know about her?"

"Who's he?" Prudence demanded.

"Officer Moran is Rose's true love. I do think he ought to be involved as well . . ."

"Oh, bloody hell!" Prudence snapped, and Felicity gave Fred a brave wink. Parsimonious Prudence might be, but, like all Godmothers, she was a sucker for true love. Her expression softened and she said to Fred, "Very well, then, on the house. Off you go."

A Coast Guard cutter pulled up in the vacant ferry slip, and Fred ran to the dock and vaulted aboard.

As Hopkins fell overboard and Gigi was knocked in after him, Rose dove for her and caught her ankle before she fell all the way overboard and was sucked under the boat.

Hopkins thrashed mightily as he was dragged beneath

the bow, and although the water was several feet below the level of the car deck, the spray from his struggles wet Gigi's body and Rose's hands and arms, making her grip on the child slippery and her fingers numb with cold.

Gigi dangled and twisted, crying "Mommy, Mommeee!" Trying not to let the child's head go under water as she shifted her grip, Rose slid forward to clutch at Gigi's waist.

Her grip on the leg slipped as if the little girl was a freshly caught fish. She slid farther forward until only her hips and legs were on the bow and her front end hung off over the water. Once more she tried for a more secure grip, felt her fingers closing on the child's trunk.

Suddenly the ferry stopped dead still in the water, and the momentum it had picked up while traveling tore Rose's fingers loose from Gigi and sent her sliding over the bow, her belly and thighs scraping on the narrow metal lip between the deck and oblivion.

She started to scream, thought better of it, and took a deep breath that was almost shocked out of her as she plunged into the bone-numbing, flesh-crystallizing cold of the water. The water closed over her head, and she felt herself sinking.

Automatically, from years of swimming in lakes and off the warmer beaches, she let her arms fall to her sides and shot back up to the surface—panicking a moment before she did so, thinking her head would encounter the bow of the boat.

But she surfaced almost a yard from the boat.

She was almost too cold to think by then, but someone had thrown a life preserver, and the crew lined the bow.

"Where's Gigi?" she called up to them, just as she saw the top of a blonde head, like that of a wet golden Labrador, break the surface of the water. She dived for the child but missed her as she sank again, so she dived deeper.

It was difficult to see in the murky water, but a little sunshine broke through this close to the surface and glinted from the girl's bright hair.

Rose grabbed the hair, felt the weight of the child as the slight body rose to the surface.

She hadn't the strength to hand the girl up to the crew members, and she wrestled with feelingless arms and fingers to lay Gigi over the life preserver. The few feet she swam pushing the preserver was the longest distance she had ever traversed in her life. Nothing she did seemed to bring her any closer.

The words of the crewmen meant nothing to her water-logged ears.

Gigi lay pitifully still and silent across the preserver. The crew members made a human chain, and the woman in front leaned down to lift the child to the deck, then scrambled away so that the male crew member next in line could lift Rose.

But about that time another boat crossed in front of them, and the wake from it swamped Rose.

This time she didn't have the strength or the brainpower left to hold her breath or swim. When the wave washed over her, she swallowed saltwater and sank.

Fred watched, transfixed, aboard the Coast Guard cutter as Gigi Bjornsen was pushed toward the ferry and hoisted aloft by the crew.

Not until it was too late did he realize the effect the cutter's wake would have on the wet-haired swimmer he barely recognized as Rose.

"Shit!" he yelled as the wake swamped her, and he kicked off his shoes and dove, nearly colliding with a ferryboat crew member who had done likewise.

Between the two of them, they found her and hauled her

back onto the car deck and commenced CPR. The other crew members had just managed to get a heartbeat and breath from Gigi.

Fifteen compressions and five breaths later she coughed, spat and sat up to wipe her eyes. "Hi," she said to Fred.

"Hi, Rosie."

"How's the baby?"

"Breathing," he said, smiling at her as if he'd invented her personally.

"I'm cold," she said, though she was wrapped in an assortment of jackets from crew and passengers who had suddenly converged to see what the excitement was about.

"Me too. And wet."

As soon as the Coast Guard cutter loaded the three of them, the engines of the ferry started again as if by magic.

Rose awoke and promptly wished she hadn't. Every cell in her body ached. Her last clear memory, which she had carried into her dreams, was of kissing Fred good-bye. She didn't remember this room—a hospital room with pale apricot-colored walls and shiny linoleum tiles on the floors and metal furniture and the inimitable hospital smell, part antiseptic, part bandage and part pureed beef and weak soup.

"How are you feeling, dear?" asked the throaty Britt-tinged tones of Felicity, who rose from her chair to come and stand beside the bed.

"Not too bad. Haven't seen much of you lately." Her voice sounded like a whisper.

"Yes, well, there were difficulties. There are a number of reporters waiting to talk to you, and a policeman outside your door. I'm afraid I need to move on pretty soon, but I did want to say good-bye before I go. I want you to know,

Rose, that I did the best I could, but I'm afraid I've left a great deal undone."

"How's Gigi?"

"Fine, poor little thing. Her father's with her. The police have located her mother and are questioning her now, but they haven't located her brother yet. I certainly hope they can find that poor boy."

Rose was puzzled by her friend's uncharacteristically worried tone. "Of course they will. We have you to see to that, don't we?"

"Actually—er—not. Not much longer, anyway. I seem to have exceeded my budget, and I need to return for reassignment first. I'm just waiting for Bobby to turn up again."

"Where's he gone?"

"I don't know exactly. I lost him when I was doing a bit of—counseling—at Sno's father's home."

"I don't think you could say you lost him, Felicity. That was one toad with a mind of its own."

"I suppose," she said with a sigh. "It's just that now that I've used up my luck for you, everything I do on your behalf goes wrong—even borrowing a wish from Prudence. When the ferry stopped, according to witnesses, that was when you fell into the water, and when Fred arrived on the cutter, that caused you to nearly drown."

"But I didn't drown, and neither did Gigi."

The door to the room swung open, and another familiar face peered around the corner. This one was dirty, with tangled hair and smelled a bit of horse.

"Rosie, hi. Gee, I can't tell from the crowd outside if you're world-famous or notorious. How ya doin'?"

Felicity sighed. "I'm glad to see you made it back to town safely, Cindy."

Cindy shrugged. "It was no big deal, actually. Once I gave the medics the joint the little toad found . . ."

"Toad?" Felicity asked. "Where?"

Cindy shrugged. "I don't know. I thought he might be yours, but after he brought the joint, I had to tie Punkin up and catch up with the others. I wonder if the toad knew it had strychnine in it and if it knew, how it kept from getting poisoned itself. Anyway, when I came back for Punkin, the toad wasn't there. Burt Stalling took Punkin back to his ranch to board for me, and by that time, Neil had heard about what happened to Rosie so Hay Henderson gave me a lift back here. Sorry I didn't bring any flowers or anything."

"They found Sno, then?"

"Uh-huh. Some guys had her. Apparently they gave her the joint . . ."

"That's not right!" Felicity said. "Didn't she tell them that's not right?"

Cindy shook her head, and a leaf fell to the floor. "I don't think she's able to. Apparently she's on a respirator in intensive care."

"But that's not right, that's not right at all," Felicity repeated.

"She'll tell them when she wakes up, then," Rose whispered, raising a hand whose fingertips were alarmingly black to pat at Felicity's hand.

"But what if she doesn't? This is all going so wrong. If only I'd been more careful."

The door swung open again and Fred entered, carrying a bouquet of supermarket flowers. He was back in brown.

"I just love a man in uniform," Rose said.

He ignored the others to kiss her so tenderly she expected it to thaw all vestiges of hypothermia. "I hope you'll still feel that way by the time this is over, Rosie. Miriam Fagan, the detective in charge of the Throckmorton case, has some very hard questions to ask you."

Rose sighed. "God knows I'll try. But why? Didn't Throckmorton tell them that Hopkins was the other person involved?"

Fred shook his head. "He's claiming you made all that up, that Hopkins was escorting the girl to shelter because she had been at risk in her former situation . . ."

"I'll say!"

"And that your calls to me, the message, the phone thing, were all an attempt by you to get revenge on him for firing you."

"What about Gigi? Where's Hank? Did they check Hopkins's home?"

Fred shook his head. "Hopkins's housekeeper thinks he's been away on business for the last few days. His wife apparently divorced him long-distance from Vegas a couple of years ago and took the kids with her. I think he's got another place where he's stashed the kid, but either Throckmorton doesn't know or he's just not talking. Chuck and Smitty picked up the mother yesterday. She was in bad shape, drug withdrawal and beat to a pulp, but she went nuts when they told her about how Gigi was found and that Hank hadn't been located yet. That woman has one bad conscience. The father's frantic over both kids, but he seems resigned that the boy's been killed. Gigi's been delirious but she calls for her brother, so that seems to me like a good sign." Fred took a deep breath at the end of this recital; then added, gently, "The hard part is, Throckmorton's selling Fagan on the idea that you killed Hopkins . . ."

"How does he explain being in possession of *my* car?"

"All a part of your criminal genius, I guess. All that's saved you are the witnesses who saw you go into the drink after the little girl. But nobody apparently saw Hopkins fall the way you describe."

"Shit. And meanwhile nobody's searching for Hank?"

"Kind of. But they don't know where to start."

Felicity excused herself. When she returned, she looked somewhat more pleased with herself than previously.

"How are the hands?" Fred asked.

"Yucky. I wonder what else I almost froze off," Rose said. "I hope I won't have a permanent punk manicure."

"Is Sno awake yet, officer?" Cindy asked.

"No, but her parents are at her bedside."

Felicity looked suddenly alarmed. "*Both* of her parents?"

"Well, yeah. Her father was pretty tired, though. Against orders, he joined the search for Sno and hasn't had any sleep, so the stepmother is keeping the bedside vigil."

"There's not a moment to lose!" Felicity said.

"What?"

"Oh, boy, here she goes again," Rose said. "Somebody get me a wheelchair in case I froze my tootsies off too. I'm not about to miss this."

With Fred looking extremely official, the cop at the door and the reporters made way for their parade as it advanced toward the ICU. Rose in her wheelchair felt like a tank in an invading army, leading Fred, Felicity and Cindy down the hall with herself in the vanguard. She really ought to have a flag to fly.

On the elevator, they met Sgt. Edmonson from the Whatcom County PD. He was on his way to see Sno too. He and Fred exchanged a few words. Under one arm he carried a bouquet of flowers, though there was a briefcase in his hand. In the other hand, he carried a horseshoe made from what looked like crystal. He seemed unaware that something in his jacket pocket was wiggling.

Thirty-one

HANK WAS COLD and scared, and except for the terrible smell of the room, he would have been really hungry. It was dark down there, and he didn't know if he was more afraid of being left alone in the dark or of the footsteps that would come down the stairs to get him. What had happened to Gigi? Where did the man take her? He couldn't hear very much down here, and he knew why. That was so the kids the man had killed down here couldn't be heard when they screamed for help.

After hours and hours, a tiny shaft of light appeared where the newspaper covering one of the basement windows had peeled away at the corner. Hank hung on to that shaft of light, watching it as if there were a TV show playing in it, but it left him alone in the dark again. Even if somebody peeked through that hole, they wouldn't be able to see him here in the dark.

He peed in one corner of the cell and realized that part of the smell was because other kids—the ones whose parts were in jars there?—had done the same thing. He tried to slip his wrists out of the handcuffs, but all that did was cut him up.

There was nothing to do but wait, and dread what would happen when the wait was over.

* * *

"Puss? Puss, I need your help."

Puss was so startled by the voice intruding on her dreams that she sat up and fell from the rail onto the fire escape, where Dico was hanging out with Ding's pack of thugs.

"Felicity, I was asleep."

"I beg your pardon, but there's another matter I think you could help me on. I want you to ask all of the cats of your acquaintance to ask all of the other cats to ask all of their acquaintances to be on the lookout for a child hidden away somewhere in an empty house or apartment. Can you do that?"

"Sure, and I could run for dog catcher too, but it wouldn't be easy."

"Who you talkin' to, Puss?" Dico asked.

"Felicity. She wants me to organize the area's cats into a search party. She obviously doesn't understand that organization is contrary to the nature of cats."

"What's she want you to look for?" Ding asked.

"A lost boy. The littermate of the little girl I rescued yesterday." Puss yawned. "Really, you'd think human beings with their opposable thumbs and cars and can openers and things could look after their own young!"

"You don't think the other cats will listen to you?" Dico asked.

"Why should they? There's nothing in it for them."

Ding grinned a wily grin. "There might be. If one of the Guerillas went to each neighborhood with some fish heads for a reward if the cat would come to him so he could call you to interpret, would they help then?"

"Only if there are no cracks about how much cats taste like chicken," Puss said.

The plan worked better than she thought. Not all cats cooperated, of course, but there were always those who liked to wander anyway. The hardest thing for Puss was keeping track of which cats were helping where, but there her human speech came in very handy, as she would translate for Ding to write down (since Dico was not a very fast writer). "The gray tom who lives in the house with the red steps down the street from the grocery next door to the McDonald's in the Federal Way Shopping Center" was one address.

"This ain't ever gonna work," Dico said, but as Puss pointed out, it was better than doing nothing, and cats *could* and did search in places where humans couldn't, just out of general interest, so why not do it with an aim in mind?

Bronski, a black-and-white neutered male, wasn't normally a joiner, but neither was he normally one to turn down a nice piece of fish. Not that he got much lately. His beat was the weeds and woodpiles of the abandoned development. It boasted only a tiny scattering of occupied houses, and these were few and far between. The rest made fine hunting grounds. No fish ponds, though.

So when Bronski heard about Operation Catnet, as the humans involved so unfortunately dubbed the search, without committing himself, of course, he told his contact that if the human with the fish should be standing on the corner near the ramp to the highway at a certain time, Bronski might have news of interest to relate.

As it turned out, he would have done it without the fish. He had entertained a dislike of a certain house for some time. It used to be empty, one of the best places for finding rats, voles, birds and garter snakes. Bronski had, lamentably, not been the only cat who appreciated this prime location. One big gray-striped queen used to lounge on the windowsill like the place belonged to her. She didn't mind Bronski using the backyard too much, as long as he didn't disturb her nap. She was fat anyway and didn't do a lot of hunting. After the man moved in, Bronski saw him shoo her away a couple of times, and then, one Saturday, when the rest of the neighborhood was a little on the dull side and Bronski went over for a chat, he arrived in time to see the man at the door, offering the queen some tuna.

Bronski's nose was better than hers. He smelled a rat. The big queen followed the man inside and *never came out again.*

Sometimes the man brought children to the house, but Bronski never saw them playing in the yard afterwards— much to his relief, actually. The children at his own house were one reason he roamed the neighborhood. A couple of times he'd seen one or two other cars there as well, but that was in the evening, which was when Bronski preferred to be at his own food dish and sitting on top of the television warming his weary paws.

The man put up silly-looking wooden things that were too skinny to perch on. Bronski enjoyed jumping on them and knocking them over, but they weren't much good for anything else. And now that the house was occupied, a lot of the small game moved on to less populated places. Bronski only came near the house out of curiosity. Because he was *very* curious about one thing.

About a year after the man moved in, Bronski had begun to notice the smell. It was an intriguingly *bad* smell. At first Bronski thought maybe the man had killed the big queen and left her rotting someplace, though humans tended not to do that much. But the smell continued long after the queen would have been nothing but bones.

Bronski had sniffed all over while the man was gone, had jumped up on the little porch and sniffed through the letter slot, sniffed in all the windowsills, but the smell was strongest around the base of the house.

Maybe it wasn't what the Catnet was searching for, but

there was something fishier than any reward going on in that place.

Today he circled carefully, sniffing the edges of each of the windows. If what Catnet said was true, there'd be no man coming to chase him away or threaten him.

Finally, he found the little place where the window covering had peeled away and peered inside. From within the house came a shriek that sent Bronski darting toward the human waiting near the highway ramp.

Gerardine had finally controlled her hysterics after thirty minutes of screaming into the mirror at her mutilation, her ruination. Fortunately, no one had heard her, and she had the presence of mind to realize she wanted no one near until she could find a way to camouflage the warts or hide them.

No one must see her like this. No one. Without her beauty, she had nothing. Raydir would divorce her, her rivals would make fun of her, her enemies (and they were many) would laugh at her misfortune. If it hadn't been for that awful child, she would never have had to call Svenny and make contact with that sadistic monster of a shapeshifting hit man who had bungled the job he was supposed to do and then was crazy enough to blame her. Sexual revenge she could have handled. She had long practice at manipulating the lusts of men and all of their odd little desires. But disfigurement! Her life was over! Since the toad had long ago hopped away, she couldn't just kill it. She never wanted to touch the filthy things again! Not that she had ever deigned to do so previously.

No, she knew who was responsible for her mutilation. How could she have let the little twit die so easily? She should have skinned her alive, cut her into pieces.

Raydir never came home that night at all, and during

that period, Gerardine had time to calm down enough to try to decide what to do. She called her plastic surgeon, but he was in Switzerland and wouldn't be back until the following week. She wasn't about to trust a stranger with her secret.

She slathered on a thick mud pack and stayed in her room all day, telling the maid she was preparing for a shoot in Turkey, which would explain both her absence and why she might be wearing veils until she could rid herself of the warts.

Time and again, she returned to the mirror and stared with horrified fascination at her blighted face. Anger grew inside her. Even in death that rotten child had revenged herself.

Surgery, even the best surgery, was bound to leave scars.

She wept again, making mud puddles of her eyes and the pillows she wept against, crying for her lost beauty until she was trembling with dehydration.

She wept until she fell into a fitful sleep where she saw Sno's unblemished face mocking her, her finger pointing at her, and the toad hopping up and down with glee. Hatred woke her and kept her planning all the deaths she would have liked for Sno if she hadn't already killed her.

Then her personal extension rang. She didn't feel like talking to anyone, so she let the machine get it. It was Raydir's voice.

"Gerry? Just wanted to let you know we've found Sno alive but just barely. They've just flown her to ICU at Harborview. I'm—"

She picked up the phone and said, with her appropriately trembling and raspy voice, as if her tears had been for her lost stepdaughter, which in a way they were, "Ray, darling. I'm here. I'll be right there as soon as I can get there."

"You sound—funny."

"I've got a little cold—" she said, and thought of the perfect cover. "I'll wear a surgical mask so as not to infect poor dear Sno. Don't tire yourself too much, darling. Gerry will be right there."

Dressing quickly, she snuck down to the gardener's shed and borrowed one of the masks they wore to spray the garden, and a teensy bit more strychnine powder. Too bad to be so repetitive, after all her planning, but at least this way she would get to watch the little bitch die.

As she drove to the hospital, she felt, in spite of everything, a thrill of vindictive hatred. So darling Sno was clinging to a thread of life after all, was she? Well, little Gerardine was going to be there with the scissors.

Every vein in her body pulsed with hatred when she saw the girl lying there, breathing through a tube, Raydir, *her* husband, bent tenderly over the little twit.

The mask suffocated her and rubbed on the warts as she hugged Ray and told him he had to get some rest, that she would watch over the girl.

Ray, who looked horrible, as if he hadn't slept in years, agreed that he could go outside and smoke and maybe bring them both back something to eat.

That would be time enough. Gerardine, doing her best Madonna with Child imitation, hovered over Sno until the nurses all became occupied with an emergency on the other side of the unit.

·Then she pulled the little paper packet of strychnine from her pocket and reached for the tubing to Sno's respirator.

Rose, her friends and the Whatcom County deputy were all moving toward the ICU when they heard a "Code five, ICU, Code five, ICU" on the PA system, and a couple of doctors ran past them in the hall.

By the time they reached the unit, a cluster of people in

scrub clothes was gathered at the door of one of ten glass-fronted cubicles opening on three sides of the nursing station, which was situated in the middle of the large room.

Only one person still stood at the near end of the room, an expensively dressed willowy blonde figure, incongruously sporting a scrub gown over her designer suit and a surgical mask on her face. She had been bending over a form animated only by the husky bellows of the respirator to which she was attached.

Ignoring the sign on the door stating that patients in the intensive care unit could have only one visitor at a time, Felicity pushed Rose into the room, hissing, "That's her! The stepmother! That woman must not be alone with that girl!"

"I can see that it's too early to try to question Miss Quantrill yet," the Whatcom County deputy said.

Fred nodded. "We'll let you know if she regains consciousness."

The deputy turned to go, but before he had gone two steps, something hopped out of his pocket and hit the floor with a wet plop, and a small green toad gave two mighty hops toward Sno's cubicle.

"What the hell?" the deputy said.

"Go ahead," Felicity said, seeming to address the floor. "This doesn't take a bit of magic."

The toad turned and cast a stern eye upon them all, its demeanor conjuring up Dirty Harry inviting them to make his day.

Felicity, only too happy to oblige, opened the door to the cubicle. The woman with the mask stopped fiddling with the respirator tubing long enough to look up and see the new visitors. In the hand not holding the tubing, as if ready to yank it loose, the woman held a little package of something yellowish.

"Seize her, deputy!" Felicity cried with a flourish of her silver-clad arm. "She's attempting to murder that poor child again!"

"Ma'am, I can't . . ." he began.

The blonde glared pure hatred at them and then turned back to the girl, the tube and, with a very brief hesitation, the packet.

"Let's see what you've got there, ma'am," Fred said, starting to cross to where he could grab her.

But just then the toad hopped up onto Sno's bed, and onto the woman's hand where it touched the tubing, "Ree," it said. "Deep."

The woman snatched her hand back as if it had been burned and screamed as if demons were chasing her with pitchforks. The hand with the yellow packet flailed, trying to knock the toad away, but the toad hopped, a mighty flying hop, straight into the woman's face, knocking aside the surgical mask.

Rose stared in amazement at the woman, who wore no makeup below the eyes. The rest of her face did not much resemble the flawless, well-publicized features of Gerardine Quantrill, but rather someone suffering the initial stages of the Elephant Man disease. The formerly perfect nose sprouted a massive wart on its perky tip and two or three warts on each perfect nostril. Clusters of warts accentuated the frown lines from nose to mouth on each side and formed a mustache obscuring the cupid's bow of her upper lip. A huge hairy wart wobbled on her chin, flanked by two smaller ones on her lower lip.

"No!" the woman cried, brushing away the toad and the dangling mask at the same time. Raydir Quantrill dashed into the room behind them.

"What's this? My God! Gerry?"

She turned away from him, hiding her face, but the toad danced up to her and she scuttled back from the corner, kicking at it, throwing the little packet of powder at it. "Keep that thing away from me!"

Fred picked up the powder packet. Cindy said, "Why, that's the same color as the stuff in the joint I found near where Sno was picked up!"

"Can you tell us what this is, Mrs. Quantrill?" Fred asked. "We'll have it analyzed anyway."

She glared at him, but about that time the toad hopped on top of her head and sent her into another spasm of kicking and clawing, this time at her hair.

"Take it away, take it *away*! That damned Svenny! Why couldn't he send me a *normal* hit man to get the wretched little bitch? Why did I have to get one that turned into a warty little horror?"

Felicity bent down and extracted Bobby from the blonde tangle.

"Excuse me, ma'am, would you care to repeat that?" asked Fred and the Whatcom County deputy simultaneously, and in unison began, "Although you have the right to remain silent . . ."

"What's this all about?" Raydir demanded, sounding exhausted and anxious as he was after the search and his long vigil at his daughter's bedside, as if he were about to cry.

"Ray," Cindy said, sympathetically touching the arm of the man she knew as Ray Kinsale.

"Your wife, sir, has tried three times to murder your daughter," Felicity said.

"Gerry?" He looked down at the grotesque face of the woman on the floor.

She threw her hands up to cover her face and said in a muffled voice, "Don't you 'Gerry' me, Ray Kinsale.

That girl had you bewitched. You always felt so guilty about her and her damned mother you never had time for *me . . ."*

Raydir Quantrill, still clad in jeans and hiking boots and his REI pullover, crossed the room to put himself between his wife and daughter while Fred dropped the powder packet into an evidence bag and the Whatcom County deputy called for backup.

"She's my little girl, Gerry," he told his wife in a tone as cold as her own heart. Turning his back on her, he leaned over the figure on the bed and said, "Sno, baby, come on and wake up. This bitch will never come near you again. I'll stop drinking, stop partying, give up the road and just do recordings. My only wish is to have you well and home again."

"That's my cue," Felicity said, winking at Rose. "New client, fresh magic. So be it!"

The entire medical staff, now finished with their other emergency, had migrated to the door of the room and were pushing their way through to Sno's bed, as Fred and the deputy, who had returned from phoning at the nurse's station, hustled Gerardine out the door.

Suddenly, one of the nurses stopped in her tracks as Sno stirred, no doubt stimulated by all the activity. "Look! She's trying to breathe on her own! Get her doctor over here now. Let's see how she does off the respirator."

Several taut minutes of medical drama later, the machine was gone and Snohomish Quantrill opened her eyes and smiled weakly at her father.

A little later, in Rose's hospital room, a well-dressed woman detective tapped the pointed toe of her smart purple high-heeled shoe. Two uniforms and three reporters, including a camera crew, were outside too, but the woman shut the door behind them as Felicity wheeled Rose back to her bed.

Fred had gone with the Whatcom County deputy to arrest Gerardine. Ray was allowed to stay in the ICU with Sno. Cindy and Felicity remained behind with Rose, cautioned to remain available for questioning as witnesses to Gerardine's third murder attempt and partial confession.

But the detective was not interested in them, or in Sno. The minute Rose was back in the room, the woman said, "I'm Detective Lieutenant Fagan of the Seattle Police Department and I have a few questions to ask you, Ms. Samson, regarding the death of Mr. Norman Hopkins this morning."

"It was an accident, Detective Fagan," Rose said. "Hopkins made a misstep while he was trying to drown both me and Gigi Bjornsen, but if he hadn't had the accident . . ."

"Well, Gigi Bjornsen is still unconscious, Ms. Samson, and a little young to vouch for you anyway. So in your own words, tell me again what . . ."

Just then the hallway erupted with noise, including what sounded like a cat with his tail being stepped on. The door was flung open once more and another policeman preceded Dico Miller, Puss and Ding and his gang into the room.

Dico was bouncing up and down with excitement. "Rosie, guess what! I found the little boy!"

"*We* found the little boy, you mean," Puss said, jumping up on the bed, her tail lashing.

"I'm sorry, but you *cannot* bring animals in here!" a nurse hollered rather futilely from the doorway, where reporters were crowding to see what was happening.

Just to confuse matters Puss hissed, broadcasting loudly enough that everyone including the reporters could hear. "Don't you go dissin' *this* cat, woman! Like there was anything in here I'd want. Just chill while my man Dico and me tell my friend Rosie here how I saved her butt and I'm outta here faster than *you* can pull a Band-Aid off a hairy ass."

"And that," Felicity told the meeting of the Godmothers' Sorority, "was pretty much that. Of course, none of that nonsense at the end with the police blaming the good for the deeds of the evil would have been necessary had Prudence not cut me off. Because of Raydir Quantrill's wish I ended up invoking magic again anyway in a sort of double-header, but that project was not nearly the magnitude of the one Rose asked of me. I trust that you will find my duties well executed and within the boundaries set . . ."

"Ahem," Prudence said. "There are a few little matters. Gigi Bjornsen, for instance, woke up to verify Rose's story the moment Puss and the gang arrived."

"Children heal quickly," Felicity shrugged, studying her silver fingernail polish.

"Then there's the matter of the police believing the gang members got their information from a cat . . ."

"Many policepersons have cats as companions," Felicity said. "The police are not such fools as people would like to believe."

Her Majesty, no longer a sprite but now a regal dowager, gave Prudence a firm look. "You've performed your task well enough, Prudence. Let us hear Felicity out. What has become of the Bjornsen children, Flitters?"

"They're staying with their father while the mother finishes detox, and the whole family is in therapy with Rose. She convinced the father that the kids had to have treatment after their trauma, and the experience has helped both parents do a lot of reevaluating. I got in touch with Haisley Henderson in a *purely nonmagical way, Prudence*, when I learned that Hay manages a tree-planting service for an international ecological organization. They've given Harry a good job so he can stay home with the children. Candy will take more work, of course, but both parents do acknowledge their share of responsibility and . . ."

"I suppose you'll try to tell us that happened without the benefit of magic as well?" Prudence said with a superciliously lifted eyebrow.

Felicity was honest enough to blush.

"And Cindy Ellis?" Her Majesty rescued Felicity with the question.

"Yes, and the so-nice men the Sno girl stayed wiz . . ." Dame Erzuli added, the brim of her large straw garden hat quivering with excitement.

"Oh, yes, let's see now. Raydir Quantrill, once Sno was found, was very grateful for the advice he had obtained from Cindy Ellis, but he had been too distracted to remember her name or much about her except that she was quite pretty and had considerable empathy and common sense, a commodity of which rock-and-roll stars seem to have a distinct paucity. He was also grateful to her for supplying the piece of evidence that identified the substance which had harmed Sno. But, since she was there through my devices, no one ever knew exactly who she was or where she lived. All they knew was that she had been riding a horse which later came up lame. That's why the Whatcom County sheriff brought in the shoe. When Cindy identified it, Raydir asked her to return home with him and Sno, when she was released from the hospital, to manage his stables. Actually, if the story runs true to form, he has rather more in mind, although I'm not sure he's as good a match for Cindy as I might wish. I might have to do a little altera—"

"Flitters!" Prudence hissed.

Felicity shrugged. "The seven vets, having duly bonded

and cleansed their psyches and bodies of impurities, and having saved a young girl's life, are all back at their former jobs with somewhat greater self-esteem than before, which is all that they ask. My contacts will be keeping an eye on each of those gentlemen, however, and should they run into medical, financial, or employment difficulty, a certain grateful father is willing to intervene on their behalf. This same father has also made a generous contribution to veterans' causes in their names, and has booked benefit concerts for disabled veterans."

"The boy with the cat?" Dame Charity asked. She herself had fifty-four cats, and some considered her more of a cats' godmother than a humans', a charge Her Majesty, ever a patron of woodland creatures, dismissed as discriminatory.

"Ah, Dico! Both he and Ding's Guerillas obtained plenty of publicity from this. Everyone has quite forgotten about Puss . . ."

"Now, how," Prudence said dangerously, "could they forget a thing like that?"

"Well, Ding, who as you know is musically quite gifted, has discovered that he and Dico have that gift in common. Ding learned this when Dico, who has never touched a musical instrument before, played all of 'Scheherazade' on Ding's bamboo flute. Of course, the press also knows Dico as a ventriloquist, which is how they accounted for Puss's speech. Now that the seven-day spell has worn off . . ."

"Wait," said the newcomer in the corner. "I thought spells lasted seven *years*."

"The life of a cat is rather accelerated, so the spells are briefer accordingly . . ." Felicity explained.

"Reedeep," said a sulky voice from her pocket.

"Except for those who've earned a longer period of rehabilitative enchantment," Felicity said into the pocket. "Your Majesty, I must commend to you Bobby Hunter.

Once he figured out which side of the metaphorical lily pad was wet, he got properly into the spirit of things and was of great assistance in the conviction of Gerardine, formerly Quantrill, now Inmate #36984. Back to what I was saying, Dico Miller is now in Ireland studying with the great John Kinsale, who happens to be a relative of Ray's. Puss meanwhile is staying with the Nguyens when she wishes to sleep dry and be fed fish."

"Doesn't young Ding resent his friend for out-achieving him?" asked Dame Erzuli, who knew perhaps even better than the rest the havoc envy could wreak in a human heart.

"But he hasn't, Zuli!" Felicity assured her. "Music is only one of Ding's *many* talents. He was offered the chance to go with Dico and study with Kinsale, but he's a bit preoccupied at the moment. You see, he and the Guerillas received such praise in the press for his assistance in finding young Hank Bjornsen that interviewers who discovered his problem in getting into school have called for a massive investigation. Meanwhile he and his friends have been offered scholarships to the schools of their choice, and people have sent in money and offers of help. More importantly, because Dico was so intrigued by the stories of Ding's parents, Ding himself decided that the time had come to write those stories down, and he is working on a book about his parents' odyssey from Vietnam to America and all of the tribulations they have braved. It will, of course, become a bestseller."

"Flitters, you are shameless," giggled Dame Charity.

"And how would you assess your fulfillment of Rose Samson's original wish?" Her Majesty leaned forward, her eyes watching Felicity's face intently.

Felicity dropped her eyes. "I tried, ma'am, but frankly, the job was beyond me. If it hadn't been for Rose and all of the other helpful mortals, I wouldn't have made a dent. I'm afraid, considering it strictly as a godmother's assignment, that I made rather a mess of it."

The newcomer stood up, protesting. "That's not true at all! Because Felicity made things happen, the sleazy, corrupt people who kept Family Services from helping people the way they were supposed to were caught and the governor, in view of the publicity, was forced to appoint a new department head. He was practically forced to choose Rose, as a matter of fact. And she learned from Felicity how to cut through the crap and get things done."

Felicity looked embarrassed.

"Not to mention," the newcomer added, "that Rose and Fred are going to live happily ever after. They are, aren't they, Felicity?"

"It's their choice, but, yes, I think so."

"Very good, then," Her Majesty said. "On to new business. But first, We have something We wish to say to Dame Felicity. Flitters, dear, We think you have done very well with one of the most difficult assignments to challenge Our agents since the sorority's creation. If the city of Seattle is not living happily ever after, at least some people are happier than they were, and a great evil within the city's fabric has been vanquished. Besides which, the unselfish young woman who invoked your assistance on behalf of the city has herself found true love, and that is the best that can be hoped for of all fates. Therefore, as a special boon, We wish to grant *you* a wish. What wish would you have, Dame Felicity?"

"I wish," Felicity said, looking directly at Dame Prudence, "that since chaos and disaster and degradation and pain are so lavishly bestowed upon people, I wish, Your Majesty, that when it comes our time to dole out *good* fortune and wishes, we might be able to execute our duties under the auspices of those who are—or will become—rather less penny-wise and pound-foolish."

Her Majesty sighed. "That is a very great wish, Flitters, but We will take it under advisement. However, it is not what I had in mind. Have you nothing more tangible you would wish for?"

"Actually, Your Majesty, I have. I would like to grant Rose one more wish . . ."

"Out of the question!" Dame Prudence cried indignantly, but Her Majesty silenced her with a look.

"It isn't. I used my previous magic to grant *Rose's* wishes, which were all unselfish. Nevertheless I anticipate that her marriage to Fred Moran will be a brilliant success and they will live happily ever after. However, I have recently heard from former trainee Linden Hoff, who has returned to her home in Seattle from our Advanced Wish Fulfillment Training Seminar, which, as you will recall from commencement, she passed with—ahem—flying colors. While beginning her practice as a novice godmother, she will continue keeping tabs on the Seattle area while managing Fortunate Finery on our behalf.

"Linden is, of course, a great friend of Rose's. She tells me that with her new duties as department head, the poor girl hasn't had time to shop for a trousseau. Therefore, ma'am, *my* wish, which I am wishing on my own behalf, is that I may give Rose a present, that present being an open gift certificate to Fortunate Finery with the stipulation that whichever garment Rose chooses shall fit her to perfection."

Her Majesty smiled and nodded, and all of the other godmothers applauded except Prudence, who tapped her pencil on her ledger a couple of times before setting it down and clapping too, trying to suppress a slight smile that brought out a surprising dimple at the side of her mouth.

"Granted, and so be it," Her Majesty said. "Now, then, Flitters, who, pray tell, is this newcomer?"

"Your Majesty, may I present Snohomish Quantrill, an apprentice who, having been victimized by a woman who cared for nothing but her own beauty, wishes to spend her summers with us learning something rather more substantial."

"And how does your father feel about such a choice, my dear?" the Queen asked the girl, who was now less vocal and quite dazzled by the royal presence.

"He thinks I'll be studying cosmetology with Dame Felicity, Your Majesty," Sno replied.

"And so shall you be, child. So shall you be."

NOW AVAILABLE IN HARDCOVER

ANNE McCAFFREY

FREEDOM'S CHALLENGE

PUTNAM